Dark (

By

Margaret Jocelyn

ISBN: 9781916696693

Dedication for Dark Clouds

For my husband Michael and my family.

Special thanks to Jean for her encouragement.

About the author

Margaret Jocelyn lives in Newmarket in Suffolk. This is her first novel, written during the Covid-19 lockdown.

Chapter 1

Willow Bridge February 2020

There were five of them altogether sitting in the waiting room. Two men and three women, all looking serious and some looking down at their feet; none of them smiled. However, Elizabeth realised that a dentist's reception area wasn't the place of anyone's choice and some of them may be far more nervous than she was even though she was only there for a check-up. After a while she absentmindedly bent forward and picked up the local paper from a low table in the middle of the room and one of the advertisements caught her eye.

An email address appeared at the bottom and just as she was considering it, she heard "Mrs Wallis?"

She returned the paper to the table once her name had at last been called and followed the dentist's assistant along a narrow corridor to the consulting room. As she sat in the chair with her mouth wide open, wishing that the dental assistant wouldn't keep talking to her as she could hardly answer with all that gear filling her mouth, she began to think about the advertisement she just read. She decided that she would look at it again on her way out. The newspaper was still there where she had left it. She re-read the piece and fumbled in her handbag for a pen and her notebook so that she could record the details, as it sounded as if it was just what she needed. It was time that she met more people with similar interests and she had to admit her life was becoming rather mundane after her recent retirement but little was she to know then what lay ahead.

She had been following usual routines but found she enjoyed less and less the browsing in shops, especially the charity shops, where she would often have picked up something unusual or even useful. Sometimes she would meet up with friends for a coffee, and she did at least still look forward to her monthly book discussion meetings but was this enough? Up until recently she had enjoyed her retirement going out and about, improving the home and not having to leave the house early in the mornings, especially during the winter months when she would leave home in the dark and also return in the dark; that was one thing she did not miss. Now the novelty of it was gradually wearing off.

It was a while after she returned home before she considered the advertisement she had uncovered; her reasoning for not taking action was possibly down to her laziness, she was sure, but eventually she had decided to look at it again and felt it couldn't do any harm to make some enquiries.

Are you interested in Art?
If you would like to be involved in forming a group to discuss art and painting, please contact me.

A reply to her email had followed almost immediately and she was encouraged by the friendly message from someone called Jerry Smith who asked if they could meet up. Then she picked up the phone to her close friend Marilyn with the hope of obtaining some moral support.

"Marilyn, it's Elizabeth" she said and she explained about the contents of the email "You're keen on art and I wondered if you'd like to join me in a meeting with Jerry, I don't want to go on my own."

"Yes, of course I'll come."

Marilyn had always been the one to think things through sensibly and she had been pleased that Marilyn had taken a positive and decisive action; she could always depend upon her. They had known each other for about fifty years now, first meeting when they had worked together in London. They had kept in touch even though both of them had moved around for different reasons, mainly for job changes she seemed to remember. Nevertheless, despite this they had visited each other once or twice. At work Marilyn had always looked well turned out and her short fair hair had always looked immaculate; she was tall and slim whereas Elizabeth who was also slim was short in stature and her unruly curly hair, however hard she tried, tended to look bedraggled most of the time. Then, after her retirement a strange thing had happened. She and Edward had been settled in Willow Bridge for a while now after so many moves and it had been Marilyn who had once remarked, "You really have messed up my address book" and they both laughed.

But soon a move was afoot for Marilyn and her husband Robert and Elizabeth had received a long, newsy letter explaining that she and Robert were shortly moving from their large house in Norfolk, where they had lived for some time, to a bungalow in a village near to Willow Bridge. Surprisingly Marilyn hadn't caught up with the modern age and refused to correspond by email yet the letter had been a joy. After all those years imagine becoming almost neighbours, at least within easy visiting distance of each other. Their first get-together after their move had quickly brought them up to date with the past, chatting about old times and the people that they had once known, but now their previous working lives had faded into the background as they dealt with present times.

"Where are we to meet this man?"

"The Coffee House in Willow Bridge High Street."

"Is he young, old or what?"

"Going by his email it sounds as if he could be retired although there is something a little odd - am I the only person who has replied?"

"Well, we'll soon find out won't we."

Two days later Elizabeth joined Marilyn in the café where they had arranged to meet. It had recently opened after the old carpet shop had closed down and the place had been vacant for some time; the new owners had turned it into a popular place to relax with a coffee or a welcome snack and it was always busy. She looked around her at all the pine tables full of friends, families and even people on their own sipping their beverage with a couple of shopping bags beside them. It was buzzing with activity and this was a place that had been convenient for all of them to meet as Marilyn lived in the next village, and apparently Jerry also lived close by. That was the one thing that she had learned when he had suggested the meeting place.

Elizabeth and Marilyn sat on comfortable chairs around a small table waiting for the man they were about to meet, and as people came in through the door, they crossed off women, couples and the very young as they assumed he wouldn't be included in that group. Eventually a man, maybe in his sixties, appeared and started looking round; he was smartly dressed and had probably been handsome in his younger days. Elizabeth stood up uncertainly and he came over to their table

"Jerry Smith?" she asked.

"Yes, that's me."

He sat down and explained his objectives while Elizabeth beckoned to a waiter for another coffee. To start off with, he had said, they would discuss artists, paintings and hobbies of the participants, and even possibly drawings and paintings that they had done themselves. He seemed to be trying to include a large mix but this could either attract more people or on the other hand it could put others off.

"Do you have many who are interested?"

"One or two."

A long uncomfortable silence followed, so Elizabeth took the lead. He really hadn't thought this through; nevertheless, she was becoming more enthusiastic about the tentative idea and his hesitancy didn't bother her. Perhaps this was what he wanted, ideas from other like-minded people. She wasn't confident enough to display any of her art of course, such that it was, and she hadn't picked up a paint brush seriously for many years. Briefly she smiled to herself when she thought of all the paint brushes that she *had* most certainly picked up when they had been painting and decorating their homes throughout the years when trying to spruce them up. Their last big project soon came to mind as she did some mental arithmetic and realised that it had been about forty years ago and she remembered the anguish she had encountered at the time. Elizabeth had never liked long lacks of communication and so in the end she became aware of something rather vague that fluttered into her mind.

"Perhaps we could visit some art galleries as this would be attractive to most." and Jerry nodded.

"Where would the group meet up? Would you have to hire somewhere in which case

there would have to be a small charge to cover the cost of the venue?"

"Yes, that's true but I would have to see how many people we would have first of all."

It all sounded rather ambitious but certainly feasible and she did wonder how many people he was expecting to take part? Even so Elizabeth felt that it still looked promising as the three of them enthusiastically put their suggestions forward; all recommendations were welcomed although she was a little embarrassed because she had come up with more ideas than the other two, even though she had to admit to herself that this was a project that she was becoming quite passionate about. On impulse she asked if they would like another coffee. There was now a small queue standing at the counter and none of them were quite sure whether they needed to join it or whether a waiter or waitress would come to them again so Elizabeth got up.

"It's OK, I'll get them" Jerry offered.

Over the second coffee, the third for Elizabeth and Marilyn, they spoke about other things in general and then they left the cafe with a promise from Jerry that he would get in touch.

"I wonder whether he will get in touch?" Marilyn said doubtfully.

"I think he will" she replied.

She wasn't wrong. The next day she received an email from him.

But the shock of it struck her violently, it came unexpectedly out of the blue and she was nearly in tears when she phoned Marilyn.

"I can't read it out to you because it's too dreadful but basically it said 'Who on earth do you think you are? You're a nobody trying to be important and you even expected me to pay for the coffees.'

"What on earth did I say to make him act like that?"

"He seemed like a pleasant, normal person but he must be unbalanced. There's obviously something wrong with him - perhaps he's got schizophrenia or something."

"Maybe, perhaps I should reply offering an apology."

"I think you should just ignore it, what he says is absolute rubbish and if he had taken exception to something he should have said so at the time."

She wished afterwards that she had taken Marilyn's advice but feeling resentful she decided to reply to say she was sorry if she had offended him and offered to refund him for the coffee, but also wanting to demonstrate that her reply was reasonable and not abusive. He replied straight away saying that he would come and find her and that she would be sorry. She decided not to tell Edward but instead contacted her friend again.

Marilyn had told her that it was only an empty threat and that she was sure that she had nothing to fear. It wasn't exactly something that you could report to the police, it was only words. Nevertheless, Elizabet kept going over and over it in her mind, trying to piece together the conversations they had had over their coffees but she couldn't think of anything to trigger such a reaction. Had she mentioned where she had lived? She was certain that she wouldn't have done so but she couldn't be certain. Although her uneasiness about this remained in the background it was still there ready to spring back at any small reminder of the incident. Eventually the stinging words of his email had faded and she had deleted it and anything else that had any relation to their, what could have been, a pleasant encounter but turned out to be quite the opposite and instead had turned nasty. So much for her good intentions and ideas, she would have to think of something else instead. Although she had been only too glad to forget about Jerry Smith something far worse was to follow a few weeks later.

Chapter 2

Willow Bridge March 2020

It had been the noise of the dust cart that had awoken her; the clink of the bins being fed into its deep pit and the rumble of them being returned to the pavement which was the normal Monday cacophony. It was only then that it dawned upon Elizabeth that today was not a normal Monday and that nothing could be normal for the foreseeable future. In the distant past if she had woken from a bad nightmare, it was always such a relief to realise that the catastrophe that she thought she had been living through wasn't real. She didn't often have nightmares these days, not like when she had been a child and had woken up screaming because she was being chased through a field by a helicopter flying just above her. This time it was real and she couldn't just shake it off. Everyone was now being confined to their home, unable to see family and friends; a prison sentence. She thought of those people who had been wrongly convicted of a crime and had been imprisoned knowing that they were innocent, although she knew that this was totally different but nevertheless everyone had lost the freedom that they had always taken for granted and Elizabeth couldn't stop thinking about all the implications that would no doubt follow and it felt as if they were now living under a dark cloud.

The virus had appeared from nowhere with little warning. Initially it had been announced that there had been cases of it detected in China and their whole country had been locked down; all the shops, markets and schools were closed and there had also been people dying from it so that nobody was allowed to go out. Everyone here had been shocked hearing about all those dire restrictions, not to mention the large number of people who had died. They had become accustomed to hearing about dreadful events in other countries such as China but nobody in their wildest dreams thought that anything like that could possibly happen here. All of a sudden, their worst fears were to come true when not long afterwards the virus, known as Covid-19, had spread to Italy and Spain and, like China, they were also having to lock down which was something completely unheard of in Europe. Other countries like China no doubt, but surely not here. The news on the radio and in the newspapers was terrifying especially as the virus had resulted in so many seriously ill and dying patients.

"The number of people dying from coronavirus in Italy has risen by 475 in one day to nearly 3,000 – the biggest increase since the outbreak".

The UK was not going to escape either but was to follow with large numbers hospitalised and the tragedy of many deaths which had brought them into this current situation.

"Stay at home, protect the NHS" was the Government's message after the devastation of so many lives being lost worldwide. The NHS were inevitably being put under enormous pressure and it was questioned how they could possibly manage to cope.

Most of the people who had been taken to hospital, many of them to die from a shocking death, were the elderly and although Elizabeth had to count herself and Edward in this group, she also felt relieved that it wasn't affecting the young as had been the case during the Spanish flu in 1918. Nevertheless, the threat of them catching it was still an unpleasant possibility. None of this was anybody's fault but freedom and the recovery of the economy could well take a long time and the uncertainty surrounding it was alarming. She now realised that they were all under 'house arrest'.

Essential shops were able to remain open but other shops, restaurants, pubs, schools and entertainment venues were now closed. Older and vulnerable people were advised not to go out and others could only venture out for essential shopping or for exercise. They weren't used to staying at home; they were accustomed to going out when and where they wanted. To visit friends and family frequently was the kind of life that they had always been used to, but not anymore. It would all take a long while for it to sink in.

"It's surreal" she said aloud."

Had she started talking to herself now? Perhaps she was going mad, she thought.

Another result of the latest plunge into this void was that a good number of the working population were forced to work from home if they were able to. Elizabeth and her husband, Edward, had both been retired for some years now and as Edward had pointed out

"Thank goodness for retirement."

But they had a son, Francis, who fortunately was an accountant in a large company and he was able to work from home but, as he pointed out, he was one of the more fortunate ones. Others were likely to lose their jobs, through no fault of their own, and many had been put on 'furlough' meaning that they would have to stay at home on temporary leave. The Chancellor of the Exchequer had announced a scheme providing grants to employers to pay eighty percent of their staff's wages and employment costs each month, and it seemed like some sort of a temporary solution and would no doubt help many. She knew of one or two people who were on furlough and some of them were doing voluntary work such as delivering food to the vulnerable who were unable to leave their homes. She had also heard of those who were sat at home glued to their computers playing games and no doubt looking at undesirable sites that she didn't wish to think about. She knew that the consequence of this would be lack of exercise, amongst other disadvantages. Her last thought had been brought home to her when she had seen an ambulance draw up at the bottom of their road as she had dropped a birthday card into the letterbox nearby. She didn't know the family but a couple of days later a paragraph in the local paper had caught her eye and she was sure that it had applied to the young man who lived in that house.

Paul Davies of (and yes, that must be his address) *was rushed into hospital with a suspected stroke. He is twenty years old and had been spending all of his time sitting at his computer, never leaving his chair. It looks as if he is likely to make a full recovery but medical staff have warned that, during this crisis, everyone must make sure that they get some form of exercise each day.*

Elizabeth showed Edward the paper

"You would have thought that his family would have

dissuaded him from living his life like that."

"You forget how difficult it is to talk sense into youngsters and how were they to know what would happen?"

She nodded, trying to remember some of Francis's exploits when he was younger and hoped that their grandchildren were as sensible as she had been led to believe. She did recall the time when Francis had 'borrowed' her car and taken it for a spin; he hadn't passed his driving test and naturally he wasn't insured. He had managed to drive her car into a ditch and they had had to go and rescue him. As she smiled at the memory suddenly something else occurred to her and she went to fetch her diary, noting that most of the events filling its pages had been crossed out and cancelled. Yet she did have a routine hospital appointment booked and wondered if that would still be going ahead.

As the date drew nearer and she had heard nothing, she assumed that she would still need to go along. In many ways she was relieved that they hadn't contacted her to tell her not to go but she was a little bit nervous when she set off on the day for the park and ride stop. This would have been a normal everyday venture but this time she didn't know what lay ahead. Just supposing the appointment wasn't to take place after all and somehow, she hadn't got the message; but hope and curiosity spurred her along. She was surprised to find that the traffic was hardly any different from usual, plenty of cars on the road and in the car park behind the waiting area for the bus. Perhaps this wasn't real after all but just an unpleasant dream; if only it was true. The bus arrived as scheduled and she was careful to wear gloves and as it wasn't too busy, she was able to keep her distance from others. Upon reaching the hospital she did find that it was less busy but the first thing she did was to grab some of the hand sanitizer gel which had already been provided. Surprisingly, she didn't have long to wait for her yearly check-up. The hospital wasn't heaving with people going about in all directions and despite all that extra space she decided to wait outside in the grounds until just before her scheduled time. It was a pleasant day with plenty of sunshine and although not exactly warm it was pleasing to sit on one of the seats in the paved area with flower beds and a few trees. Then she entered the waiting area inside the clinic in good time but found that instead of several rows of patients, there were just one or two chairs arranged spaciously and she appeared to be on her own, leaving her the choice of about five chairs.

After the appointment she wondered if it had been a waste of time but maybe she was lucky to be seen; they had taken her blood pressure which they said was fine and told her that she should contact them if she felt concerned. She soon found herself ready to leave wondering what the questions had been that she had intended to ask but she was more than happy to be on her way home again despite everything going so smoothly. One thing that she had noticed was how tired she felt and found herself walking along just like a zombie with no energy or enthusiasm to think; one foot in front of the other and little interest in what was around her, it must be due to the shock and the anxiety about the general situation, she told herself.

As she had known it would be, the true reality of the lock down was just beginning to sink in. It had been just like a rock having been hurled at her but the dark clouds weren't going to lift any time soon. Like most other people, she had got used to how things were now although getting over it wasn't exactly how she would have described it. It was of little comfort that the whole world had been affected and not just herself. As the days passed by acceptance soon came but the news was still pretty grim showing dreadful pictures of hospitals full of sick patients on ventilators and attached to tubes with the medical staff covered from head to foot in protective equipment and face masks, fighting to save them. Dreadful announcements giving out the increasing number of deaths became more and more depressing as was watching television and seeing patients on stretchers in hospital corridors and exhausted medical staff fighting to cope. Of course, as everyone knows hindsight is a great thing but even so many people in this country were asking why our government hadn't taken note of what was happening in other countries and look at how *they* were dealing with such a dreadful pandemic and why hadn't we locked down sooner?

Then they received the phone call. With everything that was going on she had completely forgotten that many months ago they had booked a river cruise where they would be stopping off at various different countries in Europe and they had never before had such an extravagant Holiday. There had been a few trips abroad and a longer one to visit family in South Africa, but apart from these and the holiday cottages that they had enjoyed in the UK they had never planned anything like this.

"We should go while we are still young enough to enjoy it." Edward had said.

There was also something rather appealing about the cruise as everything was being organised by the travel company; the air flight to the hotel, where they would be staying for the first night, and everything else involved even a taxi had been booked to take them to the airport. Elizabeth had enjoyed and agonised in turn over what she would need to take. As well as the new clothes she had purchased they had also bought a new large suitcase on wheels plus two smaller ones that would be suitable for hand luggage on the plane. She had packed nearly everything that she could a good while before their planned trip and just hoped that she had thought of everything.

"We're not going yet" mused Edward.

Once she had prepared everything and the cases had been placed in their spare bedroom, she was able to relax and look forward to what would be the holiday of a lifetime. She pondered on the interesting people that they would meet and the leisurely meals they would eat in amiable company. She only hoped that she would have enough clothes for the different occasions and for the possibly varied weather but she determined that she wouldn't worry too much about this. She definitely wouldn't mention her concerns to Edward as he would laugh at her. She had bought him a couple of new shirts but he still insisted on clinging to his old favourites which she had reluctantly washed and put in the suitcase. Their trip was now imminent and Elizabeth had emailed friends and relatives to let them know about their trip and to make sure that they knew her mobile phone number.

Edward had answered the call and she could hear him saying

"Yes, I quite understand. Thank you for letting us know."

He turned to Elizabeth

"Due to this coronavirus situation our cruise holiday has been cancelled; we can either get our money back or it can be kept for a future booking when all returns to normal. I said we'd let them know within the next hour."

Even though this should have been expected, the shock was still acute.

"What do you think?"

"We'd better get our money back because we don't know what the future will hold."

"I agree, I'll let them know. Maybe next year we can book something else."

Elizabeth took one more look at all her careful preparations that had been going on for months; suitcases on the spare bed and the passports that they had had to renew plus all the travel documents. She closed the door firmly; she couldn't face unpacking at the moment and anyway it looked as if she would have plenty of time as the empty days stretched ahead of her. Neither did she feel like notifying everyone about the end of their longed-for holiday arrangements just yet and anyway that would be the last thing on people's minds; there would be far worse things such as the anxieties about catching the disease, being confined, employment worries and so much more.

They were getting used to the restrictions, there was no choice, and she noticed how everyone else she talked to on the telephone or met when venturing out for the permitted exercise were accepting the situation. She hadn't heard any complaints. However, whatever her thoughts were, the day stretched before her like a long, boring empty road without any relief for many miles so she would have to decide on a course to take. First of all, she would tackle the mundane things that she would be doing anyway; she started on the shopping list and then glanced at the washing basket and scooped out the clothes for the washing machine and before she knew it, she had filled in time not with exciting things but with chores that had to be done and now it was coffee time already. During the next few weeks coffee time, lunchtime and their evening meals all became occasions to look forward to in the same way that they had previously looked forward to their frequent outings. She would find herself looking at her watch and as the hours ticked by. She would be relieved when she noticed the day was coming to an end as they were certainly beginning to drag, whatever undertakings she found to tackle in order to pass the time. Sometimes she did begin to wonder if some good was coming out of all of this despite, what seemed like the longer days, because previously it had seemed like normal human nature to complain about trivia, but conversations these days were not about the frequent laments

"What awful weather we're having, look at all that litter on the grass verge, that shop is selling inferior goods at higher prices" and so it would go on.

Now they were saying how lucky they were that the weather was good whilst they were locked down so that they could sit in their gardens. Although that would be if they were lucky enough to have one because unfortunately, they knew that there were people living in flats with no outside space. She and Edward could go out in the fresh air for exercise or visit a shop for necessary items although it looked as if there would be no wandering around shops casually looking for the odd impulse buy and most people found themselves 'in the same boat'.

Being grateful was one thing but being upset by the news certainly wouldn't go away and other cheerless information kept seeping through about people they only vaguely knew. There was one young couple who lived in a top flat in London with three young children and with no outdoor space except for a park a good walk away; the young mother had said it hadn't mattered so much before with friends coming round with their own children and sometimes all going off to the park together. Two other acquaintances were unable to go out as one was undergoing cancer treatment and her husband had chronic asthma; she wished that she could visit them but that wasn't possible just now. Many others as well were relying on neighbours and family to get their shopping and prescriptions and one lady who lived in a small cottage with only a small courtyard outside had said

"I haven't been outside the front door since the start of the lock down."

This made her feel so thankful for the little freedom that they did have and she really should just move on to the 'new normal' as it was now being called.

The following day she found the courage to wander into the High Street in Willow Bridge; she, like so many, was rather nervous of taking any possible risks but she really did need to get out and blow away any uneasy feelings that she had been harbouring. Walking around the quiet streets around her was eye opening but she did miss her previous routine such as window shopping or trips to the library and now wondered how she could ever have thought of it as being mundane. As she turned into the main, usually bustling street, she found herself in a ghost town; she had never seen anything like it even on a Sunday in the days when most shops were closed on Sundays.

She felt somewhat isolated as there were so few people about and the only shops open were pharmacies, those selling food and in some cases newsagents. The other shops and cafés were closed and shuttered as if it was the middle of the night, except that it was daylight with the sun peeping through the clouds. She had walked along trying to take it all in; the uncanny silence, empty pavements, little traffic or parked cars at the side of the road and the unease of waiting for something unexpected to happen. There was no jollity coming from the doors of the pubs that opened up onto the high street; nearly everyone was locked up at home. As she came up to the top of the hill, she noticed that Lloyds Bank was open with a queue of about eight to ten people waiting outside with such a big distance between each customer that they were spread out past several of the closed shops. There was also a member of their staff in uniform standing outside on the pavement waving in one customer at a time; thank goodness that she didn't need to visit the Bank.

As exercise was one of the things that they had been allowed since the lockdown she and Edward had made the most of it to save themselves going mad. One or two people she had had phone conversations with said that they would be staying in the confines of their own homes and gardens; and no, they wouldn't be going out. Although many had relatives close by and neighbours who had agreed to help with their shopping there were others who were not so lucky, such as two acquaintances that she had already spoken to. She learned that one lady, who had reached the age of ninety and lived on her own, had tried to get her shopping delivered from the local supermarket that she had been using frequently for many years; after all, hadn't the government encouraged this so that the vulnerable people could stay at home. Regrettably she was told that she would have to wait three weeks for a delivery. She was too proud to ask for help and so she ventured out to her corner shop nearby where she could get enough provisions to last her for a little while. The owner was most helpful and would have liked to have offered her a lift home in her car with her purchases, some of them quite heavy, but under the tough restrictions she realised that she couldn't do that. This had meant that her elderly customer had had to tackle the ten-minute walk home with her shopping, pausing every so often for a rest. She had remembered that there had been some seats and benches *en route* to her home but these appeared to have been taken away, so it looked as if sitting down was no longer encouraged. The old seats looked rather uncomfortable but at least they were somewhere to rest and to put down the shopping. Regardless she had trudged along the empty streets and after half-an-hour had arrived home exhausted. Apparently, she hadn't been the only person to suffer from a lack of assistance as another lady who was wheelchair bound and normally extremely self-sufficient had relied on her cleaning lady to help in other small ways, such as getting much of her shopping done. This regular help was no longer available as she was unable to come any more; seeing all the dust accumulate around her was the least of her worries. She now had to rely on her daughter, who lived nearly fifty miles away, but was allowed under the complicated government restrictions to visit and to bring her food and other essentials. Nevertheless, she had to think about the hundred-mile round trip for her daughter and hated disrupting her life so much, however willing she was.

The rules about going out were somewhat sketchy after the 'Stay at Home' message was first given out as if it was an offence to venture any further than outside the front door. Elizabeth sometimes felt guilty whilst walking around the block for exercise and chatting, from a distance, to people she had not met before as they all had something in common. They weren't supposed to socialise. This was due to the government announcements on the television

"Stay at home unless absolutely necessary. Help the NHS."

In the 'small print' they would be told that they *could* go out for exercise and essential shopping. Well, here she was once again. Edward was tackling the garden and so she had left the house on her own.

Where should she go today? Up the road she decided in the end and having reached the top she met a lady exercising her Labrador; the dog was called Toby but she hadn't thought to ask the name of his owner whom she had not seen before. It was indeed lovely to meet someone new and their conversation was initially about the virus of course, but Elizabeth learned much more. In the old days her walks mostly took her to the shops and occasionally she would see a neighbour or acquaintance with whom they may or may not have talked about things in general, but mostly they were in a hurry to get back to prepare the lunch or to get ready to go to a coffee morning or a meeting with a group of like-minded people. Now there was a good deal of unfilled time and she did enjoy seeing strangers. The Labrador owner explained

"If it wasn't for Toby, I suspect I wouldn't get out of the house."

Elizabeth said that she didn't have a dog any more but she did like to walk each day to fill in some time, not to mention to get some exercise.

"Yes, I know what you mean. How do you keep yourself occupied?"

"I read a lot and tackle crosswords; I've also bought myself a jigsaw puzzle" and she couldn't help but laugh about this as the last time she had done a jigsaw must have been with the grandchildren some time ago. "I've tidied out a few cupboards but it is less rewarding as time goes by. How long have *you* lived here?" she asked.

"I've been here for most of my life but I'm still exploring its history, especially now that I have more time. Although it's disappointing not to be able to visit some of the places I have on my list; hopefully I can continue when we have our freedom back once more."

"Edward and I moved here after we sold our business and although we are completely retired now, we do seem to keep ourselves busy – at least we did until all this happened to disrupt all of our lives. Do you have anything on your list that we should know about?"

Elizabeth asked this just to make polite conversation as she felt that they had by now got to know the area pretty well. She assumed that this lady was maybe a bit older than she was; despite walking with her dog, she was smartly dressed but wearing sensible walking boots and her short grey hair looked as if it had been newly coiffured. Elizabeth rarely thought about or even mentioned their old shop that they had once bought and eventually given up all those years ago; but she felt that she had met a kindred spirit, thus her freely volunteering information about her past. They had moved into the house in Willow Bridge after they had sold the shop that they had run together and she had loved and appreciated the modern central heating and the quietness of the road where they had moved to.. The rooms were smaller than they had been used to but it had been a small price to pay; before they had been unable to keep their bedroom windows open due to the traffic noise and fumes but here, on their first night she had flung open the windows and it had been a joy to be woken up in the morning by the birds singing. Edward would have preferred a larger garden at the time but otherwise it had suited them well and their son, Francis, had been easily able to keep in touch with his school friends.

After Francis had left home for university, they had wondered about moving again, or rather Edward had, as he still hankered after a larger garden, but nothing suitable had come up and these days Elizabeth found that the garden was plenty large enough. Even Edward was beginning to agree with her. They had made many improvements over the years and the extended kitchen looked out onto a secluded garden and the sitting room, also extended, overlooked the back garden also.

The lady continued "There's an excellent restaurant, when they can open up once more, it's called The Shambles, in the next village two miles away but don't be put off by the name. They serve excellent food. I sometimes go there with a friend, well at least we used to" she added as they both remembered what they were no longer able to do. "Although one of our local pubs The Crown, does deliver food free of charge. There is also an interesting park just half a mile from here and," she pointed behind her "it's still open, possibly because it's hidden away. It's the second turn on the left down a narrow alleyway, you can't miss it."

Toby's mistress mentioned one or two other places of interest and Elizabeth made some mental notes for the future, but especially about the park as that was something for the present and after all the years that they had lived here she hadn't remembered coming across it, although surely, she must have done at some point. Of course, these days there was certainly more time to cook, trying out different recipes and experimenting, it would make a change for them to have some food delivered to their door and she decided that ordering from *The Crown* was something they could easily do. Toby was getting impatient so she thanked the lady for the information and went on her way wondering if they would ever meet again. It was hard not being able to see family and friends and the awful part of it was that nobody knew what lay ahead; there would be no days out and dropping into somewhere for lunch on impulse and no longer would there be meetings of their various interest groups.

In the first week of the virus's emergence Elizabeth had telephoned friends, family and even acquaintances to see how they were getting on and the conversations rarely went beyond the current crisis but everyone was bearing up. She had gone through her diary and crossed out lunch and theatre bookings and there was also a cancelled coach trip that she had been looking forward to. Francis, who lived in Wiltshire, had been due to visit them with his wife and the four grandchildren but this could no longer go ahead so there was disappointment all round. All schools were closed and examinations were cancelled and this would affect the young badly and their own grandchildren were all feeling upset about it. John would be unable to take his GCSE exams this year and he had worked so hard and had been predicted to do well. It also looked as if it was unlikely that the twins, Alice and Sarah, would be able to take their GCSE exams next year either. Peter, the oldest, couldn't sit his A level exams which he had also been expected to do well in and therefore had decided to defer his university place. She felt great concern for them as they had all had good futures mapped out for them until this year, and now their term work was to be assessed instead of taking the exams. Where would it all end and what damage would it do in the long term? She herself still felt unsettled and anxious about the whole situation but it was so much worse for the younger generation and she asked herself how she would have coped if it had arisen when she was at school, it just didn't bear thinking about. Although she did remember going to pieces when exams were on the horizon and when she sat down in the examination room her mind would go completely blank resulting in her being unable to answer some of the questions that she would have known the answers to the day before.

Maybe for her an assessment, instead of an exam, would have been a good thing. On the other hand, the thought of not being able to visit friends outside of school or to be able to queue up at the swimming baths just didn't bear thinking about and she expected that she would have been bored at home. It now came to her that she would miss her meetings at the monthly book discussion group and when she spoke to one or two of the members on the phone, they had all agreed to carry on reading and to post their reviews on their website. It wouldn't be the same but they could still keep in touch remotely and they had to be grateful for that at least. The bookings in the Hall where they used to meet had been cancelled and so there would be no sitting around the table to praise or criticise what they had read and neither would there be chats over cups of tea and coffee about the world in general. Often conversations took place after the meetings had finished when they were clearing away the chairs; it was mainly small talk about holidays, family matters and sometimes even the weather. Sadly, that had all come to an end as suddenly as if someone had slammed a door shut; little had they known at their last get-together what was about to hit them.

These days Elizabeth often walked on her own around places that in the past she had only driven down to reach a particular destination. One of her favourite walks followed a quiet road around the corner from their house, so far unexplored. It wasn't until now that she would have even thought of strolling around the area close to where she lived, why on earth would she even if she had had the time? Yet now it was almost essential to do so with such a change of their customary habits; although it felt as if she was away from home, on holiday perhaps, as nothing looked familiar. She was aware of neatly cut front lawns despite the brown patches due to the lack of rain, yet there were flower beds full of colour with their variety of plants but she had to admit her ignorance regarding their names, Latin or the commonly known ones. She couldn't see any weeds – not that she was particularly looking for them – it was just the enjoyment of seeing such artistry on display; she had always been a lover of trees and all their beautiful spring colours which she was now able to appreciate to the full. It was then that she noticed two lone daffodils in someone's almost empty flower bed bending towards each other as if they were about to have a conversation which put her in mind of Wordsworth's famous poem about daffodils dancing in the breeze. There were more cars sitting on drives, no doubt because their owners were working from home or were on furlough. All the cars were beautifully clean because residents had been looking for something to do with more time on their hands; she couldn't help noticing the hose pipes and the water in the gutters but it didn't look as if any of them would be going anywhere much in their gleaming cars.

As Elizabeth wandered home after these eye openers, she pondered on the challenge that she and Edward had before them; they would need to stock up with food and she was not looking forward to this at all. She already knew that some people were afraid to go out; she wasn't afraid exactly but she had already heard that there had been long queues outside Tesco and she had always hated and avoided queues in the past. She had understood too that the shops and supermarkets would only welcome one person in at a time, so it would no longer be possible for her and Edward to wander into Waitrose together as they had done previously. They used to make a joint decision as to what they would eat on that particular evening and Elizabeth would often dissuade Edward from his impulse buys

"What on earth do you want those for? We've got a cupboard full of tins of baked beans."

"Oh, have we? I hadn't noticed I thought baked beans on toast would make a change from cheese or eggs for lunch."

When she went on her own, she would stick to her ready prepared list; her well thought out and organised lists were something that Edward used to tease her about. Yet now, once he was let loose in the supermarket there was no knowing what form his impulse buys would take. In some ways it could be interesting if he bought something that she would never have thought of even if he was tricked into the 'buy two and get one free' trap; three was usually rather excessive for just the two of them and it wasn't even as if they would be inviting anyone round at the moment. The walk to Waitrose took her about twenty minutes and it was less busy than she had expected it to be; she found a trolley and wiped the handle with an antiseptic wipe and joined the other customers standing two trolleys apart. This fitted the two-metre social distancing rule; nobody spoke. She would never have expected to find herself in a queue as previously she would have gone out of her way to find somewhere where she could walk in, pick up what she wanted and find a till where there were no more than two people in front of her. She would also check to see how full their trolleys were before joining them. These days she had to admit that she wasn't in a hurry to go anywhere so she may as well break the habit of a lifetime. At last, her turn came and a member of the staff beckoned her to get closer to the door. Suddenly a man appeared from around the corner; he was maybe in his thirties and athletic looking wearing a tracksuit and he rushed past the lady who had just waved to Elizabeth to enter the shop, nearly knocking her over – so much for social distancing. But there was not much the young lady could do so they waited for another customer to exit before Elizabeth could make her entrance. She was amazed at how patient and civilised most people were, they followed the rules like school children waiting patiently for morning assembly. Elizabeth entered the shop and grabbed things off the shelves without examining them thoroughly as she had always been accustomed to doing before; she couldn't wait to leave the shop and get home although she was certain that she may have picked up one or two items that she hadn't intended to. Possibly there would be foods with high fat and sugar content, but it really didn't matter as she wanted to get this over and done with. She walked down one aisle where all the shelves on either side were empty, there were no toilet rolls, kitchen rolls or boxes of tissues and once more she couldn't believe what she was seeing. She made her way to a cash desk and to fill in the time started examining what the lady in front was buying; there were six loaves of white sliced bread, a couple of jars of jam, several tins containing peas or carrots and others with some kind of meat and there were also two packs of doughnuts. There was no fresh fruit or vegetables and Elizabeth wondered if the lady was running a Bed and Breakfast or housing students only to realise that during the lockdown this would hardly be likely. Nevertheless, if it had been a B & B, it would not be one that she would have chosen if she was offered tinned meat and doughnuts for breakfast. At this point she wondered when would be the next time that they would leave home for a couple of nights away. Before she had the chance for further examination it was her turn and she moved up to the till; she glanced to her right and noticed a man standing with his trolley at the next till, although she couldn't see his face from the side view, she thought that she had seen him somewhere before. When he turned, the realisation of who it was had suddenly hit her, she started to panic and hung on tightly to her trolley, her hands becoming moist and her stomach doing somersaults. She was relieved that he hadn't looked her way so he wouldn't have seen her, but he did look just like Jerry Smith. He paid for his goods and left and as she walked home with her two bags of shopping, she acknowledged to herself that she had probably imagined it, he could have been anybody and she was probably becoming paranoid. Although, she did turn round once or twice even though it was rather unlikely that she was being followed even if it had been him, and she was sure that he hadn't seen her. Yes, she was getting obsessed and laughed at herself silently as she told herself that he had been in front of her anyway. Then she turned her mind to the fact that she had just had a new shopping experience and nothing to do with that dreadful man. She had calmed down by the time that she had reached home; she unpacked the shopping and went to sit down with a welcome cup of coffee after all her exertions and started thinking about what was happening to them all at the moment with the arrival of the pandemic. She couldn't help looking back to previous difficult times in her life, although none had been quite like this, a different world altogether.

Chapter 3

The North of England 1977

It had been a really good year, well so far anyway and especially for Elizabeth. They had lived in their lovely house since it had been built six years ago and it had a large garden at the back, overlooking fields. It was situated in a small market town near Sheffield where Edward worked for a large engineering company in charge of the Sales department. Francis, now aged six years, had settled down well at school and was making friends and Elizabeth enjoyed chatting to the other parents, mostly mothers, outside the school gates in the afternoons when she went to fetch him. When the weather was good, she and Francis would wander up to a park at the top of the road with swings and a slide; occasionally one of the other children would come back home with them to play with Francis. She had to admit that she was a little worried about one of his special friends who was rather boisterous and they would often land up jumping on the furniture when he came round.

"Do you do that at home, James?" she chided.

"Mum won't let us inside the house." So that answered her question. She hadn't met the mother but sensed that maybe she was houseproud and preferred her son to make a mess in someone else's home and yet there was no excuse not to keep the boy in check. James, like Francis, was an only child so they had much in common and it was good for both of them to have each other's company.

"Why don't you go and play outside?"

The weather was warm for the time of the year and even in the north they did get their share of sunshine, especially in the summer. She had remembered being a little annoyed when a relative living in Scotland had said

"It's always cold where you live, we have much better

weather in Edinburgh."

"You only seem to visit us in the winter months," she had retorted although she did sometimes wonder why this was, although they did appear to spend much of their summers abroad so why would they bother to come and visit relations with whom they had little in common?

She sighed with relief when surprisingly the boys left by the back door and ran down to the end of the garden, at least she was still able to keep an eye on them.

She often wondered what it would be like if Francis had a brother or sister; but she and Edward were still holding out their hopes. Most of the time she gave it little thought but there were other occasions when her longing sat heavily upon her shoulders; the cot and pram that they had bought for Francis were still sitting in the loft and she wondered if this was tempting providence and maybe she should sell them; after all they could always buy new ones if the time came. While the children were at school, a few of the mothers were accustomed to getting together for a morning coffee and today it was her turn to invite them to her home. Two of them brought their children who were under school age with them but despite Elizabeth's slight envy of their younger offspring she was happy on these mornings when they could talk about non domestic matters. Sometimes their discussions involved their various interests such as places that they had visited or their next holiday destinations. One of them was describing somewhere in Devon which sounded ideal for a family holiday and she thought she would mention it to Edward as she knew he would love the idea of a wooden chalet in a perfect rural setting but near enough to a secluded beach. She was just about to ask for more details when the telephone rang, a rather annoying interruption but she had better answer it just in case it was important and anyway an ignored ringing phone was such an irritation. Little did she know at the time that this call was to change her life forever.

"Edward, what on earth are you doing phoning at this time of day?"

She could hear the two small children making a noise in the room that she had just left, one of them screaming, and the mother saying

"Give it back, it's not your toy."

She closed the door behind her as she found herself grabbing the phone firmly so that her hand became damp with sweat. What on earth could be wrong? She had so often read in novels about someone's 'heart missing a beat' and this was exactly what it felt like as a worrying anticipation latched on but she waited for Edward to speak

"I thought I would let you know that I have been offered another job in the South of England; I'll tell you more about it this evening. It would mean moving but of course the money and prospects are much better. I'll see you later."

As she made her way back to join the others, she turned the surprise news over in her mind. They had lived in this peaceful, friendly place after having moved from London just a few days before Francis was born. The completion of their new home had been delayed but the baby had also decided to wait until after his or her due date; Elizabeth had already wondered if the two events would coincide, especially once the predicted date for the baby's arrival had come and gone. She had packed a suitcase of the things that she would need to take to the maternity home and stowed it in the car, just in case.

When the furniture van had arrived there was still no sign of the new addition to their family which came as some relief as it had meant she should be able to get the house organised before the baby arrived, and especially the nursery. They had been given a cot and had bought a small chest of drawers which Elizabeth had painted white and then had added some transfers of nursery rhyme characters. She had already informed the removal men where things should go and then carried on trying to empty boxes of books and kitchen implements; she had been amused when one of them had said

"Shouldn't you be sitting down?" He was a friendly, fatherly figure and she assumed that he had children of his own.

"There don't appear to be any chairs to sit on just yet" she had replied. After making the men numerous cups of tea eventually the furniture had been installed leaving them with countless boxes in every room and the washing machine waiting to be plumbed in. The carpets were due to be delivered and fitted but unfortunately not until the following week, so she knew they would still be in a bit of a mess for a while. Although the more she could do now before the new arrival the better it would be. The day after their move she had been searching for cooking pots in one of the boxes so that she could fix them something simple for their meal that evening but had to stop when a sudden pain had gripped hold of her. No, she had told herself it can't be the baby yet I'm not ready, and anyway the pain went away again almost as soon as it had come. On the other hand, she was still hoping that it wouldn't be too much longer even though a neighbour had told her that first babies were nearly always late in arriving.

Edward was busy looking into plumbing in the washing machine as they both knew they would soon be in even more need of this than usual; then soon the pains became more pronounced and with less time in between and she tried to remember what one of the nurses had said

"First babies usually take a long time........"

But at that point she had had to call Edward in a bit of a panic and he had driven her straight away to the maternity home, just a short distance away. Francis made his entry into their chaotic world a little while later. It was going to be some time yet before they could get their new home straight but neither of them had minded that.

When she opened the door, the conversation had stopped briefly as she slowly made her entrance to join the others; although one part of her was excited about Edward's phone call and his news she would miss her home and her friends; nevertheless, Elizabeth was always ready for a challenge. Two of her group had already moved away within the last year and so maybe it was her turn now. If they were about to settle in another part of the country this was as good a time as any, and especially before Francis started at secondary school, although that was some way off yet.

"Is everything OK? Maggie asked.

"Oh yes, everything is fine, thank you."

She wasn't ready to say anything at the moment, not until she knew a bit more and all had been confirmed.

Typically, Edward arrived home late that evening which was something she was used to by now but she was becoming impatient about what this new job entailed and she had already decided that she would send him off to get them some fish and chips as soon as he did get back so that she could hear more about his news without her being busy in the kitchen. Eventually he arrived and fetched the fish and chips; Francis had already been in bed for some time and was asleep when Edward went up to say good night. She hadn't seen Edward so enthusiastic for a long time and it had rubbed off on her too, she didn't learn all that much except that he would be earning more money and that the company was called Edison Engineering located in the South of England. In a way that was all she needed to know and hoped that it would mean Edward would be able to feel more relaxed as at the moment he worked long hours and would spend a good deal of time abroad. This move had to be better than it was now for all of them. It looked as if he'd already decided to take the job and, in her head, she was making plans such as saying goodbye to the people they had got to know which would be a little hard. Although, smiling to herself, she would look forward to the farewell to their nosy neighbour who was always complaining at the excited shouting of Francis and his friends when they were running around their garden. She was such a miserable old woman and rarely replied to Elizabeth's cheerful greetings; although in a more charitable mood she thought that maybe her neighbour had had sadness in her life and was envious of Elizabeth and her family. Anyway, that would be an enjoyable final visit but no doubt the feelings would be mutual and their neighbour would be hoping for a quiet couple who would move in without children, dogs or cats. She wondered how many of her friends she would keep up with as she could count on one hand those whom she had left behind in London and still kept in touch with, this would be more of a wrench but naturally she would meet others once they had settled into their new place. Moving house, and this was not their first time, always threw up problems and the first one facing them was that houses were far more expensive in the South of England than they were in the North.

Edward's new company had paid for them to stay in a hotel for a week during the school holiday so that they could look for somewhere to live. He would need to go into the office each day leaving Elizabeth and Francis to look round; as a colleague had agreed to fetch Edward each morning Elizabeth would have the use of the car.

They had already sifted through endless house details from several Estate Agents but out of about fifty or so there were only ten that could possibly be of interest. Some were above their price range but others were either too small, needing too much work to make them habitable or they were situated on busy main roads; in one case the house was next door to a lorry park. Elizabeth had already explained to Francis that they were going to have a little holiday as soon as he had broken up from school. He was quite excited about the idea of a stay in a hotel, usually their holidays were spent in caravans or holiday cottages, and the hotel had turned out to be quite luxurious. The two of them had driven round to look at the outsides of possible contenders and came back with a list of five that she had made appointments to view in the evenings once Edward had returned. There was one that was a good deal further away and so she made an appointment without being able to check that it wasn't situated next to a lorry park or by a river that risked flooding. One evening in particular they had arrived back at their hotel feeling disappointed that none of the houses had lived up to expectation for one reason or another. There were now only two more to view and their hopes now rested mainly on the one that Elizabeth hadn't been able to take a preliminary look at. They set off the following evening to look at a house situated in a small village and although it would be further for Edward to travel, they hoped that it would be worth it. They had some difficulty finding the house but when they did it was at the end of a narrow lane and they were in for a shock! It was surrounded by a high brick wall making it difficult to see it properly but they assumed that it was quite old, from the details they had looked at, but also spacious inside. Yet the appearance of the outside was enough to put anyone off; then Francis remarked

"Is it a prison Daddy?"

Edward turned to Elizabeth "Look there's a telephone box over there, go and phone to say that we are unable to come, I'm sure you'll think of a good reason."

As this was left to her, she climbed out of the car and made her way to the telephone box only to find that it was out of order.

"We can't just *not* turn up; it would be so rude and unfair to the vendors."

"OK, we'll go and have a quick look round and then take our leave. Maybe it won't be as bad as we think" he said doubtfully, but it certainly doesn't look as if it is what we are looking for.

This plan turned out to be easier said than done. They parked outside and walked up the long drive and were greeted by a pleasant elderly couple; the lady offered to make them some tea while her husband showed them round. The house appeared to be divided up into small rooms on the ground floor, many with a kitchenette attached. Elizabeth thought that maybe it could have been rented out as bed sitting rooms, possibly for students at some point, but the current occupants had obviously not made any attempts at modernisation. On the next floor they particularly noticed the huge bathroom with a large bath on legs in the middle of the room and more and more they really wanted to get away as soon as they could. Finally, they were shown into a beautiful garden at the back of the house with grape vines growing up one of the walls that enclosed the garden. Elizabeth felt embarrassed and wanted to let this lovely couple down lightly but she wished that she hadn't accepted the offer of tea. Fortunately, the couple chatted to Francis asking him about his school so that at least they were spared having to answer questions about the sort of place they were looking for, or indeed not looking for. At last, they felt able to take their leave.

"Thank you so much for showing us round but the place is probably a little too large for us."

When they reached the car Edward said "You didn't need to say anything."

"I know but I didn't want to raise their hopes. It would have been much easier if they had been unfriendly like one or two of the other people whose properties we have viewed."

Edward laughed.

Estate agents' photographs taken with wide angle lenses always made small rooms seem spacious and their ideas of 'a good-sized garden' made them wonder what a 'small garden' would look like. The final viewing was to another one that was also some distance away from their preferred location and they didn't dare to be too optimistic about this one even though it looked pleasant enough from the estate agents' photos. Before their appointment Elizabeth had decided to take Francis somewhere more fun during the day as he had been so patient, although she did think that he was enjoying the search just a little bit. They spent time in a park with swings, slides and roundabouts and she treated him to a beef burger lunch in a Wimpy Bar; she chose a cheeseburger and salad for herself.

Upon arriving at the house that evening into which they had put some feeble hopes, their first impression was encouraging and after admiring the large front garden they rang the bell. After a few minutes when there was no reply Edward tried again.

"You did make an appointment to view?" he asked

"Of course, I did."

At last, a lady appeared from the back of the house and let them in. She didn't appear to be too friendly but she was civil enough and duly gave them a tour. They were most impressed with the pleasant extended sitting room overlooking the garden and there was also an outdoor swimming pool. Elizabeth made a mental note to ensure that Francis was able to swim as this could be a hazard should they move here. The rest of the house needed a little bit of work doing to it but it was certainly comfortably liveable until they could get around to making one or two minor alterations.

"What do you think?"

"It's certainly comparable to what we are leaving behind and not as expensive as I would have expected."

"Shall we put in an offer?"

Their offer was accepted and their removal date was set for September so all was well as they had already sold their own house quite quickly. They were glad that at the last moment they had been saved from further searches although it did mean that they would need to rent somewhere to live in the meantime so that Edward would be close to his new place of work. From then onwards everything started to fall into place and they were able to rent a modern detached house where the owners – apparently, the husband was on sabbatical leave from his university – had gone abroad for a year and their other tenants had just left and there were only three months remaining. This had suited them perfectly as they had only wanted a short rental; a couple of the houses that they had been interested in would have meant taking the place on for a year. It also fitted in with Elizabeth as she would be able to spend time exploring the area whilst she looked forward to moving into their new home. They had already seen the headmaster of Francis's new school and at last all was well after their search and she was feeling optimistic for the future.

She had been picking blackberries in the lane by their rented house, and was wondering whether to make an apple and blackberry pie or something more ambitious. She went in search of one of the recipe books she had rescued from the ones that had had to go into store and could hear the telephone ringing in the distance.

"Mrs Wallis?"

"Yes speaking" she replied somewhat out of breath.

"I'm from the estate agents" then there was a pause

"I regret to have to tell you that the vendors of the house you are buying have backed out of the sale."

"Why?" She said, completely shocked.

"Apparently they had been selling due to bankruptcy but have now found the money they needed."

"Oh, I see, thank you for letting me know." She put down the phone being completely lost for words, and what could she have said anyway? This had been most unexpected but it was beginning to sink in and there was absolutely nothing she could do about it. They had lost the place they should have been moving into soon; no wonder it had been such a reasonable price and neither of them had thought to question it; why would they?

So, there they were back to square one again.

Chapter 4

Willow Bridge 2020

There was at least one thing they could appreciate, despite everything else that was going on, the warm weather was quite unseasonable for the time of the year, as April could be such a tricky month with its April showers and breezes. Today, even though it wasn't summer yet, Elizabeth planned to make the most of it and sit in the garden and relax as she would have done in previous years before life had moved onto a different plateau, and hopefully to try and forget about the situation they had all found themselves in. She was cheered by the sound of the birds singing and the warm wind gently blowing the tree branches, this was one of the things that the awful virus couldn't change.

Summer was ahead of them and surely optimism would follow. There was so much that continued as usual; hanging out the washing to dry in the sun, cooking, general housework and many other everyday tasks. Tackling these small things was exactly the same as it was before, the only difference being that this weird situation was always wedged at the back of the mind like an ache that kept returning as a reminder. On the other hand, shopping was a different matter entirely, as she had already found out, but the exercise that they took each day had become some kind of ritual. She had begun to enjoy these short walks especially on warm sunny days. The government had allowed exercise and essential shopping; a totally bizarre situation in what they had always thought was a free country. She now tended to plan her day around these two things, something that she would never have dreamt of doing before. It was difficult to think back to that time and she supposed that plans would have relied more on the weather or running out of something important and the casual walks would have taken place to further afield places if the mood took them. If they didn't wish to go out, they would just stay indoors. Although she had to admit that she was becoming a little restless at the moment and therefore decided that this could be a good time to wander off on her own; she checked that she had her front door key just in case Edward, who was admiring his work in the garden, also decided to go out for something. She called out. "Just going out for a gentle stroll, I won't be long." Once she had opened the front door and stepped outside, she noticed that something was not quite right and went to investigate. The fence at the side of the house had come down and had been flattened; she hadn't been aware of any high winds lately and certainly not with the beautiful calm weather they had been having. On further inspection it did look as if it had been rather badly damaged; she turned cold as an untoward thought dawned on her. Could Jerry Smith have been responsible? He had threatened her after all but was he really out to get her and why now after all this time? Surely even his mind would be concentrated on what had happened recently and she really had forgotten all about him until now; she shuddered involuntarily as the memory of his threat came back to her. Edward appeared and made her jump

"Are you alright?" he asked.

"Yes, of course" she lied so he continued

"I thought I would join you; the government rules are a bit confusing but at least we are allowed to go for a walk." This was exactly what she had been thinking and had been about to set off until she had noticed the destruction outside and that first awful thought had come into her head. As they were about to leave together, she pointed to the fence; Edward must have noticed it surely.

"Oh yes, I forgot to tell you that our neighbour phoned to say that his gardener had somehow managed to hit it while trying to manoeuvre the ride-on lawn mower. He tried to fix it but it will need more work so he's coming round to do it properly tomorrow."

She couldn't be sure whether Edward had noticed her loud relieved sigh "Phew", perhaps the loudness was in her imagination. On the other hand, she wasn't sure whether the relief or the annoyance that he hadn't told her sooner was uppermost, but then it had been her decision not to tell him about Jerry Smith. She was a little quiet at first but eventually recovered once they were on their way and, as on earlier occasions, they not only saw neighbours but also many other people who were almost strangers; they waved to each other acknowledging some kind of affinity.

Despite everything that had been thrown at them they still received cheerful smiles and certainly the sunshine of the last few days had raised their spirits. Elizabeth noticed a couple, probably about her age, walking towards them and they crossed to the other side of the road, an action that they were all getting used to and didn't take offence because they were all trying to keep their distance. Later on, a young child, walking with his mother and a baby in a buggy, called out 'thank you' when she and Edward had stepped into the narrow road. They did find that there were still some people, with mobile phones glued to their ears or texting, who tended to ignore this new precedent about 'social distancing' and Elizabeth sometimes had found herself walking up an uneven grassy bank to avoid them. As far as they could, they stuck to their old habits and Edward would glance at his watch when they had once more come back to the bottom of their road; they had been out for about an hour and it was now time for lunch, another routine that they had suddenly become more aware of and looked forward to. How sad was that, she thought, as life appeared to be slowing down into a far less stimulating pace. In an earlier life, when all was normal, they could have been planning an afternoon with friends or family or to attend a talk and the days passed without marking each small occurrence. She did have to admit that perhaps it was a good thing that they no longer found themselves dashing around as if there was no tomorrow and trying to cram a week's chores into one day; life was far more relaxed and the new experience was similar to being on holiday when they were able to amble along without any cares about their usual everyday responsibilities.

After they returned home, she quite wasn't sure why, but suddenly the thought of Jerry Smith came into her mind again; she couldn't understand what had triggered this as she had purposely put him to the back of her mind. Even in the past, if her mind hadn't been fully occupied, she sometimes remembered something untoward or unpleasant that had happened recently and sometimes even a long time ago. It was usually something quite trivial such as a comment or criticism from someone which she had been sure hadn't meant to be hurtful. Nevertheless, these incidences did sometimes come back to haunt her such as the time that someone she knew quite well had said

"Where did you get that jumper? Was it from the market?"

Elizabeth assumed that she had thought that it looked cheap and nasty, whereas after she had looked for ages to find something to match a smart skirt, which she wished she had never bought, and eventually had paid more than she had intended for it in a small boutique. Stupidly this had upset her at the time and she sometimes thought of the comment when she had worn the jumper and it rather looked as if the Jerry Smith incident would be just such an example. Most of the time she felt positive and was able to enjoy their limited way of life but now and then she felt mildly depressed. This must be one of those bad moments and instead of her usual optimism, bad things had uninvitedly crept into her thoughts and inevitably this man was one of them. Because he had sneaked into her subconscious it was important to get to the bottom of it all; it wasn't even as if she was worried that he would come and attack her as it was rather far-fetched like something she might read in a novel. The first thing to do would be to check in her diary to see if she had entered anything about this unnerving situation that could be significant. Often, she would record unpleasant things as if writing it down was a way of getting over and forgetting such an unsavoury experience. She hadn't written anything for some time now and she supposed that it was because there was really nothing of great interest to mention and at one point, she had been bemused to see that she hadn't remarked on anything positive, only the small upsets of the daily routines. Now she had good enough reason to look for her diary on the shelf in the kitchen where she had always kept it, it wasn't there. That was odd, she usually placed it back methodically after writing her entries; she would have to look for it again later.

In the meantime, she was determined to concentrate on good things such as having more free time, whether they wanted it or not. Sometimes they would have a leisurely conversation over a cup of coffee, although admittedly this didn't include future plans for the visits they wanted to or needed to fit into their schedule.

But then nothing was quite as before. Even shopping was rather like preparing for a trek to difficult foreign terrain, but they were used to that now and no longer did everything appear to be so odd. Apparently, many people had used the extra free time foisted upon them to tidy up cupboards and drawers. Elizabeth had started doing this as well and one thing she had noticed was that once she had begun this unexpected, but much needed occupation, she had found some pleasure in the pursuit. Even so she wondered if she would have been quite so keen if it hadn't been for the lock down. She did appreciate one of the advantages when finding long-lost items such as kitchen tools, clothing and books that had suddenly turned up. She had put aside at least three books that she hadn't remembered reading before, when tidying the bookcase, and it would be something to look forward to later.

Inevitably as time passed by, she had become disheartened even though she had taken up her painting and drawing again but nothing she did pleased her and one day she had grabbed her sketch pad and started tearing everything up in a frenzy. She still wondered if this had anything to do with her recent bad experience with the hostile communication that she had received after she had built up hopes for extending her hobby and her interest in art revived; but this was even before Covid had reared its ugly head. It was then that she remembered she hadn't found her diary but her reason for locating it no longer seemed important and she turned her mind to other things. The television programmes that she used to enjoy were no longer showing and were replaced by game shows and repeats of old, although just occasionally enjoyable, detective dramas. There were plenty of other things too

that were of no interest to them at all.

"Why on earth would anyone want to watch hospital dramas when we are all traumatised by the dreadful real-life events in the Covid-19 wards?" Edward protested and she nodded wholeheartedly in agreement.

Indeed, there were certainly many such programmes showing such as *Casualty* which had been going for more years than she could remember and other similar ones as well, not that she ever watched them as they were so depressing even at the best of times. Surely even people who habitually watched these things must have been tired after seeing the same old thing day after day, evening after evening. They were grateful at least for the small form of relaxation that came with some of the repeats, often of programmes that they had watched many years ago and had not remembered much about; they would no longer be going to the cinema or to the theatre which meant they appreciated these so much more.

At the end of the month something rather remarkable happened. A man they had never heard of, named Tom Moore, celebrated his hundredth birthday; not so unusual these days except that he had decided to walk laps of his garden with his 'walker' to raise money for the NHS and he managed to raise £33 million after saying that he wanted to do something to help. It made the news world-wide and it was something to feel cheerful about at last. Elizabeth felt rather inadequate after hearing this and she racked her brains to see what she could do that would benefit other people during the crisis. Needless to say, she hadn't come up with anything yet but she would no doubt continue with her telephone calls to acquaintances who lived alone. One or two of them had been pleased that she had contacted them and talked, admittedly, about everyday things because what else was there? Sometimes their conversations would last for quite a while almost as if the person on the other end of the line was hanging onto the phone trying to keep a link with the outside world.

"Thank you so much for phoning, it was lovely to talk to you."

This is what they would say after chatting for about half an hour even though there was little news to impart, although she did at least learn that they were 'doing OK'. Some were working on their gardens and others were enjoying walking their dogs; nobody was doing anything outrageous but neither were they complaining. One thing she did notice was that most of the people she telephoned never phoned her back so she took it that they were not feeling lonely or depressed and weren't waiting by their phones for a longed-for call. Some of them would no doubt have families and close friends, she hoped so anyway and had ended up by just keeping in touch with close friends and relatives.

Edward had gone off on his own to visit Tesco to stock up with food so she decided that she would try and find the little park that the lady with the Labrador had told her about. She set off and walked towards the spot and soon found the little alley way, at least she thought she had located it, and walked to the end. How odd that she had not been there before in all the years that they had lived here. Nevertheless, she couldn't see the park and thought that maybe there was another alley way so she started to make her way back and noticed an old derelict building in the distance; there appeared to be a well-trodden path leading up to it but she had to squeeze past some overgrown bushes to gain access. All around it was a big open space which looked like some kind of park so this must be the correct place; there was nobody around. She cautiously made her way to the ruin through the weeds but couldn't make out what it had been, the lady certainly hadn't mentioned it but Elizabeth was intrigued. It had quite possibly been a cottage at some time but there was little left of it now, then suddenly it dawned on her why she had not been here before, it had looked, and still looked like an entrance to someone's home, maybe at one time to the derelict cottage. She was quite amused and couldn't wait to tell Edward, although there had been many other places that they had frequented over the years so they did have plenty of choice but this was most fascinating. Then she became aware that she was all on her own and in the middle of nowhere and wondered if this was wise; during the lockdown there were less people about but how safe was she? She jumped when she heard footsteps and was ready to run when the sound of a dog barking reached her and Toby came bounding along. She turned round, she was breathing normally now, and welcomed the sight of the lady she had met previously.

"Hello, again."

"So, you decided to investigate, it's an ideal place to let Toby run."

Elizabeth realised that it would no doubt be mainly dog walkers who would be more likely to look for such a place as this.

"I was just wondering what that old building was?"

"Oh yes, apparently a couple had started to build a bungalow there, it must have been about fifteen years ago now, but they hadn't applied for planning permission and so they were forced to demolish it. I'm not sure why that section was left although I did hear that the man had since died so I don't know what will happen to it now; maybe someone else will apply for planning permission but it would be a shame in many ways as the little park could be less accessible if that happened."

So that was something else she had found out during her wanderings and she began to make her way home again ready to decide what to do next. Perhaps they should get a dog as it would give them a really good reason to walk; they had had dogs in the past but the walks had to take place even on cold or rainy days. Occasionally in the Summer it had been necessary to venture out early before the intense heat would hit them, neither would she be too keen on taking the pooper scooper and having to bend down to scoop the mess into the polythene bag and then to search for the appropriate bin, which would no doubt be full. Therefore, she immediately decided against it and anyway she didn't think that Edward would warm to the idea anyway and she quickly dismissed the thought.

Once she reached home and opened the front door, she could see that Edward wasn't back yet, the house was quiet as she walked through to the sitting room at the back where she decided to sit down whilst waiting for his return. She was surprised at how exhausted she felt these days and a comfortable easy chair welcomed her; she didn't really understand why this was so because, despite everything, she was doing more or less the same things that she had always done. She still walked, went shopping and did housework and cooking. Then it came to her that perhaps it was due to the lack of socialising with friends and family which was causing her lethargy or maybe it was just a sign of old age creeping up on her and this thought made her wonder about someone she hadn't been in touch with lately so she made the call.

"It's funny that you should say that" said the friend she rarely spoke to now, not recently anyway, "I feel tired a lot of the time, I suppose I'm just not dashing around so much these days".

A couple more telephone conversations had at least confirmed that she wasn't alone in this listlessness. So maybe this was a mystery solved but before she could think of any other possible reasons she was in for a shock.

A few days later her tiredness developed into something much worse; every time she attended to some minor chore, she found herself having to sit down to recover from the effort. A trip upstairs to fetch something left her lying on the bed for a while before she could find the energy to descend once more and for this reason she decided to go to bed early. By now she was experiencing a sore throat although she did put this down to the amount of time that she had spent talking on the phone that day. They had also been tackling the garden which was something she didn't enjoy much but the fact that all the weeds had practically filled up the bin was rewarding at least; nevertheless, the unaccustomed effort must have taken its toll. It had indeed been hard work; the only sort of gardening she enjoyed was when it was looking reasonably straight in the first place and she could just potter and preferably in decent weather. After a reasonable night's sleep, she woke on Sunday morning with her sore throat raging rather than improving; when she tried to talk her voice was gone as was any small amount of energy that she had previously had. She got out of bed and realised that she was shaking. She had been watching on the News the distress of patients with Covid-19 in hospitals all over the UK being unable to breathe. What should she do? 'Stop panicking' she told herself and went onto the internet to check for the symptoms of the Coronavirus.

She was somewhat relieved that she didn't appear to have any of the symptoms, even the cough that had just developed, although irritating, wasn't too bad and she was pretty sure that she didn't have a temperature so she didn't say anything to Edward. She had begun to feel a little better already when she realised that she was probably just coming down with a bad cold and was grateful that she had already bought boxes of tissues before the panic buying had started. Nevertheless, she struggled on for two weeks without noticing much of an improvement and the cough was annoying her. Normally after one week following a cold she would feel alright again, but not this time. It appeared to be taking so much longer and maybe it was something to do with the stress that they had all been under. Therefore, she would just have to carry on as well as she could with the mundane and just occasionally even with the not so mundane tasks. She still kept up with her telephone calls; after all what else was there to do? Of course, nobody had any exciting news about holidays and interesting visits so they spoke mainly about the current crisis and it was amazing how most were grateful that none of them were unemployed or about to lose their businesses; many could see how being retired had its advantages. Even one of her friends who had the habit of updating her fully on her medical complaints and the lack of progress from doctors and hospitals was remaining positive, despite the news becoming worse by the day. It wasn't just the elderly who were dying from the virus now but one or two younger people as well and tragically some of the medical staff who had been fighting to help all those people who had been infected, which had put themselves at risk too. The UK death toll had by now reached the highest in Europe and someone she had spoken to had said

" I am really annoyed about this because if the government had acted sooner many lives could have been saved."

"I do agree with you that it makes the UK look rather stupid in the eyes of other countries; it's embarrassing."

In the meantime, Elizabeth was still coughing although it wasn't bothering her as much and she was beginning to get used to it; after all she had certainly had worse colds and viruses than this in the past but the following day Edward remarked

"It's time that that cough of yours had gone away after so long."

She was a little surprised as he wasn't usually quite so caring. Until he had mentioned it, she hadn't been feeling ill and certainly not as she had done in the beginning, and yet now realised how tired she still was and she was also aware that she was walking around like a zombie. Then before she had had the time to think he announced

"I think we should go for a Covid test; they are doing them in a supermarket car park only a few miles away."

What more could she say, he was probably right and so she left him to book them both a place. They set off a couple of afternoons later just as if they were going for an outing or to visit a National Trust property, even so Elizabeth looked upon it as another experience that they would be embarking upon. There was little traffic on the road and they would be early for their appointment, but better early than late as they wouldn't want to miss their slot. As they got nearer to their destination, although they had been to this supermarket before, everything looked unfamiliar. There were road works and unclearly marked detours.

"I'm sure it's here I've been many times before." Edward remarked

"Why didn't you put the Satnav on?"

"I would have done, but I was so sure that I knew the way."

They carried on driving as there was nowhere to turn round even though they knew that by now they were probably heading in the wrong direction. Elizabeth glanced at her watch for about the third time and had already resigned herself to the fact that they would probably have to go home and book for another day, but making sure to first check the directions properly the next time. Suddenly Edward, after turning down a side road unknown to them, pointed to a signpost.

"Look that's it, isn't it".

There it was, an arrow pointing to the 'Covid testing centre' which appeared to be just a short distance away. They followed the road and found that they were on familiar territory at last and Elizabeth started breathing properly again although they were by now cutting things rather fine. She supposed that being just a few minutes late wouldn't matter, or so she hoped. They arrived with about three minutes to spare, despite having fortunately set off so early in the first place. They joined the queue which moved surprisingly quickly and somebody wearing a mask and dressed in protective clothing came up to the passenger side of the car and asked if they were both there to be tested so she handed over the booking forms that they had downloaded from the internet. Shortly afterwards someone else appeared and tested Edward first and then came round to the passenger's side where she had opened her window. It was just as she had seen on television, a long stick with the end covered in what looked like cotton wool was poked into her throat making her want to cough and then it was removed and wiped round the nostrils and she feared that she might sneeze. It was all done quickly and efficiently so that they were soon on their way home again. Now all they had to do was to wait for the results of their tests.

"Supposing they are positive?"

“Let’s just wait and see” Edward said impatiently. He was right of course but she knew that she wouldn’t be able to relax until they received the results which should be sent in a day or two, they were told.

“If you don’t have something that causes you concern, you’ll be worried because you’re not worried” Edward continued.

A few days later they both received emails stating that their Covid tests had come back negative. Elizabeth supposed that she should have felt relieved but it was really no different from getting confirmation from the dentist or at a hospital appointment that there was no further action required. She had to admit that she had worried about so many things these days but, oddly enough, getting Covid hadn’t actually been one of them. Even though she was still feeling a little weak at least her sore throat had gone and maybe even the cough was less troublesome but despite their negative tests Elizabeth found that the lethargy was worse and getting her down; it was really all that she needed and it was making her feel depressed. These days there was no possibility of consulting a doctor unless there was obviously something seriously wrong and she was aware that everything was getting so much worse for everyone. The new variant of the virus was spreading fast and with no sign of people in this area having had the vaccine yet, in fact they had heard little about it and the headlines in the news were only confirming all the extra cases that were cropping up and, even worse, there were so many more deaths and the hospitals were being overwhelmed. One day she made a decision; surely, she should have got over this cold, cough or whatever it was by now so with great trepidation she tried the number of their GP’s surgery towards the end of the surgery’s usual hours not expecting to get a reply. When someone answered she was so shocked that she nearly dropped the phone; after all a friend had told her that she had had to hang on for hours – although Elizabeth knew that knowing her friend it would be rather an exaggeration.

“Can I help you?”

She tried to explain her symptoms and added afterwards that she had received a negative Covid test.

“I’ll get someone to phone you back.”

She had yet another surprise when one of the doctors

telephoned her at about eight o'clock that evening.

"It sounds as if you may have had a nasty virus and they often do take a while to clear. If you are no better in another week do phone us again."

Oddly enough she felt better already! She had already become aware of the scare stories going around about people who had been unable to consult or to see a doctor and yet she had had a helpful call and it made her think that although many doctors could be working from home one of them had taken the trouble to phone her long after surgery opening hours.

What a strange way of life they had now found themselves in and she started to think back to the days long ago before they could have imagined in their worst nightmares what was to occur in the twenty-first century resulting in the extra hand washing, social distancing and sanitising, not to mention the lack of casually dropping into a cafe or pub at a whim. She then found herself back in the nineteen seventies which had been another world altogether despite some of the same apprehensions.

Chapter 5

Bardent Wood 1977

Once more the search was back on and the second time round was not as exciting as it had been the first time, full of great anticipation. Once again details of houses, thatched cottages and bungalows – new, old and dilapidated ones – dropped through their letter box but time was running out and they had lost their earlier enthusiasm; they had gone through it all before looking at so many properties that were unsuitable for one reason or another. When they appeared to find what they were looking for the relief had been so profound and the anticipation of a home that would give them satisfaction once they had eventually got it to their liking. Then their hopes had been dashed and the owners of their rented house would be returning in October and Edward said

"Maybe we should try and find somewhere else to rent to tide us over until we find something suitable, we don't want to rush into a sale that we might regret later on."

This did make sense and it would give them more time. With another rental they would need to be less particular as hopefully it would only be for a short while. Little had they realised that finding a property to rent posed far more difficult than they could have imagined. Even smaller properties and some without gardens and in an area that wouldn't have been their first choice posed problems of one kind or another.

"That's a ridiculously high rent for such a small place."

Another point was that if they found a rental some distance away from the area that they chose to live permanently could mean that Francis would have to move schools more than once.

Then one day as Elizabeth was glancing casually yet again, without a great deal of hope, through some details that had arrived from one of the estate agencies she noticed a place in a hamlet called Bardent Wood. The leaflet had appeared amongst all the other inappropriate ones but this time she was encouraged to take a second look.

"Look, this could possibly be an interesting property, what do you think?"

Edward looked over her shoulder at a photo of a modern house placed in a reasonably sized garden.

"It does look more like what we had in mind although it appears to be in the middle of nowhere, nevertheless I think it could be worth taking a look."

They made an appointment and having had their hopes dashed so many times before, they drove in silence determined not to become too optimistic. Their first impression was favourable as the house, with a pleasant front garden, looked out on to a small green. As they were being shown round Elizabeth's spirits rose; the sitting room at the back overlooked an immaculate garden so there would not be too much to be done there, Elizabeth thought. My word, she had almost moved in. They didn't have too much time to ponder on its advantages or its disadvantages, the fact that they liked it was enough and so they decided to put in an offer providing that there was a school bus to take Francis to the school in the larger village a couple of miles away. Having checked this out they had their offer for the house accepted and fortunately they still had their rented place until October. Naturally Elizabeth felt anxious most of the time that something would go wrong with the sale, as it so easily could do; after all they had already experienced that trauma before. Once more they would have to check with the headmaster of Francis's new school that he would be able to start the new term before they had moved into the area. It all seemed a bit Déjà vu after the last time but again she would be able to spend time exploring the area near the house. Having at last made the decision about their future home she made a point of finding parks and other places near to their rented house that might interest a six-year-old because with the rented property at least, there would be no need to decorate or to do massive cleaning and sorting out of cupboards. This would mean she could devote her time to Francis before she became involved in what would lie ahead of her once they had moved to the house in Bardent Wood. That thought made her hold her breath 'once they had moved in?' It had to be alright this time, surely, so she put her anxieties behind her and took the opportunity of having more time on her hands by experimenting with cooking which also kept Francis interested when she tried out things that she knew he would like. After their walks around the little lanes and the visits to countryside that was completely new to them, she would make a point of coming home to sit down and read or play games with her young son. She had never really had enough time to do this in the past and she found that life had become exciting once more with their pending new home and being able to enjoy the freedom in their temporary one. No doubt once they had settled into the new place there would be plenty to do, but Elizabeth was extremely glad that they wouldn't have to rebuild the house that they were buying and it looked as if even decorating wouldn't be needed for some time at least. But the uneasiness still sat at the back of her mind although she really did have to assume that all would be well this time and she should think about the positive things such as the unpacking. This would be done mostly by herself and she wouldn't mind it at all, in fact she looked forward to it. Maybe there would be a little bit of decorating to be done, perhaps starting with the bedroom that Francis had chosen with the light pinkish walls; all the other rooms were off white, maybe a daughter had previously inhabited that room.

"Don't worry Francis, we can paint over the pink" she had promised, hoping that he wouldn't choose bright orange or some such colour although she felt fairly confident that he would go for something plain where he could put up his favourite pictures.

It would be wonderful to reacquaint herself with items of furniture, pictures, books and ornaments that had been in store since they had moved out of their last house. Everything was set for the move to take place in October during the school half-term holiday. Edward had been driving Francis to school in the mornings from their temporary place and she had picked him up in the afternoons but she wouldn't be sorry when that came to an end; driving about fifteen miles along twisty lanes was not so bad in the summer months but fortunately they should be settled by the time winter arrived and she would be able to see Francis safely onto the school bus. She knew that she wouldn't be able to relax completely until the removal van was sitting outside their new front door; the fact that they had been forced to find another house when the other one had fallen through had taken away Elizabeth's trust in good fortune. They had been cutting it rather fine as their rental was shortly due to come to an end; previously they had thought that all was going to plan but it had turned out that nothing was ever straightforward so until the contracts were signed and exchanged, they still had to wait patiently. The days dragged by; by now the date had been fixed for their move and a removal company had been booked. One part of Elizabeth's brain looked forward with excited anticipation and yet another part was filled with fear. At last, the day eventually arrived when everything was signed and the relief was so overwhelming that she felt that she had been living on the edge of a cliff for a long time. Edward opened a bottle of wine that evening to celebrate and they sipped it as they relaxed for the first time in ages. In the end it turned out that this would be one of the happiest years of her life and at the time, fortunately, she had no idea what lay ahead of her.

Their new home was one of four modern detached houses and she soon became friendly with the neighbours on either side; the other neighbours were out at work and they saw little of them. Sheila and Angela, on either side, had children at the same school as Francis and each morning they would all stand together outside their houses waiting for the school bus to arrive. On her first morning Sheila had invited Angela and herself in for a cup of coffee and afterwards it became a habit to take in turns to meet in each other's homes after seeing their children off to school. It was beautifully casual so it didn't matter if they hadn't tidied up their breakfast dishes or run around with the Hoover and it was just like old times in the days before their move south. All this meant that Elizabeth had plenty of freedom and was already planning her future for the time when Francis was old enough so that she could look for a job. For the moment during school hours, she was able to decide whether to go out for the day or to stay in and do domestic things such as cooking, gardening or housework; it was certainly a good life. Not quite like *The Good Life* in a television comedy series shown on the BBC in 1975 starring: Richard Briers, Felicity Kendal and Penelope Keith. Unlike that couple the Wallis family were not growing their own vegetables or making do with handmade or second-hand furniture. Elizabeth's neighbours had become good friends and she asked herself what more could she want?

But as these delightful months went by with her relaxed and busy way of life, she was oblivious to an underlying problem. She had enrolled herself in a course in Art History at a technical college nearby although she usually had to leave early in order to be back in time to fetch Francis from school. This wasn't much of a problem as she wasn't all that bothered about sitting the exams at the end of the course as she was doing it more for enjoyment than anything else. Her neighbours had helped her out quite a bit by collecting Francis from school if necessary but she really didn't wish to put on them too much. Then she realised that something had started to bother her, although she couldn't quite put her finger on it, they had lived here for almost a year now and Edward was spending more and more time away from home, often abroad. One of the things that had attracted him to this job was that he had been away from home so often in his previous one and had worked long hours anyway; the offer of more money had certainly been an enticement but seeing more of his family had propelled him to take up the offer. However, it did look as if now he was not much better off than he had been before they had moved here. Just as the three of them had begun to enjoy weekends exploring places in their new area their carefree weekends had begun to diminish because Edward had kept being called away on business trips. It had been then that she had begun to notice the men in her neighbourhood mowing their lawns at weekends and felt a pang of envy if it was one of those times when Edward would not be back for the weekend and she could see the disappointed look on Francis's face. Admittedly sometimes he would only be away for a couple of days but there were other occasions when it would be for more than a week, rather like it had been in his previous job. On one particular Sunday she could smell the freshly mown grass and hear the hum of lawn mowers and although Edward was due back that evening, she reluctantly went to the shed and fetched their mower; she had difficulty in starting it but was determined not to ask for help and was relieved when it started up at last. It was therapeutic walking up and down trying to keep the lines straight and admiring the neat look but then she remembered that time recently when Edward had been in Scotland and she had had a phone call from his boss.

"We need him to come back urgently for an important meeting in London, can you ask him to leave the car in Scotland and fly down. He can fetch it at a later date."

She was aghast and wanted to say something but thought better of it, as it wouldn't do to make an enemy of his employer; after all he was well paid and she should be grateful for the luxurious living it was giving her. Neither did she feel compelled to find a job to keep a roof over their heads, as some women had been forced to do, giving them nightmares about child care; this was costing so much that it took away from the money they would be bringing home. When Edward had telephoned her that evening, he wasn't best pleased about having to drop everything but nevertheless he did as he was instructed. The last straw had been when he had had to go off on a trip to Russia and just before he had been about to leave, Elizabeth could see that what she had been suspecting for a while now was really true; she was happy with her life but he was not and it looked as if history was repeating itself. He had already started applying for other jobs and had asked her to post his applications along with the accompanying Curriculum Vitae, which she had done, once he had left for the airport. She tried not to think too far ahead and carried on as usual. Once more she had tackled the garden that weekend, fighting ground elder and bindweed when Francis had come running out

"Mummy, the phone keeps ringing."

"Don't worry, I'm just coming."

"Edward, what is it? Is everything OK."

"Yes, fine but I won't be back just yet as British Airways are on strike, in fact there don't appear to be any planes setting off at all at the moment. I'll see you soon though. Sorry I'd better go."

That was all she needed and just as she was trying to count her blessings and not feel too dissatisfied with the way things were turning out she had answered the phone rather half-heartedly as it was unlikely to be Edward again so who on earth could it be?

"It's Colin from Edison Engineering, I gather Edward is stuck in Russia..........”

she was just about to elaborate on the inconvenience of the situation when Colin continued

“There are no flights from Russia for the foreseeable future so it looks as if he’s well and truly stuck there, thank goodness that it isn’t me. It may be that he can get home on a sea voyage although it would no doubt mean getting through Europe somehow, goodness only knows how long that will take.”

But she had heard enough, she was already worried and really didn’t wish to hear any more from Colin, although she was sure by his sympathetic tone that he meant well.

“Thanks for calling, Colin. I’ll let you know when I next hear anything. I’m sure Edward will find a way to get home, he always manages to overcome obstacles that put themselves in his way.”

She had used her optimistic, positive voice for Colin but it didn’t mean that she believed in what she had said. Thankfully, the next call was from Edward.

“I’ve managed to book onto a Russian flight....Aeroflot. I’ll be arriving at Heathrow on Friday.”

She couldn’t help laughing with relief and longed to phone Colin but she would wait until she had picked Edward up from the airport first. On Friday there wasn’t too much traffic *en route* to Heathrow although she and Francis had set off early as the roads could have been packed with people trying to get away for the weekend, although she suspected that mostly they wouldn’t be setting off until the afternoon after leaving work early. She and Francis arrived in good time and Elizabeth looked forward to giving Francis a view of the aeroplanes setting off and coming in to land which she thought would be a good excuse for keeping him off school for the day.

“We are still a bit early for Daddy’s flight so why don’t we go to the cafe, would you like an ice cream?”

She had ordered the ice cream and a coffee and as she drank her coffee leisurely, congratulating herself that all had gone well, there was an announcement over the tannoy to say that the flight from Moscow had arrived. She was staggered, she had never known a flight to be early, that had to be a first; in her experience flights were usually either late or cancelled altogether and if they were on time, it was a bonus. She threw back her coffee and had to persuade Francis to reluctantly leave his last mouthful of ice cream and they appeared just in time to see Edward, wearing a Russian hat, standing with his hand luggage waiting for them. So far so good but little did she know at the time what was to follow.

"That was quick."

"It's because I only had hand luggage and didn't have to queue for hours at the conveyor belt. "Where's the car?"

"We had to walk a long way from the car park to get to the correct terminal as it wasn't clear at first where it would land so we will have to walk back to where I parked."

Edward had been happy with that until they had reached the correct car park but she couldn't remember where exactly she had left it, she had kicked herself for not making a note of the floor and the actual space. It wasn't quite the same as trying to locate one's car in a supermarket car park after all and so much time was wasted looking for it.

"This is definitely the correct floor isn't it, Francis?"

"Yes," he said doubtfully.

"It was in the middle somewhere."

They walked around and she could see that Edward was getting a little fed up, which wasn't surprising after a trip that he hadn't been too keen to make.

"I thought you said that it was somewhere in the middle."

She couldn't quite understand why she had thought that. Suddenly Edward spotted her small blue Ford car near to a corner and sandwiched between a BMW and a camper van; at least there it was and it hadn't been stolen which had been something that had crossed her mind at first.

Eventually things began to settle down a little after the Russian trip and Edward's erratic hours appeared to stabilise but a week or two later when Elizabeth had been busy enjoying herself once again, she failed to notice that Edward was still having regrets about his latest move and was not happy with the company who had taken him on. None of his job applications had been successful so far, but at that point she did wonder if another move was inevitable. Yet Edward was not the only one to be feeling unhappy with the way things were going at work; his colleague, Colin, apparently was feeling the same amount of dissatisfaction. Anyway, an uneasiness had already begun to find its way into Elizabeth's daily thoughts although she told herself not to panic yet. Then one evening at about six o'clock she was beginning to assemble the food items that she would be needing for their evening meal; Francis had already devoured fish fingers and peas soon after he had arrived back from school. He was always hungry and fish fingers were one of his favourite foods although he would have had a good substantial lunch at school, or at least she assumed he did as he never complained about the school food as she had done as a child. The phone interrupted her just as she was about to start her preparation. She loved cooking in her delightful kitchen although she never knew at what time Edward would return. Last Christmas he had bought her something special to keep the food hot, it was called a Hostess Trolley and it had been such a valuable gift and the food never seemed to dry out. She picked up the receiver only to hear Edward's voice.

"What now?" she thought.

"I'm bringing Colin home with me for a meal; he says he has some exciting news."

"What......" she began, but he had already rung off saying that they would be there in about an hour.

Elizabeth set to work cutting up the two pork chops that she had bought for the two of them; she coated them in batter which would eke them out to make enough for one extra. Once she had set the table, looked out a large packet of long grain rice, some soy sauce and a bottle of wine, she felt pleased that she was well prepared for an unexpected guest. She fetched some mixed vegetables from the freezer to cheer up the rice; not strictly an authentic Chinese meal but under the circumstances it would now have to be some sort of Elizabeth Wallis variation and she only hoped that Colin wasn't a fussy eater or a vegetarian.

Everything was ready and keeping hot by just after seven o'clock but there was still no sign of Edward and Colin. An hour later she realised that she had been looking at the clock every five minutes, where were they? Just as she prepared herself for a call from the Police to say that there had been an accident, she heard the phone and grabbed it.

"Colin and I have stopped off at the pub and we'll be there in about twenty minutes."

The twenty minutes was nearer to half an hour but fortunately the food didn't appear to have spoiled, thanks to the Hostess Trolley. Relief flooded over her once they had arrived; the fact that they hadn't been involved in a car crash and that the food was still edible stopped her being annoyed; as a peace offering Colin handed her a bottle of wine which looked, from her limited knowledge, rather an expensive one.

Over their meal and having consumed the other wine that Colin had brought, as well as the one she had provided, he put his latest grand plans before them and his route of escape from the company they both worked for.

"We've bought a restaurant and a couple of holiday cottages in Brighton; you'll have to come

and visit us once we have settled in, in fact you can stay in one of the cottages."

After he left Elizabeth said

"My word he hasn't lost much time."

"Good for him, he certainly doesn't let the grass grow under his feet. I will miss him when he's gone. Maybe we'll take him up on his offer of one of the holiday cottages."

Soon after this enlightenment they started making plans to stay in a cottage for a weekend that Colin had offered them in Brighton, before the holiday season kicked in. Even Elizabeth was impressed with Colin's ambitious plans now that he had given in his notice at Edison Engineering. Their weekend in Brighton had been planned for a couple of weeks later and by the time they arrived it looked as if Colin and his wife had spent time on doing the place up; it was still old with low ceilings and beams and an inglenook fireplace but the bathroom and the small kitchen looked fairly modern. They also looked forward to eating a meal in Colin's new restaurant, which they had also been doing some alterations to, on the Saturday evening. They were delighted for Colin and his wife, Sally, that the restaurant looked fully booked and busy. They had asked for an early sitting being a more suitable time for Francis and the food was excellent; Colin was a great host going round all the tables and pouring wine and chatting to the diners then he drew up a chair at their table and joined them with a glass of wine in his hand. It was not until afterwards that they learned Sally had been slaving away, almost single-handedly, in the kitchen; she had previously had experience working in restaurants but Elizabeth couldn't help wondering if she had realised what she had let herself in for.

Having seen Colin's enthusiasm for another way of life this began to take firm hold in Edward's mind and eventually, albeit reluctantly, Elizabeth's interest was aroused when he suggested that they should take a leaf out of Colin's book. The thought of seeing more of her husband had some appeal, but there would be consequences no doubt. They certainly wouldn't want to invest in a restaurant, but what about a shop?

In the end it was difficult for Elizabeth to understand why she had agreed but nevertheless they spent the next few weekends studying the Exchange and Mart paper and looking around different parts of the country for suitable businesses to invest in. They had ruled out restaurants, but also book shops, newsagents, off licences, food shops and even a boat yard as well. Luckily even Edward with his great enthusiasm had not liked the idea of early mornings in the case of newsagents and food shops didn't appeal to either of them. The book shop idea, which they had initially rather fancied, really threw up far too many restrictions and the living accommodation above the one they were interested in was far too small and without a garden for Francis to play in, just a small courtyard. Then, one day a hardware shop was advertised in one of the newspapers in a place called Trintley near Cambridge and just a couple of hours drive away from Bardent Wood. It had large living accommodation attached to it and a garden, so they set off on one of the hottest days of the year, in the sweltering heat, to have a look. She had been planning to sit in the garden to enjoy the sunshine but it wasn't to be. Once they arrived in Trintley, they found themselves in a pretty village but Elizabeth had a shock when the owner of the shop named House Supplies, opened the door to them.

Here was a man, maybe in his forties, with nicotine-stained teeth and trousers held up with braces over a grey shirt that had probably once been white. Elizabeth gulped and tried not to show her disgust as he invited them in. They started the tour in the shop first and afterwards moved into the house adjoining it, but needless to say Elizabeth had already ruled it out. The shop area itself was vast with a cellar below and it seemed a bit dreary but no doubt had some potential, although that wasn't really of interest to her. There was a door from the shop into the house where they were taken to the top of some stairs leading onto a large landing with a big kitchen on the left and through the kitchen were two more rooms. Outside the sun was blazing hot but the inside of the house was pleasantly cool, although a little dark, as all the curtains had been drawn across the windows. The bathroom at the top of the stairs was large but altogether rather awful which made that other bathroom that they had once seen in an earlier house hunting trip, seem luxurious in comparison. In total there were four good-sized bedrooms on that floor and downstairs there was a room at the front overlooking the road. At the back a big sitting room with a fireplace, blocked up with hard board, had French windows overlooking a garden – the current owner had obviously saved the best room until last but Elizabeth wasn't fooled. As they entered that particular room Edward gasped in surprise when he noticed the small round window to the left of the French doors and he looked at it with fascination for a moment or two and then turned to Elizabeth and said,

"I'm sure that this is the same house that my brother rented and lived in for a while about twenty years ago."

Elizabeth said nothing as she looked at the little window which didn't open, but she supposed it was some sort of feature which, with a stretch of the imagination, could be making the room a little lighter. She imagined that this was common enough in houses of this age. Edward had already mentioned, when they had first seen the property advertised, that his brother had once lived in Trintley and that he had actually stayed with him once all those years ago. Neither of them expected that they would be entering the same place that his brother had rented all those years ago and she wondered afterwards if this coincidence could have made Edward more interested than he would otherwise have been. After the viewing they went out into the sun and walked round the village, Elizabeth enjoying the escape and the clean air noted that it seemed a pleasant enough and quite large village. Even Francis, who had been fairly quiet, seemed relieved to be outside once more and became especially interested in a duck pond in the park nearby. Edward admitted that this shop was certainly the best place that they had seen.

"It's undoubtedly spacious and low in price for the size, although it would need a good deal of work and money spending on it." Edward was full of what it could be like when it was renovated and Elizabeth could almost picture it too, with the emphasis on the almost. Yet she had quickly put the dreadful aberration to the back of her mind once that they were on their way home. She wasn't too worried anyway that it could even be a possibility as they would still have to sell their own house first, and she had to admit that sometimes Edward would come up with what seemed to be an excellent idea only to change his mind at the last minute. She was confident that this initiative would be short lived; then the unexpected happened. After the three weeks that their house had been on the market a cash buyer had come forward which propelled Elizabeth once again into what might come about. Edward said

"We'll never find anywhere as spacious as the place in Trintley with a garden and also it is located in a pleasant area. It's a good price so there would be money left over from the sale of our house to get it into shape."

Before Elizabeth had had the time to think about it too much or to try to dissuade Edward, they had made an offer at the Estate Agents in Cambridge. At the time she was rather relieved to hear that another offer had been put in but Edward was determined and contacted the Agents again.

"The people who made the first offer still have a place to sell so if you were willing to increase yours a little more you could probably be in with a chance."

"What should we do?" Edward asked.

But she already knew the answer and their new offer was duly accepted. By then she was beginning to imagine getting in a company or companies to modernise the place and could almost picture a spacious home with all the modern facilities. Once more there was much emphasis on the *almost*. What had they done?

Chapter 6

Willow Bridge 2020

Elizabeth's daydreams stayed with her and the memories of past times were so vivid that it seemed as if she had gone back in time and was living through those years again and she couldn't help wondering if what she had been through before had been worse than this, or maybe just different perhaps. Of course, she had been much younger then and she had got through it with many happy years to follow, but she was less sure about now. In those past days they were in control to some extent with what happened but they were certainly not in control this time. She was woken abruptly from her thoughts of the past when the phone rang making her jump. She was a little surprised to hear that it was Stephen, someone she had rather lost touch with. She had been friendly with his wife, Janice, but after their last move she had seen little of her and their main connection had been mainly the brief notes in their Christmas cards mentioning family and what they were currently up to.

"Elizabeth. I'm afraid I've got some bad news."

She waited; she didn't know what to say. What could it be? Was one of them ill with the dreaded virus perhaps? Stephen sounded healthy but his voice was shakier than she had remembered but then they were all getting older.

She reached out for the chair and sat down.

"Oh dear," was all she could say.

Then she remembered that the last time she had spoken to Janice was at the start of the Covid outbreak when she had phoned so many people she hadn't spoken to for a while. Janice had been one of them and they had chatted for a while reminding her of Janice's sense of humour and how they would laugh at the silliest things. It had been then that she had mentioned she was suffering from a heart complaint but in her usual way had made light of it and had added

"The doctor said that losing weight could help. But it's not as if I overeat although I could do to get more exercise, but I do so hate walking just for the sake of it."

Elizabeth had sympathised but still wondered about her idea of 'not overeating'. She had always been fond of cakes and biscuits and in the days when Elizabeth had passed round a plate of biscuits when a few of them had gathered for morning coffee, Janice would say

"I really shouldn't", but nevertheless helped herself.

"Anyway, with the current situation I'm not able to have routine check-ups any more but I have tried walking. Stephen keeps dragging me out of the front door although all the exercise I need is proving difficult, especially as I can no longer go to the swimming baths which have had to close. Swimming has been a great help but there are many others so much worse off than me."

"I'd forgotten that recreation facilities have had to close" she replied.

She couldn't remember when she had last been swimming on her own; it had all been such an effort getting to the swimming pool, changing, making sure to walk through the foot bath and plunging into a pool which was usually crowded. Then there would be the youngsters diving just in front of you, although she supposed it would have been different if she had been a good and keen swimmer.

"*And* I don't eat *quite* as many biscuits," she continued. "I've also tried sweeteners in my tea and coffee, although they say that these are not good for us either but when I ran out, I went back to the sugar."

Well at least she was making an effort Elizabeth had thought at the time.

She quickly turned her attention back to Stephen again anticipating that something was terribly wrong.

"Janice died yesterday."

She hadn't been expecting that, it really had come as a shock and left her feeling badly shaken.

"Oh no, I'm so sorry."

There was a big pause, the shock had hit her and she didn't know what to say'

"Are you alright?" asked Stephen.

“Yes, yes of course. I just haven’t taken it in, that’s all.”

“She was taken into hospital two weeks ago and they said it was some complication due to her heart condition. Because of Covid the family and myself had to take it in turns to visit her. Then she died rather suddenly.”

“I’m so, so sorry Stephen,” she repeated “ I just don’t know what to say. Is there anything I can do?”

She realised that people always said that but of course what could anyone really do for those who had just lost someone close to them? She tried to remember all the good times that she and Janice had had together; the shopping trips, getting lost when they were to meet up with other friends, sitting down with her in a cafe when she had twisted her ankle and feeling embarrassed at the length of time that they had spent there and quickly ordering more coffee and cakes. Now she was dead and it still hadn’t sunk in; what about poor Stephen though? She felt that Stephen was fighting back tears.

“I wasn’t with her when she died,” he said.

What more could she say? After a while he added

“We can only have a small family gathering at her funeral but hopefully we will be able to have some kind of memorial service when this is all over.”

Elizabeth was stunned that she wouldn’t even be able to attend the funeral.

It was terrifying enough to think of those dying from Covid, alone without family to comfort them and only a member of the medical team at their side as it was dangerous to admit a relative let alone more than one of them. When she had heard about such cases on the news, she had tried to imagine the feelings of loneliness and being abandoned and not having someone close to you by your side; however ill you were while you were conscious it must have been a devastating feeling of great loss. Even with another illness apparently there were limits as to how many family members could be there at once and certainly no other visitors, although at least Janice’s family had been able to see her even though the visits were fewer than they would have liked.

She thought back to when her mother had died, following a stroke, and how all her family had been there for her during the last days of her life and Elizabeth had been at her mother’s side on the day t she died, even though she wasn't sure that she would have been aware of it. But she had been there all the same and she couldn't help feeling grateful that mother hadn't had to live through these current times. Even her funeral had provided a get-together for her friends and family and they were able to reminisce and remember the good times. There would be none of this at Janice's funeral or any others for that matter whilst Covid threatened.

Just as she had come to terms with this sad news something else untoward was to follow. She and Edward had started off for their customary walk a few days later, glad of the fresh air and now at last free of her lingering cold symptoms, treading carefully as they didn't want to risk tripping on an uneven pavement. What a thought! Accident and Emergency departments were to be avoided at all costs at the moment and what had happened next was rather ironic. Later that evening it occurred to her that the dustbins would be collected the following day and so she decided it was time to empty the overflowing kitchen bin; she grabbed the bag of rubbish from the bin and opened the back door ready to take the few steps to the dustbin; the back door slammed behind her making her jump. It didn't matter of course as it wasn't as if she was locked out. It wasn't until afterwards that she realised what a mistake it had been for her to look back at the closed door and she couldn't be sure why she did so, instinct she supposed, but her lack of concentration was certainly the cause of what was to follow; she carried on with her task then, wham, down she went. She was lying on her front beside the dustbin and the sudden shock left her unable to move for some time before she was able to call out for Edward; but it was unlikely that he would be able to hear her from one of the rooms inside the house. She wasn't quite sure how long she had laid there before she had managed to get up, it couldn't have been that long even though it had felt like an eternity. Just at that moment Edward had appeared in the kitchen and as he glanced through the window, he had noticed the open dustbin lid and his wife trying to struggle to her feet.

"What on earth happened?"

By then she was standing up but leaning heavily on the water butt.

"I don't know, I was being careful as usual but suddenly I landed up on the ground."

With his help she managed to struggle into an upright position, a dizziness gripping hold of her and together they slowly made their way to the sitting room where, thankfully, she was able to sit down with her foot on a stool. Her eyes had become droopy after she swallowed a couple of painkillers, and she eventually dropped off to sleep.

That evening she hadn't felt hungry and Edward had brought her a light meal and a glass of wine and finally, feeling more relaxed, she had eventually limped to the kitchen and found an elastic bandage for her aching ankle and had settled down to watch the television. Not that there was much of interest these days on TV but they had found a programme that, although they had watched it probably at least twice before, it took her mind off her ankle and she was able to loosen up a little.

After the ten o'clock news she decided to prepare for bed, but when she tried to stand up she found that she was unable to put any weight on her foot and her ankle was painful and swelling up under the bandage like a huge balloon. She really was stuck now, she couldn't move. Edward went off in search of an old walking stick that had once belonged to her mother, but where it was now was anybody's guess. In the end she pushed the foot stool forward and by bending and hanging onto it was able to push it and move herself to other pieces of furniture and door handles that she could hang on to and was then able to get herself to bed by dragging herself up the stairs in a semi kneeling position, not knowing how on earth she had got to the top she found a chair to hang on to thus managing to continue with her slow movements to the bathroom and eventually into the bed. Edward had brought her some more pain killers in the hope that she would eventually manage to drop off to sleep having already broached the subject that she really didn't wish to think about,

"It looks as if we may have to take a trip to the A and E department tomorrow at the local hospital."

That was a grim speculation as they already knew how emergency services were overstretched and she was in total despair about her predicament, and extremely frightened but determined not to think about it just now. Although she didn't sleep for a while, she did eventually manage a few hours of peaceful oblivion. In the morning the dread returned but nevertheless she gently tried to lever her legs out of the bed and noticed that the swelling had gone down quite a bit; she gingerly tried to put her foot on the floor and then was successfully able to limp a few steps thanks to the support of the bandage and was overwhelmed with relief. Naturally shopping and walks would be out of the question but at least she could get around the house; fortunately, it didn't look as if she had broken anything and it was probably just a sprain. The avoidance of a trip to hospital was the greatest relief of all to them both.

She wasn't accustomed to sitting around but this is what she would need to do for a while; luckily Edward was pretty energetic and happy to do the shopping and the cooking. What a lucky escape she had had. Although she had already been concerned about going out with the virus threatening them all, and especially for shopping, she still wondered how safe it was for Edward to wander off to the supermarket. Nevertheless, they had been going out, unlike some of their acquaintances who had been too scared of the possible consequences; but they had been determined not to become prisoners. Earlier, once all the dangers had been stressed by the government, especially for older people, she had phoned about three supermarkets to see if she could put in an order to be delivered; people she knew had food delivered all the time even before the Coronavirus but she had found out, like so many others, that the shortest time she would have to wait would have been at least three weeks and it was then that she remembered the lady of ninety who couldn't get her food delivered either. So there wouldn't be much hope was there for them. So much for the unhelpful Government advice asking vulnerable people to stay at home; and she had become one of them although hopefully only temporarily. Even so Edward had just had his eightieth birthday and he was supposed to be on that list. On checking the freezer and the kitchen cupboards she was relieved to find that they would have enough food to last them for at least a week. Quite by coincidence they were soon to learn about the kind and thoughtful people who were putting themselves out to help others. The next day a note was posted through their letter box from a young volunteer, who lived at the end of their road, suggesting that if anyone needed help with shopping or collection of prescriptions to ring the telephone number below. So, it wasn't all bad and it was good to know that they could get help if they needed it. Edward was stubbornly independent and they didn't take up the kind offer. As time went by she was able to walk a short distance, certainly to the nearest shop, although she took to wearing the elastic bandage all the time as it gave her more confidence. Nonetheless she was always glad to sit down and rest once she had returned home.

The News on the radio and on the television became more and more depressing, if that was at all possible, and she decided not to listen to it too much but this was easier said than done as Edward was following every single announcement. She had always appreciated music on the radio when she was doing the chores but these days there were the continuous announcements on the high number of deaths occurring and the UK numbers were still creeping up. This would be repeated later on the television which they had switched on to try and find something to take their minds off the sad reality of life as it was at the moment. Since the start of Covid all they could find to watch on the television were old repeats of Inspector Morse and other involved thrillers that they had seen before, but nevertheless it was still a form of escapism. Having had an excuse to sit with her foot up, once her ankle started aching, Elizabeth had plenty of time for reading and looking at old photographs and diaries which inevitably took her thoughts back to the past once more.

Chapter 7

Trintley October 1978

The removal date for their Trintley venture had been set for October, during half term, and exactly one year after Elizabeth, Edward and Francis had moved to Bardent Wood. She couldn't help wondering about possible significance for this odd coincidence and she had mentioned it to Edward but he hadn't even remembered their far more exciting previous change of residence, in Elizabeth's eyes anyway, Trintley was certainly going to be rather different.

The day had arrived for their move to the House Supplies hardware shop and they soon found themselves driving into Trintley, a pleasant enough place and fairly quiet at 8.30 in the morning, the scheduled time for their arrival. Because of this early start they had spent the previous night in a hotel in Cambridge having left Bardent Wood the day before as soon as everything had been packed into two removal vans from their home, so much loved by Elizabeth. One thing that had puzzled her was that they had required two vans, one smaller than the other, something that had never happened before and this time they had only lived there for such a short time; how on earth had they managed to accumulate so much stuff? Before their previous move she remembered how much she had given to Charity shops and to several dustbin collections when she had been full of ambitions for a home free of clutter and yet somehow the clutter had still managed to appear unbidden a year later. Luckily Edward was able to find a parking place close to the shop although it wasn't until later that they found there was a garage around the back. The removal vans arrived soon afterwards and they had parked in cordoned off areas; obviously someone had been organised enough to arrange this. It hadn't been something that would have occurred to her having never moved into a busy high street before, where there was no drive up to the front door.

It was at this moment they were in for a surprise. A third van draw up on the road outside and they were soon to discover that the cottage next door was also changing hands on that same day, therefore it became somewhat congested in the High Street. Mr Grimsley, the previous occupant of the premises, now owned by Elizabeth and Edward, or so they thought, opened the door and they walked into the house. Elizabeth cast her eyes around her, the place looked even worse than it had done the first time she had seen and dismissed it. She found herself half closing her eyes as if this would dispel the dreadful image before her and for the first time in her life she really had wanted to die when she thought about what she had lost and had realised her life would never be the same again. The normality she had previously known would be a distant dream. This was only the second time she had walked into the devil's lair even though Edward had already visited it again and she did wonder if she had accompanied him on that occasion as well, she could have made him change his mind. Although upon reflection probably not as in his usual way he had soon lulled her into some kind of false security.

"The rooms are such a good size and we can soon lick them into shape. The place is so much cheaper and the money we will get for our house will be enough to spend on doing it up."

He could see that she still had doubts.

"I won't be away from home as much and I'll be able to spend more time with Francis".

Briefly she had thought of the times in the past spent on her own, but more important than that she had envisaged what could be done with coats of paint and being able to spread out their furniture adequately. It was only now that she asked herself, and not for the first time and probably it wouldn't be the last, what on earth they had agreed to. It wasn't as if either of them had ever had any experience of working in a shop except for the short time she had worked as a volunteer in the OXFAM shop many years ago. That had been when Francis was about eight months old and a neighbour had asked if she would be willing to help out as they were finding it difficult to recruit, especially younger people. In fact, she had rather enjoyed herself and she and the elderly lady she had worked with had more interesting conversations than she had with her friends; these tended to be related to children and child care. Elizabeth and this particular lady, called Mrs Jones from Wales, had contemplated on what the empty shop next door would turn into; would it be another shop or even a restaurant perhaps? They both hoped it wouldn't be turned into a house as had happened recently, in a couple of cases, when shops had closed down.

Mrs Jones, in her beautiful Welsh lilt had said

"It's such a shame when we lose shops only to become houses, and usually for the wealthy who can afford to turn them into grand homes."

Elizabeth knew about Mrs Jones's feelings for those who were better off than she was; she had had an impoverished childhood and had then been widowed at an early age without having had any children of her own. Elizabeth had thought that she was probably in her seventies. Nevertheless, she was one of the kindest and most considerate people she had ever known and always ready to help others; she hadn't agreed with the building of the three large, expensive houses that were now taking up a piece of land that had been sitting vacant for a long time and had remarked

"There's enough space for many smaller houses that people could afford."

Mrs Jones herself lived in a caravan and she had told her how comfortable it was.

Elizabeth could see her point but had decided not to comment and wondered what she would have thought of her own substantial home surrounded by a large garden. One of the disadvantages during her volunteering days had been that she had felt guilty about poor Francis sitting patiently in his pram behind the shop counter during her fairly short time on duty, although customers often came and chatted to him so he did have plenty of attention.

She wondered what Mrs Jones would have thought of their current venture; taking on a shop and the thought made her smile. However, this undertaking would no doubt live with her for a long time but it was too late to have regrets. She'd just have to learn to live with it and all the difficulties that it would bring, in the slim hope that there could be advantages as well. She needed to be brave for Francis's sake and she quickly wiped away her tears and she even tried to smile when their son crept up behind them. On the other hand, Edward appeared to be excited about it all and she tried to visualise what it could be like after his ambitious plans for renovation. Presumably they would find builders, decorators and plumbers to turn things around and as the place had cost so much less than the amount that they had received for their last house, it would presumably be within their reach. This gave her some small comfort although unfortunately it did not last for long when she later learned to her horror that Edward intended to do a good deal of the work himself.

In the meantime, the Grimsleys still hadn't moved out and all their furniture was stacked in the front room overlooking the road. It was at that point, when they were wondering what to do next, that the call had come from their solicitor informing them that there had been some legal hitch and that they didn't own the property yet, which meant they were unable to officially move in. He agreed to drive over and expected to be with them in a couple of hours.

"Wow, that'll put the cost up of the solicitor's fee but what can we do?" grumbled Edward.

There they were with the vans outside containing all their furniture and finding themselves congregated in the sitting room at the back of the house just waiting. But there was one thing that they had completely forgotten about until there was a loud knock on the front door and they couldn't think who it could possibly be; not for them presumably as the solicitor couldn't have arrived already unless he had come by helicopter. She tried to imagine this austere man in his dark suit climbing into a helicopter. Suddenly it dawned on them that they had arranged for a firm to come and survey the place for wood worm on their removal day. The person on the doorstep announced

"Rentokill." This would make a difficult situation even worse but they let him in and left him to get on with the survey; however almost his first words were

"I could do with a cup of tea".

The house didn't actually belong to them yet and all their belongings were still waiting outside although she had packed tea, coffee, sugar and mugs in the car as she knew that the removal people would need frequent refreshments. The Wallis family had already spent about an hour hanging around in the empty room waiting for their solicitor and the Grimsleys were still in the kitchen upstairs and they tried to explain their situation to the Rentokil man but he had some sound advice for them.

"If I were you, I'd ask them in the kitchen if you could make us some tea. They're hardly going to object, are they?"

The man was right so somewhat reluctantly Elizabeth crept up the stairs to ask if she could use their kettle; she wasn't quite sure why she was feeling so anxious about it but nevertheless she felt uncomfortable. She didn't like the original owners much and was only too pleased to keep out of their way but as Mr Rentokill had already said, they would be unlikely to object to her request. To her surprise Mrs Grimsley amicably pointed to their grubby kettle, fortunately some instinct had already persuaded Elizabeth to retrieve the tea making equipment from the car and she had managed to purchase some milk from across the road so she was able to put a tea bag into one of the mugs. She gingerly picked up the kettle of boiled water to add to the mug and with great relief left the kitchen ready to add milk and sugar once she had reached the empty room again. She handed over the tea and the man took it gratefully, but at the same time she realised that she and Edward would have to wait a while longer for cups of coffee for themselves. She also thought about the removal men, were they used to waiting outside peoples' homes for ages before they could start to transfer the furniture? Edward and Elizabeth were standing with Francis in a dirty, foul-smelling room and there were piles of old newspapers on the floor. Fortunately, they had at last been goaded into action by Rentokil; Francis, wanting to be useful and at Elizabeth's suggestion went to the small supermarket over the road and asked if he could borrow a broom. Even though they had just bought a hardware shop a broom was not something included in the stock. The friendly manager smiled with some amusement at the small boy and found him a broom and Elizabeth, feeling embarrassed once more, went to the kitchen again and asked for a bucket of hot water into which she added cleaning fluid and bleach that they had also brought with them in the car, and at the last moment Elizabeth had even included a mop. She then flung open the French windows so that they could breathe some pleasant October air and Edward ripped the hardboard away from the fireplace and removed the newspapers outside ready for disposal later. With the bleach and cleaning fluid they washed down the walls and floor. They also decided that the removal men should start to move some of their belongings, even though they were not the owners of the house yet, so the men started by unloading the garage contents into the cellar. Thankfully by now the previous occupants had found a van and shortly afterwards removed their possessions. The Wallis family continued working with the bleach and detergent in the other rooms so that the furniture wouldn't be loaded into the squalor. Elizabeth overheard one of the removal men say

"What the hell did they want to move here for?"

She immediately saw his point, as they had just moved out of a lovely modern detached house into this. Elizabeth had been pleased to be filling in the time as she hoped that eventually their new home would legally be theirs and at least they had already made a start on an arduous task. Eventually, their solicitor arrived having sorted out the legal hold-up, whatever it was. Elizabeth showed him round and he didn't disguise his disbelief and horror. By late morning all was under control, as much as it could be under such circumstances and Edward announced that he should open the shop. Elizabeth gawped at him.

"We have to open up as soon as possible before our hopefully future customers give up."

The stock that they had paid dearly for mainly consisted of rusty screws and nails, a vast quantity of fire cement, some perished teats for babies' feeding bottles (no bottles though), loads of reels of cotton, mostly blue or pink, and a few birthday cards. Elizabeth had decided to avoid the shop on that first day but instead tried to get some kind of order into their living accommodation. As far as the house was concerned there were still some curtains left by the previous owners, all closed, and when she tried to draw them back it proved to be almost impossible because all the curtain rails were clogged up with grease. Elizabeth washed a brown pair from the landing, in the bath although they turned out to be cream with a delicate pattern on them so she was soon able to hang these, now relatively clean ones, in the bathroom. When she felt that she had done as much as she could, she reluctantly entered the shop with Francis at her heels; he wasn't at all daunted and was taking it all in. She had wondered if he had realised that this was going to be their home but anyway, he appeared to be treating it all as a big adventure. The first thing she did, once inside the shop, was to empty all the ashtrays and she even put those nasty glass containers straight into the dustbin as well, such was her revulsion.

The takings for their first day amounted to the princely sum of two pounds. Late that night they looked forward to falling exhausted into bed and she had already unpacked the bedding and put it onto a chair ready for the bed to be made up and Edward came to help her.

"What's that awful smell" he said

By now Elizabeth had gone to take the bedding off the chair and noticed that it was wet, she sniffed

"It smells like cats' wee." Then it dawned on her, the Grimsleys' cat had been locked in and occasionally Elizabeth had noticed him wandering around. At the time she had thought that perhaps the cat had been the nicest member of the family but she had quickly changed her mind about that.

"Poor thing" Edward said "he must have been locked in for ages."

Elizabeth hastily opened another packing box in order to find more bedding. They did eventually get some sleep but at five o'clock in the morning they were woken suddenly by a loud clattering and banging outside their window and, upon investigation, they found that the milk was being delivered to the store across the road. It sounded as if the crates were being thrown from the lorry and this was followed by the noise of the tail-lift being raised and finally the revving of the engine before the lorry had set off again leaving them barely two hours to try and get some more sleep. All this made Elizabeth realise that the nightmare was definitely real and she may never gently wake up again to what she had always been used to.

The following day Elizabeth took stock of her surroundings. Apart from most of the closed curtains that they had by now removed along with the grease, there was another reason why the place was so dark; all the walls were painted in dark colours. The hall and landing were a hideous dark green, one bedroom had maroon walls and a green ceiling and the other rooms all had dark wallpapers with large flowery patterns. The paint work varied from mauve to the green that was used in hospitals and government buildings. In the kitchen there was a shiny deep blue pegboard just above the working tops down which slid brown grease, above this there was wallpaper, this time decorated with onions and kitchen implements and the window end was papered with a dark imitation wood finish (at a later date they were to find that it actually covered some acceptable pine cladding). The bathroom was the most bizarre of all and quite shocking; there was a Victorian bath and lavatory which reminded Elizabeth of her grandfather's house, except that this was far worse – at least Grandfather's old place had been clean – the walls were dark blue with a mustard yellow ceiling. Around the bath was a row of black and pink floor tiles and the window ledge was covered in sticky-back plastic, as were most of the other ledges in the rest of the place.

Yet, despite all this mayhem, which would need to be sorted out, it didn't take them long to realise that there is not much point opening up a shop that has virtually nothing to sell and fortunately Edward had already managed to locate a wholesaler who was willing to stay open late on their second evening. Therefore, having eaten a casserole that she had prepared beforehand, they all set off for a small company near Cambridge, about half-an-hours' drive away. They were pinning their hopes on this excursion, so they left the plates in the kitchen sink to be dealt with upon their return as they were keen to get to their destination as soon as they could. The proprietor led them into a small and inviting showroom and offered them sherry and orange squash for Francis and afterwards, having looked at some of the interesting items there that they could perhaps display in their shop, they had landed up in a large cold and dismal warehouse. However, the stock was far from dismal even though they had no idea what to select from so many things on show; fortunately, the proprietor and his wife were extremely friendly and helpful and guided them as to what they would need. Elizabeth was weary after the strain of the last days and felt terribly cold but nevertheless continued walking round the warehouse in a daze choosing everything that a hardware shop should stock from the basics such as dishcloths and brooms to the more interesting pieces such as earthenware pots, stainless-steel articles and various ornate dishes.

Finally, they loaded up the car and went to the office to find out how much they had spent but at least it looked as if they hadn't bought anything they would regret afterwards, thanks to all the sound advice they had been given. Afterwards they were to become regular customers of this friendly wholesale outfit with Elizabeth doing most of the buying whilst Edward looked after the shop. Sometimes she would join the couple for a fish and chips lunch from the shop next door, when buying stock, and these visits were an escape from what was now her daily life. The proprietors, Reg and Mary Johnson of Johnson Wholesale, were always cheerful and gave her much needed encouragement and in turn she realised how hard this couple had to work to make a reasonable living.

After their first visit it must have been after ten o'clock that evening by the time they reached home, although Elizabeth still couldn't quite think of it as home. Straight away they all helped to unload the car; Francis should have been in bed but at least there was no school the following day and he appeared to be wider awake than she was despite his delayed bedtime. The next day they had the daunting task of pricing everything and arranging it all on the dilapidated shelving amongst the grime and peeling paint. Within a week of moving, they had found a painter and decorator to paint the outside of the premises which had made a vast difference both to the appearance of the shop and to their morale. Hopefully this would last until they were in a position to employ painters for a more permanent job. By now there were plenty of customers, some of them were probably being nosy but others seemed glad that they could now buy something useful and people were buying a metre of sticky back plastic called *Fablon*, that had to be measured with a circular yard rule that kept rolling off the counter. They had to weigh out animal foods from unmarked bags, trying to distinguish rabbit food from hamster mix and finding out which was budgerigar seed and where the chicken corn was. The existing stock, such that it was, was unpriced so they had to take a rough guess at the amount to charge when someone wished to buy steel wire, floor paint or some loose nails. Nobody complained so they guessed that they had undercharged rather than overcharged. Something that they had inherited was a tank of paraffin just outside the back of the shop and, especially when the weather turned cold, there were many customers who would bring their own cans to be filled up. Elizabeth and Edward had already been wondering whether the sale of paraffin would be worthwhile and had almost decided not to refill the tank once the supply had run out but, as Edward had pointed out, for the moment every bit of income was important and even something with a low profit margin. Shortly after their decision another concern had cropped up; for some days she had noticed that her hands had come up in a horrible rash and were extremely sore. She tried to think of possible reasons for this; could it be due to a new soap or hand cream she was using or was it because she was frequently handling animal foods or even coins? She really didn't know, but finding the time to consult a doctor would be difficult, unless it became much worse.

Edward had started to spend more time in the shop now that they were becoming busier and she was glad when he took over the paraffin sales. She didn't like having to go outside behind the shop leaving the door open to invite in the cold and thus leaving other customers to browse on their own. It must have been about a week later when she noticed that her rash had started to clear up and it was then that it had dawned on her that it could possibly have been caused by the paraffin so that would be another reason to give it up, although in the meantime she started to keep some rubber gloves handy. In the end, once the last gallon had been sold from the tank they decided not to re-order and they knew that they would not regret their decision as this had been a messy product and probably more trouble that it was worth; going outside in the coldest of weathers to fill up cans meant that freezing air had inevitably transferred itself to the shop, making it even less comfortable than it was already. Sometimes when Edward hadn't been around to help, she had found herself spending more and more time standing outside willing the paraffin to hurry itself into the waiting cans, thus abandoning other customers waiting to pay for more interesting merchandise. Elizabeth had rarely called for Edward's help as she hadn't wanted to delay his work on the house any more than she had needed to.

"It's not as if there is much profit in paraffin anyway." Edward had remarked. But the agreement had been mutual and a lifesaver for her so there was no need to justify it.

As if everything hadn't been difficult enough as it was, taking over the shop, but it coincided with an Industrial Action taking place during James Callaghan's time as Prime Minister, which soon became known as 'The Winter of Discontent'. It was characterised by widespread strikes by private and public sector trade unions, demanding high pay rises. This situation meant that power cuts could happen at any time, often unexpectedly plunging them into darkness when the electricity went off. One day they were caught out just at the wrong moment.

Chapter 8

Willow Bridge 2020

Eventually Elizabeth's sprained ankle returned to normal and was almost forgotten; she was lucky it hadn't been far worse and at least there hadn't been any repercussions. Her lost energy had returned and whilst wondering what she could do to put it to good use she remembered her lost diary; she really did hate losing things. She automatically went back to its usual place but it definitely wasn't there; it hadn't got underneath or behind anything so at least she had made certain that it hadn't been one of those strange cases when a lost item would eventually turn up where it should have been in the first place. She was left with the wonder of how on earth it had been missing in the first place. She started her search by taking all the books off the shelves on the large bookcase in the sitting room; she had already enjoyed replacing them in a much tidier and better order earlier but hadn't remembered quite when that had been. Maybe the diary had found its way there, after all. As she hadn't found what she was looking for, she started searching in other places as well such as in the kitchen and in cupboards and on shelves, just in case, even though she was sure that it wouldn't be found there.

She turned to Edward "You haven't seen my diary, have you?"

"No, what's it like?"

"It's dark blue and I appear to have mislaid it."

"I haven't seen it. It's not on the pile of newspapers is it."

"No, I've looked there. It doesn't matter though" although she did really hate mysteries especially when something had been lost.

Each day the news became worse; apparently there was still insufficient protective equipment for medical staff in hospitals as well as for care workers in the homes for the elderly. Shops, pubs and restaurants were suffering due to their loss of business due to having to close. It was horrifying to think that Garden Centres would have to get rid of most of their produce and pubs were having to pour beer down the drain, such a waste! But there didn't appear to be alternatives in order to keep people from catching the virus. Edward tuned into the Archers on radio four to which they had listened, on and off, for many years only to switch it off again almost immediately. The pre-recorded programmes were no longer about the everyday life that they used to portray – there was no Coronavirus in the fictitious village of Ambridge. This programme was no longer going to give them the light relief that it had done previously, in fact it was rather boring learning about past occurrences in Ambridge.

At first the alterations to their own everyday life seemed as if they had moved to another country where they didn't speak the language and all the natives avoided them as if they were aliens. Even so it was quite amazing that as time had passed nearly everyone appeared to be getting used to the drastic changes, even though this didn't mean that it was going to be easy to give up their freedom. They knew that nobody would knock on the door unexpectedly

"We were just passing ...."

"What a lovely surprise, we were only thinking of you the other day. Come in and I'll put the kettle on."

That wouldn't be happening now. Freedom wasn't the only thing that they were sacrificing as they had noticed that some of their favourite TV programmes had been axed. Something else had changed as well since March, for instance, the BBC news on the television was now preceded by a collage of photos of different activities taking place separately but cleverly put together to present a rather interesting series of pictures without activity. Elizabeth loved the cats and kittens curled up in their baskets now shown on the screen, and she found the ladies knitting rather humorous because of their bizarre and colourful amateur looking results on the huge needles. Edward had pointed out

"I've noticed that the knitting never gets any longer."

Even so the individual athletes kicking their legs up high in the air became rather tedious after they had seen it so many times. There were other things that were affected in a different way and at least they were still getting parcels delivered. One day there was a loud knock on the door BANG, BANG, BANG.

"What's wrong with the new door-bell I have just fixed?"

"I suspect that no one wants to *touch* the bell because of the virus."

On the doorstep stood a friendly young man who stepped back immediately as soon as Elizabeth had opened the door; he had already placed the parcel on the doorstep and then took a photograph of it and, she imagined, of her feet in her tatty and comfortable old slippers. Then, with a smile and a wave he disappeared. This has become the practice now, maybe even an improvement to the service. She looked forward to opening the packet; she hadn't remembered ordering anything until Edward came forward muttering that perhaps it was the special tools he had been waiting for.

After leaving their house for shopping or for exercise, they became accustomed to talking to the people working in their front gardens, from a safe distance, and one or two conversations had taken place from the opposite side of the road. They no longer had those places of interest to visit or calls from other people but instead were socialising in a more unusual way such as phone calls and emails.

On day she asked herself what else they were doing and the answer was 'nothing much' but the days still went by following old and new routines and Elizabeth had become more relaxed. At least she no longer awoke each morning with a sense of dread in her heart. The weather was still treating them kindly and walks to places they had never explored became more enjoyable. The lockdown had inevitably given them more time for reading, although she couldn't help wondering why she had just chosen a novel about the second world war instead of something bright and cheerful. In some ways reading was a form of escapism in itself because it was about something that had already happened, sad as it had been, and had been lived through a long time ago. Even so, the knowledge that during the war, the population had suffered shortages, deprivations and the devastation of soldiers and civilians being killed and the horrors of it came to her as it had never done before. Her grandparents and parents had barely mentioned anything about it because it was something that they didn't wish to dwell upon, or to put those terrors before their children. There had occasionally been the odd snippet about air raid shelters and gas masks, which even young children had had to wear, but after receiving this information it had of course soon disappeared into the back of her mind. The impact of recalling the past had made her think about some similarities between then and now; she supposed that at least during their own hardships they weren't terrified that their house or those of their friends and families would be bombed. Although many had died from the pandemic they weren't being slaughtered on the battlefields, even though the loss of life of somebody who had died due to the virus was no doubt just as devastating. At least during the war neighbours could visit each other for tea and a chat, despite the scarcities of food and beverages. Nevertheless, reading about what had happened at a time that she couldn't have remembered was still a way of taking her mind off the current circumstances. Now that she was older, and especially with the current ongoing crisis, she wished that she knew a bit more about how they had coped during war time. She then spent time on the internet researching both the first and the second world wars; she appeared to have few books about them apart from novels based on those times. She did remember being amused by something her grandmother had once told her about the war

"…….you had to queue for absolutely everything; clothes, food and all kinds of essentials and sometimes the queues could be very long."

"I don't like queues" she had replied remembering the long wait she had had outside a cinema to see *Saturday Night and Sunday Morning* on a cold wet winter day.

"I'm afraid that there wasn't much choice if you needed to eat." Then she recalled something else grandma had mentioned "Once a man joined a queue, extending all the way round the block, thinking that he would be able to get some meat or other food that was in short supply. It would have been a lovely surprise for his wife but unfortunately, he failed to notice that he was the only man standing there and when he reached the front, they were selling ladies corsets."

It was both amazing and refreshing to see that the pubs and restaurants were now being extremely innovative by offering take-away food and in some cases making deliveries. They had ordered fish and chips from one of the pubs they were not normally in the habit of visiting and it was delivered to their door promptly and she didn't remember when she had last enjoyed fish and chips so much. She wondered if this was because they had become much more appreciative of the simple things that they had always taken for granted in the past. Another of the good things to come out of this were their daily walks and sometimes Elizabeth would set out on her own. She tried to explore even more different routes and realised that some of the roads she took she had never been down before; there were many intriguing little alleyways leading off these roads and interesting houses perched up on a hill or displaying beautifully manicured lawns, some of the houses had balconies with pots of colourful flowers.

Elizabeth still found it quite remarkable that since the restrictions had started the population as a whole appeared to be taking everything in its stride and perhaps even getting used to it, not that it had made it any easier, just a realisation that human nature had the habit of making the best of bad times. One fact was that so many of their favourite television programmes had been sacrificed and what was on offer didn't give them much release just when they needed it more than ever. Oddly enough there were small things to amuse them such as when they found out *The Russian Ballet* was still performing and there was a televised clip of the dancers pirouetting around furniture in their sitting rooms and even finding space in small kitchens with the sink and cupboards behind them; it was a joy to see. Question Time on the BBC was showing again but without a live audience and those that did wish to participate were appearing via a video link.

It now seemed such a long time ago that Elizabeth used to wake up in the mornings and look in the large diary in the kitchen. She had been forced to buy it in order to fit everything in, as the pages would fill up with so many events. It was barely two months ago since she had checked for engagements and all she could see there were the crossed-out entries. Planning is also rather different. On the to do list there are just the names of people to phone, others to email and perhaps the title of the next book she wanted to read. There were no dentist and hair appointments, let alone social gatherings. Plans for the day, although rather mundane, would be a trip to buy a newspaper or even a book and feeling thankful that at least Smiths were allowed to remain open. She still kept looking at her oil paints and crayons; this really was the time to get absorbed in something like this but somehow, she couldn't get excited about the thought, not just yet anyway. This made her feel guilty when she heard about one friend who was writing poetry about the Coronavirus and another was spending hours working in her garden, but they all admitted to being depressed when they listened to the News. Especially distressing was when it was about the lack of sufficient PPE equipment that the hospitals so badly needed. Added to this there were mixed messages coming from the Government; one day they would say that they could test for antibodies and a few days later they couldn't, on another day they thought that masks should be worn and the next day they decided that they wouldn't have any benefit. There was little that was the least bit positive about it not to mention the consequences of the actual virus itself.

As the days passed Edward remarked about the amount of time that Elizabeth was spending on the phone, she pondered on this and supposed that it tended to be women more than men who would make a phone call just to talk; telephoning was just not his way except for the essential calls to his sister-in-law and to an elderly neighbour who had been recently widowed. His wife had been ill for a long time before she had died just before the virus had appeared; he was completely isolated now as friends and even family were unable to visit him and all he had were the welcome phone calls. Because his wife had died just before the outbreak it had meant that she had been able to have frequent visits from her family; she and Edward had also gone to see her in hospital and at the time hadn't realised that this would be the last time that they would see her. There had been a large gathering after her funeral at a local hotel which was something that could no longer happen. Currently, funerals were being limited to close family only in the church or cemetery and they would be unlikely to have a gathering afterwards. Elizabeth and Edward had heard of friends and acquaintances who had died during the lockdown, although none from Covid, and they had been unable to attend their funerals and sadly this had included Janice's. Even worse was the fact that they had been invited to their niece's wedding the following month, which could no longer go ahead. Alex had phoned Elizabeth in tears.

"All those months we have spent booking and planning have been wasted and we don't even know if the deposit for the hotel, where the reception was to be held, will be refunded."

"What will you do?" Elizabeth realised that she had asked a silly question but Alex continued,

" We can put it off until next year but how do we know what will happen then? A school friend of mine had already moved her March wedding until the summer but it looks as if it still may not go ahead. We can of course still get married quietly with just the witnesses present and Paul is in favour of this, but I'm not so sure that it is what I would want."

After many moves in their earlier lives Elizabeth and Edward had settled well into their friendly neighbourhood; houses had changed hands, sometimes several times, but recently the young people in their area had been a great support to those who were vulnerable or who had needed to self-isolate. They collected prescriptions, did essential shopping and made contact generally; one of their ninety-year-old neighbours had said that it was just like the wartime spirit.

Elizabeth bent down to pick up a note that had been dropped through their letterbox; it had come in a smart cream envelope with their address written on it by hand.

"What a lovely idea" she said as she handed the note to Edward which outlined the plans for a 75th anniversary of the Victory in Europe day, commonly known as VE Day. Despite the lockdown there was to be a street party celebration on the eighth of May, organised by their younger neighbours.

That particular day in May presented itself with warm sunny weather and Elizabeth and Edward joined the other residents in the road with their tables and chairs spaced out by the two-metre ruling on the pavements outside their homes. She and Edward stuck to the tradition with a pot of tea and cake, others had provided wine or beer accompanied by sandwiches. Many walked up or down in the middle of the road, keeping well apart, and met neighbours they didn't even know. Edward remarked that not everyone was keeping to the distancing rule but agreed they had to live dangerously from time to time, after all they were given to understand that being outdoors was safer. If it hadn't been for the current situation this unexpected socialising would probably never have taken place and it had turned out to be an enjoyable localised event and in turn, they learned so much from others about places that were delivering meals to people's doors and that fresh vegetables could also be sent from one of the local market stalls. It brought home to them how encouraging it was to see how the eateries, so badly hit by the lockdown, had rallied round providing take-away foods which made Elizabeth decide to make more use of this welcome service.

There was one thing that hadn't changed during this perturbing time and that was the British climate; the beautiful weather much welcomed for the street party turned into winter the following day, cold and miserable. All they could do was to be grateful that the event had been held the day before and the celebration had given everyone a lift and made many of them feel that perhaps things weren't so bad after all despite finding it hard not to be able to see their family and friends.

Shortly after this short uplifting moment Elizabeth found out about something else that could be of great benefit and apparently it was something called Zoom. She'd never heard of it before but Marilyn had told her that she'd been 'seeing' relatives from far afield by meeting up on Zoom.

"You can see them and talk to them once you are logged onto it."

Following this enlightenment, she decided to do a trial run with Francis and his family and, after a bit of help from the grandchildren, she felt that she would be ready to try it out with her reading group. Initially actually 'seeing' and talking to the family was altogether an eye opener but because it was something new their conversation was a little stilted at first until Edward appeared in the background and waved to them, making faces which made them laugh politely. She had spoken to them on the phone recently to catch up with what was going on, which was certainly not that much at the moment, but she had already asked about their school and university prospects so there was no point in going over old ground again. Eventually the grandchildren became bored and wanted to get back to what they had been doing; nevertheless, she had loved seeing their faces despite being a little disappointed that they didn't wish to prolong the session, but as Edward pointed out

"They're teenagers, it's pretty normal I would have thought, to return to something more interesting than talking to grandparents."

She had to agree as after all Peter was eighteen years old and extremely tall and his younger brother, John, was sixteen. The twins, Alice and Sarah were fourteen and Elizabeth was impressed that none of them had complained about their restrictions which she felt must have been so much harder for youngsters. Although it was a long time ago, she vaguely remembered her youth and the constant socialising and meeting up with friends; but at the moment they had been denied something that she and her contemporaries had always taken for granted.

After her practice run, she decided to set up a meeting for the Book Group with this new innovation and most of them were keen on the idea and as she explained to them in her email

"I'll try to set up a practice meeting first to discuss whatever you like and not necessarily any of the books."

About ten of them decided to take part, not everyone had been eager to try it out and some hadn't wandered into the computer age apart from the sending of emails. Their first Zoom meeting turned out to be most successful once she had got the hang of it; they had many laughs when, due to her inexperience, there would be times when she couldn't admit them to the meeting or she would lose their faces or the sound, but eventually she felt that they were ready to have meaningful discussions about the latest book even though it wouldn't be quite the same as before. The idea was appreciated and most of the group would be able to participate each month on-line instead of their previous face-to-face meetings. Even during their first experience one of them had said

"It was so lovely to see your face again; hasn't your hair grown long."

She had indeed noticed how unruly her thick, curly hair had become but of course most of them were in the same boat as there were no hairdressers open. She had kept sweeping the fringe away from her face, imagining that there was something in her eye, and from time to time she would cut little bits off it. The fringe looked better at first but eventually when she got carried away it looked worse than before and hairdressers had been closed for nearly three months now.

The next thing to happen was when the Prime Minister made an announcement regarding the current lockdown. There was one problem though; because of this announcement everyone had become even more confused than before. Those who had been working from home were now supposed to return to work straight away but they were advised not to use public transport! That would no doubt cause a few problems especially as there would presumably be no car sharing allowed either. Then, if nobody was using the buses or the trains there would be a loss of work for all those drivers.

Edward said " What a muddle, it is so fortunate that we are retired."

Elizabeth replied "I feel sorry for those who lost their jobs ,either temporarily or permanently, and are trying to deal with all this.

Suddenly Friday had come round again and once more Elizabeth realised how quickly the time had passed by and was grateful that time wasn't hanging around unfilled. Edward had opened a bottle of wine to accompany their evening meal which they had been doing for a while now, mostly at weekends, so they would enjoy sipping a glass of Cabernet Sauvignon, Bordeaux or Burgundy with their fish or chicken. During these difficult times it seemed to be far less of an indulgence but on Mondays, they would revert back to nothing alcoholic until the following Friday. Elizabeth did wonder if they would resort to extending the weekend customs into the rest of the week during their current rather less interesting way of life, but so far, they had not fallen into that trap although one friend had admitted to drinking wine every day now following the crisis. She did wonder how many new alcoholics Covid would produce, not that she could imagine this happening to that friend in particular.

These days there were a good deal of extra expressions that had been introduced and words that would no doubt be added to the Oxford English Dictionary, and other dictionaries as well.

They had been talking about the ‘new normal’ and furlough had been brought to the forefront of everyone’s mind; PPE (personal protective equipment) came up frequently, lockdown was used in everyday conversations and social distancing was another well used phrase but COVID-19 was no doubt one of the most frequently used terms.

Having spent a good deal of time trying to find something worthwhile to watch on the television to take their minds of those times of boredom or ‘what shall we do next?’ moments they did eventually discover one or two interesting entertainments such as “Have I got News for you”, something that Elizabeth had rarely watched in the past. These days the programme was recorded in participants’ homes in front of bookcases, kitchen appliances, exotic flower arrangements and interesting pictures on the walls giving them a rare view into other people’s lives. One evening Ian Hislop’s cat insisted on joining in and someone else had to calm down his boisterous dog. Although Elizabeth and Edward were able to fill in their days quite successfully with walks, shopping, phone calls and now even Zoom meetings there were times when Elizabeth would glance at her watch and was glad to see that morning coffee, lunch or supper time had come round again and she wasn’t sure whether she was sad or grateful that their lives were slowing down. They were no longer rushing about but were instead making the most of the small things. This didn’t alter the fact that there were still mornings when Elizabeth would wake up feeling uneasy and it wasn’t just the fear of catching the virus and all the uncertainty, it was something deeper than that and she tried to analyse this emotion without much success. However, they did find all the unclear government messages extremely irritating as they certainly didn’t wish to break any rules but what exactly were they? To add to the confusion the inhabitants of Scotland, Wales and Northern Ireland had different, perhaps even more sensible rules. In England, apparently you could now drive as far as you liked to exercise, even though there would be the risk of joining the commuter traffic now that people previously working from home could go back to work. There was some humour in this she supposed and she wondered why anyone would wish to drive more than a couple of miles to go for a walk.

"What about all the train and bus drivers' jobs?" Elizabeth had queried once more now that workers were forced to use their cars instead of public transport. In a way it was a good thing when they could find something to laugh about and recently, they had been ridiculing the United States President who had originally denied the existence of Covid-19.

"It is nothing serious!" he had announced, "just a minor condition." Yet, shortly afterwards he had suggested injecting disinfectant as a treatment although later on he had been forced to admit that it had been just a joke. Instead, he said that he was taking a malaria drug despite being advised against it. Oddly enough, it was surprising to learn afterwards that a trial was being done in the UK at Oxford on anti-malaria drugs to see if they could prevent this virus and there was also some ongoing research into a vaccine. There was another piece of humour to cheer up their day when they were given somebody else to ridicule in our own country; the Prime Minister's chief adviser, despite all the restrictions set by the government, had decided that he was exempt. He drove his children hundreds of miles away to get child care at his parents' home and then had driven thirty miles to Barnards Castle to check that his eyesight was good enough for driving when he had been feeling ill. If another parent had taken their children to relatives so far away, they would have most certainly have been penalised. Surely, the risk of driving if unsure of how your sight is, would be foolhardy. This will no doubt be a joke that will keep coming up for months to come and already Barnards Castle would often be mentioned in humour.

"...If you are thinking of getting a new pair of glasses, why don't you just drive to Barnards Castle?"

One day Elizabeth decided to look up the similarities between Covid-19 and the Spanish flu epidemic that had broken out in 1918 and she had read that it had killed one third of the world's population; it had affected those between the ages of twenty and forty years old but the elderly appeared to have escaped. This information led her to look into her family history to see if she could find any instances of her past family members having died from the Spanish flu; she did find that one great aunt had died suddenly and without reason in her forties. Her grandmother, even though she had sometimes spoken about her sister Florence, certainly hadn't mentioned why she had died so young, leaving a young family behind. Being curious, Elizabeth had applied for Florence's death certificate only to find that she hadn't gone down with the Spanish flu but had died from Cancer.

While she was logged into the computer, she decided to take part in a questionnaire as she was always looking for something else to fill in her time. In the end she became frustrated as some of the questions were so ambiguous and when one of them asked how the epidemic was being handled by the government, she suspected that she had ticked the opposite of what she had meant! Her real feelings were that if the government had taken earlier action quite possibly many lives could have been saved but when she had checked, too late, what she had replied it looked as if she had ticked the box saying that the government had handled it well. How annoying, but if they can't put the questions in a straightforward way instead of adding unnecessary complicated language this could be expected. However, she did fear that her brain was acting less coherently since the pandemic started and this did worry her. How much damage could all this do?

Chapter 9

Trintley Autumn 1978

It was early in the evening when Elizabeth decided to take some polythene sheeting and a box of drawing pins into the sitting room to try and cover the broken window in the French doors. She was unsure how long it would be before they could get a replacement pane of glass. Francis was still exploring the garden and she hoped there weren't too many hazards out there especially as dusk was descending upon them; still at least it would give her a chance to sort out the window. She glanced outside and all appeared to be well even though the light was fading; she switched on the light in the rather dim room so that she could see better to get on with her task. As she pondered on the neatest way to do what at least should only be temporary, she heard a loud bang behind her making her jump. Then she noticed the door leading to the hall had slammed shut and she automatically took hold of the handle in order to open the door again, but it fell to the floor with a clang. She picked it up but there appeared to be no likelihood of being able to re-attach it to the door and just as she was cursing her bad luck and not expecting that matters could get any worse, suddenly the power went off leaving her in semi darkness.

She shook the door in anger and frustration, as if that would do any good, but she had no idea when Edward would return from his search for a place where he could buy replacement shelving for the junk they had inherited. She was now locked in a room where there was no torch in any of the half-filled drawers; neither were there candles, matches or a screwdriver that could possibly be useful in any way, even if she could see what she was doing in the gloom of the evening. Indeed, it occurred to her that they would have been unlikely to keep such items in the sitting room anyway as the kitchen would be the most likely place to store tools, or at least it would be if they ever managed to get the place reasonably straight. Anyway, as she was trapped in this room access to anywhere else was not possible. Francis was not in the least bit put off by his exploration outside in the failing light, and no doubt thought that it was fun, fortunately it was pleasantly mild weather for the time of year. Nevertheless, she had better go and rescue him so she let herself into the garden through the French doors to explain their predicament. They decided to go round to their new neighbours to see if they could lend them anything to help. They were a friendly couple who had introduced themselves as Ann and Tom; they were of a similar age to Edward and herself and it had been such a relief to have pleasant people living next door. So far, they had always been lucky with their neighbours but one never knew, there were sometimes tales of people having to move because their neighbours were so detestable and there were others who were not on speaking terms with the person or persons next door to them. Once more it looked as if all was well, and not even with an eternally barking dog as had been the case at their last house. The dog's owners had been so pleasant that they really didn't wish to complain and at least the dog didn't keep them awake at night. Their new neighbours, having only just moved in themselves, were unable to lay their hands on a screwdriver or even a torch but they did find them a couple of candles and some matches. She expressed her gratitude and with Francis in tow returned to a now candle lit living room where hopefully Edward would soon return to rescue them. Francis was usually a good-natured child but after a while she could see that he was getting bored and already he was starting to look a little grumpy.

"I know. Let's play I Spy until Daddy returns, he shouldn't be too long now." Elizabeth said with more hope in her voice than in her heart.

"That's boring and it's too dark."

There were no books or games to hand as they were still busy trying to get everything unpacked and there were still plenty more unopened boxes scattered in most rooms in the house. Not for the first time she thought to herself, why on earth did she agree to all this madness as it had turned out to be. Although she was making a big effort to be positive, she had noticed that Francis at least had thought that the change of circumstances was quite exciting, although being locked in was another problem entirely. She went to try the door again and to keep Francis occupied she asked

"See if you can open it."

He looked around as she had done but of course there was nothing of use to try and force it open. He pushed the door with some force.

"I think it opens inwards, not outwards" which made them both laugh.

It was only half an hour later, even though it had seemed like many hours, when Francis said

"I can hear a noise."

At last, there was the sound of a key in the front door.

"Daddy, Daddy we're locked in the back room."

She and Francis were finally rescued when Edward was able to open the door from the other side. It looked as if he would have to spend more of his valuable time repairing the door handle and lock but for now Elizabeth was able to sigh with relief. It was at that moment that the power was restored almost as if by magic. She reminded Francis of a story book that she used to read to him when a spell had been cast so that they could escape from a locked room into the light.

Elizabeth had had so much on her mind lately but her first priority had been to get their home and shop straight enough to live and work reasonably comfortably, and also to learn to accept the small advantages that she did have as well as the bad things. Running a shop was an interesting challenge which she was beginning to enjoy, if only they were not living above it. They could never escape or forget what they had taken on, there was no chance of driving or walking a short distance to a home away from it all. Initially they had been bothered by customers phoning at all times of day when they were closed and sometimes quite late at night. One evening a man had phoned just before ten o'clock as a leg had fallen off one of his chairs.

"I haven't got any screws that will fit and I thought that you might have some that are long enough."

"Why don't you pop round in the morning as soon as we are open and we can maybe find some suitable ones." Edward asked reasonably.

"But nobody can sit on it without the other leg, I know the length of screw that I would need." Edward reasoned that he must have other chairs, surely. The trouble was that Edward was too soft and anyway it was important to keep their customers happy.

"Yes, we do have some that size. I'll grab a packet for you and you can pay me in the morning."

Elizabeth was furious and made sure that Edward had answered the door to him when he came to collect the pack of screws.

Shortly after that incident they had arranged to get an ex-directory telephone number installed in the house and they shouldn't hear the telephone in the shop when it was closed. One of the reasons for their move in the first place was that she and Edward would see more of each other and at least now she didn't have to worry when he was a long way from home; admittedly that was one thing that had been achieved anyway and she did wonder if she would ever be satisfied or, was she just being ungrateful. She had to admit that many of the problems were solvable such as the broken door handle and the old house itself had plenty of potential for improvement which couldn't come soon enough and she still lived in hope.

There had been one thing that they had both been longing for some time now, and that was the wish for a brother or sister for Francis before he was too much older. Oddly enough although it had been constantly on her mind before the move and the inevitable upheaval this wasn't Elizabeth's priority at the moment. There were so many other things just now and she had almost forgotten about her many disappointments over those last months, therefore it came as rather a surprise when she thought that she might be pregnant. She decided not to mention it to Edward just yet, after all it could be a false alarm and she had to take into account that she had been under a lot of stress lately. One half of her was excited about the possibility the other half wondered how on earth they would manage; it certainly wasn't the best time just now. If only they were a bit straighter but at least they did have plenty of space for another child and she would still be able to work in the shop and do the accounts unlike if she had been employed elsewhere. Still there were plenty of immediate issues to be sorted.

They had already applied to the council for an improvement grant and the surveyor had been round so that they really thought that they would get some help towards the cost of central heating, a new bathroom, replacement windows, loft insulation to name but a few of the essential requirements. Of course, they should have known that nothing is ever that straightforward and they were soon to learn that if there had been no bathroom at all they may have been eligible and as it happened, before they could get a grant for any improvements, they were told that they would have to raise the ceiling in the room that led off the dining room. This would have been extremely costly and added to this they didn't feel that it was necessary for the ceiling to be higher anyway, so getting a grant would have defeated the object somewhat.

"Are they trying to make sure *t*hat we can accommodate people over six feet tall?" queried Elizabeth. In the end it would have looked as if they would have had to spend the grant on things they didn't want before they could have the things they needed.

"No, it's just a ploy to stop us getting anything from them and to save the council money and also to put people off applying for these grants" replied Edward cynically, "so we will just have to go it alone."

At least they did get a small amount to help towards the loft insulation from a separate grant, so that was something at least. Because of their failure to get anything towards improvements one of the first unpleasant jobs Edward had to do was to rip out the old lavatory in the bathroom which was in a dreadful condition and didn't even flush properly. Francis had preferred to go and use the one outside which seemed to be in better condition, although that wasn't saying much. Edward had already been out to buy a new lavatory but had come back with a complete, new bathroom suite in avocado green, which had been greatly reduced in price. Elizabeth was rather thrilled with it even though the bath and basin were to sit in Francis's bedroom for some time. The avocado didn't exactly match the dark blue walls either but it was a start towards civilization. Despite their lack of getting any financial help they were doing quite well, thanks to Edward's hard work and his ability to do so many DIY jobs. But having a new baby would give them other priorities and all of a sudden, she felt able to put her general dissatisfaction to the back of her mind and to concentrate on the present.

After taking over the shop one of the most important tasks had been to open accounts with all the suppliers they would need to deal with because they couldn't get everything from Johnson Wholesale. This meant looking around for paint, garden and pet food providers to name but a few. After a search through the various catalogues and directories that had been left behind by the previous occupants, Elizabeth eventually found a rather dishevelled list of wholesale companies providing the sorts of things they would need and chose one which looked suitable. Before picking up the phone she checked that she had noted down all the things that she would need to know.

"Hello, my name's Elizabeth Wallis and my husband and I have just taken over the House Supplies hardware store in Trintley and we are looking for a paint supplier."

"Sorry we can't do business with you, just pay your bills, there's a good girl" followed by a rapid replacing of the receiver.

Her mouth was still open in her complete amazement at the response to her call; she stood there without moving for some time after the totally unexpected shock and it took her a while to shake off the hostile attitude. After a while she decided this would be just one unfriendly company they would not wish to deal with anyway, if that was the way they talked to a prospective customer. She looked for another one and dialled their number only to be surprised and shocked to be greeted with a similar response. After trying a couple more and each time, as soon as she announced the shop's name, she received the same reaction. Some of them were rude enough to slam down the phone and others firmly said that they couldn't deal with them, even when Elizabeth emphasised that they were the new owners, but it made no difference; these businesses were owed money by Edward's and Elizabeth's predecessors. By then she was in tears but before mentioning anything to Edward she decided to telephone their solicitor to explain what had happened as by then she had assumed that this was all to do with the Grimsleys whom she was beginning to dislike even more.

"Ah yes," he said, "you will most certainly need to change the name of the shop."

By now she had calmed down and went to find Edward.

"Why on earth didn't he tell us that before?" he asked.

"I don't suppose he knew that the Grimsleys were in such financial difficulties. Why would he?

"Maybe. Still, we'd better think of another name."

They pondered on suitable ones for a while, realising that they didn't have much time to get it all sorted out if they were to stay in business.

"We'll have to avoid the words House and Supplies," Elizabeth decided.

"How about Everyone's DIY."

"Um...., doesn't exactly trip off the tongue, does it? What about Trintley DIY?"

"I like that, but should we use 'Trintley' as House Supplies is connected to Trintley?"

"I don't see why not; wholesalers will realise that there will be other shops and stores in Trintley." Elizabeth turned to Francis

"Shall we call our shop Trintley DIY?"

"What's DIY?"

"It means Do it Yourself."

"I've thought of a better idea," said Edward "we could call it the Trintley Hardware Store."

Francis approved and so finally satisfied they decided to go ahead with that name and all they had to do now was to register it, get a new sign made up and deal with all the other paperwork involved. It looked like a mammoth task and yet fortunately for them it didn't take as long as they thought it could have done, to become the Trintley Hardware Store.

Not long afterwards they were able to stand back and look up and admire their bright and more modern shop sign that had replaced the old one and after that day they never looked back and were able to open accounts with many wholesalers, even with one of the grumpy ones, and they continued to get excellent service from them. They got to know many of the sales representatives quite well and a couple of them used to take lunch with them on their visiting days, which meant that they could put in their order without the inevitable interruptions that they would normally have whilst trying to serve customers at the same time. Soon after the new shop sign had been put into place, they found a couple of young painters to decorate the whole of the outside of the shop.

"New beginnings" Edward had said.

Yes, indeed and at last Elizabeth found a little more enthusiasm and began to count each improvement as a step forward.

Not long after they had put the House Supplies debacle behind them and successfully moved on, they had a nasty shock. It was Elizabeth who had answered the door of the house to find two men, one of them was well over six foot tall who must have weighed over twenty stone, the other one was slimmer and shorter but looked to be more threatening. They announced themselves and it appeared that they were debt collectors. By then Edward had appeared when he heard the alarm in Elizabeth's voice and at once realised what was happening. He immediately pointed to the smart new sign now displayed above the door of the shop and introduced Elizabeth and himself as the new owners. Elizabeth couldn't understand how they had not noticed how different the place looked now, but then they may not have visited before and so were unlikely to appreciate the efficient looking retail outlet that had replaced the run down shabby one. All the same she was concerned that they could be in for the same treatment that they had had before when trying to open accounts, but this time the men apologised and asked if they knew where the previous owners were. Elizabeth had good reason to be angry with the Grimsleys and what they had put them through after they had taken over and was about to say something when Edward kicked her lightly so instead, she said

"We've no idea, I'm afraid" and off they went wishing them the best of luck.

Edward said "They'll find them easily enough I'm sure, but it's none of our business after all."

Following their move Elizabeth had been without the use of her washing machine and was making frequent trips to the launderette, which luckily was close to one of the wholesalers she used to visit. After a couple of weeks of inconvenience, eventually, in the middle of all the other jobs that Edward needed to do so that the shop could function, he found a spare moment to plumb the washing machine into the kitchen on the first floor. She hadn't mentioned anything about the pregnancy to Edward yet but thought to herself that she would most definitely be in need of the washing machine. What joy! She was so excited that she would be able to say goodbye to the launderette and immediately filled the machine, switched it on and went into the shop. She may well have had a satisfied smile on her face as she greeted the people who came in to buy items and sometimes to ask for advice on some of the products. As often happened after a small queue had formed and the customers had gone away with their purchases, the place emptied ready for the next rush and she seemed to have encountered a moment of solitude. Suddenly, she was aware of an alarming sound as if a train was passing by just above her head, followed by bits of plaster falling from the ceiling and Elizabeth had a dreadful thought knowing that the kitchen was just above the shop and their sturdy old Bendix washing machine had started its spin cycle. As soon as she realised what was happening, she rushed upstairs to switch it off. It wasn't until after this calamity that Edward had realised, rather too late, that it was probably not such a good idea to have a washing machine in a first-floor kitchen with a decaying floor, and especially not an old and heavy Bendix. So much for that!

Recently one of the things that had given the shop project a bit of a sparkle was that the painters, they had employed, were so cheerful and helpful and they had many laughs together when Elizabeth had shown them the unbelievable colour schemes that they had inherited inside the house and the sympathy they gave had been just what she needed. One day the younger of the two had turned up to replace a window pane that he'd broken whilst he was painting the outside of the house. He really thought at first that he'd got himself a good bargain when Edward approached him; if only he had known!

'I can replace the glass if instead you would help me carry our washing machine downstairs into the cellar.'

'Of course!'

He was pleased to get out of the boring job of replacing the glass although he may have had second thoughts when he realised how heavy this machine was. The two of them practically slid it down the first flight of stairs, ripping more bits off the stair carpet. Trying to get it down the curved stone cellar steps was another matter altogether and nothing short of a nightmare. Elizabeth stood at the top of the stairs, her stomach doing somersaults and her brain meandering off into an unknown direction, feeling helpless and anxious. Her concern was that if they had let it slip there was nothing she could do, except probably to call an ambulance. After what had seemed like an eternity eventually it was securely situated in the cellar and all of them were able to sigh with relief, especially Elizabeth.

Chapter 10

Willow Bridge 2020

At the time it was great news that the lockdown was easing a little after so many long weeks of restrictions. There had been no shopping for interesting items, no meeting up with friends or family, no meals out and certainly nothing impromptu such as unexpected visits from friends or even for planned guests. Life had taken off on a totally different route which appeared to have been accepted. Even though the latest disclosure was a relief in many ways to most people, there were some who wondered if it was too soon. They had been left scared about what could happen next, even Elizabeth, longing for some form of normality just as everyone else, was left feeling a little uneasy. She was pleased that at least the government had come to their senses and had agreed that face coverings should be worn on public transport and eventually in other places no doubt; it was horrifying to hear that Britain has had the highest death rate in Europe and is also high on the world's list. Elizabeth knew there was nothing that she could do to change the situation but it left her feeling that she personally was living in the wrong country and she felt embarrassed that England was being shown up in such a bad light.

For the first time since his childhood, she and Francis had had a disagreement when she had expressed her current concerns during his last phone call; she felt that caution was still necessary. As a child Francis had always been easy going and had rarely complained about school or parental decisions, their worst battles being over the untidy state of his bedroom. After much cajoling she had eventually tackled the mess herself by removing the yoghourt cartons which appeared to be culturing mould before putting them into the bin and then she had removed the clothes on the floor straight to the washing machine not knowing whether they had been worn or not. Fortunately, he had eventually married someone who liked tidiness and they had come to some form of compromise. But now he expressed his feelings firmly about what was going on.

"It's about time too, the lockdown is doing too much damage to the economy which will be left in a dreadful state" and so speaks the business man she reasoned.

"As it is, all the attention is devoted to Covid so that routine hospital treatments and operations are being cancelled and more people will die from other diseases that are not getting attention, not to mention the increase of mental illnesses."

It was rather unlike him but he did sound pretty angry.

"What about those seriously ill patients with Covid who are inevitably putting the National Health under great strain? They can't be just left without any medical care to die a painful death, can they?" she protested.

Eventually she did manage to change the subject as she could understand Francis's point of view but nevertheless facts were facts, even if Francis was trying to make light of those poor people who were suffering from or dying from Covid. She knew that Francis's mother-in-law had been waiting for an operation on her knee and was in a great deal of pain; however, as she wasn't classed as urgent, she was having to live on painkillers instead. This meant that she was unable to be as active as she had previously been, which was just another example of others having to suffer indirectly. Of course, Elizabeth could sympathise. Francis had offered to pay for his mother-in-law's operation but she wouldn't hear of it although she did say

"I could have been doing so much more while I have had time on my hands but on the bad days, I can't do anything much at all. Then there's the constant anxiety of not knowing how much longer I will have to wait but there are so many other people who are far worse off than I am."

Elizabeth had agreed with her that if she had been given a definite date it would have been more reassuring.

"Francis has been looking into how much it would cost to be treated privately and if it gets more unbearable maybe I will want to follow that route but I really don't wish to jump the queue."

All Elizabeth could see these days was bad news followed by more bad news in the newspapers, on the television and radio and even from friends and relatives. Francis's mother-in-law wasn't the only person she had come across who had had her operation cancelled. Apparently, there were many living in pain and unable to walk due to the cancellation of knee and hip replacements. Worse than this was when she had learnt of the suicide of a particular young man called Jo; she knew that there had been one or two such cases following the Covid situation but she was unable to get this tragedy out of her mind and couldn't stop thinking about him. She had once been introduced to his mother by Francis because the family had moved into a village not far away from where she and Edward lived and they had met up once or twice, although not recently of course. Jo just couldn't cope anymore; his girlfriend had left him and he felt totally alone, unable to get out and about and to socialise because of Covid. His parents had been unaware of the state he was in as he had covered up his disturbing feelings, no doubt to stop them worrying, his mother had tearfully declared. Following this dreadful news Elizabeth had tried even harder to think about more positive things, she was really racking her brain but it was so difficult at the moment. It was too easy to give up and fall into despair as she was sure that many people had done despite all the positive thoughts that she had heard from a good many.

Then at last she did hear some good news intertwined with all that was bad; apparently the Puffins had returned to Farne Island after climate change had caused their disappearance, and now they were back again. Residents of Venice had noticed a vast improvement in the quality of the canals that ran through the city as they were running clear for the first time in years, and fish can even be seen in the usually murky waters. The lockdown has left Venice's streets empty and a drastic drop in water traffic means sediment in the canals has been able to settle. In fact, carbon emissions have been less everywhere. Unfortunately, only a small amount of news time is given to something more positive although these things would presumably be only temporary as one day everything would no doubt carry on as before. Another fact that had come out of the situation had been about the use of less electricity, good in some ways but bad in others as it had led to problems with the National Grid and engineers were having to work hard to keep the system stable.

There is no doubt that the coming of the Coronavirus had disrupted everyone's lives and worse still had caused many deaths and there didn't appear to be a single moment when they could think of anything else. For some time, there had been another huge concern that climate change would cause devastation if something wasn't done about it right now. There have been constant reminders that the world will continue to suffer from extreme events including heat waves, droughts, heavy downpours, floods, tornadoes, and hurricanes. Already we have seen the devastation of people's homes being washed away on the one hand but also seeing dying animals where there is drought. Regrettably it looked as if the Coronavirus had put this crisis to the back of many minds, although others had not forgotten the threat for the future.

Better news did follow, however, in that it was now possible for six people to meet up in each other's gardens and Elizabeth was looking forward to seeing one or two of their friends they hadn't seen since before all this started. Although she knew she should remain positive, she still felt nervous after she had invited three people round; it should have been four but one was still reluctant to meet up with others, even in the garden. In normal times this sort of occasion was something that she wouldn't have given much thought about and it would have been a relaxing occasion. They had known each other for many years and had often met up for a meal in a restaurant or in one of their homes, but this time more planning would be required. She had already bought sanitizer and hand gel and would leave the back gate open so that they wouldn't have to walk through the house; although this had meant spending a good deal of time cutting down overhanging branches and trimming the bushes that had strayed onto the path at the side of the house. Under the current constraints she wondered if she should offer them biscuits with their tea or coffee. Before all this had happened, she wouldn't have even needed to think about it but she laughed to herself about her anxiety, and was sure that she wasn't the only one giving what were once normal things a great deal of extra thought. Now she was planning just the smallest occurrence, weighing up any risks. It now seemed that she was having to treat good friends, who had always greeted each other with a hug, like distant acquaintances. Today she wondered if they would be warm enough in the garden; Edward had already arranged the deck chairs in a sheltered part and once they arrived, they would be able to sit and chat just as if nothing untoward had happened. They had come prepared with warm jackets but the weather had been pleasant enough and these were not needed.

After they left, she wondered why on earth she had not been at ease right from the start as all had gone perfectly well and she had fully enjoyed the afternoon. Her restraint and anxiety left her as soon as she brought out coffee and tea on a tray and pointed to the biscuits, carefully moved from the container with tongs and placed on a plate, so that they could help themselves. It was almost like normal, but not quite.

This new confidence prompted her to think about inviting the Book Group to meet in her garden although this presented a bit of a quandary as there were about twelve of them and according to government ruling, she could only invite five, making up the maximum number of six including herself.

"You could always arrange for them to come on two consecutive days."

Edward suggested.

She pondered on this for a while and in the end, she decided to find out those who would be interested. As it happened some of them were still wary about venturing out, and yet again, even into the open air of someone's garden. This certainly made life easier as it looked as if there would only be six of them anyway. Again, she prepared everything as before having learned much from her recent venture. This time they each brought a copy of the book that they had previously chosen and read but after their initial comments on the novel, *Miss Garnet's Angel* by Salley Vickers, they quickly turned their minds to other subjects as meeting up in person again was a novelty. In the end she had decided not to offer them tea or coffee, as she had done with her other friends, although she did feel that it was bit unfriendly but it was unfortunately a sign of the times yet nobody seemed to mind and they enjoyed the afternoon. As it happened, after chatting to this small group, she got to know a little more about them. After the book group had been set up, they had concentrated on the merits or criticisms of the selected books more than they had talked about those things closer to home, only it was a little different this time. A couple of them had lived in Willow Bridge for most of their lives and the others had moved in more recent years as she and Edward had done. It was quite amazing how normally you wouldn't give a second thought to what the people you meet had done in their past lives, there would just be a glimpse about the arrival of a new grandchild or about a past trip to an exotic place where one of their chosen novels was set. This time she had learnt more about what their sons, daughters and grandchildren were up to and the places they themselves had visited worldwide. Although it meant that Elizabeth had felt somewhat humbled at first about their achievements and travels, she had also felt more of a kinship with them and inevitably the general topic of conversation, which was on everyone's minds, had come up. Coronavirus was never far from their thoughts.

Lately she had noticed that they were all making less phone calls; there was little news to exchange anyway apart from the situation they found themselves in, and now that some limited visiting was allowed it was perhaps less crucial. One of their neighbours phoned them a couple of days later to invite them to sit in his garden under the welcome shade of his large oak tree; the weather had become extremely hot and they had little shade in their own garden so it was a welcome change. Instead of the cups of tea that they were expecting he brought out some chilled white wine. She and Edward had looked at each other and smiled, it was only three o'clock in the afternoon, but needless to say it looked as if they had all been having similar thoughts

"Anything goes during such times as these" and they agreed with their neighbour and were determined to enjoy the hot weather while it lasted.

The welcome sound of children's voices coming from the nearby school playground once more was most welcome, as due to all the schools having been closed there had been an ominous silence. It was totally unlike what usually followed after the children had broken up for the holidays; this time it was as if all the children had been whisked away somewhere, rather like in the story of the Pied Piper of Hamelin, but luckily the children were back again at last.

The pleasant weather still held which had given her the incentive to wander down the road to the Post Office, the unusual stillness during all those weeks of lockdown had been disheartening but all the same she did not look forward to this trip as previously. When she had to send a parcel in the old days, she would find herself driving to the next nearest village to avoid the long Post Office queues. Today, although glad that the non-essential shops had opened once more, she was still uneasy about her decision. However, she was in for a pleasant surprise as there was no queue at all. She had remembered, in the past, the long row of people waiting outside the General Post Office in all weathers which she had avoided like the plague; what on earth were all these people sending or buying? It wasn't as if this happened only at Christmas, it would be all the year round and so she would walk on. So, this experience meant that not everything was so bad and it was quite new for her to walk straight up to the counter after just one other person had been before her. She was soon on her way home again; she glanced at her watch and there had only been a few minutes to wait. These days, she never took the opportunity to browse around the shops leisurely, if she needed to buy something she would grab it off the shelf and depart as soon as she could. She had started to follow a routine once she arrived home, where she would wipe down all the shopping with sanitizer before putting it away. In addition to this she always tried to leave the mail unopened for seventy-two hours, unless it looked important. In such a case she would open it carefully, throwing away the outer envelope, and then wash her hands and carefully retrieve the piece of paper inside. Once more she could see some humour in this. She could still remember how agitated she had felt upon her first realisation that everything had changed so dramatically and yet she was now taking everything in her stride. She was sometimes lulled into a temporary calm when she listened to the traffic announcements on the radio and the weather forecasts on the television; they were exactly the same as they had always been and the weather announcements on the television were still given out with a bright smile, even when snow or gale force winds had been predicted. Covid hadn't changed the weather nor even the flow of traffic.

The novelty of tidying cupboards had already worn a little thin although taking all the books off the bookcase for rearrangement and shelf dusting had been far more enjoyable as she had stood back and admired their new orderliness; unfortunately, it hadn't filled in as much of her time as she would have hoped. Edward, on the other hand, was far more fed up than she was and had suddenly come up with a startling announcement. She had been leafing through a recipe book to see if she could make something that wasn't too much trouble and that she had had all the ingredients for, when he dropped his bombshell. She dropped the heavy book she was holding and it fell to the floor, loose pages scattering at her feet.

"I've decided to refit the kitchen with all this extra time on my hands."

"What?"

" It's looking a bit tired and ...."

"How on earth will you get all the things you need at a time such as this?"

"I've already had a look and I can order most of what we need online."

She had tried, only half-heartedly she had to admit, to put him off but he was determined and she had realised that it would keep him busy and less downhearted. In the end, she would be the one to benefit from a hopefully updated kitchen. Once the decision had been made, she became almost as enthusiastic as Edward. He had gone ahead straight away and ordered kitchen units they had both liked and a new double stainless-steel sink. When he showed her what it would all look like when finished she had to admit that she was quite impressed, the only trouble would be the upheaval of it all.

"I'm glad you like it and this company can deliver it in two weeks whereas with most other places there would be at least a six week wait."

"No, I agree it looks good and the sooner you can start the better." Thinking to herself let's get it over with.

"There will be a longer wait for the sink but I think I can get around that somehow."

Elizabeth couldn't see what was wrong with the old sink but she supposed a new one would look better in the end, all shiny and minus the scratches, to fit in with the rest of the new units.

She had benefited from a new kitchen many years ago, most of it completed by Edward, but they had been so much younger then. She remembered how the time had dragged on and on and seemed to take for ever, and they were also running a business at the time. However, she also remembered the joy that it had given her in the end, even when they were still waiting for a few small things to be finished off. Another Déjà Vu moment came two weeks later when the 'new kitchen' was settled in the garage and the car sat on the drive where she suspected it would be for some time. The units were piled up in their cardboard boxes because the old ones would have to be removed first, which was probably one of the worst things that needed to be done. She vaguely remembered the last kitchen undertaking and the interminable length of time it had taken. Then there were all the hidden nasty things such as the bare plaster, bits of splintered wood and the thought of all this having to be put to rights again. However, she had agreed to this and Edward was much more cheerful now that he had a new project. Elizabeth's mood had been neatly divided into two; one half of her was excited about the thought of the completion but the other half was dreading the mess, the inconvenience and the endless time it would inevitably take. She knew from experience that it would drag on longer than was hoped. She couldn't look back now as the contents of the existing kitchen cupboards and drawers had been removed and scattered around the rest of the house and one of the best outcomes was that many items were now waiting to go to charity shops and some even to the dustbin or to the local tip.

Suddenly she was awoken from her dark thoughts when Edward called out

"Look what I have found."

She half-heartedly turned towards him expecting to be shown a mouldy piece of food or a dead mouse that had found its way to a hidden section of the old kitchen, but he was holding a blue book in his hand.

"Is this the diary that you were looking for?"

"Where on earth did you find that?"

"It must have fallen to the back of one of the old units."

She'd long since forgotten all about it and couldn't remember why she had been searching for it in the first place and then it all came back to her. Wasn't it something to do with Jerry Smith? He still puzzled her and so she put the diary aside to look at later but now she needed to concentrate on kitchen matters. Strangely enough the clearance hadn't taken quite as long as she had expected and before they knew it the skip had been taken away containing the old units and there they were standing in an empty room. It made sense to paint the walls before they started to put the new cupboards together; the microwave was sitting on the kitchen table and the contents of the cupboards were mostly in the dining room. There was a small space on the dining table for the washing up bowl where she had to wash dishes using water from the downstairs bathroom. Although the lockdown had been much released, they would no doubt still be relying on fish and chips from the local chip shop or an Indian take-away, from time to time. Elizabeth wanted to get on with the painting so that they could start on the real work but Edward was a perfectionist.

"While we have the opportunity, we must make sure that it's done to a high standard."

Therefore, the woodwork was sanded followed by two coats of gloss paint and the walls also needed to have two coats of the creamy coloured emulsion that they had chosen. It had an exotic name, although to her it was cream or magnolias. If she hadn't protested Edward would have done three coats.

"Look, most of the walls will be covered by the units won't they."

After what seemed an eternity, to Elizabeth anyway, the sink had arrived at last and was in place. The kitchen now looked so much lighter with the new paler units and the light-coloured worktops and tiles. By now she looked forward to filling the cupboards and at least she had managed to get rid of a good deal of surplus stuff and wondered why on earth she had hoarded so many things that she never used, and was unlikely to use again. Everything was looking good but whatever would Edward want to tackle next? She hoped that this achievement would keep him content for a while at least. At the back of her mind was the distant memory when Edward had fitted a kitchen a lifetime ago when life was stressful, in some ways maybe even more so than it was today. She realised that the stress levels of now related to everyone and it was a different kind entirely as they were living with such uncertainty as they were unaware of what they would have to confront next. On the other hand, new kitchens always had something in common; first of all, there was the mess and the upheaval and then later on there was the joy following the completion and at least today they weren't having to work under the challenging circumstances of the past. Even with the kitchen upheaval the rest of their home was reasonably comfortable unlike in the nineteen seventies.

Chapter 11

Trintley 1978

Elizabeth's worries were beginning to settle down now that she had come to terms with the life that she could never have envisaged a few years ago; she had accepted most of the challenges and no doubt more would lay ahead of them and possibly some that would be more difficult. Thus, a new optimism had come with their plans for the future but now there would be something else; she still hadn't told Edward about her pregnancy as it was still early days but still quite exciting.

They were now waiting for their next half closing day as they had decided to drive into Cambridge to look for ideas for furnishings and fixtures in hopeful anticipation for when they would be required. This would be a well-earned day out just for themselves and she couldn't remember when they had last been able to enjoy a treat such as this, as most of their outings had been business related. They should have just enough time before they needed to be back home to collect Francis from school and she was especially looking forward to this trip. They would be doing something to benefit themselves for a change instead of going off to find stock for the shop.

They arrived at the first place on their list, having parked the car a couple of streets away. There appeared to be plenty of choices of furniture, curtaining and blinds which should have enlivened her recent enthusiasm for the improvements they wished to make. She had ignored her feeling of tiredness assuming it could be due to her pregnancy but it wasn't going to stop her plans for what she wished to do. She felt annoyed when this fatigue had become rather more pronounced but her determination for enjoyment remained. She tried to remember back to the early days when Francis was on the way, but it was a long time ago now. She probably had felt tired but there would have been more time to rest in those days. Amongst the excellent choice of everything an occasional table had attracted Elizabeth's eye. A helpful young man, tall with fair hair, came up to them; he must have only been in his teens but looked smart and wore a friendly smile, giving the impression that he was actually enjoying his job.

"Is there anything in particular you are looking for?" he asked

Suddenly Elizabeth became alarmed.

"Is there anywhere I can sit down?"

"Yes, of course" and he showed her to a chair.

She noticed Edward looking at her curiously with his impatient look that sometimes came over him when he was displeased about something, and she felt that she needed to explain to him and the young man.

"I'm so sorry, I fear that I am feeling terribly tired" and then added rather lamely "I must have been overdoing things a bit."

After her earlier excited anticipation for their day out her enthusiasm evaporated due to this extreme fatigue which had suddenly come over her and she tried to gather herself together.

"We're just looking for ideas really for our new home......" She trailed off and Edward turned to look at her; her eyes were drooping and it was amazing that she hadn't fallen off the chair. Her first instinct was just to choose the first thing she saw because she just couldn't wait to get home, then she thought better of it and maybe this would be the wrong decision after all. She remained seated and silent.

Edward failed to understand.

"What's the matter with you? You must have some idea what you want and you were so keen."

"Can we just go and sit down somewhere else, perhaps in the cafe over the road?"

"If that's what you want but we don't have that much time left."

"There is something I like but I'd rather think about it and come back another day rather than rush into it."

"OK. we'll go home then" Edward said in exasperation. He strode off to find the car with Elizabeth dragging behind him. Eventually she struggled into the passenger seat.

"Look, I wasn't going to tell you just yet, but it looks as if I may be pregnant."

A smile came onto his face "That's wonderful news, let's get you home then."

She went straight to bed, then the dreadful pains started so Edward called the doctor; they had only just found the time to register with the surgery the week before so this at least was fortunate. Their new doctor arrived and told her that her chances of losing the baby were about fifty-fifty and that his wife had had a threatened miscarriage and went on to have a perfectly healthy baby. He was a pleasant, sympathetic man, probably in his forties and must have been over six feet tall. She had a feeling that she had seen him driving around in a mini and looking as if he had had to be folded into it neatly in order not to crush his head on the roof, oddly enough his name was Doctor Little.

He prescribed some pain killers and advised her to

"Stay in bed and I will return tomorrow. It's alright, the painkillers won't do you or the baby any harm." She had been a little concerned about taking pain killers but she also felt certain that she could put her trust in him.

She felt bad that Edward would have to look after the shop, the cooking and Francis. A week had passed and she had remained in bed and Dr Little had been as good as his word and had visited regularly. There was of course no renovation work or decorating being done.

"Mummy will be alright soon; she's been working too hard and needs a rest."

The pain killers had helped and she felt a little better but this also meant that she felt well enough to be embarrassed, when the doctor arrived. There were bare floorboards with only a couple of rugs hiding the rough surfaces as their bedroom was the last on their list for a makeover. Her radio, which he had kindly offered to switch off for her, had been balanced on a plank over a few bricks. What must he have thought? This didn't bother Edward

"He knows that we have just taken over a practically bankrupt shop and just moved into rather run-down premises."

They were not to know at the time that Dr Little and his wife would become two of their most valued customers.

Their new home had no central heating and once the colder weather arrived Elizabeth had to wear several layers of clothing.

When they moved in, during a reasonably warm autumn, there had been just one paraffin heater and two, soon to be defunct, electric fires they had brought with them. They had bought another fan heater to replace the now useless one only to find that when they got it home that the new one didn't work either and its replacement made a dreadful noise. In the end it was a case of ‘third time lucky’ when they actually found a suitable one. This was just the moment when Edward had come across an advertisement in the local paper for several storage heaters for sale at an extremely low price and the place was not too far away. Edward decided this would be an opportunity they couldn’t afford to miss so that Sunday Edward said

“Will you be OK; I’ll take Francis along with me.”

“Of course, if this will stop us from freezing to death during the winter.”

She’d been in bed for just over a week now and wondered how much longer she would have to rest in order to save the baby; this had been something they had both wanted so badly but this set back had meant that a great deal of pressure had been put onto Edward’s shoulders. She picked up her novel but, after reading a couple of pages, she realised that she hadn’t really taken in what it was about. Edward had moved the radio on its bricks to within easy reach so she switched that on instead and listened to some music and eventually drifted off to sleep. She was woken up suddenly in dreadful pain again, but far worse this time. She knew what this must mean and struggled to the bathroom. Eventually she returned to bed and dozed off until about half an hour later when she heard the key in the lock and Edward appeared with a big smile on his face and Francis presented her with a large toy rabbit with floppy ears.

“We found it in a shop on our way home” and then he scampered off and Elizabeth burst into tears.

“I’ve lost the baby, Edward.”

His face fell “I’m so sorry, but we knew that this could happen. It’s a good thing that we hadn’t mentioned the new baby to Francis.”

“Yes, that’s just as well and at least now I will be able to pull my weight again; Dr Little

is coming tomorrow.” Then she had another thought.

"The rabbit?"

"It's OK, I told Francis that you would love it and that it would cheer you up."

Elizabeth had known a new baby at the moment would have been difficult to deal with and she was right when she had told Edward she would be able to pull her weight again now, but she was bitterly disappointed nevertheless. They would have managed somehow and a baby would have taken her mind off the other chaos in their lives, but it wasn't to be and life had to go on.

Never would Elizabeth have thought she could get so excited about the old-fashioned storage heaters Edward had bought. The people he had purchased them from, at a pretty reasonable price, had wanted rid of them because they were updating their system with gas central heating and radiators which she herself had always been used to in the past But, she knew she couldn't look back and these would certainly serve their purpose adequately, having left their previous civilised life behind them. At least they would still be much better off for heating than when they had first moved in; these large heaters should fit well enough into their spacious rooms and would be of great benefit.

"They look much better than I had expected; once they are in place with the bricks put back, we should soon have adequate heating."

They appreciated that the size of their rooms could easily accommodate the heaters without them sticking out like sore thumbs; although Edward now had to replace all the bricks that had been inside and had had to be removed in order to make them light enough to lift into the car. He would also have to make a return journey to collect the others he hadn't had enough space for. In a day or two the storage heaters were in situ and didn't look at all out of place but as was no doubt to be expected during these days of home improvements there was to be a problem.

First of all, they had to wait patiently, maybe just a day or two as they were promised, for the Electricity Board to come and inspect them. Then they were told that they would need to put in a white metre and even then, they would only be able to use two of them because the electricity supply was insufficient for any more. After another, even longer, wait the Electricity Board came to rectify the matter and they really did believe they would soon have a fully heated home. However, it soon transpired that the solution to this was that the Electricity Board would have to dig a large hole in the pavement outside their home, presumably to put in the necessary cables. Some men from the Electricity Board arrived one morning, shortly after this piece of information had reached them, and started digging the hole so that soon the cellar had become exposed to the outside world. As if on cue the heavens opened and torrential rain bucketed down to soak everything and everyone in sight including the flooding of the cellar. Afterwards the insurance company had pointed out that they couldn't make a claim, as this was 'an act of God'. At least Edward could see the funny side of it.

"So, insurance companies don't take into account all the atheists that are insured with them."

Fortunately, as it happened not too much damage had been done and although they landed up with loads of soggy stationery their predecessors had left behind, everything did eventually dry out.

After Elizabeth's hopes had been dashed and there was not going to be another child just now, she decided to channel her energies elsewhere. Although she still missed the modern house they had left behind and the friends she had made, not to mention the freedom that she had had, there was a plus side. She was enjoying running the business and had got to know many people, some of whom had become friends.

She still didn't like the old house but they were slowly making improvements in the space that had acquired. The best thing of all was that Francis had settled in well and really enjoyed giving them a hand when they needed it, he had suddenly become old for his age and Elizabeth had thought sadly that it could have had something to do with his being an only child.

Although they had lived here for just a few months now it felt more like many years and she could see that the expectations of turning the place into a comfortable home in a few months, as promised by Edward, had evaporated. Everything was taking far longer than she had hoped and she knew that getting their place completed to a good standard would take years rather than months. There she was being pessimistic again but Edward was enjoying doing most of the work himself and was in his element and she had to admit that what he had done was excellently completed; she was also aware that if they had paid someone else it would have been at a high cost and no doubt the result would not have been as imaginatively achieved.

Chapter 12

Willow Bridge 2020

At last, the lockdown had ended after four months of severe restrictions and in many ways, it was cause for celebration although the recent threat still stayed with them. Elizabeth, like so many others, was treading carefully. All non-essential shops were now open, at least those that were able to, but sadly many had been forced to close for good due to their lack of business for so long. Nevertheless, despite the inevitable apprehension, it still seemed both weird and yet encouraging to be able to visit a shop selling luxury goods even if they were items not appearing on the shopping list. It was certainly a great relief to see doors flung open in the high street bringing more people into the area and making it look normal.

The forecast for unemployment had been depressing as it was thought that it would inevitably rise causing even more concern. Working from home had now been eased although some companies were still encouraging their employees to continue this for the time being; Francis's company was one of these and fortunately, being an accountant meant that much of his work could be done from home anyway.

"At least I don't have the hour's commute and sitting in traffic every time they decide to dig up the road and less time is spent queuing up at the garage for petrol, not to mention the cost."

"Yes, that is certainly an advantage for you" Edward had agreed.

"Although I do miss meeting clients and work colleagues and I seem to spend far more time sitting in front of the computer, I do try to get some exercise each day even though it is easier said than done as Helen keeps finding me jobs to do around the house."

Edward had laughed, despite the pandemic and being retired he still hadn't managed to tackle all the boring jobs; the more interesting ones he was spending more time on which was keeping him occupied and away from those chores that he should have done long ago. He wasn't much of a DIY man although he had done his fair share of decorating and putting up shelves. After the last repair to a shelf that had fallen down, he had said to Elizabeth

"There's far too much stuff on it, no wonder it has been looking so precarious."

She supposed that there were a couple of casseroles that she never used so maybe she should get rid of those.

They were soon to find out that there were downsides from working from home; it didn't suit everybody. In the bigger cities, and especially in London, the cafes, pubs, restaurants and shops had always been kept busy with customers working close by in businesses and offices; vast numbers of sandwiches were sold at lunch times and trying to keep on top of the queues often meant that they had needed to take on extra staff. Even when the rush had died down there were still enough people buying coffees and cakes and even something to take home for their evening meals. This had abruptly come to an end and these enterprises were struggling and needed to release some of their staff, especially those they had needed to take on so that they could cope in busy times. Other home workers had often had to get by with their young children under their feet and those who had lived on their own, would get depressed as they were no longer meeting up with others.

Elizabeth decided it was now time to get out and about a bit more having been released from the limitations that they had become used to. Unfortunately, this was not as easy as she had thought. Having been confined for so long it was going to take a big effort to continue with what had gone before; it was difficult to describe how her self-confidence had taken a knock and although she knew that she would go out if she had to, it would only be if it was absolutely necessary. She was reminded at this point that she hadn't driven the car for a long time and the ideal opportunity had presented itself for her to visit a small picturesque village that she had been meaning to drive to for some time, but had been stopped by the lockdown. There was no excuse not to do so now; Edward hadn't been particularly interested when she mentioned this place to him, so there was nothing to stop her going on her own. The thought of getting behind the wheel again after so long terrified her and to think that a few months ago she wouldn't have had the slightest hesitation about taking such a trip. She could put it off until tomorrow; but tomorrow came and went and so did the next few days. Then quite unexpectedly a friend, or rather more of an acquaintance, had phoned

"It's Monica here, I wondered if you would like to come over for a coffee? I haven't invited anyone round for ages."

"I'd love to" she replied and she really did mean it as she hadn't seen Monica for many months.

They had originally met at a retirement party of someone she had once worked with and she and Monica found that they had much in common. They had visited each other's respective homes for cups of tea or coffee a couple of times in the past but even before Covid, these visits had more or less stopped. Elizabeth assumed that they were both living busy and fulfilled lives.

Monica lived in an isolated village no more than three miles away so Elizabeth looked up the directions again to refresh her memory and then had put the address into the SATNAV. Here goes, she thought, as she had got behind the wheel once more willing herself to set off. Her confidence had returned once she had covered the first mile and she was able to sit back in the driver's seat instead of being perched on the edge, with her hands tightly gripping the wheel. She relaxed with a huge and loud sigh of relief. By now she was nearing the village and it was just before eleven o'clock, the time that she had agreed to arrive. A few minutes later the SATNAV told her that she had reached her destination and she found herself in front of a large farm house standing alone, but it was nothing like the small bungalow that she had remembered from before. She continued down the road, knowing at least that this was the correct route, and started looking for the house number; unfortunately, none of the residences appeared to have numbers and a few more homes had been built since she had last visited. She continued, looking for bungalows on both sides of the road, her new found confidence rapidly evaporating and she couldn't understand why she appeared to be lost when she had been before. At least she had arrived safely in the village and surely near her destination, so she congratulated herself, but by now she had left all habitation behind her. Only an open road, lined by trees, presented itself ahead of her. She turned round as soon as she could, although it must have been a good mile from the place that she was looking for. Coming from this direction she soon noticed three or four familiar looking bungalows set back slightly and was grateful to see the correct one; a large extension had been built onto the neighbour's home including a loft extension, so it wasn't surprising that she hadn't recognised Monica's place. She hadn't known Monica all that well and had been both surprised and pleased to get her phone call; she knew that she lived on her own and didn't appear to have any family or at least none that she had mentioned. Looking back, she tried to think about the last time they had met and seemed to recall an art group they had both attended for a short time, long before the Jerry Smith debacle had happened. Apart from thoughts of that man she realised that it was going to be enjoyable to meet up with Monica again. She showed her into a large, sunny sitting room and soon returned from her kitchen with a tray containing mugs of coffee and a plate of shortbread. Although they had much in common with their interests Monica gave out little about herself and Elizabeth feared that she had spent a good deal of time telling her about what she herself had been getting up to. With guilt, she realised that she should have found out more about Monica's activities and family but she was always afraid of being nosy. She did hate nosy people; she remembered in her past being asked what she earned, did she have a boyfriend and other such irritating questions. Then surprised she looked at her watch and noticed that it was half-past one.

"Oh, my goodness I'd better be getting back, Edward will wonder where I have got to."

They agreed to meet up again and she made her way straight home without any further complications along her route.

Saturday arrived and Elizabeth was aware once more how quickly the time had passed by, especially since the lockdown had eased. She decided to wander off to the high street which she hadn't done for a while except for a quick dash into Boots and even to Smiths for a newspaper. These had been the only places able to remain open during lockdown and presumably they were classed as essential retail. Oddly enough she still stuck to these stores without going much further and today there were plenty of people out and about and for one brief moment she forgot what it had been like since that dreadful announcement in March when life in general had come to a sudden halt. Then she noticed that on one side of the road there were three neighbouring outlets all boarded up; previously there had been shop closures but now it looked as if there were even more. Nevertheless, there was certainly a big difference now that the ghost town experience had left them and shops that hadn't had to close down on the high street were open once more. Many of them were buzzing with activity as men, women and children walked about in the old sort of way, except that most were keeping a good distance from each other. There were lighted displays in the windows, their doors open and welcoming in the customers again; but one of the differences was that inside customers had to keep to the two-metre social distancing rule and some shops could only take in limited customers at a time. There were arrows providing a one-way system along pavements and in the shops but sometimes they were rather unclear leading to confusion. It had to be noticed that retail outlets as well as banks and building societies had all made a tremendous effort to comply and to make everything as easy as they could do under the circumstances that they had found themselves in. Although she was still dubious about shopping and had mostly confined herself to just one shop in any one day, it was a start and she expected to gradually gain more confidence. It was an absolute joy when she was able to make an appointment to visit the hairdresser again after so long. She still had three weeks to wait but had never thought that she would look forward to it so much and had kept looking at the diary, counting the days as if she was about to go on an exotic holiday. She still had a nagging doubt; supposing she became ill, perhaps with Covid, and couldn't go or what if her hairdresser got the virus? The what ifs clouded her mind to some extent but at last the day was upon her and she was on her way to the salon. She suggested that he didn't cut it as short as usual.

"Just thin it out and trim it and don't bother with layering it and then I will be able to cope with it better should there be another lockdown"

Tony looked at her questioningly as much as to say, surely it won't happen again, but he did as she asked and agreed that it suited her.

"See you again in about six weeks."

What a wonderful hopeful statement.

Chapter 13

Trintley 1978

One of their biggest decisions, and no doubt one of their best, so far was about to be put into effect. After taking over the shop they had made big changes and improvements and, going by the increase in trade, those efforts were obviously paying off. They had automatically taken over the hours of the previous owners which had included closing on a Tuesday afternoon. They were always extremely busy on Tuesday mornings, almost as if the customers were frightened of running out of something they couldn't do without during the afternoon the shop closure. Although Tuesday afternoon was a welcome break for them, they were limited as to what could be undertaken in just half a day which made the situation a bit impractical. Elizabeth had taken it all in her stride without questioning it but Edward, on the other hand, had obviously been mulling it over for a while. Then, in his usual casual way as if he had just decided to go shopping, he had announced

"I think it would make more sense to open all day on Tuesdays as we are always so busy…"

Elizabeth was about to protest before he could continue

"… and we could close all day on a Monday instead, which would give us a full weekend and would benefit Francis as well as us."

"That's a really excellent idea and I wonder now why I hadn't thought of it; after all Mondays are often rather quiet."

"We could also extend the other days by half-an-hour and then nobody would feel that they were losing out."

Shortly after their decision had been made, they had put up a notice announcing the change of opening hours which they had decided should start the following week.

"Although I don't expect many people will read it."

Strangely enough there were no complaints about the new

regime and in fact most people liked the idea and said as much. They would now have the opportunity to plan some time away from the shop as they would have a full two days off; this would have to wait until Francis had broken up from school but it would be something to look forward to.

Sadly, they were unable to give it any more thought for a while as something untoward happened on the next particularly busy morning in the shop. They never had been able to predict either the hectic or the quiet times, but a couple of days after their exciting change to their working week she had started off with just a small queue in front of her. She didn't envisage any difficulties as she had dealt with longer ones before when Edward was absent, either buying stock or working on the house. The first person left satisfied with his small purchase and the lady behind him moved closer to the till.

"I've been looking for something that has been advertised lately but I can't remember its name."

Elizabeth waited for her to give at least some hint as to what it could be as she noticed the woman behind her fidgeting with impatience.

"It's something used for polishing furniture and it's supposed to help with scratches."

Elizabeth hadn't seen anything advertised recently other than the usual polishes and took her to the shelf where anything related to polish was displayed, in the slight hope that she might find it or maybe something which would jog her memory. This gave Elizabeth a little time to serve the next customer who seemed relieved that it was now her turn and she placed one or two items on the counter and started fumbling in her handbag. It was now the turn of the next customer to become impatient as the fumbling continued.

"I'm sorry I must have left my purse behind on my kitchen table…."

Therefore, Elizabeth ignored the ringing phone hoping that Edward would appear soon to check that all was well. That was just one slight disadvantage of having different telephone numbers in the house and in the shop, so he wouldn't be aware of the insistent ringing. However, they really had appreciated not getting phone calls from customers at all hours and it had been worth it. In the end she felt that she would be forced to pick it up because the persistent ringing was getting on her nerves, it couldn't be helped even though more customers were arriving. In the past she had often found herself irritated when she had been waiting in a shop when a call had come through and the person serving her had answered, interrupting their transaction. In fact, fairly recently she had visited a place that sold mundane everyday things, in order to purchase a basic item. If she could have found it, she would have grabbed it and waved it at the man behind the counter but although she knew he sold them, they were nowhere to be seen. The man hadn't even acknowledged her presence and carried on talking on the phone; it wasn't anything to do with the business either.

"How's Mary? Is she OK? Good, good. Yes, I also have a dentist appointment tomorrow..."

The call had gone on and on and he didn't even nod at her and say that he would be with her in a moment. At that point she had walked out and decided that she wouldn't be returning there ever again.

Fortunately, just at that point she was grateful to see Edward's appearance; wiping his hands on an old towel he made his way towards the phone. She could vaguely hear his conversation above the steady hum of customer conversation and the clinking sound of the opening till. Then he was silent for a while presumably as he was listening to the person on the other end of the line.

"Yes, I understand. How bad is it? Don't worry, someone will be there straight away." He rang off and turned to Elizabeth

"That was Francis's school, he's had a fall in the playground and he's been taken to hospital."

Elizabeth went white. "He must be badly hurt if they've taken him to hospital."

"Apparently, he's still conscious but one of us needs to go. I'll come and take over here."

She immediately forgot about the customer who was looking for some kind of miracle polish, the one who had lost her purse and everyone else and went straight to the house and grabbed her bag and car keys. She briefly returned to the shop, on her way out, to remind Edward that there was shortly to be a delivery. As she approached the exit a woman had come up to her; she wasn't someone that Elizabeth had particularly liked.

"Oh, I see you are going off on a jolly leaving that poor husband of yours to do all the work."

She ignored her mainly because of her worry about Francis but also because she would no doubt have been tempted to say something that she would later regret. Instead, she rushed off to fetch the car; one or two other customers turned to look at her, probably rather surprised that she was leaving Edward to cope with an even longer queue that had formed by now. Typical, she thought, of all the times to be extra busy but then Edward always remained calm and would cope admirably. Perhaps he would explain what had happened, although this was probably rather unlikely and at least not everyone was judgmental or critical. Just as she was about to get behind the wheel of her car that fortunately had been parked on the road outside, one of her favourite elderly customers, whose name she thought was Polly, approached her

"Are you alright dear?"

She hurriedly explained the problem.

"Don't worry, I'll come with you. You shouldn't have to go on your own."

Elizabeth was so glad of her company as she tried to take her mind off the worrying news and concentrate on driving to the hospital; she had been so fearful and her brain had gone numb although she was still functioning like some kind of robot. She had already been assured that Francis was conscious, but that didn't mean a thing. If it hadn't been for Polly, she would most certainly be thinking the worst. Francis had only just turned seven years old and at this point she was reminded that she had promised him a birthday party but it hadn't actually happened yet, and she couldn't remember why. Had they been too busy or was it because she had still been recovering from the miscarriage? Anyway, a good reason hadn't come to her and instead her thoughts turned to dread. Would they be able to save him? Other dreadful feelings were being kept at bay, thanks to Polly, and she was somehow still functioning.

"Children are extremely resilient, you know. I used to be a nurse and if the hospital were concerned, they would have informed you."

"Thanks, and thanks for coming." Although she had realised after Polly's kind words that the hospital wouldn't have been able to get hold of her whilst she was in the car and of course neither would Edward be able to contact her. Luckily, they were nearly there now so she wouldn't think about it.

They had just reached the hospital and Polly said

"Pull up outside Casualty and I'll take your car to the car park so that you can go and see him quicker and I'll come and find you."

Elizabeth was thinking what a lovely, kind person she was as she made her way to the reception; she was close to tears when she thought of kindness as opposed to that other woman's nastiness – although to be fair she couldn't be expected to know what had happened. By now she was a little calmer, thanks to her new friend, but still extremely anxious. A nurse led her down a long corridor, would they ever get there she wondered. Eventually they came to a cubicle and she peered in where she found Francis sitting up in a bed with a big grin on his face.

"I've got a broken leg and they are going to put it in plaster."

Suddenly she was breathing normally again and relief flooded over her as she was able to smile at Francis with relief. At that moment a nurse came along and explained that an X Ray had shown that it was a clean break; then a smiling porter came along to push him along to the place where the plaster would be applied and he beckoned her to follow them.

They arrived home, just as Edward was closing the shop for lunch, complete with some crutches and she and Edward were left to wonder how he would manage the stairs. He could always sleep downstairs but there wasn't a bathroom on the ground floor, only an outside toilet. They needn't have worried, as Polly had said 'children are extremely resilient' and after Edward had carried him up the stairs to bed that evening, he had soon found ways of getting about. But he had become far too ambitious; the doctor had said he needed to keep his leg up, but for a seven-year-old it appeared that this would be a difficult accomplishment and especially as he was looking forward to returning to school to show off his plaster. No doubt he would get it full of signatures as had happened to another boy who had broken his arm recently.

As word got round, and she sincerely hoped that it had reached the customer who had accused her of letting her poor husband do all the work, many people telephoned to see how Francis was. That evening there was a call specifically for her.

"Hello, it's Jimmy's mother. I was sorry to hear about Francis but I thought I should let you know that Jimmy said a boy had pushed him, did he tell you?"

"No, he didn't mention it and I didn't think to ask as I was so relieved that his injury wasn't too serious."

"Maybe you should find out more and contact the headmaster, bullying should definitely be stopped."

"Thanks for letting me know."

She decided not to say anything for the moment but couldn't help thinking about those worrying moments she had had when she had first heard and how scared she was until she had found Francis sitting happily in the hospital and smiling at her, when she had envisioned him lying there prostrate with tubes and other appalling contraptions beside his hospital bed.

Elizabeth had already forgotten the guilt she had been feeling about the non-event of the birthday party when Francis said, from his position on the sofa

"Mum, could I have a dog? I would really love to have a dog."

Elizabeth was already concentrating on the white marks on the dark cover of the sofa from the plaster on his leg and thinking that it would easily come off she was sure, and anyway it was the least of her recent worries she reminded herself. She turned her attention back to her son

"You know that if you had a dog, you'd have to take him for walks."

"I'd like that."

Although she realised that she and Edward would be the ones having to walk the dog in all weathers in between all their shop duties, she seemed to remember Francis asking for a dog once before but when the request had fallen on deaf ears, he hadn't mentioned it again. Naturally he was taking advantage of what had just happened to bring it up again and completely oblivious to his mother's misgivings over the birthday party.

"I'll tell you what I'll mention it to Daddy."

In the meantime, Polly called to see how Francis was getting on and how they were all coping.

"Pretty well thank you, under the circumstances. I'd like to thank you again for all your help and support, without your kindness everything would have been so much worse."

"It was a pleasure and one other thing I was going to tell you is that my daughter's cat has just had kittens and we wondered if Francis would like one? Maybe something to take his mind off the mishap."

"Thank you for thinking of him although I'm not sure......"

"It's alright they won't be able to leave the mother just yet, you can come and have a look at them if you like, or rather if Francis would be interested."

"Thank you, we'd love to come and look at them."

That evening, once Francis was in bed, Elizabeth told Edward about Francis's request for a dog and also about the kittens.

"I don't think we can cope with a dog until he's older as you are right about the onus falling on our shoulders, but there's no reason why he shouldn't have a cat."

The following day Elizabeth asked Francis if he would like to go and see some kittens and he immediately cheered up and sounded interested.

Polly's daughter lived on a farm fairly close by but they hadn't been prepared for the unexpected; Edward drove along a bumpy track with the car lurching uncontrollably along with mud splattering the car as the puddles presented themselves and he tried to avoid the potholes. Just as Elizabeth was thinking that the journey was taking forever Francis said

"Are we nearly there?"

She realised how uncomfortable the ride would be with a leg supported by a plaster cast and she really hoped that it would be worth it.

"I hope so." She answered uncertainly. "Are you alright?"

"Yes, it's OK."

His face lit up as at last when they saw the big old house. As they had been instructed, they went round to the back door and were shown into a cosy farmhouse kitchen where the mother cat sat in a basket with her kittens. Francis's eyes opened wide.

"Can we have one?"

"If you'd like one, of course" said Elizabeth "Which one do

you think?"

Immediately Francis went to the basket and asked if he could hold one. He picked up a tiny black and white kitten and immediately fell in love with it.

"If you'd like the black and white one, we can save him for you." Polly's daughter offered.

"I'd love him. Can I take him?"

"He's not quite ready to leave his mum yet but you can come and collect him soon."

Edward was already thinking about the journey back along the road that he had already commented on

"It won't do much for the suspension."

"And" added Elizabeth "we'll need to clean the car."

They all laughed. Francis was happy and the return home didn't seem half as bad as their earlier experience. Once they arrived Edward asked Francis what he was going to call the new addition to the family.

"Charlie," he said.

Elizabeth and Edward exchanged a questioning look but Edward said

"Charlie it is then."

Elizabeth realised afterwards that Charlie was the name of a hero in one of his story books.

The time soon came round for them to collect Charlie although the journey didn't seem as bad as before; there had been no rain for a while and some of the pot holes appeared to have been filled in and added to that there was excitement, especially for Francis. He was out of the car as soon as they stopped and started up the drive as fast as he could manage.

"At least the dog has been forgotten."

"Yes, thank goodness." replied Elizabeth.

A little while later they were on their home with Francis gently holding the furry bundle on the back seat.

Chapter 14

Willow Bridge 2020

She and Edward had made great plans for the following weeks, although upon reflection maybe they weren't so great, just more ambitious than before. There would be plenty of places to visit for meals, as the pubs and restaurants were open once more, and they would also be able to wander around the grounds of National Trust properties nearby where they would also be able to eat lunch in their cafes. They set off happily on this campaign but little were they to know then that later on they would be glad they had taken every opportunity to go out and to make the most of visits to and from friends and family. The beautiful weather had not only meant eating in the gardens of pubs and wandering round the grounds of one or two National Trust properties, although the stately homes themselves were not yet open, but at the moment this wasn't something that they would wish to do during such lovely weather. There were other places on their doorstep and in the meantime, Elizabeth had also been able to arrange for some of the book group to meet in her garden now that the earlier rule of six had ended and thus ruling out the previous problem if there had been even just one more than five friends or family members. She had been so careful to stick to the rules and possibly may have concerned herself a little too much, if anything.

"At least we are trying to do what's right but I'm not so sure that everyone has been following the rules or even using common sense. There always seem to be several cars parked on the drive outside the house a few doors down the road........"

"Maybe there's someone coming to look after them." Edward mumbled.

"That's true the lady is quite elderly, but surely several cars at any one time are a bit
much."

"Perhaps she is having a party.... Or maybe lots of parties."

They laughed.

"Anyway, it's most unlikely that anyone will come and check up on our road as it is rather off the beaten track."

There were a few more gathered at the book group meeting this time although their carefully chosen novel had been picked long before Covid had ever been heard of and the novel's gloomy contents regarding someone's misery had lost its appeal. These days misfortune appeared to be something that they were all experiencing to a certain extent and they did not wish to dwell on it just now. Their conversation had soon been steered away both from the book and also from what was so frequently on their minds at the moment.

"How are you getting on with the book you have been writing?"

"Quite well as it happens albeit rather slowly; it has certainly been something to keep me occupied."

Barbara had been a keen writer of poetry and had also written short stories and a couple of her books had been published but she had started on a novel when she was stuck at home on her own during the early days of Covid.

One of the others congratulated her

"That's absolutely great, it must be a form of escapism."

"It's certainly that."

Another of them mentioned something else. "Oddly enough after many years, I've started baking cakes again and to my surprise some of them have turned out quite well. The only problem is that we have to keep eating them."

The afternoon had continued with laughter but their attention also focussed on other issues, such as what they would be doing next and what could be ahead of them. Gradually it was becoming a little chilly and so they all began to wander off.

"That has been a wonderful afternoon and thank you so much."

She had been pleased she had arranged the gathering and as she started to put everything away, she realised how enjoyable it had been and looked forward even more to her next get-together when Francis and Helen would be visiting them at the weekend. She was a little disappointed that the boys wouldn't be coming, but at least she would see the twins. It was rather a long way for them to come for the day but Francis didn't mind the drive and so they all intended to make the most of it. Edward got out the barbecue and she made some bread rolls and prepared a variety of salads; she had also set the garden table. However, when the wind blew cooler and the paper cloth had waved about, leaving a large tear in it, and the cutlery had started to jangle about, she moved everything into the conservatory.

"At least this isn't against the rules anymore, we can meet inside" she said more to herself than to anyone in particular but there were still many mixed messages from the government; Northern Ireland, Scotland and Wales had different regulations anyway.

"Apparently, we are told, meeting outside is safer" Edward had said "But let's just use some common sense shall we."

She had already cleaned everything thoroughly with sanitizer and it was almost amusing to think what she had done even for her close family. She did rather miss all the hugs but caution and safety had been on all their minds lately and she dwelt on the fact that there was plenty of fresh air in the conservatory with the doors and vents open. Once again, this family occasion had turned out to be another lovely day and much appreciated as they had all been able to relax and forget about everything else that was going on around them. Francis and Edward had cooked sausages on the barbeque and there was also the chicken that Elizabeth had started off in the oven; Edward had made some beef burgers and there seemed to be an awful lot of food and she wondered if they would get through it all. Helen helped to bring the salads from the kitchen and despite the hand gel and surface cleaning sprays scattered around everywhere they gave the bizarre situation little thought and caught up with their various snippets of news.

Elizabeth was tempted to mention the Jerry Smith saga to Helen and Francis to see what they would make of it but the moment passed and afterwards she was glad that she hadn't brought the subject up; by now it did look as if she was making rather too much of it.

One topic they did touch on was the confusion coming from the government. They were trying to get as many employees back to work as possible in order to save the economy, which was naturally most important except that they still needed to keep the virus cases down and for this reason people had already been advised not to use public transport.

"It's a 'Catch 22' situation isn't it." quoted Edward.

"Being retired certainly has its advantages; imagine how workers will be put off going to work if they are afraid of public transport and their only other alternative will be to get back into their cars, which is something the government has tried to discourage. It will lead back to the days of long traffic jams." Edward added. "At least we don't have the worry about losing our jobs or businesses".

A new routine had come into effect in the early days of the pandemic when their Thursday evenings had turned into some kind of social event. On that evening, every week, their meal needed to be well organised in advance so that they could go outside at eight o'clock to join their neighbours. This was also happening in other towns and villages, the clapping for the NHS to show their appreciation for all they had done during the crisis. It had become well known that all those working in hospitals were working tirelessly under tremendous pressure to care for extremely sick and dying people who had contracted the virus. However impossible their tasks were, they had battled on regardless working long hours and risking their own lives and sometimes becoming casualties themselves. This was no doubt inevitable as they were working so closely with patients suffering from an extremely contagious disease. This small gesture became known as Clap for Carers, Clap for the NHS, Clap for Key Workers or Clap for Heroes; it was a movement created as a gesture of appreciation for the workers of the United Kingdom's National Health Service and other key workers during the global pandemic of Coronavirus (Covid-19).

When they had first heard about the idea Edward had said "It will be something that people in the larger towns will be taking part in and it's unlikely that anyone here will bother; although it's a great idea."

He was completely wrong about that though, because on that first Thursday evening they had turned on the ten o'clock TV News as usual and saw pictures of hundreds of people standing on their doorsteps clapping; small towns and villages took part whether they lived on a busy road or a side street and they found out later that many of their neighbours had joined in the new custom and they had regretted not to have joined them. Therefore, on the following Thursday evening Elizabeth and Edward had ventured out and were amazed to see that about seventy to eighty percent of their neighbours living in their quiet road were on their doorsteps and many of them were elderly. Because they themselves lived at the top end of their street they had got into the habit, each Thursday evening, of walking down the middle of the road both to clap and chat to other people standing on their doorsteps.

The new general relaxation had been great news; even though social distancing was still important. One good thing was that at least the panic buying appeared to have stopped and most essential items were back in stock in the shops. Then one day Elizabeth received an unexpected telephone call from a lady from their local library whose voice she hadn't recognised. There had been all those months of being unable to spend time leisurely browsing round the shelves and going home with as many books as she could carry, even though she wouldn't have had the time to read them all. It had been a long time since she had been near the place after the realisation that the shutters were closed, leaving just an unwelcoming building. This had meant that most of her reading matter had been from books from her own shelves or one or two that she had secured second hand on-line. Even the second-hand book shops were no longer open.

She quickly turned her attention back to the unfamiliar, although friendly voice.

"I'm just phoning to let you know that we are opening up again and that books can be ordered once more."

Elizabeth had been amazed, after receiving this useful information, at the length of time they had chatted about various topics from books to cookery and wondered if she would be doing the same with all their regular borrowers. Once the call ended, she was determined to return to the library straight away even though she still had plenty of books to hand. A couple of days later she set off happily and was pleased to see, from her first glance, the library looked a little more like it had done in the old days but once she had stepped inside, on closer inspection, she noticed that there was something different. Not only had all the books had been rearranged but the shelves themselves had been moved round and a one-way system had been put in place; she wandered slowly along the rows and by the time she had reached the end of the alphabet in the fiction section she was reminded of a particular novel which had been previously recommended to her and that she had been trying to get hold of for some time. She immediately set off in search but the author's name was Rutherford; she spent a while looking for authors beginning with the letter R and yet there didn't appear to be any and as she was about to give up, she found that the shelf with the Rs came after the S's instead of before. She hadn't found the one she wanted anyway, but assumed that eventually the library organisation would progress and anyway this was a really good start. It would no longer be possible to sit on one of the comfortable armchairs, previously provided, to peruse books and magazines and she wondered if anything would ever be the same again.

Elizabeth had vaguely wondered whether the event of Covid would have changed the topics of peoples' conversations because they had all been confined to their homes. She suspected that there would no doubt have been many arguments and probably complaints as well, especially among teenagers, whose lives had been disproportionately disrupted due to no fault of their own making. On the other hand, she tried to imagine the difficulties people living on their own faced; loneliness would presumably cause misery for many. These days, as doubtless in most other households, she and Edward's usual topic was about the way the government was mishandling the crisis and she felt that many other people would have similar opinions to themselves. Although there were one or two who felt differently and sympathised with the Prime Minister for having a serious health crisis to deal with so soon after he had taken office, which had certainly been most unfortunate although it appeared that the First Minister of Scotland was now getting more praise than her earlier criticism. She came over as concise and to the point unlike the muddled thinking here. She had already made it compulsory for everyone to wear masks in shops as well as on public transport, no doubt giving people more confidence to venture out. But the Minister for the Cabinet Office amongst other things, had said that he didn't think that it should be compulsory in England – just a courtesy. Previously politics had never been a matter of much prevalence but all of a sudden it had forced itself to the forefront and she had tried to cast her mind back to their previous discussions and supposed that these had basically concerned local everyday events. The general feeling now was that it was beneficial to have something or someone to criticise or laugh about during such a worrying time especially as a good deal of their earlier optimism had evaporated now that the Government was giving out more facts about the disease. Recently there had been a warning that there could be another spike in infections as the autumn and winter months emerged and there were also concerns about the economy and naturally about the Brexit saga, and as time went by there would naturally be other problems to add to the list. As it happened, they weren't far wrong about the pessimistic prognosis as there were still high incidents of the virus and the UK had landed up with the highest number of deaths in Europe. Other countries had closed their borders but people were still flying into the UK without any restrictions, and especially to England, from other countries and including from those where they had had large cases of the virus. So why hadn't we stopped importing it? Passengers had been flying into England from South Africa, India, Italy and from elsewhere and our cases had increased even more, so at this point it would have seemed sensible to stop this from happening. Although looking at it from a different angle it is particularly devastating for the airlines, travel companies and all their employees and it brought it all home to Elizabeth when she learned that one of Edward's nephews, a pilot on the long-haul flights, would have to retrain but it would take two years before he could start. They also knew of those who were on furlough but who also lived under a dark cloud as to whether they would have a job to go back to when this all ended. Something that she had found even more disturbing was when she had read an article in one of the daily newspapers about people known as Covid sceptics. Apparently, a number of people in the UK thought that Covid fatalities had been exaggerated or non-existent and had become dedicated to downplaying the pandemic. They refused to take any sensible precautions.

"Have you seen this, Edward?" she said "Surely nobody can ignore the dreadful scenes that we see portrayed on television, in crowded hospitals."

"I agree but a good deal of this has been started on Facebook which I don't have much time for although I also feel sorry for those people who have had routine operations cancelled."

"I know, that is so awful too, but what can hospitals do? Just leave Covid sufferers to die in dreadful pain?"

"It's certainly a dilemma but many Covid sceptics are regulars at street protests, members of the far right and football hooligan groups. Yet there are also others who are simply small business owners who have suffered major personal fallout and all share a conviction that there is something that the mainstream is blind to."

Just two years ago the current situation couldn't have been dreamt up; it would have been something that would have occurred in a fantasy futuristic novel, the sort of novel Elizabeth had never chosen to read. This sort of chilling literature could have been an escape into another world, but they were now living in another world. Nevertheless, the views of todays' sceptics still made alarming reading.

"I'm not wearing a mask, what's the point" she had often heard it said, and "Covid, is just a myth, loads of people are dying from flu and numerous other complaints and cancer patients are being ignored." Of course, sadly so much of that was true.

Everyday life now included the use of sanitizer gel provided in all shops and hostelries and even in their own homes. At last face masks had become compulsory in shops for which she was glad, despite their inconvenience. Having just reached home after a shopping trip she had glanced at the goods lined up on one of the work tops; the kitchen had now taken on a different look as the items would have to wait there patiently until she had wiped everything down with sanitizer first. The box of biscuits she had treated them to looked at her accusingly as if to say if you are not going to open me shouldn't I be in the cupboard? Certainly, the sooner they were out of temptation the better. Other new items dotted around the kitchen were the sanitizer and hand gel sitting on the window ledge above the sink with the soap, not to mention the face masks now lying-in wait since they had become mandatory since the twenty- fourth of July. Although Elizabeth felt that it was a good step forward and in line with other Countries, she found out that not everyone was of the same mind. Everybody had a right to their own views, it was a free country after all, so why was she getting so wound up about it? To distract herself she busied herself by making a cup of coffee and sitting down to read, certainly not the newspaper though as that would depress her too much, and so she would escape into an old Agatha Christie novel where a murder was about to be solved by Hercule Poirot. Then eventually she would get around to putting her purchases away but in the meantime her mind had wandered off to how things used to be long ago.

Chapter 15

Trintley 1978

Francis had been looking forward to his return to school, not so much because of school itself but he was expecting to be treated like a hero such as the one in the book that he and Mum had been reading together. The hero was a brave boy called Charlie and lots of exciting things seemed to come his way although not falls in the playground. Elizabeth had been a little concerned as Francis had been told not to put too much weight on his foot but how on earth could a boy of his age be expected to think about that; in the end she had decided to phone his headmaster.

"Even at home he keeps trying to walk on his plastered leg so I believe that he would be better off at school."

"I agree and I'm sure he will be alright. He's a bright boy and it will keep him occupied. He won't be able to take part in the games lessons but he seems to prefer reading and doing sums anyway."

The next day Elizabeth drove him to school. He had only just started to go on his own but he wouldn't be able to do that again for a while now. Then in the afternoon after she had fetched him, she had asked how it had gone and he had sounded enthusiastic.

"Yes, it was good at school."

However, after a few days he became quiet and less willing to go. She couldn't get anything out of him and began to wonder if there was any truth in what Jimmy's mother had said. Was he being bullied? But she wasn't able to give it much more thought as everything in the shop was keeping her occupied at that moment. Two representatives had appeared at the same time that morning as one had missed his usual day due to problems with his car. The rep dealing with the pet requirements was young, quietly spoken and tall with a dark beard; nevertheless, he was extremely good at persuading her to buy things that she wasn't sure they really needed.

"You won't regret it, I promise you" and oddly enough she rarely did feel that she had made a mistake.

"Yes OK" she had said as he noted something else down on the list.

"If you think that it will sell, go on then".

In the end she had given him quite a large order and hoped once more that she wouldn't regret it, but her first thoughts still remained with Francis.

The other salesman was older and more talkative and they bought a good deal of their general hardware requirements from his company. He was called Frank and had often turned up at lunch time, maybe he did this on purpose as he knew that they would be closing the shop and going off for a snack lunch in the kitchen. Although as it happened, they didn't mind offering him a sandwich whilst they put in their order; it suited them all because they could do so without interruptions. Today she was trying to put in the two orders while at the same time concentrating on serving customers as they wandered in, but Frank was most helpful as he pointed would-be purchasers to the correct places in the shop. She felt less at ease with the Pet rep and consequently had paid more attention to him as he had been standing around waiting patiently, but at least he had now got his order Then Frank asked

"Where's Edward today?"

"He's gone off to fetch some wallpaper a customer ordered ages ago and had threatened to cancel as it was taking so long," she looked at her watch anxiously "he should be back by now though."

Frank said "I can well understand the customer's frustration because if you're going to decorate a room you don't want to put it off for too long as there's always the danger of changing your mind, although it wouldn't be too good for you either."

It wasn't until after the two representatives had left that she really began to worry, where on earth was Edward? By now the place was less busy and it was getting on for lunch time and she was sure he would want to be back in time for it, but there was still no sign of him. She went into the kitchen and made herself some coffee and grabbed some biscuits and cheese; soon after she had cleared it all away it was time to open the shop again,

Edward still wasn't back. Surely, he would have contacted her and if he was on his way home from the warehouse and had a problem with the car there must have been a call box somewhere along his route. It was now nearly three o'clock and as Francis couldn't walk back from school at the moment, she would need to collect him, but no Edward and no car! She grabbed some paper and a pen and wrote out a note to put on the shop door.

Back in ten minutes
then she scribbled it out and wrote
Back in twenty minutes

Just in case, one never knew and after further thought she added the time that she would actually have to leave to fetch her son. There was a reliable taxi service nearby but the number rang and rang and rang, so in the end she put the phone down and looked for another company but at that point several customers appeared at once as if on cue, and unfortunately one of them was always rather impatient, thinking no doubt that she was more important than everyone else. Elizabeth groaned but nevertheless continued looking for another taxi company after giving a brief smile and a wave that she hoped would look like some sort of apology for keeping them waiting. Then at last Edward appeared.

"What on earth ...."

"There has been an overturned lorry on the main road and I waited in the long queue for absolutely ages, unable to do anything else. About half an hour ago the police turned up and managed to get all the traffic into one lane so that eventually and slowly the cars and vans were able to get past the lorry. The bad news is that the traffic is going to have to be diverted down our High Street until they can remove the lorry. Elizabeth was so relieved about Edward's return that she didn't give those particular implications any further thought. She waved her *Back in ten minutes* sign at him

"I was trying to get a taxi so that I could fetch Francis."

"It's OK I'll go now, just in case the traffic here has started to queue up although there shouldn't be a problem going in that direction."

Edward left straight away and Elizabeth sighed and returned, in a far better frame of mind, to the customers.

That night, she had settled herself into bed with her novel even though it had been rather late and eventually she found herself nodding off; Edward was already fast asleep. After a short while she was woken up suddenly to the sound of heavy traffic thundering past their house and as the night wore on the noise increased and although there appeared to be less of the lighter traffic, such as the odd car or two where the drivers may have been returning home from or setting off for a late shift, the flow of lorries increased and a steady loud rumble continued and the house seemed to shudder and shake, but one after another the heavy vehicles kept coming. She gave up trying to sleep and picked up her book again, being grateful that it was a good page turner so she was able to read on with the steady noise continuing beneath their window. When they had been about to buy the business the estate agent had impressed upon them that the High Street had been bypassed some years ago but this information had gone in one ear and out of the other, yet now she understood why the man trying to sell the property to them had somewhat laboured the point. This must have been what it had been like before, although she suspected that over the years the road would have become even busier still with all the extra freight that successful businesses had produced. Naturally Edward was by now wide awake and she remembered what he had said about the traffic having to be diverted past their home. Despite the dreadful tumult eventually she felt her eyes drooping and put the book aside and drifted off to sleep. Just one hour later the alarm clock shocked her awake and all was silent outside.

Chapter 16

Willow Bridge Summer 2020

By the time Summer arrived there had been weeks, in fact months, of a dreadful sense of deprivation. Apart from the loss of many lives there had also been the loss of freedom but now there was new optimism and time ahead had been welcomed as never before. There was hope for long sunny evenings and even the prospect of a holiday. Wide-ranging changes had come into force in England and the Prime Minister has said that although the pandemic was "far from over" he vowed that "life is returning to our streets" so families could be reunited, drinkers could enjoy a trip to the pub and people were actually able to book a holiday. Social distancing was cut from two metres to "one metre plus" and indoor gatherings involving two separate households would be permitted, including the possibility of an overnight stay, but social distancing would still need to be maintained meaning that there could no longer be hugs with friends or even with close relatives. This was a sobering thought but not to be dwelt upon at the moment as there must be some kind of sensible reasoning behind it and everyone appeared to have accepted this because any sign of improvement would be a bonus. Nevertheless, even though she could understand the necessity she did wonder if some would view the outlawing of hugs with family and friends of sinking this country into a dictatorship regime like those such as China. At least in China they had been used to wearing face masks due to their extensive pollution, so it would have been no hardship for them at least and now it was also becoming a way of life here as well. Another thing that Elizabeth often wondered about had been the two-metre rule because unless you went around with a tape measure how on earth could you know whether you were far enough away from each other. Although there had been occasions when she had found people were far too close for comfort although at least this was mostly when being outside which was apparently safer; but shops had measured out the correct distances with arrows and also lines to stand behind, which did help although at first it seemed rather strange.

The Government had decided to introduce an "eat out to help out" scheme in order to support the struggling hospitality section. At the time it appeared to be a most welcome idea and a wonderful way to support pubs and restaurants after the hard times they had been through. It was great to see cafes, pubs and restaurants were now filling up and many of their friends and acquaintances were taking advantage of this offer. Some of them had been out nearly every day, being delighted with the benefit of cheap food and being able to go out and meet up with others again.

"We were able to take the whole family for lunch and it was such a treat and without too much expense."

"What did you have?" asked Elizabeth

"The youngsters had beef burgers but we had the all-day breakfast with bacon, egg, tomatoes and all that came with it. It was certainly filling."

Yes, it would be she thought, and her stomach turned at the thought of such a large fry up, it would have been the last thing she would have chosen. Another friend had enjoyed a pub meal with food piled high on their plates. However, Edward had said "If we do decide to dine out, I would rather go to somewhere more special and treat it as an occasion and I don't think that I could cope with a large plate of unexciting food" and she had wholeheartedly agreed with him. For this reason, they decided not to take part in the scheme as they felt places not offering discounts would be less busy and they also presumably still needed and deserved the custom. They decided to visit one of these instead; it wasn't as if they had been splashing out on holidays or on meals for some time now. In the end they had agreed to visit the restaurant which had been recommended by Toby's mistress. Elizabeth still thought of her as 'Toby's mistress' and wished that she had asked her name but never mind they would see if they could book themselves in to The Shambles in the next village, just two miles away; these days it was essential to book in advance. The Shambles was an old building, possibly dating back to the seventeenth century and had recently been refurbished following a fire that had raged through what had apparently been a beautiful old building. The work had been completed and had reopened after being closed for over a year. Then coronavirus had struck shortly afterwards and tragically they had had to close down once more due to the lockdown. Although it had been a hard time for all restaurants the virus couldn't have struck at a worse time for this one especially. They both looked forward to the occasion in more ways than one; eating out once more in what was now a beautifully renovated venue and also in the hope that they would be two of many who would support them. Upon their arrival they noticed that the car park was almost full, which was certainly a good sign and they parked and wandered through the front door. They noticed that the work had been tastefully done and after closer inspection it looked as if they had been able to keep many of the old features from the original place. The tables had had to be spaced out due to the new safety rules and would not be set in advance as had usually been the case before. The staff were cheerful and friendly, bringing cutlery and glasses to the table as required. Elizabeth was impressed as she had wondered if the new owners would have taken the opportunity of the fire to modernise the old building but fortunately this hadn't been the case and Elizabeth could imagine how it must have looked before. Despite the inevitable limited choice on the menu, no doubt due to the rather different circumstances resulting from the Covid situation, the food was of a good standard and although it was quite expensive it was good value. She had always preferred quality to quantity and hated to see amounts of chips and vegetables piled up willy-nilly on a plate which immediately tended to spoil the appetite. The last time she and Edward had eaten out in this village, at the time being unaware of the existence of The Shambles, had been a long time ago. They had met up with a couple of friends who often joined them for a meal at places that had been recommended and they had visited a pub not far from The Shambles, but set back off the main road. This venue was always busy so that even in those days they had needed to book up well in advance. The pub had also been old and in those days the tables had been placed close together so they were able to exchange pleasantries with couples at adjoining tables, and in the winter months there was always a log fire and the table near to it could be a little uncomfortable, but that was a long time ago. About twenty tables used to be arranged in the front portion of the restaurant and yet now there would probably only be between eight to ten tables at the most; she couldn't help wondering if this eating place was still trading, especially with the competition from The Shambles. Elizabeth couldn't remember the last time they had had such an enjoyable meal out on their own; maybe it could have been on one of their birthdays but that was like delving back into history.

The good weather had continued but now a heat wave had descended upon them, even though this was fairly unusual in August. In fact, it was so hot that they were unable to sit outside because even their large sun umbrella wasn't able to protect them and the tree in their garden didn't give them much shade either so they were confined to a small, rarely used room, at the back of the house which had been the coolest place. It would appear that they were never content as during their earlier days in lockdown they had longed for good enough weather so that they could get outside and especially when they could meet with up to six friends or relatives. Now they could meet up outside or inside, but at the moment not in comfort, and the severe heat had drained their energy so that they couldn't attend to the garden or do household chores and neither did they wish to invite anyone round either, although they knew that this heat wouldn't last. Edward's earlier frustration by the lockdown and the restrictions had appeared to be much worse for him that it had been for her; he was not one for sitting down and reading and the renovation of the kitchen had really helped to keep him occupied. She on the other hand was still trying to come up with other ideas to pass the time; there was a limit as to how much time could be spent reading or tackling crosswords and although these activities were pleasurable, they didn't actually produce anything useful. She had found that listening to music had been a great way of escaping from it all and both of them were still watching repeats of old TV programmes as a way of relaxation in the evenings. The BBC, despite the fact that the licence fee had now been extended to the over seventy-fives, were no longer putting on programmes that they found were worth watching and definitely nothing much to their taste. Edward remarked

"I expect they are trying to attract younger audiences."

"But do the younger ones actually watch TV? They seem to spend most of their time staring at their I Pads and phones" she had pointed out.

"Well, their achievement will be that they are losing the older audiences."

She had been standing in front of the patio doors, looking out at the garden for a while thinking how good it was looking, albeit from a distance she had to admit; she took several glances at her watch to see if it was time to make some coffee.

It was then that she suddenly remembered the lost diary that Edward had found in the kitchen and so she picked it up before sitting down with her feet curled up under her and opened the first page. She had wondered why she had been looking for it in the first place but then it suddenly come to her. Her entries at the start had mentioned interesting snippets about what she had been doing or who or where she had visited and for instance, she had noted in detail a day that she had gone to a National Trust property that they used to visit regularly when they had been members. It had been glorious weather and far too pleasant to look round the historic house but the grounds and the gardens were idyllic. Since then, they hadn't renewed their membership as they had visited the local ones so many times already and these days they tended to travel less to other parts of the country and so it made sense just to pay for each visit. Yet on that day in particular, when Edward had offered to help a neighbour repair his fence, her initiative was to visit the Wimpole Estate where attractive gardens had included an interesting house, a good restaurant and not to mention the second-hand book shop. Although she had been many times before and had set off with confidence, she found herself completely lost upon reaching the vicinity. In the end she had landed up by eating her lunch in a pub instead of in the Wimpole restaurant as she had intended; she did eventually arrive after a few more wrong turns and had enjoyed the rest of her day and without getting lost on the way home.

Having read that little snippet, the diary had become rather boring with descriptions of how hot or how cold the weather was, visits to and from friends, a pleasant holiday but even that appeared to concentrate on the weather. The biggest event appeared to be a power cut that had lasted for several hours. Then she came to the piece she had been looking for but unfortunately the entry for that day hadn't given her many clues; she had written firstly about her initial impression of a seemingly normal man whom she had communicated with and had arranged to meet with her friend. Then followed the exact words of Jerry Smith's offensive email received after their initial meeting. She thought back again, and not for the first time, what she could have said to offend him but she had still come up with nothing. She could only think that he had some kind of personality disorder, she had heard of something like this but couldn't remember what the condition was called. Anyway, it made her feel better to think that she had made her own diagnosis and so, as Marilyn had suggested, it would be best to forget about him and she had done exactly that until his name had cropped up again. She had read something in the local newspaper about a Jerry Smith, although at the time she had realised that there could be many men with the same name, and the mention wasn't something outstanding enough for her to remember what it was about anyway and whether it was the man she had met or someone else altogether. There had been occasions, fortunately not so many now, when the name had come back to plague her and it did seem totally irrational.

To stop her gloomy thoughts, she decided to wander into the town instead of taking her daily walk around the block. By now there were even more empty shops, many having had to close due to Covid but with some of the others their days had already been numbered and presumably this latest catastrophe would just have been the last straw. One of her favourite shops had been the Oxfam second hand book shop where she used to browse for ages even if she didn't find the particular book she was looking for, but it was always rather exciting when she found something unexpected that looked interesting. She normally started with the letter A in the fiction section and continued until she had reached the end of the alphabetical sequence; quite often she would find a couple of books in excellent condition that she knew that she would like to read when she had the time. Afterwards she couldn't resist browsing around the rest of the shop at the old leather-bound volumes of classics and children's books in an inviting pile, not to mention the shelves of cookery books. She wasn't sure why she looked at those as she had plenty at home and invariably found suitable recipes on the internet instead of searching through her own books. She was going to miss the closing of this shop in particular, and this was another pleasure that had been denied to her, although what had made it even worse was that it was one of so many charity shops that had shut down. There was no doubt that some would have gone anyway, even without the pandemic, that was the way of things but now the shutters on her favourite shop had come down for good. There was also another charity shop she used to love and it had become a barber's shop so there would no longer be the joy of looking at the bric-a-brac and chatting to the volunteer who was on duty that day. She couldn't bear to count the boarded-up shops in all categories that had shut because of the crisis and would never open again. She became more cheerful, though, when she saw people sitting outside pubs and cafes again as in the old days, and she did always try to look for the positive things that were happening amongst all the gloom and doom. She was still pondering on this as she walked home again, pleased that she had at least had a bit of exercise even though she wasn't carrying home an intriguing purchase.

Then she was reminded of one of her friends who had told her "I no longer listen to or watch the news on the radio or television because it is becoming far too depressing" and she seemed to remember that this hadn't been the first time that she had heard these sentiments, especially as she felt just the same. Everything was now looking precarious again after all their previous optimism. She tried not to pay too much attention to the news like the others she had spoken to, but Edward always appeared to be worried that he would miss something important and kept the radio on during the day and became upset or annoyed if the time for the BBC television news was altered.

"Whatever is happening now will still be the same in a few hours' time" she would say.

Now there was talk of pubs and restaurants having to close again due to increasing cases of the deadly virus so everyone was holding their breath, but life goes on. She had no sooner kicked off her shoes inside her front door ready to sit down for a bit with her book or the paper when there was a loud knock on the front door, nobody seemed to use the bell any more. They didn't get many callers these days but as soon as she opened the door, she remembered that they had ordered some new bedding and she saw there was a parcel sitting outside. As was the recent custom, the delivery man stood back and took a photograph of the parcel and the open door instead of asking for a signature. This was another thing she was getting used to which had made sense, and this had come about all because of the virus. They could no longer stand too close to anyone else or handle foreign items. Once she had picked up the package, she took it into the kitchen for eventual unpacking and washed her hands.

Chapter 17

Trintley 1978

After her lack of sleep the previous night Elizabeth felt extremely tired; she was rather like a zombie wandering around in a somewhat sluggish way, being unaware of what exactly she was doing. She had finished her novel by reading through the night as the traffic had rattled by and hoped that she would have time to visit the library today for another book, and preferably another page-turner as the last one had fortunately been. Although she did wonder if a boring one would have been more likely to have sent her off to sleep despite the noise. Towards the early hours of the morning, she had eventually drifted off only to be rudely awoken by the alarm by which point everything was quiet outside.

"They must have managed to remove the lorry." Edward had announced.

"That's a relief" replied Elizabeth, "perhaps we will get some sleep tonight."

After their disturbed night, Edward set off after a hurried lunch to see two of their regular wholesalers while the shop was still closed, although Elizabeth was used to opening up and managing on her own however busy things became. She put the cheese and ham back into the refrigerator and the bread into its container and went to fetch the keys ready to open up at two o'clock. That was odd they were not in their usual position on the hall table; she was a little annoyed that Edward had not replaced them but she went off searching in all the other possible places. She had known him to leave them in the kitchen or in the bedroom but they were nowhere to be found and time was marching on and by now she had searched everywhere she could think of. Already she noticed a queue outside and someone banged on the door even though there was still another ten minutes to go yet. She had another look round just in case she had missed the hiding place where they might be. Becoming a bit frantic, she started looking in the most unlikely places such as in the bathroom and various cupboards and drawers throughout the house. It was no good; Edward must have accidentally taken them with him, that was the only explanation. What should she do? First of all, she tried to undo the lock with a screwdriver which turned out to be impossible, well at least this meant that the place was secure but not much consolation to her at the moment. The queue had spaced themselves out and it was now nearly time to open up, normally she would have given in and flung open the door, but she couldn't do that today. There had been one man looking on curiously as she had been fiddling around with the screwdriver in a most unprofessional way; but she had been pretty desperate. There hadn't been much point in telephoning wholesalers as it would take Edward half-an-hour to get back and that would only be if she could track him down. There was only one thing for it. She found paper and a pen and wrote:

If your requirement is urgent
Please ring the bell on the house next door

and duly attached the notice in a prominent place on the window above the shop door. Naturally, every single customer's needs were urgent and Elizabeth spent a hectic hour or so taking people through the front of the house and into the shop and then letting them out again. She tried to ignore the embarrassment of escorting all those people who were mostly strangers, past the dreary dark green walls, bare floorboards in the hall and the shredded stair carpet, because she had no choice in the matter. She did wonder if they would query why the owners of a hardware shop would live in such shabbiness or hopefully, they would remember that they had only recently moved in and would be working on the improvements. She didn't think about it too much while she was being kept so occupied, maybe later the bizarre charade would hit her.

Eventually there was a lull and Elizabeth had no idea how long it would last so she decided to try and track down Edward's whereabouts; if she could halt the discomfort of what she was having to do by even half-an-hour it would be worth it. Anyway, he must surely be ready to return soon. Unfortunately, both of the places that she would have expected to find him said that he had already left but after some hesitation, feeling that she needed to give them an explanation for her sudden need to talk to him, she told them about the keys because they were always so friendly. Both companies thought that it was hilarious, so eventually after her initial anger and frustration she began to see the funny side of it too and she supposed that at least it had amused the customers as well. In those days people on the whole were amiable and she had not been at all worried about any security risk, even though they did experience *some* shoplifting at a later date.

The humour of the situation was beginning to grow a little thin by the time Edward returned; surprisingly he didn't laugh, which would probably have annoyed her even more but his response was rather more irritating when she had asked

"Why on earth didn't you put the keys back in the usual place? I assumed you would have done so after you had locked up."

"Never assume" and he was right, she should have checked.

"So, it's my fault, is it?" But she made a mental note to do a double check in the future and realised that there was no point in arguing about it.

However, it was just possible that maybe this minor crisis did lead to some good fortune in the end, at least. Soon afterwards on one of their closing days when Edward had gone off to collect some wood they had ordered, a bout of depression had come upon her with a vengeance and was possibly more aggravated because of her recent experience of having to reluctantly invite customers into her home. These attacks of depression sometimes did hit her after their move into the dilapidated place. She dropped down onto the floor of the landing with her head in her hands and wept, once more regretting their rash decision, how on earth was she meant to live like this? Then she looked up at the dark green walls and the ghastly pink ceiling, resulting from the place having been inhabited by chain smokers; even with light coming through the window the hall and the landing were still dark. Then, on impulse, she dried her eyes and sneaked into the closed shop, hoping that nobody would see her and think that she was open for business. She took a large tin of a creamy coloured emulsion paint from the paint section, a paint roller and tray and a broom handle. She went back into the hall and poured paint into the tray, fixed the broom handle to the roller and set about painting over the green walls and disgusting ceiling; the broom handle attachment enabled her to reach over the stairs and also up to the ceiling. She would have preferred a white ceiling but maybe that could be achieved at a later date.

After just one coat, and it would need several, the place already looked lighter and cleaner. Following this activity there was no stopping her and she was soon standing back and admiring her handiwork which had resulted in light, clean walls and gave the hall and landing a feeling of space and light. A couple of weeks later she had gratefully accepted the hall and stair carpet that had been offered to her by one of Edward's relatives. Even though the carpet was in good condition and of high quality his uncle and aunt were replacing it with a new one; apparently, they often became fed up with items in their home and replaced them. It wouldn't have been her choice with its colourful pattern, but she was thankful for the gift. Maybe these relatives had decided on something a little plainer, but whatever their reasoning it would be of great benefit to them.

Chapter 18

Willow Bridge 2020

Six months had passed since the virus had made nonsense of their lives and the realisation that it was actually half a year made it sound even worse. Even though the time had passed quickly enough, for them anyway, this didn't mean that it had been easy, far from it. Naturally it hadn't been the same for everyone and she knew of people who had told her that time had dragged because they hadn't even stepped outside their front door. Yet gradually they had got used to how life had suddenly turned out after the initial shock and uncertainty. It was as if they had just lost something valuable such as a piece of jewellery, they had been wearing every day and then suddenly it had been lost; she felt that she understood what it would feel like. As it happened, life did have a habit of changing gradually as the years went by such as with the new technology which they relied on all the time and if the internet went down, for instance, they were left helpless. But the latest change was far more sudden and hadn't crept up upon them gradually so they had all been totally unprepared.

During the Summer months with the advantages of the lighter evenings and warmer weather there was less need to be shut indoors. Now Autumn was on the horizon with Winter ahead and a certain amount of extra anxiety because nobody had expected this to go on for so long. It should surely have gone away by now, as with the influenza that came around each year and diminished during the summer months. Scaremongering in the press as well as from government ministers became more alarming, sending shivers of despair to deposit themselves at the back of the brain. Elizabeth knew that there were so many people much worse off than she and her family were, but that didn't stop her pondering and worrying and it wasn't even as if it had made her feel grateful that they were suffering less than others.

The truth was they didn't know what lay ahead. The government didn't know and neither did the Scientists and certainly not the badly stretched National Health Service. It was far too easy to think of the worst scenario without getting more factual information. Although for Elizabeth there were some moments when she was continuing as if nothing untoward had happened, yet there was still something at the back of her mind that didn't sit right. Maybe either she was deluding herself or she was just making the best of it.

There was an absolute terror of being admitted to hospital, even for something other than for COVID, after what she had heard and seen so far. Apparently there had been cases of hospital patients being admitted for a different serious complaint and then contracting Covid, which had put their lives at risk more than the disorder that they had gone in for. There were others who were waiting for non-urgent, but nevertheless important surgery, which had had to be cancelled. She had always been a great worrier and this wasn't about to change but she did mention some of her thoughts to her friend Marilyn who had then asked

"Do you know of anyone who has either had or died from Covid?" and she had to admit that no, she hadn't heard of anyone.

She glanced out of the window at the houses opposite but everything was silent; there were a few cars parked on the road but otherwise there was no activity, not even at the house nearby where they had been having a loft extension. A wasp, or maybe a noisy fly, had flown in through the window and was buzzing around spoiling the short feeling of tranquillity. She could do with something to take her mind off the uncertainty but all her initial enthusiasm for new chores and exploration had wandered off somewhere. She thought that at least the schools had gone back, but there had been a warning that this could bring more cases of the epidemic and the threat of a spike in the winter was most probable. Despite everyone being relieved that the children were allowed to continue with their education, having missed so much, there were still doubts and yet more doubts. First of all, the youngsters had lost the ability to meet up with their friends and many would fall behind with their schooling. Some parents were struggling to become teachers as well as parents; many would be able to cope somehow but others wouldn't. One young child had said tearfully when he had been asked if he was missing school

"I do miss my friends, it's lonely at home with just my Mum and she is having to work a lot on her computer to earn some money and I don't want to disturb her."

It was certainly much harder for those children who did not have any siblings when they were separated from their friends; but there were also parents who were looking after several children in a small space. The children were at home but their parents were also trying to work from home as well as keeping an eye on their offspring. She could understand all these problems, they were highlighted enough on the news and added to this there were cases where people had lost their jobs due to so many pubs, restaurants and shops being closed. Apparently, many more people were coming forward with mental health issues and this was not surprising under the circumstances; although it also meant that these people would have to wait a long time for advice and treatment as the health service was already over stretched. Another consequence was that those waiting for routine operations had no idea when they would get the crucial appointment and now it looked as if there was the possibility of there being another lockdown; could they take any more? Just in case this was to happen again, she made the decision to make the most of eating out while they still could and she also realised that it would be wise to make another hair appointment sooner rather than later and then she immediately reached for the phone. After marking the date for a hair trim in her diary, she began to look at restaurants and pubs. These thoughts and plans brought so much uneasiness as they just didn't know how long their liberty would last. She took pleasure in booking a table in an Italian restaurant for the two of them; without their previous social interaction planning such a small event had now taken on a different aspect altogether. Spontaneity and routine had gone. After she had fixed the hair appointment and booked the restaurant, she went on to feel a certain amount of excitement about which shops she would choose to visit while they were still open. She had become used to only buying items such as food and housework essentials, and to be honest did she really want anything else, even the thought of new clothes or another handbag failed to excite her.

Getting older had never bothered her before but now she was becoming more aware of age creeping up as never before and she did wonder if it could be put down to Covid. She remembered her mother and even her grandmother saying

"It's not much fun getting old" and they were reasonably fit and healthy but Elizabeth now knew exactly what they had meant, and Coronavirus had really brought it home to her and apparently to the friends she had spoken to as well. They had been warned that they were in the higher risk category, which appeared to be the case as you aged, and this was uppermost in their minds although she had to admit that it wasn't worrying her too much at the moment. The fact that she had always kept busy and had been involved with so many activities after her retirement had undoubtedly kept her feeling young, but this had suddenly changed. Involuntarily she had become less active which had altered her previously philosophical view of life. Unpleasant thoughts started to filter through her brain once more when she remembered her friend Janice who had died just after the Covid outbreak and there had been another colleague who had also died recently from something not related to COVID; both of them had been younger than she was. She shook herself as the last thing she needed was to get morbid, especially as she and Edward had muddled by over the last months and were now feeling freer and more confident about visiting shops and places in general, which was indeed an improvement. Edward, having completed the kitchen renovation, was looking for and often finding other smaller DIY jobs that would certainly not have been tackled before, such as putting up hooks in the tall broom cupboard and even tidying the garage. She was less keen on the practical jobs and after her initial cupboard tidying surge the novelty had worn off, especially when she found that some of her neat shelves had become just as untidy as they had been before in such a relatively short time. She really would have to look for other things that she could do and so she lifted out some sketching and drawing pads once more thinking that maybe she could try the grandchildren's coloured pencils instead of using her paints; she had also bought a couple more jigsaw puzzles. Many years ago, she had tackled jigsaws with her grandmother; she had only been a child but she had enjoyed picking out all the straight bits that would form the border as Grandma had instructed. At the time she felt she was being helpful and they had both exclaimed with delight each time they found a piece that had fitted in.

She opened up the first jigsaw which looked as if it would be a charming picture that would look good framed and hung on the wall, but there was a large amount of sky and also a lake which would no doubt be somewhat challenging. She decided to do a crossword in the weekend *Telegraph* first and perhaps come back to jigsaw later on; just as she was thinking about this there was a loud hammering on the front door. She cast her mind back and tried to remember what they had ordered; nothing came to mind but anyway she eagerly went to answer it as a welcome distraction and by now she was used to the new way of accepting deliveries. But instead of a cheerful delivery driver ready to step back from the doorway with a parcel already placed on the ground outside, stood a young man, he couldn't have been much more than eighteen or nineteen years old. He was short and thin and wearing a well-worn jacket although he looked reasonably respectable otherwise; he came closer to the door than was the usual custom these days.

"I need money, I'm unemployed, having been discharged from the army. I want your help; your neighbour across the road is a really lovely old lady and was most generous."

Elizabeth squirmed at the thought of the lovely old lady handing out some money she could probably least afford and immediately felt annoyed that her vulnerable neighbour, living on her own, had felt that she needed to be generous. She also wondered what the lady's family would think about it.

"I'm sorry, I never give out money on the doorstep" and it wasn't as if he had asked nicely.

Instead, he looked angry as if she had insulted him in some way and she regretted that she was on her own because Edward had just gone out shopping and would be gone for a while yet. She wasn't quite sure what she should say but nevertheless repeated that she didn't give money to anyone who came to the door. With that he flounced off with a resentful look on his face leaving her feeling uneasy. Would he come back and do some damage to get revenge? Surely not she was making far too much of it. Nonetheless, she made sure that all her doors were locked being left with this disturbing thought, until she told herself not to be so ridiculous. She had never experienced anything like it before even the youngsters, selling dusters in the past had always left politely, even when she hadn't taken pity on them and bought items that she didn't really want or need. She still had a drawer in the kitchen filled with inferior dusters and dishcloths that she had accumulated over the years and she no longer felt the necessity to buy any more. It wasn't as if she didn't feel sorry for those who had lost their jobs, especially during the current crisis; all the same she no longer handed out money on the doorstep as she had heard of so many dreadful things. There had been one case when an elderly woman had thought she was getting something useful done when a man had offered to clear her gutters; whilst they were talking on the doorstep his friend had gone round to the back of the house, where there had been an open window, and had robbed her. Although this was the first time she had ever felt threatened on her own doorstep there was something uncomfortable about it. This had reminded her about her apprehensions concerning Jerry Smith a little while back and she wondered if she was becoming paranoid. Maybe all this distrust was another result of the COVID crisis and with too much time on her hands to think about untoward consequences. She was sure she wouldn't have been quite so bothered about such things in the past and it was time she put all these uneasy thoughts behind her. She should dwell on more positive things, but oddly enough as she stood there for a while, staring at nothing in particular, once again she was taken back to her past.

Chapter 19

Trintley 1978

The renovation work in the house was making progress, although of course not fast enough for Elizabeth. The rest of the avocado bathroom suite was still situated in Francis's bedroom and both Elizabeth and Francis were delighted when Edward announced that he was going to replace the last of the old bathroom with the new suite and at the same time, by taking a section off the large adjoining bedroom, he would be able to make a separate shower room. Eventually the two new bathrooms had been completed and even though Elizabeth was overjoyed she was unable to understand why she wasn't feeling elated. She supposed that the inevitable extra length of time that it had taken, including all the upheaval, had been rather painful which must have prevented her from feeling 'over the moon'. She likened it to a similar situation that she had had as a child when she had looked forward eagerly to getting the new bicycle she had been promised. She had already learnt to ride on one belonging to her friend but when her own shiny new one had been presented to her on her birthday, her mum had told her that when her dad had returned from work, he would take her out for a ride on the country roads near-by. It had been some time later when he had arrived home but she had had to wait for him to finish his meal and then for him to read the newspaper. By then the best of the daylight had gone and he suggested that they should go out for a ride in the morning as it was a Saturday. Sometime later she had ventured out on her own to meet up with friends and it hadn't been long before she had forgotten her desperate longing for a bike and the delay in her being able to ride it. This reminiscence made her guiltily try to remember what it had been like when they had been using the old original disgusting bathroom, now that she had become used to the two new ones. Edward had worked really hard and Elizabeth had appreciated it more than she could say, but he had enjoyed doing it whilst she had found all those weeks rather excruciating.

Some weeks after buying the shop, she had purchased a five-year diary and her first entry had expressed a wish that she had started the diary when they had first moved in, to record the progress and other happenings. Better late than never, she supposed and jotting down her feelings each day had turned out to be therapeutic; unfortunately, after a while the diary had concentrated mostly on the least pleasant aspects of the venture which was perhaps not such a good idea after all. It had become obvious that the whole thing had become far too much for her as many of the entries had demonstrated. Added to that she noticed that there was far too much repetition about the cold weather with the mention of the number of thick jumpers she needed to wear, the place never feeling cosy; the turmoil they inevitably lived in cropped up rather too often. Each time one task was completed or a problem was solved another had always turned up. One day, when the shop was closed, she had sat with the diary on her lap and her pen poised in her right hand only to find herself gazing out into the garden; it was a dull day and there was nothing to attract her for long, the distant trees in other peoples' gardens had lost their leaves and looked somewhat bereft and their one and only small tree was no doubt a candidate for being dug up as it appeared to be dying, so she went back to her empty page again but was reluctant to enter any more negatives. She thought about all those famous diaries such as those written by Samuel Pepys and Anne Frank, but then she wasn't exactly trying to follow in their footsteps. Anne Frank wrote coherently about dreadful things when she was only a teenager and what she herself was experiencing was hardly in that league. There was only one page per day in her own diary and flicking back she noticed that some pages were full and overlapping into the following day, whilst other days, such as today would probably remain blank. At least she was heartened to notice that she had written about achievements as well as about the weather so she made a decision; why not ignore the dates and just enter the more interesting things whether it took up a page or several and that was what she intended to do.

Whilst she was embarking on her diary project Edward had determined to catch up with the twentieth century and the latest technology. They had already decided to buy a computer, and had settled on a Commodore PET, Edward had done all the research on it first, and she had also become quite excited about it and they began to call it the 'PET' once it had been delivered. Soon after its arrival Edward proudly put it in a window of the shop and he and Francis kept going out to look at its display of hardware items. Later, Elizabeth joined them and was most impressed; especially as it looked as if they were doing something really innovative and it was bound to invite the curiosity of their customers; it was certainly something different even for those used to technology. After a few days, they were flabbergasted; not one single person had remarked on their new window display. If they had left the window empty for a few days somebody would no doubt have remarked on it or queried the reason. They could have adorned it with cabbage leaves and this also would have brought in comments yet when they did something completely different, even the most friendly and chatty customers had failed to notice.

"We could just as well have filled the window with the contents of our dustbin."

"That would definitely have caused some comments." Elizabeth replied.

"So much for our new idea at trying to attract custom, you would have thought that someone at least would have made a comment."

Unfortunately, the customers showed no enthusiasm and walked straight past the window. Consequently, little more than a week later following Edward's surprise and disappointment, he gave up and took the computer into the house where he and Francis enjoyed using it instead. Elizabeth redressed the window with some saucepans and a few other things that she had used before but the display gave her little pleasure. There again, people had got used to seeing everyday items that were on sale in the shop and this display was not mentioned either and they had to be grateful that most of the enthusiasm was inside the shop.

Later, whilst reflecting on this episode and also on her decision regarding her diary she heard a rustling noise behind the settee; then Francis's kitten suddenly appeared tangled up in a ball of wool from her knitting. She wasn't quite sure why she had taken up knitting again after so long, maybe it had been another attempt at therapy, although she was already regretting the complicated pattern of the short-sleeved jumper that she had chosen. Charlie was bouncing about and by now he had the ball in his mouth; she got up to untangle him and he seemed to be getting bigger already. As she had already said to Francis

"They don't stay kittens for long and he will soon be a cat."

"I'll still be able to keep him, won't I?"

"Of course." He had become part of the family and this was one decision that they had had no regrets about.

Chapter 20

Willow Bridge Autumn 2020

The wind had been getting up and there was definitely a drop in the temperature which no doubt was something to be expected at this time of the year. Edward still had his days of restlessness and spent a good deal of time on the internet trying to find things to make life easier or better, or Elizabeth thought, maybe even more complicated. The kitchen renovation had been a success but she was still wondering what would happen next. Edward thought their heating system should possibly be updated and he also decided they should buy a more up-to-date cooker. However, most of his ideas had been ruled out either because of the expense or the impracticability, but at least these thoughts were keeping him occupied. His latest decision had been to replace a couple of the radiators in their extension with electric ones instead of the original ones being fed by the boiler; these had coped before the extension was built but not so much afterwards as the heat was finding it difficult to get through to the extra radiators.

"I'll go and have a look round because even if I can buy them on the internet, I would prefer to actually look at them first."

She had agreed and soon heard the front door slam behind him as he left. Everything had gone quiet so she picked up yesterday's newspaper, which she hadn't got around to reading yet although she couldn't understand why as spare time often hung around her. One thought was that the newspapers only gave details of disasters and problems and she yearned for some good news to reach them, but the only positive information was about the wins in sporting events. Suddenly her contemplation floated away as she became aware of footsteps; that was odd unless Edward had forgotten something and returned. In which case surely, she would have heard him and anyway he would probably have put his head round the door

"I've forgotten my wallet?" or some such comment.

No, Edward definitely hadn't returned but she could still hear the footsteps. She always made sure that the outer doors were locked, especially when she was alone, nevertheless she went and double checked but everything was secure as she had expected it to be. The footsteps stopped so maybe she had imagined it; then the tap of walking feet continued and it fleetingly crossed her mind that perhaps the young aggressive young man had broken in to get his vengeance, but quickly ruled it out as being most unlikely and also rather impossible without her noticing. Her other bête noire of course was Jerry Smith and even she wasn't crazy enough to think that he was likely to appear out of nowhere. The steps appeared to be coming from the downstairs bathroom and she went cold as that was the one place where she had probably left the large window open as the small one had become too stiff and difficult to manage. As she went to investigate, she thought of those people who had suspected a burglar and had gone to fetch a kitchen knife or a heavy implement first, but this thought had made her laugh. It was the sort of thing that happened in films, so she forgot about weapons. She opened the door gingerly and noticed that the window was shut after all but no longer could she hear the footsteps. Suddenly a gust of wind came with a vengeance and at the same time the sound of footsteps were there once more. Somehow the sound was different now that she was nearer to the source and as she approached the window the branches of the small tree outside lashed against it. She laughed aloud with relief and she would certainly not be telling anyone about her irrational fears, even though she could now see the funny side of it. She was reminded that on the news recently an elderly woman, living on her own, had been robbed and attacked in her own home and at the time Elizabeth wondered if the lady had locked her doors properly. This thought made her change her mind about not admitting to her nervousness about someone breaking in. Once Edward returned, she told him what had, for a short time, worried her slightly; even though he was amused he had gone straight to the shed for something suitable for trimming the offending branches of the tree.

At the moment she couldn't be sure whether everything was

going backwards or forwards and if it was good or bad that something called a three-tier system had come into force in England on the fourteenth of October. This meant that, for example, people should work from home; weddings should consist of only a maximum of fifteen people; journeys should be reduced but retail was to be fully open again. At the end of September, the Prime Minister had announced that "we were at a critical moment in the crisis and he would not hesitate to impose further restrictions if necessary."

They had counted themselves lucky because their area had come under tier one and so they were able to meet with up to six people inside their homes as well as outside which was something positive to think about. Therefore, once more she and Edward were definitely going to make the most of this freedom not knowing how long it could last. Those living in tiers two and three had more restrictions as they had had higher cases of the virus. Being in tier one meant Francis, Helen and family would at least be able to visit them again following the last time in July. Elizabeth hoped that perhaps this time the boys would come as well, although it would mean bending the rules as there would be eight of them but these rules were so complex and changing all the time so they really didn't know where they were.

Previously she had felt upset for the grandchildren and for other people's children and grandchildren as they had all quite unexpectedly been plunged into an unknown and formidable situation. Less than a year ago they had been totally unaware of what was about to befall them even though, at the end of 2019, the World Health Organisation had been informed of a cluster of cases of pneumonia that had been detected in Wuhan City, Hubei Province, China. There had also been something on the news, but it wasn't in the headlines and there was always something untoward about China to read about; and our country was far away from there. Therefore, the general public here and in the rest of Europe had gone about their usual business worrying about possible inclement weather, what to buy family members for their birthdays or Christmas, the uncertainty as to what to wear for a particular occasion or what they should eat for a change. Never in their worst nightmares could they have envisaged what lay ahead of them. In order to cope with the reality, they had needed to concentrate on small things they could be grateful for, although there would still be those who had little to be thankful for. When she thought of employees who had lost jobs or who were financially insecure, she could, once more, see the advantages of being retired. Also, it was fortunate that Francis was an accountant even though he was fed up with working from home at times; but at least he wasn't working on his own in a tiny flat or bedsit. Anyway, they were now all looking forward to a better future and the next visit from their son and his family was a joyful thought for Elizabeth.

At this point she had started on plans for the Book Group to meet in her home but once again there was the quandary as to how to keep the number below six people as there were normally about twelve of them. She started off by sending them all an invitation by email, but once again there were only five of them interested which at least made everything easier. She was a little sad to think that so many people she knew had a great fear of leaving the safety of their own homes. She could well understand the worries of Jo and Helena as they both had husbands with medical conditions so they needed to be extremely cautious about meeting people outside their families. On the other hand, replies from Peggy and others tended to be negative.

"Thank you so much for your invitation, I would love to take you up on your kind offer but at the moment I only leave the house for essential shopping or for medical appointments."

Although Elizabeth could understand their reasoning, she had decided to take a few minor risks right from the start otherwise she would have become insane. This meant going out and meeting and talking to people, even if from a distance. She couldn't help wondering if those who were scared to venture out were doing themselves harm in other ways such as being isolated, but then they all had different priorities no doubt. Sometimes when she left the house to go shopping, she would meet even more people *en route* than in previous times and they often had longer conversations. Admittedly it wasn't much but it certainly helped to lessen the sense of isolation which was inevitable at the moment, even for those who didn't live on their own. She was still extremely careful and thought a good deal about safety and her planning for the meeting of their group was well thought out.

Once the day arrived, they were able to be well spaced out as fortunately she had plenty of room, and she had made sure there was sufficient ventilation. They were soon able to forget about the restrictions that had crept into their lives and had once more enjoyed a couple of hours indoors, discussing many matters other than what they thought about their selected book.

It turned out that it had been most fortunate they had made the most of these small amounts of freedom. They had eaten out once or twice at different restaurants and pubs, entertained the book group and other friends and appreciated the company of their son and his family for a large roast lunch. Now this comparative normality was to come to an end once more. At the end of October, a second lockdown was to be put into force due to the rise of infections but it was to be called by a different name this time. The number of the tiers had been extended to include a tier four, which most of the country would come under, even those areas that had previously been in tier one. There were only a limited number of places in the first tier now such as Cornwall and the Isles of Scilly; the rest of the country, including Willow Bridge, would find that once more pubs and restaurants would be expected to close, apart from takeaways; non-essential retail would close and there would be no household mixing. Construction, courts, schools and universities could remain open which was a slight improvement from the original lockdown.

"I don't know why they are calling it tier four, why not just announce that there is to be another lockdown for everyone?" Edward muttered.

"Apparently The Prime Minister, in his wisdom, has decided to call this 'tougher national measures' rather than lockdown."

Edward raised his eyes to the ceiling but even so his attitude was that there was nothing they could do about it however confused and annoyed they were with the handling of the situation. Despite their joint build-up of frustrations Elizabeth suddenly felt the need to talk to someone else and as she hadn't spoken to Marilyn for a long time, she decided to ring her for a chat. It was rather odd though, because immediately after Covid had struck they were forever on the phone, but lately they presumably thought there was not much of interest to talk about any more and she couldn't remember who had phoned the last time they had spoken. She and Marilyn had always had much in common such as the books they liked reading and places they had visited, although she had to admit that since both of them had retired their ways of life had differed more. Marilyn had suddenly become less adventurous and in fact she had cut down some of her interests such as her frequent visits to her local History Group.

"I thought I would give it a break for now" and that conversation had taken place before Covid.

Elizabeth wondered if it had been because of her husband, Robert's recent ill health, and maybe they were just trying to be cautious. Also, they no longer talked about the people they had worked with; so much water had passed under the bridge since then. This time Elizabeth supposed she was using her more as a sounding board. She had started off with:

"Here we go again in a second lockdown. Last time it was all new to us and although somewhat terrible it was another experience; this time we know only too well what it entails but it is going to be far worse with the colder weather and the darker evenings. There will be no sitting in the garden or walking in the sunshine" she had hardly stopped for breath but continued all the same "aren't the news bulletins depressing; the UK have the largest number of deaths in Europe, we are told, and they are not so much creeping up but climbing at an alarming rate." Then it occurred to her that it was time that she paused after her long tirade.

Marilyn being more of an optimist replied

"Well, they are hoping that this lockdown will bring the R rate, as they are calling it, down to a more manageable level."

"I only hope you are right. None of us know what is going to happen and as if we aren't worried enough about the virus there is also devastation to the economy."

"It's good news at least about the vaccine, they say that some may be ready before Christmas."

"Let's hope so but they will not allow us too much optimism, will they? That would never do." she finished sarcastically.

"Yes, you are right about that. I suppose they're unsure how it will work and how they will deliver it to the whole of the population. Apparently, GPs are getting worried as to how they will cope with its distribution. Robert says he's not sure whether he will take the vaccine because of possible side effects he's heard about, and he is not alone."

"If enough people don't partake, we could be in for a range of lockdowns for years to come and we will become prisoners and how will we ever recover, not least the economy?"

They had been talking for over half an hour without embarking on any lighter kind of subject but instead wondering how people they had once known had been coping, and what each of them were doing to relieve the monotony. Yet neither of them had decided to take these uncertainties any further

"Have you phoned or heard from any of them?"

"No, I can't say that I have."

It was looking as if they were too busy concentrating on their own predicaments instead.

Elizabeth felt quite humbled that Marilyn had set up a sort of Samaritan's group and had a list of phone numbers for lonely or depressed people; each of the group took it in turns to ring them. Why on earth hadn't she thought of doing something like that? There had been many times before, even in the past, when Marilyn had put her to shame. She had always been the first one to suggest benevolent activities and had often joined the charity box holders shaking their tins in the High Street collecting for Cancer Research or Oxfam. It had been Marilyn who suggested they should visit an acquaintance of theirs who had been diagnosed with dementia and had needed to go into a care home. Elizabeth had been reluctant to go as these places were so depressing.

"We didn't know her that well."

Marilyn replied

"She used to be an interesting person to talk to and it was so sad that the dementia should have hit her so suddenly and she doesn't have any family. She would probably be grateful for a visit even if she doesn't recognise us." So, they both went along.

"We don't know what lies ahead of us do we?" Marilyn had commented afterwards.

After Elizabeth had put the phone down following their long conversation, she was unsure whether it had made her feel better or worse. Although recently the population in general had become more optimistic because they had heard there were now three possible vaccines on the horizon, despite a few question marks, it was hoped the vaccine could be available to some people before Christmas. Then the optimism dropped a little and everything had gone rather quiet as safety checks still needed to be done first. People as a whole had had high hopes of freedom by the following Spring, she wasn't quite sure why they had started setting themselves deadlines but she supposed that nobody would have expected the virus to last more than a year. But the goal posts were moved again and this fictitious date had been moved to the end of next year. Wow, more uncertainty. But how could anyone really know what was ahead?

Elizabeth had nearly fallen over the kitchen stool in order to switch off the radio in a hurry when all the gloom and doom was filtering through to her brain. It made her feel depressed and even angry, if that was the right word, as this was nobody's fault. Anyway, she had nearly broken her neck when she couldn't face listening to more of the despair, she really would have to be more careful; the last thing she wanted was to land up as a casualty. Even so she had still learned there had been protests about the latest new four tier system and people were out on the streets in crowds, without wearing masks and presumably helping to spread the virus. One man had more or less said "and you know what they can do with the vaccine...." Indeed, there were people who think we shouldn't have lockdowns at all; just let the virus run riot. Some didn't believe in the vaccines either. Once more feeling outraged, she voiced her concerns to Edward.

"You shouldn't take any notice of those people," he said. "They are most likely just a minority who need something to rebel about whether it's about climate change or a lack of pay rises and some of them will join any protest whatever it is. And…" he added

"…it's obvious to most now that if we don't try to keep the virus in check with vaccines, it's not just old people who will become seriously ill or die. It won't help the economy if medical staff, teachers and the people who are trying to keep the economy running go down with Covid-19. Already people have died from other serious diseases because the doctors can't cope and how can we keep the schools open if there is a shortage of teachers due to them having to stay at home? Also shops and restaurants won't flourish in the long term if they don't have enough staff who are virus free."

"You really should have gone into politics, Edward."

"And another thing" he said "although I think the government has dealt with this whole thing badly, they are now trying to find the best way of getting to grips with it and if the new harsh tier system works it will have been worth it."

"It's not me that you have to persuade but I do agree that all these dissenters are making a bad situation much worse. Where will it all end?"

Chapter 21

Trintley 1978

They had been living in the large flat above the shop long enough to find time to unpack more of their boxes and cases. Already they had worked extremely hard to get the shop itself into some kind of order and although every spare moment, when not working on that undertaking, was spent on improving their home, progress was slow. The list of jobs to be done appeared to grow longer and they didn't have enough time or enough money to proceed as quickly as they would have liked, so it looked as if they would be living in chaos for some time yet. Edward didn't mind this at all; in fact, he thrived on it and was enjoying the challenge. Elizabeth, on the other hand, had found it most unpleasant cooking a meal in an old-fashioned and shabby kitchen with dirty walls, even though she had spent a good deal of time with cleaning materials and had become quite an expert at removing unwanted grime. Added to this she found it difficult to concentrate on the necessary paperwork involved with running a shop, as she looked up and noticed the ghastliness all around her. One day when imagining that these problems could never end, Edward suggested she should take a day off, certainly a day away from the shop and demanding customers would be beneficial. She had some tempting thoughts about walking round the shops and buying something frivolous, losing herself in a Stately Home or exploring the countryside nearby to be followed by a good lunch in a pub or cafe. To do all of this while Edward looked after the shop was most enticing but of course afterwards she would have to return to the real world of turmoil. Nevertheless, she did take a day off although in the end it took a somewhat different direction as some magnetic force kept her housebound. She wandered into their dining room papered with blue flowery wallpaper and in just a few minutes had started by stripping it off, which turned out to be most therapeutic. The majority of it came off easily and she was soon left with the bare walls, but this was just the start. They would now have to order some new wallpaper as this was the only option for the uneven walls. Afterwards they spent a good while trying to find one that was reasonably plain. At last there it was, a paper they both liked; unfortunately, as they were soon to find out, it happened to be one that was not in stock and they would have to wait a few weeks for it.

"I hadn't realised that there were so many other people with such good taste" Edward remarked.

As they liked it better than all the other choices Elizabeth agreed that they would just have to wait; there was no point in choosing second best as they would regret it afterwards and Edward was less concerned about the long wait.

"There will be an awful lot of other work to be done on the room before wallpapering can begin."

Elizabeth groaned, although she didn't regret that she had started on a task that needed doing, she really had no idea what she had let herself in for. First of all, the electric wiring needed to be chased in behind the walls instead of dangling loose, and at the same time Edward was able to put in extra power sockets and was able to move the ceiling light from the edge of the room to the middle.

"Why would anyone in their right minds try to light a room from the extreme edge of it?" she wondered aloud.

They had already found out that the sliding windows would not open and somehow had just accepted it as they had with all the other inconveniences; but now was the time to rectify this. The existing window frames were not standard which meant that some would have to be specially made and fitted which would delay everything even further. This wasn't much of a surprise to either of them, everything seemed to be complicated. Just as the old frames had been removed ready for the replacements the weather reached its coldest so they were open to the elements as a bitterly cold wind blew through. At least they had to be grateful it wasn't raining as it had done that time when the cellar was flooded while the electricity cables for the storage heaters were being put in. Even so, her day off stripping wallpaper was to lead to weeks of hard work in the house, mostly for Edward, while she ran the shop on her own. During the inevitable upheaval they decided to rip out the old window seat so that their sideboard would fit neatly under the window, thus increasing the size of the room. This was a bonus in the end, even though originally Elizabeth had not had anything against the window seat as initially it had lent an old-fashioned charm. The work on just the one room, as usual, expanded into an eternity because with these old places the unexpected was invariably found the minute a seemingly simple job had to be tackled.

While the dining room was out of commission, they were forced to take their meals in the dreadful old kitchen. One particular Sunday Elizabeth had put aside to tackle the first VAT return, which would no doubt take quite a long time, she had spread all the papers over the kitchen table but found concentration difficult. This was partly because Edward was still working on the dining room next door and Francis and a school friend had decided to make the kitchen their secret lair, not to mention the usual distraction of the shabbiness. Normally Elizabeth would have encouraged Francis and be pleased that the boys were having fun, but even though his friend was a little older than he was they still needed some supervision. Nevertheless, she was becoming near to despair until Edward came to her rescue as he could see the frustration on her face. He had looked ahead and had already lit the open fire in the sitting room where he suggested she should be able to work in peace.

"I can keep an eye on the boys" for which she was even more grateful.

She realised that no doubt work in the dining room may have to slow down a little, but she also had a deadline which was getting rather close. She went down stairs and proceeded to set the papers out on the large rug they had laid on the bare floorboards and soon began to make progress, even without a table. All was quiet and peaceful until she decided to go and see how everything was going in the kitchen. As she approached, she could hear laughter and was curious to see what could be amusing them all. Francis's friend had decided to give some toffee to Charlie and the poor cat was putting his paw into his mouth trying to deal with a bit stuck in his teeth, and shaking his head as he had done with the toys he had had when he was still a kitten. It was rather humorous she had to admit, and once she had come to Charlie's rescue Elizabeth didn't have the heart to scold the boys. Edward was pleased once the VAT return had been completed successfully as he hated paperwork; he preferred the practical side of the business. So that evening he had offered to cook and when the food was ready, delicious as it would no doubt be, she had had to prepare herself for eating in the unpleasant surroundings. However, she was in for a lovely surprise! Edward had put a tablecloth on the kitchen table and pulled it out into the centre where he had placed some lighted candles and put off the glaring light from the fluorescent tube. In the subdued light with the glow from the candles they were able to enjoy a tasty candlelight supper with the disorder pushed away into the background and Elizabeth had felt so grateful.

Chapter 22

Willow Bridge 2020

The population at large had become accustomed to and had put up with a diluted way of life; ordinary times seemed like a distant memory. An article in a magazine Elizabeth had been flicking through, about a place called Holt in Norfolk, had reminded her of the time long before Covid had even been heard of. They had visited this interesting place where they had enjoyed a pub lunch and had wandered around admiring antique shops and boutiques as they mingled with the crowds who were also out for the day. Many of them would squeeze into small shops and although Elizabeth had never been a lover of crowds the holiday mood had taken away her inhibitions and she had joined the gatherings. Now she wondered if she would she would ever go there again or wander round places such as this without a single worry about the rising cases of Covid-19 and deaths from it, restrictions when going out and not knowing what was in store for them.

November arrived bringing with it the cooler weather and darker evenings which in itself had brought more anxiety. It had dawned upon them all that there would be more need to stay indoors. Then came more disquieting news; the government had had to announce a second national lockdown to come into force in England; this would be far worse than the first one with the colder weather and it could no longer be looked upon as a novelty like the first time. They had been bemused that such a thing could happen in the twenty-first century in their own country. The sunny weather they had the first time had alleviated the feeling of isolation somewhat, but this time there would be a much heavier price to pay.

Elizabeth had already spoken to one or two people who had admitted to being bored now, after having already coped for about eight months by getting on with chores that had been on the to do list for a long time; they had been looking forward to their release from it all. She had convinced herself she wasn't bored, just fed up; she had always been an avid reader but the number of books she was absorbed in now had definitely increased as she escaped into the fictitious characters' lives. When the libraries had to close, she hunted through old books on her bookshelves and enjoyed one or two she hadn't remembered reading before. After a while she missed browsing in the library and even in the charity shops, where she often found second hand books, but they were closed as well. This meant she had been compelled to buy one or two on the internet, mostly second hand, which was all very well but where on earth would she put them all? She had inevitably accumulated more than she would have normally done. She had been able to find extra space on the book shelves but even this was beginning to run out. Edward had persuaded her to get rid of a few of their older books but it had been a difficult choice and now they were piled up in the spare bedroom waiting for the charity shops to open again. At least if she did change her mind, she could easily retrieve any of them from the pile. She had found in the past that when she removed unused items, and especially clothes she no longer wore, from cupboards and drawers they would sit in charity bags waiting for their disposal; then after a while she would rummage through them and rescue one or two of the things that might still be useful.

Her daily walks had filled in a good deal of time and sometimes when passing the newsagents she would buy a newspaper, not so much for the news, but for the pages of crosswords and puzzles which she had become addicted to during the last months. She had already considered various other projects to help to pass the time and one of these had been to knit another hat. During her walks in the cold weather and her much longer hair falling over her eyes, she had dug out one she had knitted a few years ago, but why on earth she had chosen such a bright colour was beyond her. Possibly at the time she thought the bright orange would be more fun to work with but now as she contemplated wearing the orange hat with her red anorak, she decided she must replace it with something more sombre. This decision made her venture out, although she doubted whether anyone would notice her orange hat. Oddly enough Edward hadn't remarked on her odd colour scheme but it was possible he hadn't even noticed; nevertheless, she would feel much happier if she could remedy this state of affairs. She was lucky to find a shop open where she could buy some wool; it was a pleasant surprise as she wouldn't have thought that this particular shop was an 'essential' one, but then she supposed they did sell some basic food items even though they appeared to be mostly tins; there were also sweets and chocolates of every kind which were obviously essentials, she thought sarcastically. Anyway, at least they sold wool and she chose a creamy colour; she would no doubt still have some knitting needles but wasn't so sure about a suitable pattern and this shop didn't appear to sell them anyway. She expected that it was because of Covid as it would doubtless be thought to be unsafe for lots of people to touch all those paper leaflets. Once she had arrived home with her purchase, she rummaged around in a drawer in the spare bedroom, this room having become more like a junk room with various bags of items resulting from some earlier sorting and tidying. This particular drawer contained many items and she was unsure why they had been kept them, but she found a knitting pattern and some needles. However, the pattern was for a different type of wool and the needles were the wrong size but she was ready for a challenge which certainly faced her now. Even though she told herself she wasn't really bored, she realised this small thing could be something to look forward to.

The government was about to make its biggest mistake yet. The Prime Minister had been going round in circles and really didn't know which way to turn; he genuinely didn't want to ruin Christmas for everybody, which was good of him, but he still needed to keep everyone safe, so in the end his promises were probably rather rash. Despite the latest harsh restrictions, he had now decided to open up the Christmas holiday season so that families could get together which meant that anyone could travel to and from anywhere in the UK such as from Land's End to John O' Groats, thus spreading the virus. There was already much unease amongst politicians and scientists about the prospect of there being a spike in incidents of the virus but unfortunately the Prime Minister felt it was too late to change his mind and say "NO socialising over Christmas". If he did that there would be an outcry from so many but on the other hand the cautious would be critical about the risks he was taking; whatever he did he would upset someone. His later announcement made things far worse when he warned that there could be a spike in January but even so he told everyone to enjoy Christmas! He advised everyone to keep their windows open and not to play board games and the use of disposable plates and cutlery was advisable. Of course, most people would be careful anyway but there would be others who would throw caution to the wind.

"Imagine keeping all the windows open at Christmas with snow falling or icy conditions outside causing us all to shiver." Edward said facetiously.

Following his words of wisdom, the Prime Minister announced three households would be able to meet up during a period of up to five days over the Christmas period.

"How ridiculous is that?" she thought and inevitably they would all suffer from the consequences.

Chapter 23

Trintley 1978

Elizabeth was still making an effort to remain positive but this was easier said than done, nevertheless she had been pleased with her efforts in the hall and on the landing; the dining room was now a pleasant eating space with only one or two other small things that still needed to be completed. Added to this they were comfortably warm. The novelty of their new venture had worn off by now and the permanent mess everywhere was something she was trying not to dwell upon too much. At least Francis appeared to be happy enough and was often a great help both in the shop and in the home. He had even tried his hand at cooking and amazingly at tidying up as well. She knew she should encourage him with his basic cooking even if it did cause chaos at times. One day he said he had discovered a way of peeling onions without suffering from watering eyes. This had brought a smile to Elizabeth's face when she saw him standing at the sink peeling onions wearing a pair of swimming goggles.

By now they had added Calor Gas to their increasing list of items for sale in the shop, which meant there was the arduous task of moving the empties out into the drive every week so that the supplier could replace them with the full ones. In turn these needed to be put away into the back of the barn. Edward did this religiously every week and she thought this may have been the cause of some trouble he was having with his right arm; the full canisters were extremely heavy and even the empty ones were not particularly light. When the replacement ones were delivered there was the deep clunk, clunk, clunk sound of the full ones being dropped off and the metallic clink of the empties being returned to the van. She supposed this was not quite as bad as the old paraffin days, but it was still a chore that took up time and a great deal of effort. After she had struggled with a full canister herself, on one occasion, she came to a decision which presumably Edward hadn't thought of. Or maybe he had ruled it out in the belief that it wouldn't actually work. One day the opportunity of putting her idea to the test presented itself when she was on her own.

She put on her feeble young lady act and persuaded the next customer, a charming middle-aged man and regular visitor to the shop, to bring his empty canister and follow her to the place where the full ones were lodged outside. He was perfectly happy to leave the empty one and pick up a replacement. So far so good. But the question was, would she be able to persuade the less obliging customers to do the same? This was a good start anyway and it seemed to be working. Soon they managed to train the customers to pay for their calor gas canister first, and then to bring their empty one outside and exchange it with a full one; soon it became a normal and accepted routine. Of course, Edward still had to prepare for the changeover from the company that supplied them, but he had to admit this was an improvement and gradually they would learn how to improve various other customs and practices in the shop.

Little did they think how much enjoyment and amusement Francis's cat Charlie would give them. Recently Charlie had started to join them in the shop when Francis was at school, and would curl up on the counter receiving plenty of attention from the customers. One day Elizabeth appeared just in time to see his tail sticking out of a bag of rabbit food and wondered what he could find so fascinating about the food meant for rabbits. He certainly wasn't going hungry as she feared that sometimes Francis would put down another plate of food; even after he had finished the dish of Whiskas, she had already given him. Afterwards he would skilfully slink away licking his lips. She pointed out the amusing spectacle to Edward who looked inside the sack. Then he immediately removed Charlie back to his favourite place on the counter, picked up the sack and took it to the back door. He appeared shortly afterwards and replaced the sack whispering to her

"There was a mouse in it."

So, it looked as if Charlie had saved the day as she didn't think customers would have been too happy to get a free mouse with their pet food. On another occasion a lovely, friendly elderly lady came in to buy her favourite furniture polish and some dusters.

"Oh, my dear how are you?"

It seemed to be a rather more effusive greeting than usual, but Elizabeth thought little about it until she realised that the lady was talking to Charlie and not to her.

Chapter 24

Willow Bridge December 2020

There had been nine months of lockdowns and varying restrictions and now it was December. Francis had agreed that he and his family would like to spend Christmas with his parents this year and hopefully it would be something they could all look forward to, although after the last months of uncertainty, warnings, and what if situations Elizabeth had one or two reservations. She really didn't want to pour cold water onto the idea especially as family visits appeared, at the moment, to be permitted by the government. Nevertheless, the provisos were somewhat disturbing and the thought of keeping their windows open and not playing board games could cause some disquiet for them. She kept turning it over in her mind until she thought she had come up with a satisfactory solution to her concerns. One of them was regarding their safety and the other was being able to enjoy the company of their son and daughter-in-law and the grandchildren without too much anxiety. She decided they could move their dining room table into the conservatory, which was large with plenty of ventilation; she remembered once before they had done this when they had been entertaining a large number of guests. Thinking back, she thought it could have been for their wedding anniversary celebration but it seemed so far in the past now and long before Covid. This would also make sense for this occasion and it would be better than using the small and cosy dining room on Christmas day; hopefully they wouldn't get too cold and they could possibly introduce some form of extra heating if necessary.

She remembered the Prime Minister's promise that Christmas would still be the sort of festive occasion they had all been used to and yet many people were having second thoughts about entertaining after the latest grim warnings. Some had decided not to take up his cheerful invitation to have merry family gatherings and had decided to stay on their own. On the other hand, Edward and Elizabeth's preparations appeared to be safe enough even if not quite what they had been used to in the past.

Even though everyone had come to terms with a different way of life after so long, with the inevitability of the days becoming much colder as they had moved into winter. Damp foggy mornings would not encourage stepping outside unless absolutely necessary. Non-essential shops had reopened on the second of December and their High Street had once more turned from the ghost town into what it had more or less looked like earlier, although Elizabeth couldn't help wondering how many more full lockdowns there would be. She cheered herself up as she walked down the main street of their market town and saw so many people bustling along, no doubt many looking for Christmas presents and there were queues outside some shops and those that had opened again were looking festive and welcoming. As well as finding cheer in shop windows she noticed the Christmas trees and decorative lights in the windows of people's homes nearby. This had always been something that had been taken for granted in previous years but 2020 lent a different slant to it; nobody was going to be beaten by the virus and they were making the best of it by carrying on with as many of their Christmas routines as they could. In the old days Elizabeth had hated seeing Christmas come to the high street so early, and seeing Christmas cards in the shops in August when they hadn't even said goodbye to Summer and Autumn. She surprised herself that today she welcomed all this frivolity and felt cheered by the signs of festivity.

After this small respite suddenly, they were plunged back into a much greater despair than when it had all started, as news had filtered through that a new strain of the virus in the South East of the country had appeared, followed by another one from South Africa.

"Which" the Health Secretary had said "is yet more transmissible than the mutated strain currently sweeping through the South and South-East."

So, this meant many of the families who had arranged to meet up at Christmas had decided to cancel after all, as the mixed messages from the government kept coming through at an alarming rate. The Prime Minister had already promised not to spoil people's normal Christmas gatherings but once more he warned that more people could be admitted to hospital after Christmas and the hospitals were already stretched to their limits. Elizabeth was reluctant to contact Francis as they would all be so disappointed so she asked for Edward's opinion.

"We should be safe enough with all your suggested arrangements and I've lost count on the numbers we are allowed to entertain anyway." He said cheerfully.

She managed to hide her own misgivings about their family Christmas reunion, then the following day their daughter-in-law phoned.

"I really don't think we should visit you this year for Christmas with all the unsettling prospects; we would hate to put you at risk as the boys and the twins have mixed with so many other young people. We'll all be disappointed of course."

"I do agree with you Helen, it could be risky for all of us. It would be better perhaps to have a late Christmas in the summer."

Helen laughed "We'll look forward to it. Here's to the summer."

Despite her disappointment, Elizabeth was relieved and not as upset as she might have been; they would be spending Christmas day on their own this year after all and despite this she was determined she would make the most of it. As it happened, they now had two white artificial Christmas trees sitting in the loft; they had been bought comparatively recently following all those years when they used to stagger from the local market with a large and unwieldy real tree. This would then have to be disposed of afterwards and they found themselves vacuuming up pine needles well into the Spring. Eventually they had come to their senses, especially now that their family were older. A couple of years ago Edward came home with a large familiar looking box, just like the one she had brought back with her earlier that day.

"Great minds think alike." Edward exclaimed.

He had opened up his box with a picture of a white tree on it when they noticed that Elizabeth's tree was identical. The trees were all being sold off as the shop had obviously ordered far too many. They laughed as they had both got a bargain thanks to shops no doubt wishing to get rid of them so as not to have them hanging around after Christmas

"So now we have two trees, I suppose we can put one in the sitting room and the other in the hall. Anyway, it will make life easier without the pine needles dropping everywhere."

They had both agreed that if they were going to have a plastic tree there was no point pretending it was real, by choosing a green fake. That Christmas they had decorated them both as it was a year that friends and family had visited over the festive period. It seemed a lifetime ago now. Therefore, after their disappointment this year Elizabeth suggested

"Let's get one of our trees down from the loft."

She would decorate one of them but leave the other where it was. She had already bought Christmas crackers and candles but instead of the traditional turkey they had decided they would have something totally different, maybe some fillet steak, and the large turkey could go into the freezer. Like so many others they had thought the government had been most unwise to open up the holiday season anyway so that anyone could travel to and from anywhere in the country. The worry was that they could all suffer for it in January with further cases and yet another lockdown. There had already been a warning about the risks from the PM but he still hadn't dared to change his mind. Many people would take advantage of the freedom to entertain their families even though Francis had agreed with his parents, like so many others had done, that it would be better for them all to stay at home.

"I just don't know why everybody makes such a fuss at Christmas when we can get together at any time. We can always move Christmas to Easter and maybe the weather will be better then," mused Francis.

"That's more or less what I said to Helen. It's just that we have all been used to Christmas as an excuse to get together rather than as a religious ceremony, and it is usually something to look forward to" then she added "when the day is finally upon us after all the kerfuffle."

She couldn't help thinking of the years of agonising about what to buy for presents, what should they eat and the last-minute rush trying to get everything organised just for one or maybe even two days. Christmas had always been fun, but only once the day had arrived. What hadn't been bought or prepared, it was too late to worry about.

At last, there was *some* good news to cheer everyone up a little; information of a new vaccine was beginning to filter through although it was still early days yet. Those responsible were being congratulated on working so hard and coming up with something so soon but there would still need to be many more tests and great care would still be needed for some time. Then came some headline news and a great deal of publicity when the first elderly lady had been injected and there were photographs of her on the news over several days.

"........A UK grandmother has become the first person in the world to be given the Pfizer Covid-19 jab as part of a mass vaccination programme."

This lady, who was due to celebrate her 91st birthday the following week, had said

"The injection I received was the best early birthday present I could have ever had."

Eventually more welcome news followed when they heard of one or two people in their eighties who had had the vaccine although there was no sign of anyone in their vicinity getting it yet. As time went by and as Edward was over eighty, she had been hoping to hear something and so when passing their doctor's surgery one day she had gone in to make inquiries, only to receive a frosty reply

"We've no idea, we haven't heard anything."

Chapter 25

Trintley Christmas 1978

It was Elizabeth and Edward's turn to stay with Kate and Geoffrey for Christmas this year, as they had tended to alternate their seasonal visits between Elizabeth's parents and Kate and Geoffrey's. Elizabeth had never particularly looked forward to visiting Edward's parents, she had always imagined her mother-in-law's critical eyes upon her. Kate must have been an attractive woman in her younger days and even now she had kept her youthful looks. She wore stylish clothes and her tall slim figure showed them off to advantage. She was also a little house proud and had some beautiful furniture and tasteful items displayed on antique tables and Elizabeth was often rather nervous around them, especially once Francis had got to the age of touching everything; although fortunately his grandmother adored him and he could do no wrong in her eyes. At least that was one thing that Elizabeth had got right, she had produced a grandson for her.

Edward said it was rubbish that his mother was judging her but nevertheless she hated the way she always said when they arrived

"Oh, doesn't Edward look tired. He works so hard."

Under her breath she would say sarcastically "of course, and I do nothing at all but just sit around with my feet up." Also, there was that other fact that she had had only had one child whereas Kate had produced two, which in her eyes would have made double the work. What was so hurtful was that it wasn't as if she hadn't wanted more children but deep down, she knew it wouldn't have made much difference to Kate anyway. Edward wouldn't notice of course, but she always felt his mother's eyes weighing up what she was wearing and on the odd occasion when she had presented her with flowers or a homemade cake the thanks she would receive would be

"You shouldn't have bothered, we don't eat many cakes these days," or "you shouldn't spend your money on flowers, we have plenty in the garden."

Mother-in-law was always immaculately turned out when she herself would always choose clothes that would be warm and comfortable; this was especially true since they had been running the shop. The shop idea had been another thing that Kate hadn't approved of although she wouldn't admit it to her beloved son. In fact, that was one thing that her in-laws had in common with her own parents; they also thought they were completely mad to take on a shop. There was a stark difference, though, in the acceptance or even the non-acceptance of Edward's and Elizabeth's decision. Kate had said little to her son but instead quizzed Elizabeth as to why they had decided to give up a civilised way of life for a shop.

"Edward had a good job, didn't he." She had said.

There was no point explaining that he hadn't been particularly happy in his job although she was rather annoyed at her next barb.

"I suppose it was your idea."

Elizabeth stood with her mouth open for a while in utter disbelief but chose not to say anything; she didn't want to fall out with Kate for Edward's and Francis's sakes and chose instead to ignore the comment. On the other hand, her parents had accepted their decision and had offered them nothing but help and encouragement.

Despite Elizabeth's usual reservations about their stay with Kate and Geoffrey, this time she decided that it would be lovely to get away from their current chaotic way of life and they hadn't seen the in-laws for a while now, which had been making her feel guilty. There was no way they would come and stay with them in their 'undesirable home' unlike her own parents who had stayed with them and helped out, and had also bought them presents that would be useful. The senior Wallis's lived in a large, comfortable house in Southwold where you could just about catch a view of the sea from the window of the bedroom they occupied when they stayed. She was also pleased that Edward's younger brother, John, was going to be there as well. Fortunately, Francis did enjoy those visits to his grandparents in Southwold and he would be especially happy that his uncle John would be available to amuse him. John, as a single man without children loved playing with Francis and would spend a great deal of time with him. It was rather a surprise to Elizabeth to find that she was actually looking forward to the break, even though it would be spent with Kate and Geoffrey. The thought of escaping for a short time into a tidy, civilised and centrally heated house was bliss and recently they had all been suffering from severely cold weather and, despite the storage heaters, the younger Wallis's home left a good deal to be desired as far as heating was concerned.

She woke early on the morning of Christmas Eve wondering if she had got everything ready so that they could leave for Southwold as soon as they closed the shop. They expected to be busy as no doubt customers would be looking for last minute gifts for the people they had forgotten, or for relatives who had decided to descend upon their families unexpectedly. She noticed that their bedroom was rather cold and the heater was not as warm to the touch as she had expected, but then they did keep the output of the storage heater low in the bedroom. Edward was still asleep so she grabbed her warm dressing gown; she had decided not to pack it for their stay at the in-laws as it would hardly be required. In the dark she made her way to the kitchen to look for her list of items to take with them. The switch there yielded no light and she cursed that the strip light in there must have gone, luckily their large torch was handy and she made her way out into the hall and pressed that switch. There was no light there either and when she returned to the kitchen to put the kettle on, she was soon to find out that the electricity had gone off at four o'clock that morning.

By now it was getting on for eight o'clock and a small amount of natural light was peeping through and they managed to eat some breakfast cereal with a cold drink each. There was no toast and no coffee. This was a day when they would have expected to have been busier than usual as people arrived for their last-minute purchases. In some ways, it had been something to look forward to. Yet as it happened this was also a day with no heat, no light and no till. They dug out the old paraffin stove again and used a Calor gas lamp and candles for light. As for the till, they had to record everything sold on a notepad; how archaic was that, but there was no other choice. Elizabeth had never been much good at mental arithmetic and kept paper and pencil handy so that she could calculate the totals. The houses and the shop on the other side of the road were not affected and staff in the shop opposite took it in turns to boil up their kettle a few times; so, they could at least have some hot drinks. Elizabeth had intended to provide a cooked meal at lunchtime as they would be setting off for the in-laws as soon as the shop had closed. They were unsure how long the journey to Southwold would take on a Bank Holiday evening, but in the end at lunch time they had landed up with cheese sandwiches instead. They hadn't expected to be needing the bread as they were going to be away, so it was a little stale and they weren't able to toast it of course. Francis hadn't complained and in fact he was finding the lack of electricity and the makeshift alternatives rather exciting. The electricity was eventually restored just before they were due to leave that evening after such an eventful day. By now the car was packed with clothes and Christmas presents and their neighbour had kindly agreed to come in and feed Charlie whilst they were away; although Francis had wanted to take him with them.

"Charlie will be happier in his own home and Ann or Tom will come round and feed him."

Having put Francis's mind at ease they were soon on their way; the traffic was not as bad as they had expected and so they arrived in Southwold on schedule. Another welcome surprise was that Edward's mother had provided an extremely welcome hot meal that evening and for once Kate appeared to be pleased with Elizabeth's help in the kitchen.

On Christmas morning Kate had got up early and put a huge turkey in the oven; there were many different vegetables as well as the potatoes for roasting. Elizabeth actually enjoyed peeling the potatoes and preparing vegetables for the large lunch which was to be provided just for the six of them – Kate, Geoffrey, Edward, Francis, John and herself. For the first time in ages, she was relaxed and forgot about what she had temporarily left behind. One thing that could be said for Kate was that she was a well organised and good cook. After the turkey, vegetables and Christmas pudding – not to mention all the wine she had drunk, she did wonder if she had consumed too much – she was glad about the suggestion of a walk afterwards. Having wrapped up well, they all enjoyed a stroll in the cold sea breeze, along the front; there were not many people around apart from a few dog walkers with whom they exchanged friendly Christmas greetings. Again, Francis didn't complain about the exercise in the cold and he appeared to be as captivated as she was hearing the waves crash onto the pebbly beach as if in anger. Afterwards they returned to the warmth of the house and played one or two board games that Francis could be included in. She then found the preparation of dishes for supper, in pleasant surroundings, and the setting of the dining room table with invitingly arranged foods most therapeutic. These foods included exotic salads to unusual cheeses and Elizabeth hadn't had to dash around the shops buying it all herself, which was an added bonus. Sitting in front of a log fire in the evening made her feel calmer than she had done for a long time; Geoffrey had kept topping up her glass with wine and John had already taken Francis under his wing until his bedtime. There was only one thing that bothered her, Kate never asked how their new venture was going although Elizabeth hadn't really expected her to be interested; she thought it was a bit beneath them and so there was no point in dwelling on it too much. Nevertheless, she had been expecting some oblique comment. Let sleeping dogs lie, she thought, and it would probably be best if nothing was mentioned after all.

She hadn't expected to enjoy the break so much but after working flat out for those months it didn't seem so unexpected after all, and therefore in many ways it was an added bonus that the shop was left unmentioned. After the break she really did not want to return home, but of course that would be what they would have to do. She wondered if she and her mother-in-law had become a bit closer and couldn't help but speculate on the change in her attitude. Maybe she had imagined it, always wanting to see the bad side of Edward's mother. Or maybe Geoffrey had stuck up for their enterprise and had pointed out how much hard work had come with it for both of them. Well, she would never know but she made up her mind she would have to show her appreciation to Kate in the hope they would be able to keep up their improved relationship. She was pondering on the idea of sending her an expensive bouquet of flowers, but then thought better of it after her last gift of flowers had fallen rather flat. She supposed that maybe this new understanding may never have happened if, firstly, they hadn't bought the shop and secondly, she hadn't been in such need of the welcome distraction.

Soon the moment came when they had to return to their chaotic life, although the respite had undoubtedly given them more energy and enthusiasm, and she especially had reaped the benefit. In the end Christmas had turned out to be one of the best Elizabeth had experienced. Once they had settled back at home, they decided not to stay up to see the New Year in. They were mistaken if they thought they were going get some sleep, though. There was a pub just across the road and another one next door, so at midnight all the jolly makers were let loose and the noise went on for some considerable time and well after midnight.

Chapter 26

Willow Bridge 2021

Optimism had come after the lockdown ended in July last year, and the fact that the cases of the virus were falling and everything appeared to be more normal, although not quite. There had still been reminders everywhere such as face masks, hand gel, notices giving warnings about washing hands regularly and staying at a safe distance from others. The Government had adopted a tier system in October, leaving some restrictions in place but it had still been wonderful to see people walking around the town again. There was still a certain amount of caution required and people were avoiding getting too close to each other. Best of all was that they had been able to visit a pub or a restaurant for a meal which was something she and Edward had taken advantage of while they still could, as there was always the lingering threat that this semi freedom couldn't last. They had been right to remain careful, as after Christmas and continuing into January everything had come crashing down again. Another variant of the virus had already reared its ugly head and many families, who had arranged to meet up at Christmas, had cancelled. Edward and Elizabeth's family had done the same due to the mixed messages from the government which were not only confusing but also alarming.

The Prime Minister had warned that opening up for Christmas could cause a peak in January and could cause more people to be admitted to hospital. Despite many having altered their arrangements over that period, this turned out to be true. Even though most people had been sensible, many others had not heeded the warnings. Hospitals were now under more pressure than in the first wave and were at breaking point; watching the devastation on television was traumatising to most people but there were still some who ignored the rules and denied that the virus even existed. The only good news was that there were some vaccines which had gone through rigorous testing and were now being used in this country. They kept their eyes and ears on the news with the hope that it wasn't just an optimistic rumour; they didn't dare raise their expectations as there had already been so much disappointment, leading to despair. Then at last they were hearing of more people, across the country, getting their vaccinations although there was still no sign of it happening in their area.

One day, quite out of the blue, Edward received a phone call from their doctors' surgery. "I'm calling to invite you to attend for one of the vaccine sessions." It was as if he had been given an invitation to a banquet; although it did mean he would have to drive to the vaccine centre a good twenty miles away. He didn't mind that, it was a small price to pay especially as they had heard of many who had to travel even further. They couldn't help wondering how many people would have difficulty getting the vaccine if they didn't have a car and there was no one else to take them. Luckily Edward did not have this worry and was not only relieved but quite excited as well, who would have thought that anyone would look forward to an appointment such as this. But there it was, almost as if he was going to be awarded a medal. It wasn't as if there hadn't been vaccinations in the past such as those they had been given in their youth, and recently there had been the yearly flu jab. Yet this one was different somehow; then they remembered all the publicity surrounding the first recipient and thinking of the ninety-year-old Margaret Keenan, the woman who had been the first to receive the Pfizer jab, Edward remarked

"Well, I'm not expecting to make the news headlines as she did."

"No" Elizabeth had replied "but you will now be one of many, which can't be bad, can it."

After this recent good news Elizabeth expected it would be her turn soon, but so far, she had heard nothing. She had decided to wait a little longer before making any enquiries, and had put it to the back of her mind.

Sometime later, Elizabeth heard the phone ringing and went to pick it up. They didn't get many calls these days as there had no longer been those invitations to visit friends, and when they did speak to each other, they had little to talk about. In the end it was another surprise, a call from the doctor's surgery.

"Mrs Wallis?"

"Yes, speaking." Whatever could they want? She couldn't remember when she had last had a call from the surgery and she seemed to remember that it was to change the date of a routine appointment. She turned her mind back to the friendly voice of one of the receptionists.

"I'm inviting you to come and get your vaccine."

Inviting again, she thought, as if it was to attend a celebration.

"Oh, thank you. Will I have to travel off to….."

"No, just come to the surgery and you will be receiving the Astra Zenica vaccine which doesn't need to be stored at such a low temperature so we now have some in stock."

"Thank you, that's great." She felt relieved as she had already envisaged the journey to where Edward had travelled for his vaccine. In the event she didn't need to drive anywhere. Since Covid she wondered if she'd remember how to handle the car again after so much time had elapsed since she had driven anywhere. So that made the news even better. After the jab she had been quite prepared to wait for fifteen minutes before making her way home, as Edward had needed to do even though somewhat reluctantly; but when she inquired, they told her that it wouldn't be necessary. As she wandered home, she suddenly felt more confident that they would be a little bit safer and more relaxed, especially as the vaccine was being rolled out quite quickly now.

Their exhilaration was not to last long as they were to hear shortly afterwards the virus was spreading faster and that there was another new strain. Once more another lockdown was announced and this time, they had no idea when it might end as the goal posts kept moving further away. Once again non-essential shops, pubs and restaurants would close and of course there would be no meeting up with friends and families. Worse than this was that the Economy would once again suffer and there was concern for the future of the grandchildren if they couldn't return to school in January. Definitely everyone's earlier resilience had dropped having coped the first-time round but they were wearying of it all now. Once more Elizabeth didn't go out again apart from taking exercise, which was less inviting during the colder and rather miserable weather. She and those she talked to were rather scared to go out once more, despite so many of them having benefited from the jabs. Edward did most of the shopping as these days they were unable to visit the supermarket together as had previously been their custom, most shops had limited their numbers and had encouraged only one person at a time unless they were in need of assistance. There were a few things Elizabeth should have bought when she had had the chance but she had become complacent and it was too late now. She had intended to buy some more of the beeswax polish to use now that she had more time to attend to her comparatively new oak table; but then it wasn't exactly urgent and there would be no pleasure in going to the shops, even if they were open. She did regret one thing she had kept putting off; she could have done with another pair of comfortable shoes as with all her walking her old favourites were falling apart. When she did eventually venture into Willow Bridge to buy shampoo and also some vitamin tablets – she had read somewhere that these might help them keep them healthy – it was back to the old Ghost Town again.

As the days passed the picture became bleaker; the only thing that could possibly raise their spirits, although maybe only for a short time, were that two vaccines were now being rolled out. Edward should soon be getting his second dose and then it would be her turn. The government had been criticised for their mishandling of the crisis but at least they were in the lead with the vaccines, although it did look as if they could be running short by now. There was also a dispute apparently, about the vaccine in the EU, which had had something to do with the Brexit agreement. This had not helped matters either. Although the EU had had nowhere near as many deaths as the UK, they were now trailing behind with their vaccine programmes as they had not put in their orders early enough as the UK had done.

Chapter 27

Trintley 1979

It was four months since they had moved into the large flat above the shop and somehow, although she was unsure how, it had become their conventional way of life almost as if their previous lives had belonged somewhere else. They had become used to it and even to the rather undesirable state of the kitchen, in the same way one gets used to a dull toothache after a while. Although she suspected that Edward didn't see it in the same way as she did, it had become an interesting challenge to him. In one of Elizabeth's energetic moods one Sunday morning, and these descended upon her from time to time, she began stripping off the kitchen wallpaper. They hadn't even finished the dining room yet but she didn't think the kitchen could be any worse without the stained wallpaper than it had been with it. Once she had started on this satisfying task, she found there were so many layers of old wallpaper that it looked as if the kitchen was going to become larger after removing all the extra thickness. It was most interesting to see all the different designs and colours that had been there before; stripping off all the layers was a great achievement and once more it gave Elizabeth some kind of hope. Surprisingly it wasn't particularly difficult as it came off so easily. She remembered occasions in the past when she had decorated a room and, even in a modern house, it had often been extremely labour intensive. There was the constant soaking of the old wallpaper and then realising, after what had seemed like hours of hard work, that there was still a long way to go. Luckily this wasn't the case here, she even laughed to herself when she decided that the wallpaper probably hadn't been put on properly in the first place which would have been typical. This bad workmanship was nevertheless of great benefit to her at the moment. She was just coming to the end of stripping one wall before turning a corner, when she stood back and admired her handywork. Then she came to a section that was even more uneven than the rest; she gave one huge tug that brought a large piece of paper off in one go, then suddenly there was a loud crash. She looked down when she saw a door laying on the floor in front of her and behind the gaping hole was another room; the piece of wallpaper was all that was holding up the door between the two rooms. She heard Edward approaching closely followed by Francis coming to investigate the noise and her cry of surprise and they all three became helpless with laughter. Later this was followed by another surprise, although quite a pleasant one as it happened.

Above the sink and around the window at the far end of the kitchen there was fake wallpaper, resembling dark wood, and once removed there was pine cladding in good condition behind it. There was just a small chunk missing and to cover this over, just for the sake of one small bit, was bordering on the insane to her mind. Surely it could have easily been replaced. Although there was still a long way to go, she felt they were at least making some progress at least. During the time she was continuing with her laborious task, the dining room was eventually finished and the shop was much improved with plenty of stock arranged as appealingly as possible. This all meant that Edward could now be freed up to tackle a seriously needed update of the kitchen once Elizabeth had started her feverish demolition of what she had hated. After all, wasn't the kitchen one of the most important rooms in the house?

Every Saturday they were kept extra busy in the shop and became used to long queues. This was most encouraging and even quite enjoyable at times. Elizabeth should have been pleased but despite their welcome popularity she was still worried about their outgoing expenditure and wondered if all their hard work would make them enough money to live on. Added to this concern she was always under pressure to meet deadlines for orders to the various suppliers, otherwise they would have to wait another whole week for the goods that people were waiting for, and then there was always the VAT return which needed to be submitted on time. Edward was not able to spend as much time on 'rebuilding' the house during the day, even during the week as they were both so busy in the shop which they had agreed was what they needed. She thought again of the expression 'between the devil and the deep blue sea' although she was still unsure where it had originated from, only that it could possibly be nautical, but there had also been songs with that title. Anyway, these words had summed up her feelings exactly as she now had to decide which was more important, to get the house looking reasonable or to make enough money to live on. The realisation immediately hit her that without making sufficient profit in the shop there would be no money for the renovation of their home. The fact that they somehow needed to do both propelled her on. They must have had boundless energy as they were frequently working late at night pricing and putting away new stock, and on other evenings they would be working on the house. Now the concentration was on the kitchen. They had already ordered some new kitchen units but regrettably a new floor needed to be laid over the old sagging one before they would have the excitement of fitting the units. These days they didn't have the energy or the enthusiasm to go out in the evenings, even given the chance, after working so hard during the day. Elizabeth did think that if she kept battling on with a goal in sight eventually the place would become ship-shape and then they should be able to look forward to easier days ahead with more outings and socialising. Then quite out of the blue an opportunity presented itself to them. A Celidha had been organised by the Parent Teachers Association at Francis's school for the following week, and she found out about it when she attended one of the PTA meetings with Pat. Pat was the mother of one of Francis's friends and it was she who had persuaded her to join the committee, and often used to give her a lift. As they drove home Pat asked

"Are you and Edward going to the Celidha ? It should be fun."

"We hadn't really thought about it as we are kept so busy and we rarely go anywhere now."

"Well, there's your chance then."

She mentioned it to Edward once she had arrived home.

"Yes, I think we should make the effort to support the school."

With some gentle persuasion from Pat, Edward's enthusiasm and the offer of a babysitter being solved by their kind neighbours, Ann and Tom, they bought some tickets. As it turned out she had been so pleased that she had made the decision to go after all the doubts that had beset her at first. She had ended up enjoying herself for the first time in ages. For two or three hours she had managed to forget about her stress and dissatisfaction and had joined in with the others in the dancing, followed by interesting nibbles and wine that had been provided by the other parents. At this point she made up her mind that she really ought to get more involved with Francis's school. Initially her decision to join the PTA was because she wanted to meet other people who had worked, but maybe she needed to take a more active part. Pat acted as secretary and they now needed someone else to help organise their events; she pondered on this and wondered whether to offer. She wouldn't rush into anything just yet but maybe by the next meeting she would have had more time to think about it.

Chapter 28

Willow Bridge Spring 2021

"It's been a year now",

"What's that?" mumbled Edward whilst searching the internet for an item that could make tidying the garden shed easier, although at the same time realising the impossibility of it.

"I was just saying that it's the first anniversary today since we had our daily life disrupted on the twenty-third of March, not really something to celebrate although it's strange how that date will be marked indelibly on the brain."

"Um, I suppose so."

"I don't think that any of us would be able to cope with another year like this but it could well happen unless the vaccine programme is extended around the world and if the protesters can be kept at bay."

According to the News large numbers of people of varying ages have been crammed together protesting about lockdowns, vaccines, masks and various other things. They were not wearing masks and selfishly not protecting other people. She had no sooner expressed her opinion on that particular article in the paper when she noticed something else; she had turned the page and had started to scan through it and something made her read it again but taking more notice this time

Several police officers have been injured as they tried to quell protests against restrictions on people's movements, compulsory wearing of face masks, lockdowns, vaccinations and other measures. A man called Jerry Smith was arrested after hitting one of the police officers with a baton......

She smiled to herself and was about to phone Marilyn when she noticed the photograph below it. It showed a youngish man, possibly in his thirties or forties, with long dark hair tied back into a ponytail and wearing a scruffy leather jacket; there was a huge grin plastered on his face. Underneath the photo of Jerry Smith there was indication that he was the son of an eminent local business man. Elizabeth laughed out loud, there was no way it was the Jerry Smith she had come across and had labelled a maniac, although it did look as if this young man was a maniac as well.

"What's so funny?"

At this point she felt the need to explain everything to Edward about Jerry Smith. After she had filled him in, he eventually replied

"I imagine there will be many Jerry Smiths around, it is a common enough name."

A couple of days later she had spoken to Francis and he also seemed to think that wearing a mask didn't matter.

"There's no proof that they give any protection and it's not such a good idea either. Have you seen all those disposed masks littering the streets when people just dump them carelessly? It is totally irresponsible."

"I agree with you there, I hate to see people tossing away their sweet wrappers and cigarette packets, and as you say, sometimes masks. I saw a young lad throwing a Mars bar wrapper on the ground and I went up to him and said "I think you have dropped something."

"Wow, did he punch you on the nose?" She laughed "no, he looked as if he was going to pick it up though" she paused "I still think that it can't do any harm to remain cautious, including the wearing of masks."

He also pointed out that some people, especially the young, did need to vent their feelings; they had lost so much. She wondered if she should send him the newspaper cutting about the man hitting a police officer with a baton, although maybe not.

Then she turned her attention back to Edward who remarked

"Apropos of nothing I think that you will find that not everyone has got used to the situation we are in."

"Yes, I suppose you've got a point although surely things should start to improve in a week or too; the worst of it has been during the winter months and larger numbers are beginning to get the vaccines now. There's much to be optimistic about."

Afterwards it occurred to her that just as everyone had raised their hopes they had been dashed again. The new Brazilian variant, with three cases detected in England and three in Scotland, was worrying especially as one of the persons concerned couldn't be traced; they could be anywhere. Experts believed that this variant was first detected in travellers from northern Brazil in January, and it could be more contagious. This is yet further proof that the delay in introducing a hotel quarantine was reckless and the continuing refusal to put in place a comprehensive system leaves our country exposed to mutations coming from overseas. Edward was usually the one to look on the bright side and sometimes complained that she always found the downside of everything. He said,

"At least vaccines can be rapidly adapted to new mutations, we are told."

It was thought that with the schools returning after Easter there could well be more cases but it would be an even worse disaster if the children's education was curtailed any more. Nevertheless, it would appear that at least the Prime Minister is treading more carefully and it looks as if most of the general public agree that there should be a gap before opening up other things that we have all been taking for granted. Naturally, there are those who don't agree with caution and there have been snippets on the news about people behaving recklessly. Although Elizabeth wholeheartedly agreed with prudence, like so many others, she was longing to return to something resembling normality with all the shops opening up again and looked forward to getting her haircut; although still feeling relieved that she hadn't had it cut really short the last time, as she had been tempted to do. At least by keeping it longer she had managed to keep it more or less under control, that is until now. In the past she would never have put up with her unruly thick, curly hair but she had bought various slides and clips which had worked to a small extent but now she had to keep pushing the fringe out of her eyes. She had taken to wearing a woollen hat when going out, at least the weather had been cold enough. Even so she had always hated hats and had never worn them in the past, even when it was extremely cold. She still had to wait patiently until next month for her hair appointment and the date couldn't come soon enough. She had felt the days and weeks dragging by and the day marked in the diary kept moving further away. She couldn't help dreading the what ifs? Supposing the lockdown had to be prolonged? Supposing her hairdresser got Covid? Supposing she or Edward went down with Covid? She stopped herself and tried to think of something positive instead, although nothing came to mind at the moment except that surely it will all be over one day but those anxieties still sat at the back of her mind. She really needed to remind herself about all those people who were so much worse off than she was even though it wasn't a cheery thought.

Chapter 29

Trintley 1979

Elizabeth was awaiting in anticipation; the arrival of their new kitchen units had been promised for the twenty-first of April. She was sure that she was feeling just like a child looking forward to their birthday or to Christmas. A decent kitchen had been one of the many things she had been dreaming about and it would be a large step towards civilization, so she had been counting the days. The result would not be an overnight miracle, she knew that, but progress was looking just a little bit nearer. She supposed that it was no surprise that the units did not arrive on the promised date and as she had learnt from past experience being let down was always a possibility or more likely a probability. Edward phoned the company.

"Sorry sir, there was a problem with the transport. You will receive them on the twenty-fourth, I can guarantee."

Bitterly disappointed Elizabeth said "Oh yes, I'll believe that when I actually see them in front of me."

Although what did a few days matter? She had waited long enough, if indeed they weren't let down again. They had already spent so much time preparing and anticipating but when they saw the van outside on the twenty-fourth, she didn't feel quite the elation that one would have expected and she felt it could be because she was always expecting things to go wrong. The delay had already proved that and taken away some of the joyful expectation. She looked at the boxes several time before she could believe what was in front of her, before they moved them to sit just outside the kitchen all ready for the first one to find its rightful place.

"Oh no," Edward muttered.

Her heart must have missed a beat "What now?"

"They've sent the wrong doors!"

So that led to yet another phone call.

"Oh well, at least we can get started with installing them, the doors can be added afterwards. And the new floor will take at least a day to lay."

That was true, of course. Then at last, the evening arrived when they needed to move everything out of the kitchen in preparation for laying the flooring the following day. Although much of the stuff had to be taken down the stairs and put out at the back it still left them only a small space for manoeuvring and they were going to be without a cooker and a sink for a day or two. It was a slow start on that Sunday morning as a piece of essential equipment, the spirit level, was faulty. Elizabeth's frustration was growing by the minute and she wasn't sure how they had eventually resolved the spirit level saga but Edward is never beaten and got around it somehow. At lunch time she and Francis went off to fetch a Chinese take-away from a restaurant a few miles away and having enjoyed the meal, which was a bit like an indoor picnic, she filled a bowl with water from the bathroom and placed it on the dining room table in order to wash the plates. By the evening half of the floor had been laid and as they stood back to admire their progress, although actually it was Edward's progress, the phone rang.

"Marilyn, how lovely to hear from you." She was trying to think when she and her friend had last spoken.

"Robert and I are staying in Cambridge for the weekend and we thought we'd drop in and see you."

"We'd love that, it's been such a long time."

Normally she would have been delighted to see them and to catch up with old times and maybe even to invite them for a meal but this time Edward didn't really want to stop his work on the floor, even though he agreed it would be good to have a break. At least she would be able to make them some coffee if she could find the kettle, which was now somewhere in the dining room with the coffee, tea and sugar. There was no way either that she would be able to invite them for lunch.

When she thought about it, she realised that she and Marilyn hadn't seen each other since they had moved here and she wondered what on earth she would think of the place. She would have to show her round and as she hadn't even visited them in their previous home this made her even more embarrassed about the place that they now called their home. Marilyn and Robert's home would be immaculate, she was certain. When they arrived Elizabeth had shown them into the sitting room which was probably the most liveable room in the house with the French windows looking out onto the garden, which Edward had managed to tidy up a little. She then went and made coffee and was glad that she had bought some biscuits. They caught up with months of news and reminisced about the past when they had worked together in London. That had been a long time ago and their paths had gone in different directions and this was even more obvious when Elizabeth had compared her life now, with Marilyn's. Marilyn had had a rough time after Robert had been diagnosed with cancer and Elizabeth felt guilty now, when she realised that their frequent phone calls after that dreadful news had soon tailed off. It became more difficult to know what to say and her friend tended to make light of it. Although the prognosis had not been good at the time, eventually Marilyn told her that he was in remission and after a while he appeared to have made a full recovery. They now lived in a bungalow in a Norfolk village and even though she hadn't visited them yet she knew she would be envious of their modern place, despite everything else that they had gone through previously.

Once they had finished their coffee, she realised that she couldn't put it off any longer, she would have to show her visitors round so she asked

"I expect you would like to see what we have been up to?"

"Oh yes, you've certainly taken on quite something and we are curious to see what you have done to the place."

It must have been even worse than they expected and Marilyn was horrified when she saw the work in the house that they had had to undertake and all the tasks ahead of them as well. In the end Marilyn and Robert appeared to be more interested in the shop itself and wanted to buy a couple of items; she wasn't quite sure if they really wanted them or whether they felt sorry for them. Naturally whilst they were wandering around the shop there were a few instances of people peering into the window and even rattling the door.

"You see what we are up against."

"Yes, perhaps we had better get out of sight."

Elizabeth certainly appreciated their sympathy, that was something that she needed at the moment although even Edward had agreed with her that this small break was something of a relief. In the end she felt she needed to show Marilyn and Robert that they hadn't completely taken leave of their senses and said, although somewhat reluctantly, not quite believing it herself.

"It should all be worthwhile once the work is complete."

After the couple had taken their leave Edward returned to the kitchen floor and as the next day was a Monday the shop would be closed, so that they should be able to continue without interruption. By Monday evening not only did they have a level floor with vinyl covering but also some of the kitchen units were in situ. At last Elizabeth's spirits rose and she only wished Marilyn had visited them just a few days later. Edward continued with the kitchen on Tuesday while she opened the shop for a busy day following the break. The weather was so cold, even though it was April, and she couldn't get warm despite wearing the layers of jumpers as she had done during the winter months; she must have looked like the large Michelin Man on the TV advert. However, Elizabeth wasn't the only person suffering from the cold as there were large numbers of customers queuing up for Calor gas.

As they were now required to go to the rear of the shop and outside through the back door for the collection, the door remained open for a good deal of the time, blowing in extra cold air. Those not requiring fuel didn't want straightforward things either, only items that needed measuring or weighing or that were unpacked or unpriced. She also noticed that people had an irritating habit of letting her add up their purchases on the till and then they would wander off to look for something else. Obviously, this couldn't be a bad thing but it did mean she couldn't ring up the next customer's goods. On a couple of occasions, she inadvertently added them to the existing total which didn't go down too well when someone was accidentally charged for the previous person's goods as well as their own purchases.

Due to their current lack of cooking facilities, she could only prepare a cold meal that evening, not as suitable as she would have liked while they were all shivering but she had little choice in the matter; nevertheless, progress was being made in the kitchen. It was the following day that she was to be in for a rather terrifying experience. At lunchtime Edward asked her to help him to lift the split-level cooker into the housing but it was dreadfully heavy meaning that she had to take a good deal of the weight while he tried to slide it into the correct position. Those few minutes she had hold of it seemed like an eternity and she was petrified that she would drop it. Then just as she was about to sigh with relief, Edward noticed that it wasn't quite straight so they had to remove it and start all over again. An hour after this frightening occurrence her sheer relief was indescribable but her arms and legs were still feeling like wobbly lumps of jelly.

At last, everything was starting to look really good; the freezing weather had come to an end and she now had the enjoyable task of returning some of the kitchen's contents to the new units. There was plenty more painting and decorating to be done but it was much less of a chore when it could be accomplished in the better weather and with items being stacked neatly away in the new cupboards. Light could be seen at the end of the tunnel and the progress was much appreciated by them both. She now had a new kitchen and she was really thrilled with it, especially now that the correct doors had arrived and were in place and after all the trauma and hard work of the past months. Elizabeth felt she may be able to enjoy life a little bit more and with this in mind she asked somebody she had become quite friendly with, and who lived in a modern house nearby, to come round for a coffee and to view the new kitchen. Edward was able to take his turn in the shop and as Elizabeth and her neighbour sipped their coffees at the table in the kitchen her friend took a long look around and said,

"Wow. It's fantastic."

Elizabeth realised that of course she hadn't seen the place before, it would have been too embarrassing to let anyone look at it in its original state although the before and after was indeed quite an eye-opener.

"If I had a kitchen like this, I would be encouraged to do more cooking," she added.

That had really made Elizabeth's day and it suddenly came to her that it did now look like a kitchen advertised in a magazine;

who would have believed a few months ago that such a transformation could happen and there was also more space than in the average kitchen found in a modern house.

For some time, she had been aware that there was something odd about their new experience of shop life that was difficult to fathom out. Sometimes there would be queues of customers waiting patiently to be served followed by a long stretch of time without any customers at all. Although the latter gave Elizabeth an opportunity to sort out paperwork and to place orders with suppliers, the lack of trade worried her a little from a financial point of view. Not for the first time she wondered if they would be able to make a living. She tried not to dwell on this too much and anyway the takings were healthy most of the time, which made the worrying flutters she was prone to calm down a little. After these qualms, all of a sudden it appeared that all their customers had decided to descend upon them at once and there would be a long crocodile of people to grapple with. Although many would find what they wanted on the shelves, others preferred a personal service and, on these occasions, when searching for an article for one person she would often get side-tracked by one or two other people asking for something else and she'd forget who she had been serving first. Fortunately, most people were patient and friendly. She suspected that theirs wasn't the only shop to experience this phenomenon and looking back she did remember times when she had walked past a busy pharmacy, post office or delicatessen only to return later and find them empty; there had been no way that she was going to join a queue and her ploy usually worked.

There were still many things wrong with the house but although they couldn't complain about the spaciousness everywhere, she noticed that as soon as they overcame one hurdle with their improvements another one would crop up; possibly it was because as rooms became more habitable, they had shown up the others in a bad light. The main bedroom, hadn't been a priority but now she looked at the two lonely chests of drawers and a bed which looked lost in the room as did the one rug on the black-varnished floorboards. Most of their clothes were still sitting in suitcases as their fitted bedroom furniture in their last house had inevitably been left behind for the new people.

However, locating clothes from suitcases was the least of her worries as they didn't often need to find smart clothes to go to meetings, social occasions and for days out. In fact, Elizabeth had stuck to her comfortable casual wear, the weather determining her attire for the day. While she had been pondering on this situation an advertisement had appeared in the local paper. Some second-hand white bedroom furniture, not unlike the fitted furniture they had had before, was for the sale. If they were to purchase this furniture it would be rather a luxury as they had so many other expenses, but after much soul searching, they decided to be extravagant as it was unlikely that they would ever see such a good offer again and they felt sure that they would not regret their decision. Edward fetched and assembled the furniture in an amazingly short time and the room was transformed; at last, she would be able to hang up the clothes from the suitcases in the hope that as time went by, they would be able to make a bit of time for a social life which Elizabeth had really missed. For this reason, she ironed out the creases in the folded-up clothes that had been sitting in cases since they had moved in, and found some coat hangers for them, in hopeful readiness for when they would need them. The time came sooner than expected, one day they made the most of an excellent opportunity when a teenager they had got to know, wanted to make some pocket money and asked if they would like her to look after Francis one evening, and so they found themselves going on a 'pub crawl'. They had made some good friends, many of them were their regular customers, and they had also had offers for babysitting. The 'pub crawl' started off in the King's Head nearby which had just been taken over by a young couple who had also become regular customers; they all had something in common in that they were also renovating their pub and living quarters. There was a marvellous atmosphere in the bar especially with the wonderful inglenook fireplace, but they too had much work to do and it was such a great feeling to realise that they were not alone in their refurbishment projects. Following this they went to the two-hundred-year-old Crown public house which had also been taken over by another couple of good customers, in a similar situation. When the owners had shown them round, she and Edward were able to observe what they were trying to achieve and this was such a tonic to see other people in similar circumstances to themselves. There was plenty of history attached to the old pub and Elizabeth could visualise how it could be turned into a welcoming place for people to meet and even the accommodation offered itself to a form of elegance, although she appreciated that it could be some time yet before this couple could fulfil their ambitions. Their own place, although Victorian, did not offer the same elegance as a two-hundred-year-old building but nevertheless she was grateful that at least they hadn't bought a public house with those unsociable hours of business. Once they were straight – whenever that might be – they would be in a much better situation. Most of the local publicans were customers but after she had consumed, by now, about three half pints of lager and Edward had had a couple of pints of beer they decided to call it a day. There were four more such places they should visit at some point; one of them looked a bit rough, so they would probably give that one a miss, but no doubt they would investigate the others when the opportunity offered itself; especially as some of them served evening meals.

Edward and Elizabeth had never had any experience of working in a shop before except for the time when she had worked as a volunteer in an OXFAM shop. Under the circumstances they were doing pretty well even though it was all rather precarious and, being a great worrier, she did have many concerns about how this would all work out, both financially and practically. Nevertheless, she had to admit that they definitely got a 'buzz' when they were busy and especially on Saturdays which was the most hectic day of the week. Edward never worried as she did and looking back, she could see that many of her concerns were unfounded. Although at one point their accountant, who had been recommended to them by their Bank Manager, did approach her to suggest that she should keep their stock levels down. It looked as if he had realised that she was the one with the business head although of course without Edward's knowledge about practical things they would certainly never have survived. After the discussion with the accountant, she became ruthless and refused to order extra boxes of anything just to earn a small discount. She persuaded Edward not to buy some of the items that he thought should be stocked and they had one or two disagreements, but in the long term her efforts paid off and as she explained to Edward

"We don't want to have money sitting on the shelves instead of in the Bank" and she made sure that they concentrated on ordering mostly fast selling goods. They did allow themselves a few extravagant things such as some bone china tea cups and saucers and a few ornaments which in small quantities usually did make a reasonable profit. Edward loved running the shop; to him it was a kind of sabbatical whereas she had sacrificed rather more than she cared to think about. Previously she had had plenty of freedom to go out and about when Francis was at school but undoubtedly, she would have soon wanted to get some kind of job to keep her mind occupied rather than concentrating on shopping, house decoration and visits to places of interest. Indeed, she was never lonely now as she had often been before as Edward no longer travelled all over the country and any problems that they had with the shop they were able to share. There were many interesting people among their customers although they did have their share of difficult ones too. One day a woman, whom they hadn't seen much of before, walked purposefully into the shop and came up to the counter and slammed down a light bulb.

"You can give me a refund" she huffed "it's a 'dud'."

Edward smiled at her

"I suggest that you take it back to where you bought it from" at the same time pointing to the Woolworths label. It certainly gave them something to laugh about afterwards. One of their customers was a millionaire businessman who used to send one of his staff in to buy paraffin amounting to a sale of little more than a pound a week. One day he asked Edward to send him a monthly bill! Not only was Elizabeth annoyed about the cheek of it, but also about the fact that he had assumed that Edward was in charge and that she was just his slave. Needless to say, they could easily do without his business.

Chapter 30

Willow Bridge Spring 2021

Once more the latest lockdown of the last months was gradually being released. The schools had returned and there appeared to have been no increase in cases but obviously there was still the warning that everyone needed to tread carefully, making it impossible to relax completely. There can be no knowledge of what exactly is around the corner despite the relief that some things could eventually feel more normal; but this had happened before only to be put back into reverse at a later date. When the day was set for the opening up of non-essential shops there would definitely be something to look forward to although maybe this time without too many 'Great Expectations.' More to the point, as far as Elizbeth was concerned, was hairdressers were opening up again and Elizabeth had already made an appointment in great anticipation. Two families or six people would now be able to meet in one of their gardens and this would be in time for Easter but there was just one problem here. Elizabeth considered this as she gazed out of the window at the pigeon sitting on her neighbour's fence; it sat on its own which was unusual as there usually tended to be several of them together. The pigeon had been there far longer than they normally stayed, almost as if he or she was watching her, but next time she looked he had flown away and for a fleeting moment she had felt sad and abandoned. She quickly began to put her thoughts back together again and to the problem she had on her mind. They hadn't seen Francis and his family since October of last year but meeting in their garden could be impractical if the weather was cold. Not only did they have all the uncertainties regarding the Covid outbreak, not knowing what was ahead of them, but there was also the mistrust in the British weather. Although it had never been easy to plan outdoor events, these days it was far more complicated now due to recent circumstances. Contingency plans had always needed to be in place in order to take into account any dramatic change in the weather and it would be no different this time although maybe even more complicated. On impulse she rang their son and suggested that he and his family should come for lunch during the Easter period. She had hesitated a little before she had rung but Francis seemed pleased

"We'd love to come and your grandchildren are longing to see you again."

She mentioned to Edward what she had done and he thought it was a great idea.

"It means there will be eight of us rather than the stipulated six."

"So, are they expected to leave two of the family behind? It will be the same for everyone wanting to see their families, big or small. Anyway, have you interpreted the complicated rules correctly?"

She thought about it

"Maybe not," her head had been spinning around far more than usual lately but she had another thought.

"I don't think a barbecue will be feasible even if the weather is kind to us, as the garden needs tidying up before we can enter into our summer outdoor life."

She was looking outside at the forever growing weeds around the patio and also at the pile of old watering cans, empty paint tins, rusty garden tools, miscellaneous strips of wood and broken plant pots, not even in a neat pile. Francis wouldn't even notice the mess but on the other hand she most certainly would and Helen also would be aware of it. She shivered as she pulled her woollen jacket round her shoulders.

"I think it will make more sense to lift the turkey out of the freezer, the one we should have eaten at Christmas." Christmas at Easter had already been mentioned before in a somewhat humorous way "but we may have to do more bending of the rules if it's too cold to eat outside." She remembered how they had done just that on their family's last visit and anyway she didn't fancy tackling the garden just yet.

"If we pull out the table in the conservatory and open the doors and vents, we should be OK. Anyway, who's to know?"

suggested Edward.

"I agree, we should be perfectly safe otherwise we would have to wait much longer before we can legally entertain them indoors. It's all common sense really and it's not as if we would want to take any unnecessary risks anyway."

Despite this Elizabeth was still anxious, especially as she had tended to be a little critical of her elderly neighbours who had entertained their families all through the Covid restrictions, although at the time Edward had said

"If they are living on their own, they will need help from close family who will want to keep an eye on them anyway."

Not that she would have said anything of course and anyway she sympathised with them because with really old people how do they know if they will ever see their families again? Consequently, the plans were soon laid for Easter and she couldn't change her mind now.

Chapter 31

Trintley 1979

Elizabeth would usually wait until the shop had closed before juggling the paperwork, the decorating and the housework; occasionally she would tackle a few straightforward things in the shop, whilst waiting for the next customer, so she never found herself with idle hands. It was a bit of a waste of time tidying up in the house while the renovation work was going on but she felt somewhat compelled to do it all the same, it was something that had been born within her; Edward continued with the improvements as well as taking his turn to cook the meals.

There was some good news at last when they had finally managed to find some white metal shelving to replace the existing patchwork of old shelves they had inherited with the shop and this was due to be delivered just before the Bank Holiday weekend at the end of May. They had planned to set off on Sunday morning to visit her parents, David and Harriet, whom they hadn't seen for some time. She felt guilty about this and they, like the in-laws, had thought that they were completely mad but had supported them and she thought that this small break would do them good. It seemed a little odd to her as well as a regret, but they had seen less of her own parents than they had seen of the in-laws. Her father was still working as a GP in a small practice whereas Kate and Geoffrey had retired, or at least Geoffrey had. Kate had for a long time been enjoying her leisure activities, playing the lady of the manor and being on various committees; she also spent a good time playing rounds of golf. Her own parents' home was comfortable but less ostentatious and her mum and dad spent their free time working on their large garden. Elizabeth had lived there until just before her marriage to Edward and although she had never been particularly close to her parents, she had appreciated everything they had done for her. She had especially valued their help after Francis was born; they had been thrilled to have a grandchild. She was definitely looking forward to the visit and fortunately the shelving had arrived on schedule and was stacked out at the back ready to be put in place upon their return, when she hoped the break would have given them both plenty of new energy.

On the morning they were due to set off they had woken up to wonderful bright sunshine but by the time they had packed what was needed into the car it looked as if it was going to be a really hot day, even a heat wave perhaps, and soon Elizabeth was aware that the heat would make the journey uncomfortable. She was right. It was hot in the car and it looked as if everyone else had had the same idea of a bank holiday weekend away and so after a while they joined a long queue of traffic. The journey took them nearly double the time that it usually took, in the sweltering heat, and Francis kept asking how much longer it would be before they arrived at grandma and grandad's house.

"We're nearly there now" Elizabeth was at last able to announce but at the same time hoping that there wouldn't be another traffic jam ahead of them. Eventually the house came into view and they had never been so grateful when they eventually arrived to spend a welcome and relaxing weekend with her parents in the Kent countryside. Her father had arranged deck chairs in the shade under some trees in the garden and she helped her mother to bring out cold meats and salads from the kitchen for their lunch. Although this delightful weekend passed rather too quickly, they were still eager to return, hopefully feeling refreshed, to spend Tuesday dismantling the old shop shelving in order to put up the shiny new replacements and fortunately the hot weather had cooled a little for their return journey.

In many ways Elizabeth was looking forward to the challenge ahead of them although of course it would mean more hard work, but she was sure the end result would be well worth it. Once again, they

were glad of the half-term school holiday as Francis was able to help with the removal of the stock from the existing shelves. Most of it filled up space on the floor but eventually the majority of the old shelves were bare. Many of the old shelves had fallen apart of their own volition without their help, except that there was one floor to ceiling one which proved to be rather more difficult. She and Edward had to lie it down on the floor to get it apart which had left hardly any space to manoeuvre and it required a few gymnastic moves as they stepped over and around it, but worse than this would be taking it down into the cellar where they had decided that they could use it for storage. Fortunately, in the end it was not as tricky as they had first imagined so this was yet another great achievement and one of the few pleasant surprises. The new shelving gave the shop a much lighter, smarter appearance and all they had to do now was get rid of the old ones, at least those that hadn't already disintegrated. They had already advertised them for sale but unsurprisingly not much of it had found a home. However, the Vicar at the local Church did have his eye on a wooden gondola shaped unit which was pretty solid and on castors.

"It would be beneficial in the Church Hall to be used as a cake stall."

So, they happily donated it to his cause and later on in the day Edward and Elizabeth, helped by Francis could be seen pushing it down the High Street, much to the amusement of the passers-by. One of the best outcomes of the new shelving was that a good deal of enjoyment was to be had by replacing the stock on the clean and sturdy replacements.

Life still continued to be totally unpredictable. At the age of three years old Francis had shown an interest in their old piano and had even sat down and surprised them enormously by playing something that sounded rather like a signature tune from a television series they were familiar with.

"It looks as if he may have inherited the musical talent from his grandparents." Edward stated one day."

Elizabeth agreed that perhaps they should organise some piano lessons for him and she spoke to a neighbour who had a musically talented daughter.

"I'll give you the contact details of her piano teacher, she is really good and we are pleased with the progress our daughter has made."

Elizabeth hadn't lost much time and had gone round to see the music teacher the following day. She also taught at the local school as well as giving private lessons. She showed interest although she admitted that she didn't have many slots left at the moment.

"How old is your son?"

"He's only just over three years old" she answered proudly.

"I don't take children until they are seven as for one thing their hand span isn't big enough at that age. I would love to teach him when he is a bit older."

With that Elizabeth left feeling deflated and rather disappointed and reported it to Edward. His reply was

"What about Mozart? He started at an early age didn't he."

Elizabeth laughed "I don't think he would be quite in that league."

Thinking back to that time, she realised that Francis would by now be old enough for some piano lessons, if that was what he wanted, although he had never mentioned it again and the piano had stood silent for five years. However, maybe this could be something he might enjoy so she brought the matter up one day

"Francis, do you remember how you used to sit at the piano, when you were younger, and you played some tunes? We even tried to get a teacher to give you some lessons."

He looked a little blank.

"Now that you are older you might like to have some piano lessons."

He paused as if he was seriously thinking it through.

"OK."

"We'll see if we can find you a teacher then."

She thought that he appeared to show some interest although she did wonder if this time it was less inspirational. Before, when they first noticed he had some ability they wondered if he could have inherited the musical abilities from Edward's side of the family; his grandfather had been a concert pianist and one of his great uncles had also had a musical career teaching talented youngsters to play the violin. Elizabeth knew there was not much musical prowess on her side of the family apart from a great appreciation of classical music; indeed, her father still had a large collection of classical gramophone records. Eventually they managed to book some lessons for Francis with a retired music teacher by the name of Mr Hanson, although Francis kept referring to him as Mr Handsome, which he certainly wasn't.

However, he had been well recommended by one of their customers and, although strict, was supposed to be a good teacher.

By now their new shelving was beginning to make a big difference but there was still work to be done and much of the stock was still on the floor, making life even more difficult when they were unable to find a particular item. One day, although they were beginning to find a home for nearly everything, there were still a few hurdles to climb with the organising and locating of some of the goods. Just as she was about to set off to take Francis for his piano lesson, a queue of people arrived in the shop, as if on cue. As Mr Hanson had once pointed out that he had a tight schedule and so it would be unthinkable that they should ever arrive late she had to tear herself away leaving Edward to deal with several things at once including the retrieval of one or two misplaced pieces from the shelving upheaval.

The May weather continued into June and was uncomfortably hot and the jokes about the unpredictable British weather proved to be so true. They had not forgotten the days of being miserable with the cold and hating being taken away from what little heat that they did have, but now all their energy was sapped because of the heat. Despite this, one lovely weekend Elizabeth bravely painted all the insides of the windows at the front of the house. Feeling that she had really achieved something she had planned to sit out in the garden on that Sunday afternoon, but that was not to be as it clouded over in the afternoon. It just goes to show how apt is the saying 'Make hay while the sun shines' and so Elizabeth had learnt a lesson, she should have sat outside and left the windows. Needless to say at least she was able to continue with the painting after all, in the slightly cooler conditions.

By now they and many of the customers appreciated the new pristine white strong shelving and they looked forward to the completion of the rearrangement of the stock which turned out to be an enjoyable experience. Often, she wondered if she was neglecting Francis, hence the idea of organising the piano lessons, although he seemed happy enough apart from the odd grumble because he was still waiting for his new bedroom, which was creeping up on the to do list. Despite this he was often a tremendous help in the shop with unloading stock and sticking prices onto it and even sometimes serving the customers; he was only eight years old and already knew how much change he should be handing out.

Chapter 32

Willow Bridge 2021

Months had gone by and Elizabeth was finding it difficult to remember what life had been like before. It is amazing how she had somehow got used to what may lie in store; it was unbelievable to think how long this virus and its consequences had lasted. They did have, or rather had continued with, spasmodic socialising when lockdowns had been released and there had also been an occasional meal out, something to be enjoyed when possible and the opportunity grabbed with both hands before it was whisked away again. They could not take anything for granted these days. She remembered a particularly enjoyable meal at a restaurant when only outside eating had been permissible; the owners of the small restaurant had gone to a great deal of trouble, and expense presumably, to make outdoor eating comfortable. There had already been a covered area outside which they had been able to fence off attractively now that the need had arisen; she and Edward had booked a table for two and Elizabeth had looked out her smart winter coat despite it supposedly being summer. She was surprised when she found they had been seated near to an outdoor heater which they had been told they could turn up if it became too cold. The hot food was extremely welcome and also excellent and this would definitely be a meal to remember. Her enjoyment was due partly to the restaurant's successful coping with the current situation and never would she have expected to enjoy a meal at a table, well spread out from the others, but still wearing her coat. She supposed the novelty of it all, after having had to give up these occasional treats, had added to the enjoyment. Now there was more hope in the air with the success of the vaccine programme in the UK giving out extra confidence to many of the population and also the gradual unlocking of restrictions in the hope that in June life could resume as before. There would still be a good deal of uneasiness as they had already had their hopes lifted only to be let down later. The open air eating out had been a welcome idea despite the fact that, as it turned out, the month of May had apparently been the coldest May for about forty years.

A traffic light system had been introduced to deal with the risks involved with travel; first of all, there was Green and Portugal sat on this list meaning that it was a country that could attract visitors without restrictions and having to go into quarantine upon return to the UK. Then there was Amber meaning that one pre-departure Covid test was required plus quarantine at home for ten days upon return. Red was for the countries deemed to be at the highest coronavirus risk and the list dictated different rules for testing and quarantining for travellers, in other words a bit of a no-go area, but nevertheless causing confusion and concern in the travel industry. Of course, without much warning, a country could find itself being moved from Green to Amber, and maybe even to Red. At the moment a holiday was the last thing on their minds and anyway as the summer weather looked like another thing that sometimes used to occur in the past; they still had the heating on indoors and their thick anoraks were also in use and hanging on the coat hooks in the hall, taking up space. There had been many times when Elizabeth had regretted leaving her gloves behind when she had gone out. The recent optimism had been good though, as people were able to look forward to the day when they could eat indoors in restaurants and also invite friends and family inside their homes. Hopefully next month they could even meet up in larger groups, according to the road map out of lockdown.

However, more bad news was to follow as it invariably did. A new variant of the virus, named Delta, which appeared to have originated in India had taken hold in the UK and especially in certain parts of the country. Elizabeth couldn't help feeling angry with the situation with all its unpredictability and expressed her thoughts aloud

"If only the government had stopped people coming in from India straight away, as soon as they knew about it. The delay has caused this awful situation and it may well be that things will not be able to open up after all next month as has been promised, the uncertainty is excruciating now."

The Prime Minister had once more repeated the message that he had given out at Christmas, "you *can* entertain; there is no law against it but maybe it would be safer not to do so." In other words, you *can do so but DON'T.* It looked as if history was repeating itself.

"The only good thing is" Edward replied "that those who have had the vaccination will feel safer this time round and will be less inclined to cancel indoor activities".

Usually by now Elizabeth had looked out her summer clothes and put away most of the winter ones. At the moment their thick winter anoraks had been demoted to the bed in the spare room as she wasn't confident enough that they would not be using them again and wouldn't tempt providence by putting them away.

Then, at last the warmer weather did decide to greet them and the beautiful colours of the May blossoms were out, giving them hope that maybe summer would follow albeit rather later than it should have been.

Chapter 33

Trintley 1979

About eighteen months had passed since they had taken on the business and moved to Trintley. The place was beginning to feel a little more like home, or perhaps more to the point was that Elizabeth had become more used to it. Apart from the hours he had spent in the shop helping customers and coping with practical things that were not within her level of expertise, Edward had already fitted a new kitchen and was now just putting the finishing touches to the new bathroom and also to a shower room which had been added by taking a section off the large adjacent bedroom. They now had space, heat, a certain amount of luxury and a thriving business and so the question was what more could they want? Maybe it was time to come up with some new plans and they had already both thought about this but neither of them had come up with anything awe-inspiring, certainly nothing that could beat the achievement of adding a whole free day to make a weekend for them. Their decision to open all day on a Tuesday, so that they could have the benefit of the whole day off on a Monday, had been most successful and they had been delighted with the outcome; there had been no negative comments and they had gained much more freedom. After Saturday, Tuesday became their busiest day and it was most satisfying. Because they now had a full weekend, even though it didn't include a Saturday, they decided at half term to make the most of their new hours. On a beautiful sunny Monday morning, the three of them set off for Frinton-on-Sea nine o'clock. For the first time in ages Elizabeth felt they were just a normal family enjoying playing with their young son on the beach as she watched Edward build a large sand castle, only for Francis to knock it down a few minutes later, followed by peals of laughter from them both. Up until now she had had a feeling of being different; who on earth would give up a lovely modern house, a well- paid job and a certain amount of freedom and exchange it for a shop with a flat above it, even a large flat. Yet, she had to admit, since the start of this insanity they had made some good friends. She no longer looked forward to arriving home after a shopping trip or an outing to be greeted by the dusty outside of their home with the front door opening up onto the pavement and the traffic. There had been a time in the past when the places where she had once lived welcomed her home as a place of comfort to return to after she had been away from home, even for a short time. There had been long exhausting shopping trips, enjoyable but tiring outings to places of interest and the sight of her front door had given her a feeling of contentment; it wasn't quite the same now but nevertheless once inside the house she could at least by now appreciate a certain amount of satisfaction.

The morning had passed watching Francis and Edward having fun and also hearing the sea gently crashing onto the beach; it looked as if the tide was coming in but she appreciated the tranquillity and wondered what it would be like to live by the sea and being able to experience this feeling frequently; although it could undoubtedly be quite wild in the winter months. She speculated on how it would have been if they had bought the shop on the coast that they had once looked at, but had ruled it out as being unsuitable. She suspected the sea wouldn't really have been much compensation as the accommodation had been rather too small anyway.

Soon after midday Edward suggested they should find a cafe for some lunch so they packed their belongings together and moved away from the beach. Just as they were approaching a small cafe a large dark cloud appeared followed by drops of rain that increased rapidly and then to turn into a heavy downpour; the people sitting outside cafes and restaurants started to scurry for shelter. They counted themselves lucky to be able to secure a small rickety table for two in the cafe and Edward quickly dragged over a chair from a large table scattered with empty plates and half full glasses of various drinks. The rain stopped almost as quickly as it had arrived and so after demolishing sandwiches and a large piece of chocolate cake each, they were able to take a walk along the seafront before leaving for home, ready to tackle the following working routine after a pleasant day.

Following their welcome break, trying to think of other new ideas came to the surface once more following their earlier success with the change to the shop's opening hours. Suddenly quite out of the blue Edward said

"You know that chap that brought in some samples of the plants he was growing in his greenhouse."

"You mean Mr James?"

"Yes, that's his name and I mentioned, partly as a joke really, that perhaps we could sell some of them in the shop."

"Yes, I do seem to remember that he took it quite seriously at the time."

"Maybe we should contact him again and see if it would be possible, I haven't seen him lately but I do believe he gave us a telephone number."

So maybe they had hit upon a plan after all.

Chapter 34

Willow Bridge Summer 2021

After the months of constraints surely there must be something to look forward to at last. The latest restrictions were being lifted and they would now have the opportunity to eat inside restaurants in England and would be able to invite friends and relatives into their homes. Having built up their optimism maybe there was to be an improvement to their current way of life. Unfortunately, suddenly these hopes were dashed again. The possible date for the release of the restraints had been set for the twenty-first of June, but now that had come into doubt as Covid cases had started to rise and another new variant, coming from Nepal had apparently, shown up. The different mutations were named after letters of the Greek alphabet: we have Alpha, Beta and Gamma and soon followed by Delta from Nepal. Elizabeth and Edward felt incredibly grateful that they had not booked a holiday abroad, as so many people had done, now leaving their plans in tatters. The twenty-first of June and the date for freedom was moved forward to the nineteenth of July when just maybe the country could open up again without so many limitations; but it was like living on the edge of a cliff. Looking over the edge gives an uneasy feeling of fear and yet at the same time stepping back from it leaves a certain amount of hope. Thus, the nineteenth of July may or may not happen but hope is still there. The cases of the Delta variant were rising rapidly and many, but not all, of the scientists are predicting another wave in the Autumn and are in agreement that we should wait another four weeks before resuming the usual routine. Politicians and businesses come over as less gloomy than the scientists, stating that the vaccines are working and that more damage will be done to the economy if further restrictions are followed. The truth is that nobody knows what is really ahead, on the one hand Elizabeth feels lucky that she and Edward's lives are less disrupted than those of the younger people and especially the ones working in the hospitality industry; many others are struggling to keep their small businesses open. However, she couldn't help looking at what they had all lost. Although eventually they may be able to resume some of their social activities, at the moment, she wondered if she would ever have the enthusiasm to invite friends in for a cup of tea or coffee. Neither will there be the spontaneity of being able to drop in, on impulse, to one of the local restaurants for a meal; for a while she had been hoping to do this once they could eat inside hostelries once more. She feared such an event would be like planning an excursion to somewhere completely unfamiliar. Although she couldn't help questioning her reasoning, they had been used to staying at home except for exercise and shopping, and it no longer seemed a problem, just natural although she wasn't quite sure what natural was any more. It had been about eighteen months since she had jumped on the park and ride bus to visit the city in order to have a good look around and to treat herself to lunch in one of the cafes. Nowadays many of the shops had closed down for good and cafes would only accept those who had already booked a table. She questioned where the fun would be in that and where would it all end?

Chapter 35

Trintley 1979

Occasionally Edward would come up with a new idea but many of them were either impractical or ridiculous, such as the time he had suggested they should remain open all through the lunch time.

"I don't think it will give us any more custom because many of the customers will also be thinking about lunch and anyway the break is good for us, even if not essential."

In the end he had agreed with her about that but the selling of plants could be a great advantage to all concerned. Many of their customers took great advantage of this and often they would look round and purchase plant food or other garden related items. Elizabeth suspected, because she was seeing one or two unfamiliar faces, some of these people came for the chrysanthemums and various other species that Mr James produced. She was not familiar with some of the species, whose names she hadn't heard of. One day she overheard someone say to another lady accompanying her

"I saw loads of flowering shrubs arriving one day and I thought the shop was about to change hands. I hadn't been in the shop before because I get most of my shopping in Cambridge, where I work. Anyway, I decided to be nosy and I was pleasantly surprised to see how much interesting stock there was and I made a few purchases."

"Will you go again then?" asked her friend.

"Oh yes, I'm sure I will."

She repeated the conversation to Edward afterwards and he responded

"Well, it just goes to show the benefits of taking on the plants and it will also benefit Mr James as it looked as if some of his produce used to go to waste."

It looked as if Mr James and his plants could bring in more

business, as they had hoped. She started searching for his telephone number to see if he could replenish the stock, she was sure she had kept it and normally would have expected it to be with all the other telephone numbers connected to the business. She was annoyed with herself as she had always been the organised one, rather than Edward. Maybe she had thought they wouldn't need to contact him as he came in so regularly and had therefore thrown it away in one of her tidying up moments.

"Have you found his telephone number?" Edward asked later.

"I can't find it anywhere but I'm sure that he will come into the shop before too long."

"Didn't you put his number in our personal address book that we keep in the kitchen?"

"Why would I have done that?"

The next moment found Edward standing before her with her address book and there was the number they wanted so Edward lost no time in contacting Mr James.

"He's going to bring us some plants tomorrow morning."

It wasn't as if any of them were making a vast fortune from Mr James's produce but, but those weeks appeared to become busier. Then one day, quite out of the blue and after congratulating themselves on their success, a severe looking woman walked into the shop. She was tall and thin, maybe in her late thirties, with long brown hair pulled back off her face; she was smartly dressed but didn't smile. Elizabeth was about to ask her if she needed any help but something stopped her when the woman started prodding things on the shelves as if they may be contaminated. Edward appeared at that moment and the woman went up to him and pointed at the attractively arranged plants just inside the door.

"It looks to me as if you are selling these illegally."

Edward's mouth opened.

"What."

"It would appear that you are not putting these sales through the till."

"Of course not, why would we? We are just helping someone out and avoiding waste. We've already agreed on a price that we will pay him and also the charge to the customers which all seems reasonable enough."

Elizabeth turned it over in her mind and really couldn't see that they were breaking any laws but it looked as if this lady was about to protest when another customer approached them.

"You are talking nonsense; many people sell their surplus garden produce from their front gardens and I don't recall there being any law against it and this amounts to the same thing."

With a snort, the woman left with her nose in the air.

"You haven't heard the last of this," she said, nodding in their direction.

Elizabeth turned to her rescuer who was a regular customer who she believed was a member of their Parish Council.

"Who on earth was that?"

"Just a trouble maker I imagine."

Although as it turned out they hadn't heard the last of it, but they were not going to dwell on the matter just now.

They had had a high turnover of the plants, so in the end their decision to give up the sale of paraffin seemed to be justified; the plants were far less trouble and less messy than the low profit margin paraffin which they had inherited when they had moved in. There followed another lifesaver when they made the decision to close the shop for a week in the summer so that they could all go away on holiday. This was something they could justify as they would need a break even if it meant a loss of income, but more to the point was that they owed it to Francis.

"If we give the customers plenty of notice I'm sure they will come back to us and those who don't feel that we deserve a break are possibly the ones that we don't rely on anyway."

Elizabeth wholeheartedly agreed with Edward even if it did make her slightly uneasy at first, but they booked a holiday cottage in Norfolk where they would go as soon as Francis had broken up.

She was sorry that their lovely neighbours had moved out of the cottage next door to them recently, as they had been so friendly and helpful and the fact that they had also shared the same removal day seemed as if there was some kind of harmony between them. But they had moved to somewhere a little larger, not far away, and they said they would still be willing to look after Francis if they wished to go out. Elizabeth and Edward had debated whether to ask them if they would look after Charlie while they were away but after much discussion, they decided to take him with them as the cottage would be quite suitable.

Nevertheless, they still looked forward to meeting the new people who turned out to be rather different. The new neighbours had started off by doing extensive alterations as soon as they moved in and consequently became good customers. As it turned out they were a couple, possibly a little older than themselves, and the Wallis family soon got used to the banging and the flying dust as they demolished and rebuilt the cottage, although initially they appeared to be friendly enough.

Housework was still a constant battle for Elizabeth but one day she thought it was time to make Francis's bedroom more to his liking, especially now the bathroom suite was no longer sitting in there. While he was at school and Edward was giving advice to a customer, she went to see what sort of decoration it would be in need, although there wasn't an uncluttered square inch on the floor and after looking under the bed she nearly gave up. So often she had tried to tidy up his room but, in the end, she decided if that was how he preferred it maybe she shouldn't interfere and it wasn't as if she had nothing better to do. Her next thoughts were that if she were to ask him what he would like to improve his bedroom it might just give him some incentive to tidy things up a little; even though the word *little* was somewhat emphasised in her mind. Having come to that decision she looked round further and saw there was no chance one coat of paint would cover the dark and bumpy walls, so she went in search of a book of wallpapers that he could choose from and she looked forward to seeing what he would pick so that she could move onto the next challenge. The sitting room was nearing completion and the old French doors had now been replaced with modern replacements; the wall lights were a great improvement too. She had to admit their home was now becoming a more comfortable place at last and added to this they had a holiday to look forward to.

The cottage they had booked was situated in a small Norfolk village, rather off the beaten track but nevertheless within walking distance of a farm and not too far from the sea. They would be able to visit places such as Beccles, Bungay, Lowestoft, Southwold and many other places nearby and Elizabeth felt that they were giving Francis a suitable holiday for a child of his age. After the strangeness of everything since their move, although this had been more of a concern to her than it had been to her son and Edward, it would still be quite an accomplishment.

By now Francis had chosen some wallpaper he liked even though she had to dissuade him from his favourite one covered in colourful monster like creatures she was sure would give him nightmares; she promised him she would start on it as soon as they returned from their holiday but in the meantime, they would all appreciate a good rest away from concerns, difficult customers, accounts and interrupted lunches. Instead, she and Edward would be sitting by the sea and watching Francis play on the smooth, flat sandy beaches in nearby places along the coast. Preparing for their holiday turned out to be quite labour intensive. They were only going for a week but by the time she had put a notice on the shop door, notified the representatives and those responsible for deliveries there was still the packing to do. As they would be staying in a cottage, they would need to take various food items because they would be arriving on a Sunday when less places would be open. They would also need to take towels and bedding. It appeared that customers, knowing that the shop would be closed for a week, had started to panic buy which had made them extra busy.

"That's a good thing, isn't it?" remarked Edward "We won't have to worry about the sales we won't be making during the week we are away. Everyone will be well stocked up" he added with a grin.

At last, they were ready and as they had already decided to take Charlie with them, Francis was happy. After they had experienced a pleasant day out to Frinton, following their change over to the new hours, they now relished the idea of a whole week away. The weather was better than they could have hoped for. The cottage was most comfortable and they had some good days out to places of interest and were able to spend time on beaches with Francis, although one of his favourite places was to the outdoor swimming pool at Beccles, where he learned to swim after Edward's encouragement. Francis also enjoyed the couple of fish and chips meals they had eaten straight out of the paper it was wrapped in.

The week passed by quickly and upon their return to the shop, as they drove towards it, Elizabeth realised that she no longer looked forward to going home as she had always done after holidays in the past. In those days the thought of wandering around their own garden again or preparing a meal with renewed energy after a pleasant break, was welcoming. This time as their old building came into view she felt as if a beautiful castle had turned into some sort of ruin before her eyes, almost as if Cinderella had been changed from a beautiful princess into a girl in ragged clothing instead of the other way round. She had to shake herself as she moved through the front door of their home, and once inside was able to appreciate all the hard work they had done to improve their accommodation. Then she tried to think more about their holiday and the extra energy and enthusiasm it should have given her. She needed to be ready to move on with the old routine, and fortunately she expected there would be good things ahead. Having returned to their old everyday life in the shop, other challenges lay ahead of them. In September there was to be a change from the 8% VAT (Value Added Tax) to 15% which meant calculating and changing all the prices on the goods for sale, which would be quite a daunting task.

They had been most fortunate in that they had been introduced to the grandson of one of their friendly customers. His name was William and his mother had died from cancer, followed by the death of his father in an accident at his workplace, a year ago. William, now aged seventeen, was living with his grandmother who had asked Edward if they needed any help in the shop either at weekends or in the school holidays; she felt it would be good for him to be distracted after what he had been through. She and Edward had decided to employ him for a few hours at weekends and it had offered them a most welcome advantage. He was a charming young man and popular with the customers; being tall he was able to reach things down for them from the high shelves and had quickly learned a good deal about the products they sold. He had settled in well at the local secondary school and maths was one of the subjects he was taking for his A level exams; he had willingly offered to help them with the VAT change.

By September 1979 they had obtained planning permission to open up the cellar beneath the shop for an extension to the sales area and everything was going well. The new staircase had been tailor-made and they had a man lined up to fit it one weekend. On the Saturday evening of the weekend chosen, after closing the shop, they moved everything away from the stair area so that they would be ready for the work to start on Sunday. They both stood back in satisfaction as they had been promised that the staircase would be all finished by Monday evening, ready for opening up on Tuesday morning. They had been assured that this was no problem and it could easily be done in two full days. Early on Sunday morning they were all ready and waiting for the man to turn up to fit the new staircase. Edward kept looking at his watch.

"What time is he supposed to be coming?" Elizabeth asked anxiously.

"He didn't give an exact time" replied Edward "but I rather understood that he would be here by nine o'clock."

"It's getting on for half past nine now" said Elizabeth, feeling that they had been ready and waiting for hours.

"Maybe he's just not a good time keeper, he'll be here soon."

About twenty minutes later she could hear the phone ringing and Elizabeth immediately grabbed it but passed it over to Edward, she wasn't sure quite why she did that but she had a bad feeling about it.

"Hello," Edward waited.

"I'm supposed to be coming to fit the stairs in your shop basement today."

"Yes?" said Edward patiently, waiting for the man to say that he was delayed and also doing calculations as to whether they could still get it all done in time.

"I regret that I won't be able to come after all as I have hurt my back. Sorry" and he rang off.

They looked at each other aghast and at all the stock piled up all over the rest of the floor and the new staircase, in sections near to the entrance door into the shop, taking up much of the available space.

"What on earth are we going to do?" Despite Elizabeth's anxiousness she still hadn't believed what she had just heard. It couldn't possibly be true but it was and she could see complete pandemonium before her. They had had it all so well planned and perfectly organised. She remained rooted to the floor. But Edward always, well nearly always, came up with a solution.

"Do we have William's phone number, or at least his grandmother's?"

Elizabeth grabbed her address book and found what she was looking for and Edward made the call while she held her breath until, what seemed like an eternity, Edward turned to her.

"Yes, he's free and more than willing to come and help."

Elizabeth thought that she must have been holding her breath for longer than was wise and released it with a huge sigh of relief. William arrived, less than half an hour later and between them, Edward and the seventeen-year-old set about fitting the stairs which fortunately Edward had kept the plan for. This included cutting the large hole in the floor where the stairs were to fit. Previously the cellar had been accessed by a narrow ladder-like contraption situated towards the centre of the shop and the new stairs would be nearer to the front. In the future it turned out to be a wonderful asset after Edward and William had miraculously completed the job in the two days, despite the initial setback.

Although there would still be much more to do to get everything sorted, at least they would be able to open the shop. That evening Edward opened a bottle of wine.

"I think we need to celebrate, if it hadn't been for William.... Well, it just doesn't bear thinking about. That's another thing, without offending him or his grandmother we must pay him a realistic amount for what he has done for us, without him we would probably have had to wait ages to get someone else to do it and probably at a high price too."

"And imagine having to move everything around again so that we could function." Elizabeth exclaimed

"I'll give it some thought although I think he rather enjoyed himself" Edward remarked.

In the end he spoke to William's grandmother.

"He is saving up for a new bicycle so something towards it would be welcome – but not too much please."

They gave him some money towards his bike and booked a table at a nearby restaurant so that they could take William and his grandma out for a meal, which they both appreciated even though William insisted on having beef burgers.

Nearly two years had passed since their rash decision to sell their lovely house and move to their current place above a shop. Oddly enough Elizabeth had found many advantages in her new way of life; she was enjoying the challenge of running the business and found all the improvements they had made rewarding. Most of the major work in both the shop and the house was more or less completed and she was enjoying organising the shelves in the shop to make the best of the extra space and they still appeared to have plenty of customers, if not even more. They obviously must be doing something right. The house was *almost* luxurious inside with all the space and modern features but one of the main problems was that being on the main road with passing two-way traffic meant they suffered from a vast accumulation of dust and dirt. In the downstairs room at the front of the house they were forever removing sooty dust which had piled up between the layers of secondary double glazing. Keeping the shop clean and tidy was a never-ending task but eventually they decided it would be simpler to employ someone to clean the house, thus freeing up Elizabeth to concentrate on the shop. In between attending to customers, she found the opportunity to keep the dust down and the floor clean. On the mornings when the cleaning lady used to come to clean their living accommodation Elizabeth would rush around picking up clothes lying on the floor – mostly belonging to Francis – removing cups and mugs to put into the newly acquired dishwasher and generally tidying up first so that there was room on the floor for the vacuum to be moved round and tables clear enough so that they could be polished; Mrs Mop, as they called her, loved polishing and sometimes Elizabeth noticed a stickiness on the surfaces where she had overdone it. Edward and Francis found all this tidying up amusing.

'Mum's cleaning up for the cleaning lady.'

Chapter 36

Willow Bridge 2021

There had been so many changes since March of last year; things that nobody could possibly have predicted or even dreamed about. Previously life had been ticking by with its various worries and problems such as what disastrous events could happen due to climate change; the horrors of countries at war; migrants risking dangerous crossings through the English Channel in order to escape what they had left behind. Those who had remained were starving and homeless and also with their lives at risk. Brexit also has been responsible for many disagreements and difficulties amongst acquaintances and families. So, everyone had their concerns. Then suddenly, quite out of the blue, Covid hit the world, intensifying those existing problems and one elderly man had even compared the Covid crisis with World War II.

"At least people were able to get together to comfort each other if relatives had been killed in the fighting or had had their houses bombed."

It had indeed been perfectly normal to go round to the neighbour and to have a cup of tea and a grumble about what was happening. Elizabeth had replied to him

"Well at least our houses may stay standing but all the deaths and suffering is no doubt comparable."

It had occurred to her that she had had this conversation with a complete stranger as she had walked past his house and noticed him standing on his doorstep. She doubted that they would have spoken in the days before the virus, even if they had nodded to each other in acknowledgement. This made her think of positive things as this crisis had brought people together because they all had something in common. Walking had now become a daily routine and she was still keeping up with the habit which, upon reflection, did differ from previous times when walks had been taken for a purpose, either to buy something or to visit someone. She felt that this was one good thing to come out of it. In the pre-pandemic days, she and Edward would occasionally go for a long walk if the weather invited and if they didn't have anything else more pressing to attend to, otherwise they would walk to the town for shopping on most days. It was different now, whether she was walking to the shops or just for exercise; it was as if she had a dog to take out as a daily routine. The Government had declared that walking was allowed and that they should go for a stroll once a day. It felt as if they were now living in a country where there was a strict regime and rules and regulations could not be broken because of the threats of imprisonment. People in this country, who were deemed to be vulnerable, had received an important letter telling them they were in a special category and should stay at home. Neither she nor Edward had received this letter warning them not to go out. Therefore, they assumed that they wouldn't have to be trapped between four walls as some people would be under those circumstances.

Elizabeth had already decided that it was fortunate they didn't have a dog after all, and was now reminded of this wise decision. The weather had been extremely hot making it too uncomfortable to go out, but when it had become cool enough, she had grabbed her opportunity but whilst on her way home she was caught out in a thunderous downpour. It reminded her of the time, not so long ago, when she had been unexpectedly caught up in strong winds and heavy rain when walking back from the hairdresser; the umbrella had immediately blown inside out and she was left trying to keep her hood up to protect her newly coiffed hair; she had never been so glad to return home. She imagined that taking a dog out in such weather conditions would not be fun, and the thought of it shaking its wet hair all over the place came to mind.

By now they had given up any ideas regarding holidays, and had decided instead to spend the money on the house. They found the name of the painter and decorator who had been recommended by a neighbour and contacted him with a view to getting him to decorate their dining room, also possibly the kitchen if she could face it, but first things first she thought. Much to their surprise he was able to come almost straight away and they were now reaping the benefit; they had moved the dining table so they could look out onto the garden while they ate and wondered why they hadn't thought of doing this before. However, one thing led to another and they made another decision to get their garden landscaped. If it wasn't practical, for the moment, to spend money on a holiday, why should they not use it to make the house and garden more inviting if they were going to spend more time at home. Trying to keep the garden tidy was becoming rather a chore and sometimes drove Elizabeth mad after she had tried to make a difference. She would spend hours on one section only to move to another part that she really couldn't face tackling, and finally giving up when she didn't appear to be getting anywhere. In a case like this, time on her hands didn't appear to be of much advantage.

Chapter 37

Trintley 1979

Their new neighbours appeared to have settled in and their contacts had mainly been when they were customers, although they seemed pleasant enough Elizabeth still missed their predecessors. One day they both came in to the shop together and formally introduced themselves as Mavis and Joe; Edward, always the good neighbour said

"If you need anything we're only next door so do let us know."

They didn't take advantage of having a hardware shop next door to them and only expected to buy things during opening hours, although sometimes Joe would ask Edward what would be the best tool to use for a particular job and they would spend time discussing the best options. Eventually they developed some sort of friendship even though they didn't appear to have much in common and one day Edward suggested

"It might be a friendly gesture to invite them in for a meal one evening."

She agreed and after setting a date for the following week she looked forward to it. They hadn't done any entertaining since they had moved and she supposed she had missed the dinner parties they used to have in the past and there was no excuse now as their living space was more acceptable. She spent a while studying her cookery books and then thought she should ask them if there was any particular food item they didn't like.

"We eat anything," said Joe "and it will give us much pleasure to have a meal with you."

She had taken a liking to Joe straight away but Mavis appeared to be a little distant and much less relaxed, although she was sure they would get along fine. She was pleased that their dining room and kitchen were by now pleasant enough, especially as she had an underlying feeling that Mavis would be scrutinising their efforts. She had got this impression due to an early conversation the two women had had which at the time she had thought was rather odd as they had only just met. Mavis had said

"You are lucky that Edward is so capable and has done so much of the renovation" and Elizabeth got the impression that Mavis thought she didn't do much towards the running of the business. Maybe she was being a bit unfair but there was something about Mavis that she couldn't quite put her finger on. She tried to remember what had put her on her guard and then it occurred to her that it must have been that conversation they had had about Edward's hard work and the implication that she herself had an easy life. If only, she thought.

She sat down with pen and paper to make a list of foods she would need to buy for the occasion; she had already decided on a starter of homemade tuna pâté followed by a ragout, accompanied by a selection of mixed vegetables and sauteed potatoes and she would make a chocolate orange mousse for the dessert. Everything was in order and ready for their meal in plenty of time on the day they had fixed. Sunday had suited them all especially as Elizabeth would be able to devote plenty of time for food preparation. She had set the table and added some candles, in the elegant glass holders, that had been given to them as a wedding present and had only just recently been unpacked after their move. Mavis and Jo arrived exactly on time and Edward answered the door and brought them straight up to the kitchen where he poured some wine. Francis was all ready for bed but came in to say hello where he was greeted by the couple he had only seen from a distance, and he appeared to make a good impression upon them.

"Francis, you'd better get into bed now. You need to be up early for school tomorrow."

She was aware that the food would spoil if she wasn't careful so she aimed for them to sit down as soon as everything was ready. Mavis looked round the kitchen almost as if she was looking for something to criticise but surprisingly came out with

"What a lovely kitchen."

She continued examining a book shelf that Edward had hastily put up to house her cookery books and which she had been pleased with.

"That's such a good idea to have a shelf for cookery books."

"Edward put that up after the new kitchen had finally been installed and it has been so handy."

They wandered into the dining room which looked cosy as she had lit the candles and placed the pâté on the table.

"Did you make the pâté?" Mavis asked. Joe tasted it and expressed how good it was.

She brought in the main course which she had gone to a great deal of trouble with and felt relieved that the ragout had turned out well after having taken her first mouthful. Mavis didn't make any comments about it though, instead she talked in full about the wonderful meal they had recently eaten in a restaurant nearby.

"It was a fantastic restaurant, recently opened. You must go it's not far away. I'll give you the address. The food was absolutely divine."

Soon they all talked about what turned out to be the one thing they did have in common, the alterations they were doing on their respective homes. It appeared that Mavis was a perfectionist whereas Elizabeth was far too keen to get the jobs done to worry about small details, although Edward certainly took a great deal of trouble with everything he did and she was always happy with the results when they were eventually finished. Elizabeth made some coffee, once they had eaten, and took it downstairs to the sitting room. Once more Mavis's eye was drawn to a small bureau in the corner of the room that Elizabeth had inherited from a relative who had recently died. It had fitted in well and turned out to be most useful. After its arrival she had spent time organising all her paperwork that was not connected to the shop, which up to now had been distributed between different places.

"I love the bureau. Is it an antique?"

"I don't think so, although it is quite old and I do love it especially as it is a good place for keeping personal correspondence and other bits and pieces."

Mavis had already spent a good deal of time analysing everything around her and then she once more turned the conversation back to herself.

"Do you like my shoes?"

Elizabeth looked at them and thought to herself, they were just shoes after all! Nonetheless she politely agreed they were extremely stylish.

"Do you know how much they cost?"

Elizabeth didn't really wish to know but Mavis would no doubt tell her anyway and so she wasn't surprised when she learned about their enormous price.

Later as they were about to leave, Mavis turned to her

"You must come and have a meal with us. I'll check our diary" and with that they were gone.

In the end Elizabeth had been pleased to get the entertainment of the neighbours over with, especially as she did find Mavis a little overwhelming to say the least. She had rather enjoyed all the preparations she had made but felt disappointed that her efforts had not been appreciated by Mavis. In the end she was unable to dwell on it too much as the next setback was about to arrive in the form of the woman who had complained about their sale of plants.

The phone call from her had come just as they had been about to close the shop for the day.

"Hello this is Miss Curtis…'

Elizabeth was trying to think who on earth Miss Curtis was, she was sure she didn't know Miss Curtis but the woman's next words were soon to enlighten her.

"You will remember that I queried the validity of your selling plants and after talking to my solicitor it looks as if I may be correct in my assumptions."

Elizabeth did wonder about her careful wording 'I *may* be correct…' nevertheless it did make her feel uneasy and she wondered why the woman would need to consult a solicitor. It did seem rather extreme. She thought about this for a while before thinking of a suitable response but she was saved from this quandary when Miss Curtis continued without waiting for a reply.

"I am planning on opening a flower shop in the empty place at the top of the High Street and your happy go lucky enterprise could affect my new legitimate business so I do hope that you will give this some thought."

Then to Elizabeth's relief she cut her off abruptly; so at least she hadn't said something she would regret later. She thought back and tried to remember the name of the customer who had come to her rescue when the matter had first come up, she thought he was a member of their Parish Council and maybe Edward would remember him. Anyway, she would now have to impart this disturbing conversation to Edward.

Chapter 38

Willow Bridge 2021

Uncertainty had become a way of life but still everybody awaited that special date of the nineteenth of July when restrictions should be removed. However, it remains to be seen and it is not surprising that many feel that it will never happen as promises have been made before and then another variant crops up from nowhere to change the plans, as in the case with the twenty first of June. Others are worried about still being too exposed. There has been much concern, and sometimes anger, in the case of football matches and UEFA officials being able to come to England without all the precautions the rest of the country has had to take. Added to this general uneasiness there was also apprehension about the G7 Summit; the G7 being an organisation made up of the world's seven richest nations: Canada, France, Germany, Italy, Japan, the United Kingdom and the United States. This Summit was still going to go ahead in Cornwall, the county where apparently cases have risen following their previous low rates of infection in the beginning.

To Elizabeth it all seemed a bit ludicrous but despite it she did find that there were some days, not all of course, that she almost forgot about the threat they were living under. She was enjoying and looking forward to things, as in the past, such as starting a new book or sitting in the garden with the beautiful smell of the mock orange bush or even planning for the future. Yet the fear would then return when the forecast from scientists and politicians predicted that there would be a peak of the virus in the autumn or winter and much has been made of this disheartening prediction. She noted how any encouraging news was kept in the background, such as that booster vaccines are being worked on. For some reason they don't want to give out too much cheerful news and the press appear to prefer giving out negative bulletins as well.

Nobody knows what is ahead of us. Everyone is waiting for D Day, which is due on the nineteenth of July, and are wondering if everything will go back to normal as hoped. Or will there be another peak or more to the point can further lockdowns really be avoided? There appears to be nothing but questions but on the other hand there is one thing that is certain and that is that Covid is here to stay but how it is dealt with is another matter entirely. Waiting for the date when all restrictions are supposed to be released, with the possibility of some form of the old life, comes with foreboding. The Prime Minister has again made a promise that this will happen and it is apparent that he is reluctant to break his promise despite the peak in cases, and the UK having the highest infection rate in Europe. Because of this many people are against the lifting of social distancing and of face coverings being no longer compulsory, yet there are others who are against any restrictions altogether so it does look as if, as they say, *you can't win* and even though the way the government have dealt with most things during the crisis leaves much to be desired, there has to be a certain sympathy with them because whatever they do there will be some people who will be up in arms. We have absolutely no idea where we will be in a few months' time and there is still great concern that hospital admissions will increase and medical staff will once more be under intense pressure. Yet again routine operations will have to be cancelled and no wonder people are scared. The nineteenth of July has been called Freedom Day by the Government but it is feared that it will be far from any kind of freedom.

Chapter 39

Trintley 1979

Elizabeth waited until Francis was in bed before she told Edward about the customer who had challenged their sale of Mr James's plants

"She's not a very pleasant woman and she rarely comes into the shop."

"She's talking rubbish and I wouldn't take too much notice of her" he replied.

"Do you know the name of the man who came to our rescue when the matter was first brought up."

"I'm not sure of his name, all I know is that he is on the Parish Council and I believe he is a solicitor. If I see him, I could perhaps mention these further developments, but just casually of course." Edward looked a little doubtful so she added

"I suppose you could, but just let's wait and see, it's unlikely that the woman can do anything anyway".

Elizabeth hadn't expected to get an invitation from Mavis so quickly and was surprised

when she had popped into the shop and invited them round on the following Saturday evening; in many ways she would look forward to it. She had enjoyed using her culinary skills to entertain their neighbours but there was certainly something rather odd about Mavis. She hadn't liked the way she had been critically examining her furnishings, anyway it felt that way to her but no doubt Edward would say she had imagined it. She had thought the meal she had prepared for Mavis and Joe had gone rather well, after all she had taken a great deal of trouble looking out recipes that she had used before and what seemed like a lifetime ago; all the planning had taken her back to the times when they would frequently entertain four or more friends and in turn would enjoy a meal in their homes. In those days she had joined a baby-sitting circle so that she could always find someone to look after Francis and she would be able to reciprocate; her Saturdays would often be spent either going out somewhere or looking after the children of other members in the circle. When they used to either visit friends for meals or join them for a restaurant meal, they had always found it an excellent occasion to dress smartly, especially the women, wearing a fancy blouse and long skirt but it didn't do to dwell on what had gone before.

Despite her misgivings she looked forward to the meal next door and at least she would have an evening when she wouldn't need to cook; Francis would be happy with some fish fingers and she turned to Edward

"I don't suppose we will need to find a baby-sitter as we can take it in turns to go and check up on him" and Edward agreed as he should be asleep before they went.

Elizabeth looked in the wardrobe to find something smarter than she had been accustomed to wearing lately and located something that had been unworn since they had moved.

"Does this look a little too overdressed?" she asked Edward.

"It looks fine." He hadn't really looked at it properly but she was sure he would have said something if it had been unsuitable.

She decided to try it on before deciding and then she noticed that she had lost quite a bit of weight since the last time she had worn it and so it was now a size too large. In some ways she was rather pleased but she did wonder how she had lost so much and maybe it was because she had been much more active since they had been running the shop, not to mention all those stressful moments, so she shrugged it off. In the end she found a belt that would go with it and feeling satisfied she went to show Edward again.

"You look great. Is it new?"

She laughed.

"Since when have I had the opportunity to go shopping for clothes? Don't you remember the last time I wore it was when we went to a party connected to your old company."

He shrugged.

They stood outside Mavis and Joe's front door, Edward clutching a bottle of wine.

"I hope they will like it."

"I'm sure that Joe will appreciate it." Elizabeth couldn't help emphasising the *Joe*.

Joe came to the door which led them straight into their small but well fitted kitchen and she couldn't help noticing the book shelf tucked into a corner, Mavis had obviously been impressed with the shelf that Edward had put up in their kitchen but she never thought that she would copy it; except that hers was more ornate. Even so she preferred Edward's handiwork and assumed that Mavis would have paid an exorbitant price for hers. There was a good smell of cooking and Elizabeth realised how hungry she was and Mavis turned round and said,

"Do go through, I'll be with you in a moment when I've just checked the meat."

Joe took them into the sitting room where a small dining table was set for four. Immediately her eyes were drawn to a bureau in one corner of the room, not unlike the one that she had inherited but in rather better condition, and as if on cue Mavis arrived making Elizabeth feel glad that she was wearing her smart dress that she had been anxiously brooding about. Mavis noticed her looking at the bureau

"Yes, do you like it? I bought it yesterday from a little antique shop near Cambridge. It was rather expensive but I couldn't resist it."

Elizabeth could see that although it looked similar to the bureau she had inherited from her uncle, it was probably much older and it could be worth a good deal of money.

They sat down to eat a delicious meal of roast beef, done just to their liking and not overdone, with fluffy Yorkshire puddings and vegetables. This was followed by a rather unusual trifle, again excellent. Unlike Mavis when they had visited their place, Elizabeth complimented her on the food and Joe filled up their wine glasses. By then it was Edward's turn to go and check on Francis.

"I wouldn't have thought it would be necessary to check on your little boy so often, he's only next door."

"Do you have any children, Mavis?"

"No, we didn't want children."

Elizabeth ignored the statement and went on to say that if Francis woke up and they weren't there he would be upset. This had been something that had bothered her a little even though he rarely woke once he had gone off to sleep. Mavis's next comment took her by surprise.

"I hope you like my dress; it came from Paris and it cost me over five hundred pounds."

What could she say to that?

Chapter 40

Willow Bridge July 2021

'Freedom Day' arrived, as promised, on July 19th and with it an increase of assurance. The end of lockdowns and everything appearing to be more as we had known it was a wonderful feeling, at first anyway. When the pandemic had arrived, it had brought with it a sensation of disbelief followed by an eventual acceptance and now there appeared to be some sort of similarity even with their sense of general relief. There was still a good deal of anxiety about what lay ahead and the speculation that there could be something worse on the horizon, possibly nearly as bad as lockdowns and nobody could put their trust in anything anymore. They weren't far wrong. Many people had downloaded an NHS app which was a check as to whether a person was reading positive for Covid. A positive reading meant that you would get 'pinged' thereby meaning you would have to go into quarantine. The downside of this was that many were getting 'pinged' even when they had tested negative, using their home testing kits, and had already been given the two doses of the vaccine. All this meant was that many had to stay off work causing some shops to close again because they didn't have enough staff. In many cases, there were empty shelves in the shops as delivery drivers were also having to quarantine amongst others involved in the food chain; there was also concern yet again about the lack of enough medical staff in hospitals due to them having been 'pinged'. This situation became known as the 'Pingdemic'. Edward pointed out

"The app is not a legal requirement and many haven't been able to download it or have chosen not to. it, so what kind of sense does that make?"

"None at all but many people are under the impression that it is the law and that they have to abide by it."

“Yes, but already many are moving the app from their smartphones, and you can’t blame them.”

Elizabeth admitted that she had also done just that although Edward hadn’t even bothered to load it in the first place.

“Unfortunately, the government doesn’t appear to have got the message about the damage that this is doing and although they appear to be making some exemptions about the quarantining they really don’t cover enough of the essential services.”

Elizabeth frequently walked past a popular cafe where a comfortable seating area had been made available outside, when the government rules had stopped the meeting of friends and family indoors. Once the restrictions were lifted it had become an even more lively place with all the tables full both inside and outside. Even though she hadn’t actually been there yet, the sight of the full tables cheered her up and made her think of past times. One day she was about to walk past it on her way to the shops but stopped in surprise; there was no sign of anyone sitting outside the cafe on this beautiful sunny day. She moved closer and noticed that the tables and chairs were stacked up inside once more, as had been the case during the latest lockdown. She was mystified until she saw the notice in the window,

We regret that we have had to close due to a member on our staff testing positive for coronavirus. We look forward to seeing you again soon.

yet another victim of the ‘Pingdemic’, she surmised. On the other hand, the news was now more positive because cases had been going down for a few days even though hospital admissions were still rising.

In July 2021 the BBC news reverted back to what it had been before; once more there were the cyclists, walkers, kayakers and others showing real activity instead of the collection of snips shown as a collage, which she supposed had been quite innovative in the circumstances. By the summer they were all able to appreciate the sight of days gone by, but there was always that uncertain feeling at the back of their minds. Would they ever be able to relax completely?

Chapter 41

Trintley 1980

It was nearly lunchtime and customers were starting to leave the shop as it would be closing shortly, although there was always someone who would linger and hold them up; sometimes this would make Elizabeth feel impatient but she had to fix a pleasant smile on her face as she hung around with the keys as a gentle hint. At the same time, she was beginning to wonder where Edward had got to; she was sure she had seen him go into the back of the shop where the paint was kept. He usually appeared when they were due to lock up, almost as if she wasn't capable of doing this, even though she did always welcome his help. It was certainly a bit odd so she turned the closed sign round and locked the door before going to look for him. There was a big old-fashioned sink at the back of the shop which was found to be most useful when needing to wipe things down or to rescue a leaking tin or a split packet. What greeted her though, was alarming. Edward was hanging onto the front of the sink as if he had been glued to it; he tried to turn round and she was shocked to see how white he looked

"I can't move, I may be going to be sick."

"Shall we try and get you into the house and somewhere more comfortable?"

"I can't move."

She was alarmed and picked up the phone in the shop; then the thought came to her that the staff in the doctor's surgery would probably be at lunch too, what should she do? Just as she was starting to panic and wonder if she should phone 999, one of the doctors picked up.

"My husband has found that he is unable to move, he's hanging on to the sink, I don't know what to do. I don't want to leave him" she realised that she was probably talking gibberish.

"How long has he been like that?"

"I don't know. I've only just found him."

"Is he conscious?"

"Yes" she spluttered

"I'm going to call an ambulance and it will be with you in about ten minutes. Stay with him and I'll remain on the line until it arrives."

"Thank you" she spluttered gratefully.

She explained to Edward about the ambulance and he didn't protest. She had given the address of the shop and went and opened the door again, hoping that nobody would try to come in. Luckily Joe next door came to find her because as he had passed by, he had realised that something could be wrong as normally they would be closed, leaving the shop empty at this time.

She explained briefly.

"Is there anything that I can do?" he asked.

"I will need to be here to fetch Francis from school in a couple of hours."

"If you are not back from the hospital by then, I will go down to Francis's school, I know the headmaster quite well."

At that point the ambulance arrived and Joe said

"I'll put a note on the door. Off you go."

By now the medics had brought in a wheelchair and were pushing Edward through the door. She locked it behind her, putting the key into her pocket and followed Edward into the ambulance.

Chapter 42

Willow Bridge August 2021

Marilyn arrived in time for coffee, something they had been out of the habit of doing since March of 2020, Covid and the aftermath. As Elizabeth showed her into the lounge, she noticed she had a newspaper tucked under her arm and wondered what news Marilyn was about to unwrap but no doubt she would soon be letting her know so she made her way to the kitchen

"I'll just make the coffee; shall we celebrate with some biscuits as well as it's been so long?"

"That would be lovely, thank you."

Elizabeth supposed that in a way it was some kind of celebration and immediately placed the tray on the small occasional table and poured coffee into two mugs. Before she could mention the paper Marilyn opened it up and spread it out on the table in front of them and pointed to a photograph on the second page.

"Do you recognise that man?"

"I don't think so."

"I don't want to bring back bad memories after all this time, but I thought you might find the bit about him interesting."

Elizabeth took another look

"Yes, the face does look a bit familiar, but the name underneath says Jerry Sutherland although he does look a little like that dreadful man who insulted me, Jerry Smith wasn't it."

"That's right, I'll leave it behind so that you can read it later."

"Thanks, I will."

She tossed it aside and immediately changed the subject. She learned that Marilyn and her husband were going to stay in Southwold for a few days at the end of the month and they agreed how delightful it was to be able to plan again; she and Edward were hoping to find a holiday cottage not too far away but unfortunately everything was getting booked up rather quickly, so maybe they would have to wait until the schools had returned again in September.

After Marilyn had left, she picked up the paper to read about the man that looked like Jerry Smith and yes, she was sure that the photograph was of him. The piece announced that Jerry Sutherland had been found dead in his home.

A man's body was found on the kitchen floor of his home early yesterday morning and the police understood that his name was Jerry Sutherland but he had recently been going under the name of Jerry Smith.

Elizabeth carried on reading and learned that

He had been a teacher but had spent a short time in prison after he had smashed up items in a shop because the elderly man serving him had spent too long attending to him, and he had become impatient. The man had fallen, as he had tried to stop further damage, but he had lost his balance and hit his head, later he died in hospital. Eventually Jerry had been released from prison after it had been proved that the death had resulted from an accident. He never went back to teaching and had taken early retirement.

Yet there was something more interesting.

Initially the death of Jerry Sutherland was thought to be suicide but the police are continuing with their enquiries.

Although the man was certainly not anyone she would grieve for, she did wonder why he would have been driven to suicide and also why the police appeared to be uncertain about his death. Perhaps he had upset someone else and had been killed. Then she realised that she had been reading too much crime fiction as well as watching, sometimes gruesome, detective dramas on the television. These had been a form of distraction for her although she didn't like the idea of something like that occurring in her everyday life, even to such a man as Jerry Smith.

Chapter 43

Trintley

After Edward's trip to hospital Elizabeth was able to appreciate all the good wishes and help given to her by their customers and neighbours; some of them she hardly knew even though they had come into the shop from time to time. Joe had been as good as his word and had gone down to the school when the children were due to leave and the Head Teacher had asked the mother of one of Francis's friends, Jimmy, to take him home with her.

Upon arriving at the hospital Elizabeth had been rather alarmed in the way they had rushed Edward into a cubicle and asked her to wait outside while a couple of doctors were examining him, then one of them came to talk to her.

"His heart's alright and it's definitely not a heart attack, but we can't be sure what has caused it, we'll keep him in overnight and do some more tests. You should be able to take him home tomorrow."

Joe had fetched her from the hospital and the next morning the shop was extremely busy but mostly customers were asking after Edward and offering any help she might need. She closed the shop that afternoon so that she could visit and Jimmy's mother said she would take Francis home with her again. It had been such a relief to realise that the customers were sympathetic and she didn't have to worry about closing for a few hours.

Upon her arrival at the hospital the next day, Edward was sitting in a chair looking healthy and cheerful.

"They still don't know what caused it but they have given me some pills just in case, although they think it is unlikely to happen again."

"But if they don't know what caused it how do they know what pills to give you and how do they know that it won't happen again ? She asked.

Edward shrugged. "They seem to know what they are doing

and think that it was probably a one off but they would do further tests if it did happen again."

Edward soon returned to the normal routine so she stopped worrying and put her faith in the fact that as Edward had said "They seem to know what they are doing."

After all, they seemed to think it was unlikely to happen again.

Chapter 44

Willow Bridge 2021

Eighteen months had passed since the outbreak of the pandemic in 2020 and yet dark clouds still loomed overhead. Everyone has once more been swept into uncertainty after the initial optimism when the vaccines had been successfully delivered, meaning that deaths and hospital admissions had dropped. Yet deaths and hospital admissions were now rising again and scientific advisors have predicted, the same as they had done last year, that we would be in for a new wave in the autumn and winter. Therefore, a good deal of the previous optimism had vanished and many were worried that there could be another lockdown and that next Christmas would be history repeating itself. On the more positive side everyone is doing what they can when they can, just in case, and making the most of being able to go out and about. Elizabeth and Edward were glad to be able to visit family and friends and they had even booked a night out in London. The previous year there had been no birthday or other such celebrations but hopefully this year they could at least have a meal out somewhere on their birthdays. But first of all, Elizabeth was looking forward to their trip to London and even started to feel more confident as the day drew nearer; surely it couldn't be cancelled now, but one never knew. As her friend Marilyn had said

"Enjoy every day as it comes."

She had agreed with her even though they hadn't a clue as to what was ahead of them.

She was still nervous about touching handrails when going up or downstairs in public places, sometimes she stepped carefully with her hands at her side and at other times she held onto the rail for safety; following this she would look for the hand gel, even though she still kept a small one in her handbag. On the radio the other day she heard that there had been several accidents on escalators on the London underground due to people avoiding the handrails, so she obviously wasn't the only one; although the spokesperson had assured them that she had not heard of anyone catching coronavirus from a handrail. Nevertheless, she could see that it was the lack of information that was still causing fear and confusion.

Whilst pondering on Marilyn's sensible advice about enjoying every day as it comes, Elizabeth started turning something over in her mind. Should they escape from the chores they had found themselves doing, such as gardening and general sprucing things up, or go out for a day or even for longer perhaps? Some of their neighbours and other acquaintances were taking holidays, even abroad, so she wondered why they were so stuck in the mud. She looked at the list she had compiled, many months ago, of places to visit but they were either just that bit too far away at the moment, or they were closed. However, more likely it was just a general lack of enthusiasm that had come upon her lately and still lingered. They do say that 'great minds think alike' and she hadn't been the only one looking for a temporary escape plan. Edward had wandered into the kitchen whilst she was staring out of the window above the sink, trying to come up with a solution for the monotony. She wasn't even taking in the pleasant autumnal view outside; although she remembered her father once saying that he didn't like autumn as it was a time that things were dying. On the other hand, she had usually appreciated the beautiful colours of the trees with their leaves in hues of yellow and red and even a few green ones hiding away. Even leaves on the ground, wet with the rain, looked appealing despite the hazard of slipping on them as she had once done, but fortunately escaping injury. She turned around to give Edward her attention.

"You know how you were reminiscing about our life in Trintley......" there was just a short pause before she answered, it had been such a long time ago and much water had passed under the bridge, as people kept saying.

"Yes, I do sometimes think about it and also about the difficulties and hardships, but we came through it didn't we."

"Why don't we take a drive over there and have a look around? It's not as if it's so far away."

It was indeed strange that she hadn't gone back again, but her friends who had lived there had moved away so there had been no reason to do so. She had put all that behind her until a reminder would sometimes crop up, usually about someone who had died or the time when they had heard that their old place was on the market again. There was no longer anyone living in Trintley that they knew well enough to visit but it would be fun to go to their old haunts and see what had changed. Now especially was a good time to make the visit and it would be something to look forward to. She had to admit that remembering their past life, many years before they had ever heard of Covid, could be therapeutic after all, so they planned their trip for the end of the week.

Once they arrived in Trintley, thoughts of people who had once lived there came back to them. They parked the car in what had become a large car park and no longer a rough piece of land where anyone could park free of charge, needless to say there was now a ticket machine. Just as they were emerging from the car park onto the High Street, they noticed a tall, elderly man leaning on a stick and slowly making his way towards them. Elizabeth thought he looked familiar and although they looked at each other, neither of them showed any sign of recognition. Then Edward said

"Wasn't that our doctor?"

"Yes, I believe you are right. Doctor Little, I think. He's certainly aged but then we all have of course. It must have been more than forty years ago since we last saw him."

The old cottage just around the corner from where they had once lived, still looked the same with flakes of peeling green paint hanging off doors and windows.

"Surely the old man who lived there can't still be alive?"

"I believe he had a daughter who spent quite a bit of time with him" replied Elizabeth

"You'd have thought she would have had the place spruced up; the woodwork has had no protection for years." Elizabeth shrugged in reply

"You would have thought it would have been sold and renovated by someone."

They walked down the road that led to the old Lloyds bank, where they had been regular customers, only to find that it had now become a cafe with seats and tables outside.

"Let's go and see the old place, shall we, and then we can have some lunch in the new cafe."

They continued strolling along the High Street taking in changes such as the small electrical shop which had been taken over by new people and looked as if it had been modernised; previously although they sold pretty well everything you could have wanted from an electrical shop, it had always looked dark and unwelcoming except for the friendly faces of the people who owned it. Edward had once remarked

"You would have thought that an electrical shop of all places would have had better lighting in the shop and also in the window."

Now it looked more spacious inside and the window had been dressed in a professional manner and the shop front had had a new coat of paint recently; it certainly looked more welcoming than it had done before although they didn't bother to go inside. The post office had moved to somewhere larger and the old place was now someone's home. Eventually they reached their old shop which had been turned into two houses and suddenly Edward exclaimed when he noticed the For Sale sign outside one of them. They looked at each other, both thinking the same thing. They made their way to the Estate Agents and Elizabeth found difficulty in keeping a straight face when Edward approached the young man, who appeared to be in charge, and pointed at the photo of the one half of their old home which had once served as the shop.

"We are interested in this property; our son is looking for something like this but he won't be able to come and view it just yet ...."

The agent wasn't interested in their son but if he thought he might make a sale that would be all that mattered, and little did he know when he interrupted them

"I'll phone the vendors if you like."

He went off to the office behind him and Elizabeth laughed

"This is the last sort of place that Francis would be interested in, and anyway we may not be able to look at it today."

She was wrong as it embarrassingly looked as if the owners were anxious to sell.

"Can you go at two o'clock this afternoon?"

They agreed that this would suit them well and they filled in time by wandering around the park where they used to take Francis to feed the ducks all those years ago.

It was a beautiful Autumn Day with just a slight nip in the air and they soon found the pond. There was a young mother with two small children each clasping a large piece of bread from which they were breaking off bits to throw to the ducks. A majestic swan swam by, ignoring everything that was happening on the bank and Elizabeth realised that she had not appreciated everything that they had had on their doorstep when Francis was young. She had been so busy worrying about the running of the shop and the stigma that she had always felt about living above it. Then they returned to the High Street; they were looking forward to eating lunch in the cafe they had once known as a Bank. It wasn't really warm enough to sit outside, although some hardy customers were enjoying the fresh air, so they chose a table inside in the corner overlooking the road; maybe this part had originally been used as an office hidden at the back and the small window, hardly noticeable before, must have been enlarged. They were served with cheese and tomatoes in freshly baked bread sandwiches accompanied by a cafetiere of coffee. Her slight feeling of guilt about the viewing of the house they had no intention of buying didn't spoil her enjoyment of a pleasant and leisurely lunch. The delightful expectation would follow of seeing what had once been their home, but she couldn't help saying to Edward

"It sounds as if these people are keen to sell their house and we are just what could be called time wasters."

"I expect they will get plenty of those anyway." He looked at his watch and said "We'd better make a move."

They found themselves standing practically on the same spot where they had stood more than forty years ago on that eventful day, when they had gone to look at the hardware shop. Elizabeth found it difficult to sum up her feelings. She supposed there was a small sense of nostalgia although that couldn't be right as she had been pleased to get away from the place, nevertheless it did occur to her that they had achieved so much and sometimes it felt good to go back in time.

Everything was rather different now, as instead of the door being answered by that scruffy man showing bracers over his non too clean shirt a young woman dressed in tight jeans and a fitted deep pink blouse answered the door with a smile. They followed her through what had once been the shop but was now a comfortable sitting room lined with bookshelves and furnished with a couple of leather settees. Elizabeth could see that, despite the original shop front with the large window overlooking the road, it was still a little dark and she remembered how they had always needed extra lighting during the day; the owners were using a couple of elegant table lamps which gave a pleasant glow from a couple of corners of the large room even though it was still early afternoon. They walked through to a small dining area behind which some steps led into a modern kitchen and a door opening onto the garden. She remembered the old sink and the covered in fireplace that had been there originally and she was reminded of that dreadful time when she had found Edward hanging on to the sink in dreadful discomfort and she had feared that he may have had a heart attack. Then they followed the young lady upstairs which had also been tastefully done with three smallish bedrooms and a pleasant, contemporary bathroom. She was perfectly honest when she told her host that it had all been beautifully done, even though she wasn't to know that they had in fact once lived in the house. Then she had to descend into Edward's fiction as she didn't want to raise the hopes of the young woman

"We love your house but it would be a little small, I'm afraid."

She wondered whether their story had had any impact on the fact that they were supposed to be looking for their son, but she was saved in thinking what to say next as Edward was more direct and asked

"What makes you want to move?"

"My husband works in London and he is fed up with the long commute and so we are looking for something a little nearer."

Edward nodded and she continued "We've seen a place in Kent, but we will have to think about it, as property there is more expensive."

They wished her and her husband good luck and left. It had been a most enlightening experience and Elizabeth wondered what Francis would think of their venture.

Once back in Willow Bridge Elizabeth said "I'm so glad that we went. It was a lovely day out."

There was also another outing to look forward to the following week as Edward had already bought tickets for a concert in London for Elizabeth's birthday, so she thought they had really started to live again and that their short trip to Trintley had been some kind of practice for a more carefree life once more. But disappointment was to follow when they received notification that the concert had been cancelled.

"We'll still go to London though, as the hotel has been booked and I'm not sure that we can cancel that."

So, she was glad that at least they would still have some sort of a break, especially remembering their last enjoyable short trip. Their arrival by train into London was amazingly straightforward and having decided to book into their hotel first, they found their way down to the underground. Elizabeth was surprised to see that it wasn't the least bit crowded, remembering only too well her days of commuting and standing on crowded platforms. If she was lucky, she was able to squeeze onto a packed train in between large and small passengers before the doors closed. Today they were able to stand a reasonable distance from the next person on the platform and most were wearing masks; once the train arrived, they were even able to find seats. They alighted at Oxford Street and once more they were shocked at what they found. As they walked down what had once been a familiar street, it appeared to be just the same as nearly everywhere else in the country; full of closed and boarded up shops, plenty of scaffolding and not many people bustling around. It was no longer busy and thriving as it had been the last time that they had visited, which must have been some time ago now, and long before Covid. Following their disappointment, they made their way to Knightsbridge on the underground which once more was nowhere near as busy as they would have expected. There was that same run-down look everywhere but Harrods still looked the same from the outside as it had done in the days when she had worked in London; but that was where the similarity ended, the other famous shops such as Woollands and Harvey Nichols were no longer there and instead they were confronted by more boarded up shops and massive road works. Inside Harrods there were few customers and even if they could have afforded the prices, there was definitely nothing they would have wished to buy. The furniture especially looked impractical and ostentatious and who on earth would want to give it room in their homes, Elizabeth thought. It had been many years ago when she had hankered after Harrods goods and had then settled for something simpler and less expensive. That evening they decided to eat in the hotel, not having the incentive to look for restaurants that in the past they had always enjoyed doing. Nevertheless, the hotel restaurant was empty apart from one other young couple placed at the other side of the large dining room. That in itself wouldn't have bothered them so much but what made it worse was the uninspiring food that was served up.

The following day, having seen enough, they decided they would catch an earlier train home, which in the end turned out to be a wise decision. They spotted the Cambridge bound train which was due to set off in ten minutes before they noticed that the train they had originally intended to catch had been cancelled. There was no reason given and they thankfully boarded the one which conveniently would be leaving shortly.

"Well, that was a bit of luck that we had already decided to leave earlier." This meant they were able to congratulate themselves that they had made a good decision, albeit quite by chance, but their good luck was not about to continue. The so-called fast train stopped at a couple of stations and there was a longer stay than usual to let passengers on and off. A few stations later they stopped yet again.

"What on earth are we stopping here for?" But they were about to find out when an announcement came through that this train would not be going any further, there again there was no reason given. Edward remarked

"The government is trying to persuade us to use public transport but I have to ask myself where is this public transport?"

In the end they had to finish their journey by using a circuitous bus service and were pleased to arrive home and even though the trip had been exhausting neither of them had had any regrets about the unexpected experience and moving out of their comfort zone and Elizabeth remarked.

"Although it wasn't quite what we had been expecting, I still enjoyed the break after being stuck at home for so long and it was quite an education to see how much has changed."

After their trip to London, they decided it would make sense to take a lateral flow Covid test after mixing with so many people throughout their journey; Elizabeth was a little nervous in case they tested positive and she imagined having to cancel her dentist appointment and other things that had been already arranged. Nevertheless, she went and fetched their test kits. After she had completed her own test, she put the timer on for the required fifteen minutes before she had the courage to check the result. She sighed with relief when her result turned out to be negative, as did Edward's test.

More good news followed when they heard that about eighty percent of the population in this country had been vaccinated. Of course, everyone knew it would be unwise to be complacent which turned out to be true when bad news quickly followed once more. Due to the pandemic, and certainly not helped by the Brexit situation, there was now a shortage of lorry drivers which had led to petrol and diesel shortages at the pumps and there were also many empty supermarket shelves due to a shortage of delivery services. Gas prices had increased enormously as had other fuel and inevitably this had affected the cost of food and other goods and services which had likewise risen. Despite this, the government had stopped the increase to the Universal Credit and the furlough scheme. How on earth were people going to manage? There had also been a prediction that the cases of influenza would rise this year so that, added to Covid, the whole country would be in for a bad time and it meant that masks could become mandatory once more and again workers would be expected to work from home, if they could. Although in many ways most things appeared to be more or less normal after the original shock in March of 2020, but it was alarming, and even embarrassing, to learn that our country is faring far worse than other countries in Europe, despite the successful roll out of the vaccines. Our Covid cases were still soaring by the day. Although the vaccine take-up appeared to be slowing down, surely the eighty percent of the population that had now been inoculated would have made a difference but it appeared not to be the case. A few reasons have been given such as less mask wearing here, more mixing in large groups such as nightclubs and we didn't lock-down soon enough, as in other countries. Also, there is more use of public transport and the immunity could be waning; those eligible for the booster jab are being encouraged to come forward but oddly enough when Elizabeth tried to get an appointment there were none available! Then the news announced that the take-up was disappointing, but no wonder. The predictions for the winter are bad and it is still only October, yet with the cases of the virus still rising rapidly the government appears to have no intention of doing anything to increase the precautions despite warnings from the opposition parties and the NHS.

Elizabeth soon found that her earlier feelings of dread, which tended to attack her first thing in the mornings, had returned with a kind of a sick and dizzy feeling. Despite the vaccines there is still a danger hanging in the air, and if there wasn't enough concern already more had been added. Climate change which has been a problem for a long time had once again come to the forefront, but with the coming of Covid-19, most of the work and incentives to tackle it have been pushed to the back, despite the fact that we are hearing about the dreadful floods and forest fires due to global warming. These will increase and we are being warned of catastrophe if we don't act now. Glasgow is to host the COP26 meeting (2021 United Nations Climate Change Conference) of world leaders, which was postponed from last year, due to the pandemic. Most nations are to get together to try and do something about this catastrophe ahead of us and it has meant that even the politicians are coming forward to warn us about the dangers of burning fossil fuels such as coal, oil and gas.

Edward had told Elizabeth that there was nothing that they could do about any of it so worrying about everything had no effect. On the other hand, he felt the they were at least trying to do their bit.

"We don't waste food, we eat little red meat, we have our solar panels and are looking into a more sustainable way of heating the house and we don't take numerous holidays abroad."

“Chance would be a fine thing at the moment, for foreign travel” muttered Elizabeth but she wholeheartedly agreed with him.

The dark clouds are well and truly settled overhead as nobody can plan anything anymore or even hope for things to go back to where they were years ago. Nonetheless, everyone would, as usual, make the best of it all.

Chapter 45

Trintley

The Wallis family had eased themselves into a gentle routine over the years and Elizabeth had gradually found many advantages with their life in Trintley. The old years, before Trintley, had begun to fade into a past some of which she had hardly remembered. They still received Christmas cards from some of the friends she had met in Bardent Wood, always with promises to visit although this never seemed to happen. She did glimpse small pieces of news from her next-door neighbour from Bardent Wood and she had been sad to learn that one of their fellow morning coffee group members had divorced and moved away. She couldn't help looking back at all the interesting conversations they used to have when she had visited her beautiful large farmhouse, never at the time having any feelings that there was or could be discord in their lovely home. Apparently, the people who had moved into their old house had been less communicative and were out at work during the week anyway, so life moves on she thought.

At least by now they had got to know many people in Trintley, partly through their customers but also through Francis's school and other people living nearby. After so many improvements over the years their living accommodation had eventually become a comfortable place to live in. She had done a little entertaining and had also held a birthday party for Francis. On that particular day the weather had been sufficiently pleasant for them to be outside and Edward had gone to a great deal of trouble to cut the grass and tidy up the garden. However, Francis's friends had preferred the messy bit at the far end, near the compost heap and old plant pots, some of them broken and ready to be disposed of. There was also an old rusty tin bath which they would need to dispose of somehow but the children had found some rope and tied it between two trees to make a rather haphazard swing incorporating the tin bath. She only hoped she wouldn't have to hand back an injured child to a parent, nevertheless she loved to see them all enjoying themselves and soon forgot her misgivings. Maybe in the future she would be able to remember these years as carefree times. Then, as so often happens, once life settles down and there are less worries and challenges ahead everything can become a little boring and although Elizabeth was beginning to enjoy herself just a little bit, she could see that Edward was still trying to think of new ideas.

Elizabeth was woken by the sound of the telephone ringing and she automatically glanced at the clock on the bedside table; it was two o'clock in the morning. The phone had also woken Edward and they both jumped out of bed and made for the landing where the phone was situated. She was there first and picked it up wondering who on earth could be ringing them at that time of night and thought back to the hoax calls that they had had many years ago at these unreasonable hours. All the same she felt uneasy and no doubt Edward would be feeling the same.

"Hello" she said, realising that her voice sounded rather subdued.

"This is Doctor Grant, I'm at your parents' house and I am sorry to tell you that your father has just passed away."

She was speechless, she'd spoken to both of her parents on the phone only a couple of days ago. Dad had been his usual cheerful self and had asked her how things were going. Her mother was the one who always had more to say than her father did, and the last time they had spoken she had mentioned something that had seemed trivial at the time.

"Your Dad's had a cold that he is finding difficult to throw off but he seems to be much better today."

She had noticed that he had sounded a bit croaky but they had all been suffering from colds lately. Edward must have noticed that she was looking rather shocked and as she had gone quiet, he took the phone from her. Dr Grant repeated his message.

"I am taking Elizabeth's mother home with me and my wife and I will take care of her until you arrive." He gave Edward his address.

"It will probably be about two hours before we can get to you."

"Don't worry, that's not a problem."

Although they were on amicable terms with Mavis and Jo next door, they had never asked any favours from them as they had always felt free to do with their predecessors, Ann and Tom. Still, Jo had been most helpful when Edward had had a suspected heart attack so Edward phoned to explain their current predicament and fortunately it was Joe who answered.

"I'll be around in five minutes or so to keep an eye on Francis for you."

Elizabeth quickly packed an overnight bag for herself and rather to her surprise, whilst waiting for Joe, she found herself tidying the kitchen just as if nothing had happened. This was really weird, she thought. It still hadn't sunk in why they were waiting for Joe's arrival before setting off on their unexpected journey.

The journey hadn't taken too long as there was little traffic at that time of night. Dr Grant and his wife were perfect hosts, handing round cups of tea and chocolate biscuits, when they arrived. Elizabeth noticed that her mother was joining in with the light general conversation the Grants had introduced and wondered what alarms could be going on in her mind. Elizabeth had known that her father and Dr Grant had met each other soon after they had qualified as doctors and had been friends ever since. A while later Elizabeth thanked the couple and she, Edward and her mother left for her old home. Mum had seemed reasonably cheerful under such awful circumstances and Elizabeth thought that although she had no doubt been relieved to see herself and Edward, the shock had probably not kicked in just yet and she supposed that she also hadn't really come to terms with the news either.Edward had to leave she and her mother to get back to open the shop and to take care of Francis, but she remained behind for another couple of days until they had informed everyone and organised the funeral. Elizabeth was to return home by train and Edward had promised to collect her from the station.

"I'll be back for the funeral; we will both be there for you. Do phone us at any time, won't you."

It was so fortunate that her mother had so many good friends and neighbours around her and one or two of them had also been widowed, so Elizabeth didn't worry too much about going home to Edward, Francis and the shop. They would have to close the shop for the funeral of course.

Chapter 46

Willow Bridge 2021

The headline news was still about the coronavirus and its consequences, little else was mentioned as if nothing else was happening around the world. Then, something else did eventually take over the news and it was almost a relief, dreadful though it was. There had been the brutal handling of a black man by white police officers in the USA in November, resulting in the man's death; his name was George Floyd. Demonstrations followed in America and elsewhere. George Floyd's name appeared everywhere and it was almost as if it had actually happened in this country as demonstrations and violence here were not now just about lockdowns but about the treatment of George Floyd as well. There was no longer any sign of social distancing and it looked as if reports about this latest fiasco were likely to go on for a long time and to take over from the other shocking news that they had become used to. Elizabeth had known it would be inevitable that there would be a small number of people, who would protest against lockdowns and vaccines, but now there were clashes in the streets giving the reduced numbers of the police force an extra struggle. Groups of people, both young and older individuals, at last were letting off the steam that had been kept under reasonable control during the pandemic and it was almost as if trapped animals had been let out of their cages. Even though the violence and conflict here does appear to be less than the turbulent behaviour going on in other countries, no doubt something to be grateful for at the moment, but nevertheless it was most disturbing. Even though pretty well everyone had sympathy for the brutal treatment of George Floyd and his family and were disgusted by the treatment of the American police, it was still a situation that was getting out of hand and there would be consequences. She noticed that even their local paper had a whole column devoted to the riots and she picked it up and skimmed through it nonchalantly, having nothing better to do at the time. Suddenly she noticed something else further down the page and once more a familiar name jumped out at her

The coroner's court finally came to the conclusion that the cause of Jerry Sutherland's death had not been suicide but that the death had occurred following a fall……

and there she had been thinking that perhaps someone had murdered him, as her imagination had run away with her. It had been a long time ago, though, and she wouldn't have wished that upon him but at least no one else would be troubled by him now.

In the month of November, the trees were still showing their beautiful reds, yellows and rich greens; the fallen leaves that had normally landed up as a wet sludge on the pavements, threatening the danger of a nasty slip or fall, had not appeared just yet. There were still crisp yellow leaves piling up under the tree lined routes and whatever was going on around us all nothing could change the beauty of the different seasons, even though the catastrophe of climate change has brought a few surprises with the seasons starting at the wrong time.

Christmas was already standing on the doorstep once more and it was disconcerting to think how the years flew by. Although the previous year with so much uncertainty had passed by quickly, Elizabeth was aware of a feeling of *déjà vue*. She remembered only too well the fears they had had then but couldn't help wondering if the normal sort of Christmas would go ahead this year or could it be possible that they could be locked down again as the cases of Covid-19 were still rising. Last year their worst fears had materialised and now they were in almost the same situation but with just a small difference. The NHS had been under unimaginable strain then and there had already been warnings that it could be worse this year, not so much because of Covid but because of staff shortages and all the other inevitable seasonal illnesses and accidents, putting hospitals in a precarious situation.

"There's not much to look forward to anymore, just more doom and gloom coming from everywhere." Elizabeth said.

Edward, always the optimist, said "At least a good deal has been learned in the last year and the vaccines are having a positive effect so there's no reason why we shouldn't look forward to a visit from Francis and his family this year."

She agreed and was pleased to notice that lately all the arrows and markers in the shops were disappearing as they had become worn, hopefully this was a good sign as people were becoming more confident now that the vaccine programme appeared to be having a good effect. Despite cases still continuing to rise fortunately there were less deaths resulting from it. After last year's hope for the Christmas season being dashed at the last minute, nearly everyone had been daring to look forward to it this year and starting to make plans to visit or to entertain families and friends, or even to go away to make up for the loss of the previous year's lack of activities. Hopefully she and Edward would also be able to do the same as others. Then followed the next bout of bad news as another variant had arrived from South Africa, yet to be named, and about fifty cases so far had been confirmed. Apparently this one could evade vaccines or spread faster than the now dominant Delta variant and might pose a significant threat as the world emerges from the pandemic. At least this time the government has stopped people from flying in from the countries affected and those who do so will have to go into quarantine. Apparently, it will be another three weeks before the world will know the full implications; it could be a false alarm or it could lead to devastating repercussions. Therefore, fear and dread had descended again until more is known. The new variant had been named Omicron and so there appears to be a leap through the Greek alphabet. Elizabeth had been wondering why they had jumped from Delta to Omicron, leaving out Epsilon and other letters, although she could understand that maybe some of them could cause some confusion.

A year ago, nobody had had any idea where the virus was leading and with this new variant it was almost exactly the same situation as previously with the uncertainty yet again as to how serious it would be and how many restrictions would need to be put into place. The only thing that anyone could do was to wait, and yet history has a habit of repeating itself again as the new omicron variant had put everyone on alert and following the last-minute cancellation of Christmas events last year it could be happening again one year later. Last year they had all accepted that Christmas would have to be sacrificed and looked forward to better times which they were confident at the time, would come soon, little did they know that one year later they would still be under this awful dark cloud. Yet again many Christmas parties that had been looked forward to had already been cancelled and the restaurants and other venues would be suffering again, not to mention the hope of their previous lack of trade being made up one year later. On top of all this the general public were incensed upon hearing that government ministers had actually had parties last Christmas, when everyone else was locked down and making sacrifices to try and keep everyone safe, worse still was the fact that these ministers had denied it.

The news had become grimmer and grimmer and Elizabeth decided that this year was far worse than last year with all the current Christmas forebodings. Last year the limitations had been accepted and she remembered how she and Edward had made the most of Christmas day and had even enjoyed it as this was going to be a unique and one-off occurrence and they, like everyone else, would be willing to accept the consequences. She thought back to all those years ago when she had entertained all their family, including the in-laws; sometimes there had been ten to twelve people sitting around the table and it had always been festive and enjoyable but had left her with a feeling of complete exhaustion afterwards and once she had said to Edward

"Wouldn't it be lovely to have a Christmas day on our own one day, when we don't have to get up early to put the turkey in the oven and to be able to sit down after the Christmas lunch without all the clearing up and the mandatory long walk afterwards."

Then she recalled the old saying 'Be careful what you wish for' and laughed to herself. The current worries and uncertainties came back to her; would Francis and family still be able to come? How much preparation should she make? She had to be prepared to be disappointed again and the second time round would not be much fun; although Edward tended always to see that the 'bottle was half full' when hers was half empty, although this time she tried to be a little more optimistic.

“We’ve mostly had the jabs and we are now able to take lateral flow tests beforehand.” Although the last time she had done one of those tests she had waited anxiously for fifteen minutes, which seemed an awfully long time, before daring to look at the little gauge and to thankfully find that the result showed negative. Oddly enough Edward was less optimistic this time and thought differently.

“It does look as if we will be on our own again this year, going by the latest news bulletins.” He was frequently checking up on what was happening by switching on the radio or the television, followed by inspection of his I Pad and this constant vigil irritated her somewhat as it wouldn’t change anything, nevertheless, once more the unknown had become excruciating.

After all the wondering and hoping during the last months there was a happy outcome in the end. The family had been able to join them for a Christmas meal which had turned out to be a happy and carefree occasion despite them all being a little cautious and they had also enjoyed a long walk after lunch in pleasant weather.

Chapter 47

Trintley a few years later

It was Mavis who had given them the news.

"Did you know that a large new store has just opened up a few miles away from here, it's called Texas Homecare?" No, she hadn't heard, she was far too busy organising things at home to research what was going on around her but she wasn't going to let Mavis know that.

Therefore, she replied "Yes, I believe someone told me."

"Well Joe and I will still be buying our goods from you, it's far more convenient. I may go and have a nose round and I'll let you know all about it."

"Thanks, Mavis."

A couple of weeks later when one lady was buying paint, she put a large tin on the counter at the same time commenting

"Gosh, that's expensive! They are selling it a lot cheaper in Texas Homecare."

Although the customer still bought it, Elizabeth and Edward decided that they had better go and have a look at this splendid new store and check out their prices, so they planned to visit on the following Monday after which they should be able to see what was ahead of them. On Monday they set off for Texas and parked in the large car park outside, ready to look at what was on offer although many of the items they would not be selling in Trintley Hardware Store anyway; nevertheless, they did notice that some of their products, such as paint, were selling at the same price that they had to pay to their own wholesalers.

"It stands to reason, when you think of it, that a place like this with branches all over the country will buy such large amounts from the big wholesalers and they are bound to get a good discounted price." Elizabeth said.

As time went by, they didn't notice at first that the newly opened super store was affecting their own business too much.

They still had plenty of loyal customers who appreciated the personal service and she and Edward were able to diverge into other areas which were less competitive. They accepted they would make little profit on items such as paint, but there were other things for instance; chinaware, porcelain, stainless steel and a few luxury goods which were still doing well. Then another customer placed some paint on the counter and remarked how much cheaper it was in Texas Homecare but he also mentioned that at least he didn't need to get the car out, which was some consolation at least. Edward made the point.

"We will still need to stock some paint, although maybe less than before, because people will run out and will also find it more convenient to come to us."

"And," added Elizabeth, they may be tempted to buy something else as well."

Edward nodded in agreement but they did wonder about possible problems that may occur in the future and had to question whether their small shop could be under threat from those large super stores that were mushrooming up at an alarming rate. They had run their place successfully for a number of years and even now they were able to rely to some extent on the items that were more of a luxury than people's basic needs. They both continued as normal although there was the slight underlying worry, especially in Elizabeth's mind.

Then quite by chance, someone Edward had worked with for many years some time ago contacted him and invited them both out for a meal. It was something of a surprise and neither of them could think why he should do so after so long. Elizabeth especially looked forward to it and it did slightly take her mind off her concerns about the viability of their business. The colleague took them to a smart restaurant in Cambridge and it was while they were waiting for their desserts to arrive that he broached the subject about a project he was working on and asked Edward if he would be willing to help him out.

"It would mean coming into the office in Cambridge for some of the time but a lot of the work could be done from home. You don't need to give me your answer immediately."

Edward agreed to think about it and he and Elizabeth discussed it between them after they reached home although

Elizabeth was sure that he had already decided to accept the offer. Later he broached the subject again.

"In the end it really is an opportunity not to be missed especially as things are at the moment with the business."

Elizabeth couldn't be sure whether their thoughts about selling up had been planted in their minds because of Edward's unexpected chance or because of so much uncertainty in recent months. There was also another possible reason though; maybe they were beginning to get tired of the sort of life they had embarked upon over six years ago and a change could be a good thing in the long run. A few weeks later, after much soul searching, they decided to put the business on the market to see whether there was any interest and they were even more encouraged to do this after Edward had accepted what had turned out to be consultancy work with his colleague. They realised that he wouldn't be earning enough to keep a roof over their heads but it was a start, and at this stage they didn't want to think too far ahead. They would need to look for some other means of earning a living and somewhere else to live, but first things first they still had to find a buyer for the shop which could be difficult if small shops were having to compete with the large chains. Due to Edward's usual optimism, they even went as far as to put a deposit on a new house nearby; it was on a small estate and the house was expected to be ready in a few months, it would hopefully fit in well and as he said

"If we do get a buyer, we would need to have found a home."

One or two people showed interest in the shop with its excellent living accommodation but that was as far as it went, they presumably all had good reasons not to buy it; after all anyone else coming after them would inherit the same difficulties they were experiencing A few months later, and having lost the house they were hoping to buy due to their failure to sell their own property, they decided to take it off the market and to try and think of an innovative way to make the business pay, but they had had no regrets at their attempt to move on.

They weren't quite sure what they would be able to come up with yet but there must be something. They had also realised that it would be wise not to let on to their customers about their wish to sell but unfortunately word had soon got round. Despite not telling anyone of their plans at this stage, one of their nosy troublemakers had soon found out and news travellled fast. They did wonder what he was doing looking at the commercial properties for sale; it wasn't as if he would have wished to buy it anyway. He had been unemployed, due to health reasons, for some time and it looked as if looking at properties was something he did to pass the time and who could blame him.

"It's a pity that he couldn't keep it to himself" Edward muttered after he had been quizzed about it by someone else. "I said that we were only testing the market to see how much it would be worth and had no intention of selling at the moment, and anyway it's no longer for sale anyway."

Happily, the rumours soon died down and they carried on as well as they could and looked for other things to give their profits a boost. As fortune would have it a local artist was looking for an outlet to sell her beautifully crafted wall plaques and although they made little money out of the sales, more customers had come into the shop to look at and often to buy the plaques, so it benefited them all; it could have been wishful thinking but they were sure that these wall plaques were bringing in more custom. Nonetheless, they were reminded of the contretemps resulting from their selling of the plants.

"That little storm passed so I am sure there will be no need to worry this time. I wonder what happened to that woman anyway?" Elizabeth asked.

"I did hear that she's no longer in business and she didn't last long anyway. Although I was also told that she had had personal problems and had moved out of the area."

"Who told you that?"

"I can't really remember; I think it was one of our regular customers who always seems to know everything."

Elizabeth was pretty sure that she knew who that would be.

It was during this unsettling period that a strange thing happened. There was a man who frequently came into the shop with an empty calor gas cylinder to replace it with a new one; there was nothing unusual about this and he would go out to the back to exchange it as was the custom. One day he was accompanied by his wife and Elizabeth thought that her face looked familiar; then after only a few minutes they both recognised each other. She and Patricia had been at school together and had even been good friends, although they had eventually gone their own separate ways and had eventually lost touch. About twenty years must have passed by and yet after all this time they still found that they had much in common and were able to catch up with all their news over cups of tea in the kitchen. Edward had taken over in the shop and had tried to make polite conversation with the regular customer, who he obviously didn't know all that well, but just happened to be the husband of Elizabeth's friend Patricia. Anyone would have thought that Patricia and Elizabeth had been in regular contact during those missing years as the two of them found the link that had joined them together before was still there now. Just as Edward and Elizabeth had done, she and her husband had moved around the country a good deal but the coincidence of them now living within a few miles of each other was extremely bizarre; just the sort of unlikely thing that happened in novels. Recently they had taken over a market gardening business nearby and their arrival as near neighbours was about to have quite an impact on their own lives, especially on Elizabeth's. They had already commiserated about the precariousness of small businesses and especially in Patricia and Ian's case because for instance, supermarkets bought their cucumbers from their wholesalers in sealed sleeves which meant that small market gardeners could not compete because of the extra expense involved. Elizabeth understood exactly what she meant as they themselves were facing similar problems with their sales of paint and related products where super stores sold them at so much less than they were able to do. It was then that she told her friend they were considering selling the shop because likewise they were up against so much competition.

But as Elizabeth confided

"The trouble is I am probably too old to get another job, even if we do sell, but we will both need to look for something else to do in case we do ever manage to find a buyer, which is looking less and less likely at the moment."

"I thought exactly the same about alternative employment" Patricia said "I mean about being able to get a job. That was until I saw a civil service post advertised, offering equal opportunities.

I was quite surprised when I was asked to go for an interview and although I didn't get the job, they said that they would put my name down on a reserve list, which was also surprising. I had completely forgotten about it and was about to make plans to go on a training course when quite out of the blue, a few weeks later, they offered me a job."

Following this conversation with Patricia, Elizabeth started looking casually in the local paper. They hadn't sold the shop although they would no doubt put it back on the market again at some point. As everything was so precarious at the moment, maybe she should study the job market more seriously in view of what Patricia had just said; it made sense for one of them to get some form of other employment anyway. Then, oddly enough she noticed a civil service post advertised in the local paper and read it through three times but if Patricia had been right and they were serious about equal opportunities perhaps she needn't worry too much about age. Elizabeth had plenty of experience both with clerical and secretarial work in the past, not to mention currently running a business. Before Francis was born, she had had a responsible job in a London company dealing with their accounts and running the office in general, so it did look as if she had the necessary experience. On the other hand, it has been a few years now. Anyway, there was nothing to lose and even if she was unsuccessful with her application, it looked as if she could be put on a waiting list. That could be an advantage as, who knew, when they would get rid of the shop. She spent some time updating her CV, making sure to add all her recent experience, and sent off an application without hoping for too much. The following week a letter arrived for her and the content of it was quite astonishing.

Dear Mrs Wallis

Thank you for applying for the position of Clerical Officer.

We would like to invite you to come to our office for an interview. It has been scheduled for Wednesday 4th October, at 10.30am at the address shown above.

Please call me on 01223 335522 if you have any further questions.

Yours sincerely

John Peters

It had been a long time since she had attended an interview but instead of being nervous, she looked upon it with interest and curiosity when she found herself sitting in large waiting room in an old but imposing building in Cambridge. There was nobody else there but as she looked around at the stark walls displaying a few lonely portraits she had a gut feeling that she wouldn't be working here; she just couldn't imagine herself being in what seemed to be rather austere surroundings. Before her thoughts had taken her any further a lady appeared at the bottom of the stairway. She was younger than Elizabeth, short and not exactly what you could call slim, but with long fair hair pushed back off her face with a slide in an old-fashioned style. She wore a multicoloured pleated skirt with a white silky blouse tucked into it, Elizabeth assumed she was probably younger than she looked as her frumpy clothes were no doubt ageing her somewhat but she smiled politely.

"Mrs Wallis?"

Elizabeth followed her upstairs to a small office where the young woman took her seat behind a large desk next to a dumpy little man and Elizabeth found herself sitting opposite them and they introduced themselves. All those months running the shop had given her a confidence she had never had before and she answered their questions without hesitation.

"If we were to offer you the job, when would you be able to start?" the man asked her.

She hadn't thought about that; she wasn't expecting to be offered a job, well not straight away.

The young woman asked "Would you have to give notice?"

She thought of Edward managing without her but he would cope somehow if necessary. Anyway, presumably these questions would be routinely asked of all the candidates.

"No, I should be able to start straight away."

What had she done? Anyway, she didn't need to worry, she was hardly likely to be offered a job following her first interview, but she would be able to look back on it as useful practice for the next time and a way of moving forward.

She arrived home just as Edward was closing for lunch.

"How did it go?"

"Quite well really, although I can't imagine myself working there somehow, although it was an interesting experience and will probably stand me in good stead in case I do need to apply for a job in the future."

They found themselves in the kitchen and she realised that she hadn't thought about what they would eat that evening and as if Edward had read her mind he said

"I've taken some fish out of the freezer and I thought we could have some frozen chips with it."

It was quite a relief that she wouldn't have to worry about food and she still appeared to be in a daze after the event and she started thinking about the next thing on her to do list. That evening she nearly didn't hear the telephone as she was still pondering on the paint order which needed to be put in by tomorrow, but she picked it up just in time. It was the lady from the interview.

"Mrs Wallis, we'd like to offer you the position of Clerical Officer at this branch and I believe you said that you would be able to start straight away."

She was so flabbergasted that she paused before coming to her senses.

"Yes, yes of course. Thank you."

"Could you start next Monday? We will of course send you the offer in writing."

"Yes, Monday will be fine. Thank you."

She put down the phone. This was quite unexpected and something of a shock and once more she wondered what she had committed herself to.

Edward had come into the kitchen to start preparing the meal and as he appeared she turned round.

"I can't believe this. They've offered me the job and they want me to start on Monday."

"Well done!"

"But I wasn't expecting........."

"Don't worry, I'm sure we will manage and it will be good to have another form of income, I'm sure William will be glad to help us out when he can and you will be here on Saturdays presumably which is the busiest day."

"Oh yes, I will only be working from Monday to Friday and as it's what they call flexi time it could be helpful as I should be able to juggle my hours a little to suit us and to fit in with Francis. I will still do the accounts and at least all the work on the house is finished so you will be able to devote more time to the shop."

"Yes, I'm sure I'll cope on my own. You used to manage when I was busy working on the house."

That made her feel a little better but she muttered

"But you were close by when I needed help."

They soon managed to get everything sorted, this included a bit of part-time help from a lady they had got to know quite well and William agreed to help out, mostly at weekends and holidays, when he could. She was now able to look forward to her new enterprise; it would be a welcome break from what she had become used to and also with a salary coming in at the end of each month. It wasn't a large amount but it would at least be of some assistance.

The following Monday morning she turned up at the stark looking government building with uniform windows all along one side of it and once inside was daunted when she was shown into a spacious office. At one end of the room the lady who had interviewed her sat behind her desk and was introduced as their supervisor. There were two more, larger desks each with three to four people seated at each of them and she soon found out that one of the empty chairs was to be taken by her. She was shown to a seat opposite a young man called Robin, whose post she was due to fill as he had been promoted to another section. Apparently, he was to give her six weeks training for the job. During those six weeks she completed a couple of notebooks with copious entries and asked Robin plenty of questions, many of which he couldn't answer.

"I have no idea why we do that; we just do."

She would reply that she always liked a reason for everything although she still couldn't see why she would need six weeks of training. Eventually he had moved on and she was left on her own with her completed note books and the work wasn't in the least bit difficult and was reasonably interesting. She enjoyed the experience of working in an office environment and especially the escape from the shop. There were nine of them in the large draughty office where she worked, and she began to feel as she had done all those years ago when she had worked in London. The people here were rather less friendly though, but she was sure that they would thaw out once they had got to know her; there were moments when she completely forgot about that other life in the shop. She hadn't regretted her decision even on the day when she had wandered into another office to use the photocopier and found a rather odd atmosphere. They all looked at her as if she had descended from another planet; nobody smiled and when she asked about the photocopier someone just pointed to it and she sincerely hoped that she wouldn't need to ask how it worked, luckily it was straightforward enough. There were the good times too, especially when work colleagues in her office had thawed out and had found much to laugh about regarding various inconsequential things. They would also take the opportunity to celebrate each other's birthdays which entailed buying a bottle of wine, usually Liebfraumilch, and cake from the shopping complex nearby. This was the life of a civil servant she supposed; plenty of rules and regulations but not having to work under too much pressure for most of the time. Weeks went happily by and the Saturdays she spent in the shop became more enjoyable than before and it was no hardship to spend time on keeping the books up to date.

One day she came home from work to receive some exciting news. Edward announced

"There's someone interested in buying the shop."

They hadn't got around to putting it back on the market just yet but suddenly a local builder had come to see Edward and had indicated that he and his wife were keen on owning a shop.

"We've been thinking about it for a while and then noticed that it was no longer on the market. Do you still wish to sell it?"

Edward replied

"We were about to advertise it again."

"I understand that the accommodation with it is quite large; we have three children."

"Would you like to come and have a look round?"

So it was that a couple of days later the couple had visited and appeared to be genuinely interested and enthusiastic; there was just one snag, they had a house to sell. As far as Elizabeth and

Edward were concerned, having lost the new house they had been interested in previously, they didn't have anywhere else in mind as they hadn't dared to think that far ahead. They casually asked the couple what accommodation their house offered and it sounded most promising and just the sort of place that would suit their needs. In turn they were invited to go and have a look at their place. The following evening Edward, Elizabeth and Francis found themselves driving through torrential rain from Trintley along dark country roads to a place called Willow Bridge. Although it was barely fifteen miles away it seemed to be taking forever to reach the house, which appeared to be in the middle of nowhere, and Elizabeth was beginning to think that sadly it would be totally unsuitable after all, even though the idea of actually swapping their properties had been attractive. Eventually they found themselves on a road with a few shops and further on some houses but it was a dark, damp evening and there was no street lighting.

The house itself looked quite inviting from the outside and the door opened onto a pleasant and comfy lit space. Once they had been shown round, all three of them fell in love with it and the distance and the journey had paled into insignificance and no longer seemed to matter. The house had similar sized accommodation to what they already had, except that it was modern, maybe just two or three years old. There was a longish drive leading off a quiet road up to the front door and at the back was a large garden looking out onto fields which they were assured would never be built on. Finally, both families decided the easiest way round the buying and selling problems was just to exchange properties. The Willow Bridge house was perfect for them and compared to the place they would be leaving it seemed just like Heaven to Elizabeth. On the other hand, the shop premises had appealed to the young couple and their children. As this man was a builder improvements and repairs would present him with no problems and he would be able to combine both businesses.

Their nosy troublemaker didn't live to see their eventual departure from the shop as he had died from a heart attack after living his life at an unhealthy rate for so long; he was about the same age as Elizabeth. She shuddered, he had certainly been a troublemaker but he had been a good customer despite his complaints and she couldn't have wished that upon him; she even felt a little sad and wondered what he would have thought about them moving away at last.

Exciting months followed, planning the exchange of properties although there was always a nagging worry that it could all fall through. Yet everything went well and the final stocktaking which they undertook one weekend, involving both parties, was a most enjoyable experience for Elizabeth, knowing that they were soon about to leave all this behind them. She had booked two week's leave from work, which she looked forward to even more than if she was about to take a holiday in some sunny faraway place. Her only concern was that although they had some savings in the bank and she had a job, Edward hadn't found anything else yet apart from the consultancy work which would also bring in a small income.

The removal day proved to be hard work as in order to save money they had hired a van but once again William was able to help. Elizabeth drove many breakables and fragile items to the house in the car so that they wouldn't need such careful packing, one of the worst problems for all of them was that so much stuff had to be brought downstairs from the flat above the shop. Edward and William had numerous journeys to the new home with a full van and they would definitely not have managed without his assistance. In the meantime, Elizabeth had packed up all of the kitchen contents and it was extremely tiring going up and down stairs with all the boxes. At long last, by late afternoon, they had left the Trintley shop for good but they still had to finish unloading the contents of the van into their new home. They had already needed to put some of their furniture, including the cooker, into the garage as both families were trying to exchange properties on the same day. William's grandma had kindly offered to cook them a meal that evening for which they were extremely grateful. But first they had to finish unloading in time for an extremely tight deadline because after their meal Edward and William aimed to get to the MFI store in Cambridge, before they closed at 8.00 pm, in order to collect some fitted wardrobes that Edward had ordered and this needed to be done before giving up the hired van.

The first week of Elizabeth's holiday had been spent packing up the Trintley home but now at last she looked forward, with even greater excitement, to her second week getting the new place straight. Their first night spent there was amazing and she thought she was just having a wonderful dream; exhausted and dazed she sat down on their old wicker chair in the bedroom. There were no wardrobes fixed up yet, just a couple of chests of drawers, the bed and suitcases of clothes on the floor. She rejoiced that they had real central heating with radiators in a comparatively pristine house. A feeling of peace and joy came over her as she realised that she had escaped after all those years into a better world. The following morning, she woke and noticed the breeze waving the curtains and she could hear the melodious sound of birds singing, something that they hadn't been able to hear during all the time they had lived in Trintley, as they couldn't even keep the bedroom windows open due to the traffic noise and the dust and fumes. Her main worry now was how they would manage financially but she was determined not to let these thoughts spoil her new found happiness and most of the time she let them sit firmly at the back of her mind.

Chapter 48

Willow Bridge 2022

Elizabeth picked up her diary again and for a while sat with the blank page in front of her, thoughts and ideas floating around as if in a thick mist, only to disappear again. Nothing had been written in it for some time even though she had religiously recorded the events that had happened during the Covid crisis and their enforced lockdown. She wondered if she was getting bored with what had been a novelty, even though it had not been a pleasant one, or whether all this could be put behind them at last. However, she couldn't help noticing that this day marked an anniversary. It wasn't exactly the sort of anniversary that would be celebrated in the normal way but nevertheless it would be a date that had to be noted and it would no doubt go down in history. It had been about two years ago when everywhere in the world had been plunged into chaos due to the arrival of the unexpected and unknown virus. At the time it had been looked upon as something that had unfortunately descended upon them and amazingly most people had taken it in their stride and done whatever it was that they had to do. But no one had thought that it would be two years before things could return to the kind of life they had once known. It seemed as if at the time they had stepped into another, different world. Even so she would have thought she would be making a diary entry noting that all was well again. Although looking back she believed she had had a similar entry exactly one year ago, but her expectations had been disappointing in the end.

There had been all those months when they had heard nothing except for Covid news covering the headlines in the papers and even more so on the television; everyday they had been given numbers of those who had died, those who were in hospital and even slightly better information about the ones who had recovered. Statistics, and more boring statistics but also dreadful visions of the patients being cared for by overworked and understaffed medical staff were still being publicised and did little to ease the tension. Once again it was almost as if there was no other news out there; she supposed they did still get the weather news but previous worries about global warming and climate change had been cast aside. The dreadful storms worldwide had appeared with a vengeance causing widespread destruction and loss of life and leaving people homeless; in this country these had been named Storm Dudley, Eunice and Franklin almost as if they were being christened like delightful babies and children, except there was nothing delightful about the storms but they were a timely reminder that greater effort needed to be put in regarding climate change and it should happen immediately. The more trivial news had been neglected and something about the man who had found a nail in his beef burger or the woman who refused to send her son to school because he was being bullied, was no longer mentioned.

In the end it had only been due to drastic consequences that Covid was to disappear from all the bulletins, even though it hadn't gone away. On the 24th of February President Vladimir Putin of Russia began a military invasion of Ukraine. It was the largest military conflict in Europe since World War II, with over 3.2 million Ukrainians fleeing the country causing the largest refugee crisis in Europe since World War II. It had been unthinkable that anything worse than the recent events could possibly happen, and yet it had indeed happened and news about Ukraine had put the world's Coronavirus crisis into perspective and the current horrors have once more terrified the population at large and it was remarked that it must have made it so much easier for Putin, with the rest of the world focussed on Covid that no one had seen this coming.

Elizabeth muttered

"Don't they say 'Be careful for what you wish for'."

In the end, the hope for a change in the headline news had arrived although it was certainly not something that could ever have been wished for. She wiggled her pen as she struggled for the words that would convey optimism. In many ways she had to admit to herself that she was beginning to gradually get back into her previously busy and fulfilling life and, despite some apprehension, she was now meeting up with people again without wearing a mask or with such strict social distancing, even though outdoor venues were still encouraged where possible. The arrows, making sure that entry to shops and routes along the pavements had become one-way had more or less disappeared so that most people were mingling freely, Although, it was to be another few months before these precautions were truly relaxed.

At last, in June, after so much had been cancelled Elizabeth and Edward booked a much-needed and longed for weekend away by the sea. The dry sunny weather was a bonus for their trip to Portsmouth where they spent one of their days at the Docks looking round the Marie Rose and the Victory and Francis and his family had been able to join them for the day; it had been a long time since she had had a big hug from her son and this was followed by an enjoyable, although rather exhausting, tour which was a welcome return to the old days. The last time she had been to Portsmouth was when she was a child; these days she was more aware of all the steps and of having to bend her head in the Victory which she presumably hadn't needed to do before.

Another bonus of this trip was that they were able to sit in the crowded café for lunch, because she hadn't forgotten those days so recently when such places were closed, only to be followed by the limitations of being spaced out when they opened up again. She noticed that hand gel was still readily available but she considered that this was altogether a good thing; other things were more as they had been before.

When they arrived home, with their holiday still fresh in her mind, the last two years had slipped gently to the back of her thoughts as she began to feel relaxed without the mask wearing and now being able to mingle in the shops and to travel on buses and trains without restraint, although a visit to the dentist did cause her some amusement. She had donned her face mask as was prudent for medical appointments; however, she was asked to remove it at the reception desk and was handed a new disposable one and it wasn't until she was sitting in the special chair that had been comfortably adjusted for her that the dentist said

"You can remove your mask now."

It was such an ordinary request but she could see the humour in it as it would have been rather difficult to have her teeth examined whilst her mouth was covered. She shuddered though when she remembered that it had been just after her last dentist appointment when she had come into contact with Jerry Smith.

Recently there had been numerous statements by so many people and especially by news readers that

"Covid was something we would have to live with" and of course on the whole people were doing just that, not knowing what was around the corner. Mostly, the 'new normal' as it has been called, is happening and people have been getting used to it and are continuing with their daily lives just as they had done before all it all started.

Elizabeth gazed out of the window as she wrote her concluding words and she could see the beautiful sky with pink tinges and the trees in full bloom and realised that whatever happened, nature and the weather conditions, good or bad, would always be with them.